Additional Clauses.

This work of fiction, titled Dark Awakening, explores themes within dark fantasy romance. It is important to note that the narrative contains sensitive and potentially distressing content, including scenes involving sexual assault, forced proximity, and explicit sexual situations. Viewer discretion is advised. The following content contains sensitive material, including sexually explicit scenes and violence. Reader discretion is advised.

ISBN

9798989234202

Content Warning

This book explores complex themes in the following pages and includes content that some readers may find distressing. I've included this warning to ensure you know the sensitive topics covered in this narrative.

Sexually Explicit Scenes: This book explicitly describes sexual situations and intimate encounters, such as forced proximity, Sexual assault, and aggressiveness. These scenes are integral to the plot and character development but may not be suitable for all readers. If you are uncomfortable with explicit sexual content, we advise you to exercise caution while reading.

Violence: The story also delves into violent and intense situations, including physical altercations, graphic descriptions of injuries, and acts of aggression. These depictions are intended to serve the narrative and character arcs but may be distressing for some readers. If you are sensitive to violence, please consider whether this book is right for you.

Sensitive Topics: Throughout the book, we explore sensitive themes, including but not limited to trauma, mental health, and interpersonal conflicts. While these topics are handled with care and respect, we acknowledge that they may be triggering for some readers.

While reading this book, I encourage you to prioritize your well-being and mental health. If the content becomes too distressing or uncomfortable, I recommend putting the book down and seeking support from a trusted friend or mental health professional.

Remember that skipping over or skimming through distressing sections is entirely okay. Your emotional well-being is paramount; I want your reading experience to be safe and enjoyable.

AWAKENIN

THE CROWN OF THE SEVEN REALMS SERIES

BOOK I

Danica

1

The antiseptic sting invades my senses—nature's way of telling you you're somewhere fun has gone to die. Electric-blue lighting streaks overhead as my heels punctuate the silence with rhythmic certainty. Room 813 awaits—my personal cathedral where I, Dr. Danica Pierce (yes, the letters after my name could form their own alphabet), commune with the gods of genetic possibility.

"Morning, Dr. Pierce." Marty Hayes's voice breaks through my mental science spiral. The poor guy's glasses are doing that annoying glare thing under the fluorescent lights, making him look like some mad scientist. Which, I guess, we both are.

"Hey, Marty," I toss back, cool as a cucumber despite the contraband vial burning a hole in my lab coat pocket. "How's life in stem cell city?"

"Patience and perseverance."

"My door's open if you need a genius consult," I offer, already mentally dissecting the experiment awaiting me behind closed doors.

Once I'm safely locked in my lab, surrounded by enough shiny equipment to make a tech geek drool, I pull out my prize—pure vampire blood, undiluted and definitely not FDA-approved. Getting my hands on this baby took more back-alley deals than I care to admit.

Vampires. *God,* what a circus that was when they came out.

Their revelation rocked our perfectly ordered world. I watched that first interview with clinical detachment that crumbled as the evidence bared its fangs. Reality shifted on its axis that night—science suddenly had new parameters to play with.

The knee-jerk legislation came fast—humans building paper fortresses against immortal beings. Cute, really. They've adapted to our synthetic offerings and willing donors, playing nice for the cameras. But whispers echo in dark corners about old feeding rituals, about arrangements sealed with a bite rather than a signature. Can't say I blame them. Though turning humans remains their cardinal sin—apparently immortality has enough baggage to sink the Titanic twice over.

And here I am, about to poke the proverbial bear with a very scientific stick.

I twirl the vial between my fingers—liquid potential. The Institute would condemn enhanced strength, immortality, and vitality—all swimming in this crimson treasure as "too risky." But risk and progress are intimate bedfellows.

With practiced precision, I load the blood into the sequencer, tucking a stray chestnut lock behind my ear. My steady hands betray none of the electricity coursing through me as fluorescent lights cast my ambition across gleaming monitors.

Hours evaporate. Each microscope view reveals impossible DNA patterns that mock established science. The hair tie pulling at my scalp becomes background noise; who cares about comfort when you're dancing with the genome of creatures that defy everything we thought we knew?

The sequencer's beep cuts through my concentration like a knife—sharp and unwelcome. The screen flashes an anomaly that sends ice water through veins I thought had frozen over years ago. This code—this beautiful, terrifying symphony of impossibility—rewrites the rulebook I've been clutching. Fear and wonder wage war in my chest as the thought crystallizes: What if this discovery isn't just breaking ground but breaking worlds?

With fingers that finally betray my excitement, I key in commands, watching data pool like liquid mercury in the dimmed lab. These strands aren't just anomalies—they're evolutionary middle fingers to everything we've established as truth. Is this our salvation or our swan song?

A knock at the door nearly sends me through the ceiling. "Danica?" Marty's voice filters through, unwelcome as a tax audit. "You've been locked in there for hours."

I freeze, eyes darting to the evidence of my scientific treason scattered across the lab. Every neuron fires with the desire to ignore him, to dive back into the genetic wonderland I've uncovered.

Answer or ignore? Let Marty glimpse this forbidden dance, or guard it like the dangerous treasure it is? Silence isn't an option—not if I want to keep this research from becoming tomorrow's ethics committee case study.

They say knowledge is power. What they forget to mention is that power has a nasty habit of exploding when mishandled.

"Danica?"

I inhale deeply, excuses lined up like soldiers ready for battle, and prepare to answer. But beneath my scientific poker face, the decision solidifies like concrete. Later, when the coast is clear, I'm going deeper into this genetic rabbit hole.

Let the consequences try to catch me.

Danica

2

The antiseptic ghost follows me, clinging like an invisible lab coat I can't shed. A flash of color cuts through my scientific haze—Emily, my personal rainbow in human form, bounces into view with her electric blue eyes practically sparking.

"There you are!" She announces, loud enough to wake the dead—which, given my current research, isn't entirely impossible. "I was about to file a missing persons report. Or check if you'd finally merged with your microscope."

Despite myself, laughter escapes me—a rare specimen in my collection of daily responses. "You'll have to schedule my rescue operations between experiments, Em. What's the outside world like again?" I ask, the weight of forbidden research momentarily lifting from my shoulders.

Emily rolls her eyes dramatically, grabbing my arm. "Still spinning, despite your absence from it. Come on, I'm starving, and you look like you've been surviving on coffee and scientific journals again."

She drags me to our usual Italian bistro, a place that's witnessed more of our secrets than any confessional. As we settle in, Emily launches into tales of her latest biochemical breakthroughs, her hands dancing through the air like she's conducting an invisible orchestra.

"Em, that's revolutionary," I say, pride warming my voice.

"Please," she snorts, though her eyes gleam with satisfaction. "Like you haven't been playing God in your lab all week." She leans forward suddenly, dropping her voice to a theatrical whisper. "So, spill it, Dr. Dracula. Did your little vampire blood sample reveal the secrets of the undead universe yet?"

My face must betray me because Emily's grin turns positively feline. "The vamp sample, Danica? Any juicy hemoglobin revelations? Discovered how to turn water into blood? Planning to grow fangs for Halloween?"

I glance around nervously, paranoia prickling my skin. "Emily, not so loud," I hiss, though a nervous laugh escapes me.

"Oh my god, your face!" She cackles, covering her mouth in mock scandal. "Relax, nobody will arrest the mad scientist at table seven. Though your guilty expression is doing you zero favors."

"You know I can't talk details," I murmur. "But let's just say the tests are...intriguing."

"Ooh, intriguing," Emily mimics, wiggling her eyebrows like demented caterpillars. "Translation: 'I've discovered something mind-blowing, but I'm too paranoid to tell even my best friend, who could totally help with her biochemistry expertise.'"

"No promises," I counter with a small smile. We dissolve into ridiculous theories and genuine laughter that smooths the jagged edges of my day.

But when Emily's expression shifts to something more serious, I know what's coming. "How's the family soap opera? Your parents still auditioning you for the role of baby factory?"

I manage a chuckle that doesn't quite reach my eyes. "As always."

A sigh escapes me, carrying the weight of unmet expectations. "Ever the loving interrogators," I admit, wrapping family dysfunction in the thin veneer of sarcasm. "Damon's still wearing his golden child crown. Should I send your warmest regards to my dear brother next time he graces me with a call?" The joke lands between Emily and me, sparking shared laughter that masks the deeper bruise.

My fractured family tree has shaped me more than I care to admit, its roots running deeper than my scientific credentials. The memories ambush me in quiet moments, unwelcome visitors I can never quite evict.

Emily and I settle the bill, and our ritual is complete until next time. I gather my belongings, already mentally preparing for tonight. "See you later at the bar!" I call over my shoulder, the promise of normalcy a welcome counterweight to my secret research.

Emily flashes me that mischievous grin that usually precedes trouble. "Eight o'clock sharp! I've got new material that'll throw us out or make you shoot wine through your nose!"

I shake my head, laughing as I push through the door. The promise of cocktails and Emily's questionable humor later is the perfect counterweight to both family drama and forbidden science.

Some equations balance themselves.

My Seattle apartment towers into the night sky, glittering with lights like a jewel box. I love this view. The open floor plan connects the living room, dining nook, and gourmet kitchen. One entire wall is floor-to-ceiling windows with stunning city views.

I close the neutral curtains, shutting out the world to create a sanctuary. My simple bedroom provides all the peace I need. I love curling up in the plush bed after a long day. I can let my scientist side loose at my desk, surrounded by books and journals.

As a bit of an insomniac, I get antsy when I'm home alone for too long. So, I picked up a part-time gig at Playful Pint for extra cash and socializing. The pub's lively vibe is the perfect break from my problems, and the festive uniform is a nice change of pace from my usual lab clothes.

The bar's signature blend of day-old hops and peanut dust greets me like an old friend the second I cross the threshold. I take a deep breath, letting the chaos of the workday start to peel away, layer by layer. My bag lands with a thunk on the counter—battle-scarred wood that could tell a thousand stories.

Looking up, John's face breaks out in familiar lines of welcome. "Ready to work your magic tonight, Dani?" he asks.

"You know it, babe!" I toss back at him with an over-the-top wink and a flourish as I jump into apron mode. John gives me a good-natured head shake. His chuckle is lost in the growing buzz of the bar.

I flow through the crowd on autopilot, trading quips with the regulars, their laughter dissolving the last traces of Dr. Pierce until only Dani remains—cocktail queen and dispenser of wit.

The night finds its rhythm until Emily bursts through the door like a human exclamation point. Her electric blue eyes scan the room, zeroing in on me with laser precision. Hair artfully disheveled, crimson lips curved in that smile that's gotten us both into spectacular trouble over the years—my chaos compass, pointing true north when my life spins off its axis.

"Hit me with your latest," I challenge, elbows propped and all ears.

Emily doesn't disappoint. Her one-liners have me howling, almost face-planting into an unsuspecting customer's drink. She's got the magic touch for making it all seem right in the world.

Until the record scratches.

John's face transforms mid-conversation, color draining like someone pulled a plug. "I gotta go," he mutters, the phone still clutched in his white-knuckled grip before he bolts, the door announcing his exit with a bang that silences the bar for one heartbeat.

Unease tiptoes up my spine, the sudden shift turning my gut into a clenched fist. Part of me wants to bolt after John, to shake the truth out of his suddenly tense frame. But the night's not done with me—not with patrons signaling for the last call. I'm left with questions and the hollow echo of the slamming door.

What the hell just sent John running like the devil was on his heels?

Rhyland

3

The wind's cutting like a damn knife tonight, whipping leaves across the courtyard. These ancient walls might impress others, but to me, they're just stone and magic—nothing special. Some stubborn ivy's managed to crawl up the sides, nature's half-assed attempt to pretty up this fortress.

"Still brooding in the shadows like a damn gargoyle?" Erik's voice breaks through my thoughts. The silver-haired bastard approaches with that warrior's stride of his, all proper and precise like he's got a stick up his ass.

"Mortal bullshit doesn't interest me," I growl, my eyes fixed on the moon casting light on his broad shoulders. "Their lives are too damn short and meaningless to give a fuck about."

Erik gives me that knowing look I fucking hate. Always trying to play the wise older brother card. "You dismiss even the appeal of romance?" His expression shifts slightly. "The local mortals have certainly captured Lucian's attention, at minimum."

I keep my focus locked on the dark woods, ignoring his weak attempt to get under my skin. "Lucian can stick his dick wherever he wants. That kind of hunger doesn't drive me."

"This sanctuary resides deep within the wilderness. You cannot deny its call to your nature." His tone remains even, controlled—trying to reason with me like a stubborn child.

I don't give him the satisfaction of a response. He finally sighs. "Very well, continue your solitary contemplation. You are, however, forsaking much. Life offers more than... this current state."

"Enough," I growl, my patience wearing thinner than cheap toilet paper. "I'm on my path. Your flowery bullshit isn't gonna change that."

Erik withdraws, acknowledging with a precise nod. As he retreats, he offers one final observation: "Even the most frigid heart can experience warmth, brother. Do not disregard this truth."

I quickly shove his sentimental garbage from my mind as I brush off the biting cold. I ripped out my weaknesses a long fucking time ago and emerged stronger, more focused. Without those emotional distractions, my mind's clear to tackle what really matters—this clusterfuck of a prophecy.

The damn thing reads like a cosmic joke—our fate supposedly rests in the hands of some clueless mortal born under whatever special star. As ridiculous as it sounds, there's no denying the doom spelled out between the lines. Our entire race hangs in the balance, and I'm expected to trust a fucking mortal? What absolute horseshit. But I can't just ignore it either.

Doubt weighs heavily, but I refuse to let it slow me down. This isn't the time for soft-hearted crap. I need to tear through this ancient text and extract the truth, whatever it takes.

The council thinks they've got the wisdom to handle this shit. Until they get their heads out of their asses and shed some real light on this mess, I've got no choice but to chase down whatever fate has scribbled out for us. Time's running out, and destiny isn't waiting for me to get my shit together.

As clouds devour the moon, the ivy and runes surrounding me feel less like protection and more like a cage. This place we've built—hidden deep in the Oregon wilderness—feels like a prison, but there's no walking away. The prophecy's got me by the balls, whether I like it or not.

With a disgusted sigh, I head toward the council's ice-cold chamber. The idea that this will accomplish anything feels stupid, but fuck it, I've got to play along. I'll deal with whatever nonsense they throw at me. What other choice do I have?

RHYLAND

4

Shoving open the heavy doors, I stride into the vampire council's meeting chamber, the click of my Oxford shoes echoing off the marble floors. Blood-red curtains drape the tall, arched windows, and tapestries depicting our history adorn the walls.

The massive oak table dominates the room like a sleeping beast, ringed by chairs that probably cost more than most mortals make in a year. My throne—because what else would you call that pompous silver and onyx monstrosity—waits at the head like an old friend about to give me bad news.

Even with those fancy-ass red crystal chandeliers throwing light everywhere, shadows still creep around the edges—typical vampire aesthetic bullshit. The council members are all dressed in their finest "important meeting" clothes, wearing expressions that say they're about to ruin my night with more problems.

These ancient bastards might look like they belong in a retirement home, but each packs enough power to level a city block. Not that I'm impressed. Power means jack shit if you don't know how to use it.

With a thought, I slam the doors behind me. One of the perks of being able to move shit with my mind—makes for a damn good dramatic entrance. Plus, it's handy when I need to throw some asshole through a wall.

The silence in here is thick enough to choke on. Everyone's thinking about the same thing—that shadow-loving piece of shit, Moretemis, and whatever hell he's planning to unleash from his demon playground.

Killian's eyes are blazing like he's about to shit himself. "Moretemis gets stronger every day. Our defenses are failing."

I think of the prophecy calling Moretemis an unstoppable evil. But I'll be damned if I let some puffed-up shadow demon bring us down. "Then we'll find a fucking way to stop him," I snarl back. "Use the prophecy, call in favors, I don't give a shit how. Just get it done."

Killian nods like a bobblehead, probably sensing everyone's fear with his empathy bullshit.

"The prophecy mentions some human's 'hidden strength,'" I growl. "Sounds like complete horseshit, but we're desperate enough to chase any lead."

Viktor, dramatic bastard that he is, slams his fist down. "A mortal? That's absurd!" The room crackles with his pissy energy.

I fix him with my deadliest stare. "Question the prophecies again, and you'll be drinking through a straw." That shuts him up real quick.

Eva speaks up, commanding attention. "How do we identify this mortal, Rhyland?" Her truth compelling power gives her words weight.

"I...don't know yet," I admit reluctantly. More uneasy whispers. My mind races, hating the prophecy's vagueness.

Cole, our resident blood-bender, looks worried. "What if Moretemis gets to them first?"

"I'm handling it," I snap. "Lucian may know more. I'll go to Seattle and get answers." The thought of that chaotic city already exhausts me.

Randal pipes up like a nervous chihuahua. "There's also that self-proclaimed vampire king in Seattle..."

My fists clench so hard my knuckles crack. Some wannabe king throwing his weight around? Perfect. Just what I fucking needed.

I rise abruptly. "Enough chatter. We have work to do. Turn over every stone, chase every scrap of information about this mortal. I expect results, not excuses."

I storm out, fury fueling each step. How the hell am I supposed to find one specific human in that teeming mortal cesspool? This prophecy makes no goddamn sense—better be worth the migraine it's giving me.

Time to hit the whiskey before I put someone through a wall.

Finally reaching my private sanctuary, I kick off these fucking uncomfortable shoes and strip out of the stuffy suit jacket. Time for the good stuff—I grab my crystal decanter of top-shelf whiskey and pour enough to make a normal man's liver cry uncle.

Dropping into my favorite leather chair like it owes me money, I take a long pull of the amber liquid, letting it burn away some of this prophecy bullshit clouding my head. The fireplace is doing its thing, flames dancing like they're mocking my attempts to make sense of this mess.

Someone's got the balls to interrupt my brooding. "What?" I bark out.

Eva strides in, her flowing dress trailing her. I motion to the liquor cabinet in offering, but she declines with a shake of her head. "We will find them, Rhyland," she says, standing by my chair. Her voice resonates with calm authority. "Have faith."

I scoff and knock back another healthy swallow. "Faith's for people who don't know how fucked they are. Right now, that's exactly where we're sitting."

She puts her hand on my shoulder—brave move considering my mood. "Yet you led us through worse odds. Your determination is what we need now. With it, we cannot fail."

Looking up at her, I feel my resolve harden like steel. Damn her for being right. Self-pity isn't my style anyway. I drain my glass and get to my feet.

"I'll leave for Seattle tonight. We'll get answers." My voice now rings with renewed conviction.

Eva's smile is knowing. "There's our fearless leader. Go raise some hell."

The road ahead might be darker than a demon's asshole, but I'm going to find this mysterious mortal if I have to tear the world apart brick by brick. Our survival depends on it, and failure isn't in my vocabulary.

RHYLAND

5

With Eva's departure still burning in my mind, I reach for the whiskey, again. Tonight calls for getting absolutely hammered before dealing with the crap waiting in Seattle.

The aged liquor scorches down my throat, a welcome distraction from the council's bullshit. My "office" is precisely what you'd expect from someone like me—all dark wood and leather, heavy drapes, and a fire that's trying its best to keep the shadows at bay. It's failing, but points for effort.

I take another deep pull, letting my mind drift back to 867. The Battle of York—Anglo-Saxon Kingdom of Northumbria—what a shit show that turned out to be. Got myself turned into a vampire that night, and holy fuck, did that hurt. But the power that came with it? Like mainlining lightning. Worth every second of agony.

I thought I could save my family, but I was too late. Wiped out. My history turned to ash. Their deaths are burned into my brain like a brand, keeping me company in these quiet moments when the whiskey isn't quite enough.

A knock jars me from my brooding. Erik. The silver-haired bastard doesn't mince words—one of the reasons he's earned my trust over the centuries. The fact that we share the same maker doesn't hurt either. From the moment we fought side-by-side, taking down a coven of witches, I knew he'd be the kind of brother worth keeping around.

He strides in, making himself at home, the whiskey untouched. I refill my glass; it's high time we discuss our sibling, Lucian. The silver-tongued devil—who also shares of our maker's blood—and need to see what the hell he's been up to. It's time to bring that cocky son of a bitch back in line.

"Lucian continues to expand his influence in Seattle," Erik reports, formal as ever. "He courts favor with both mortals and immortals of significance. However, his ambitions may cloud his judgment regarding his responsibilities to our cause."

I can't help but snort at that. "He's always been a sneaky bastard, but he's got a nose for useful dirt. Still, gotta make sure he doesn't forget his place."

Erik's expression darkens. "Adrian remains at the Obsidian Enclave, delving ever deeper into blood magic rituals."

That makes me pause mid-drink. The Enclave isn't exactly a summer camp—it's where vampires go when they want to fuck around with powers they shouldn't. "Adrian's got a good head on his shoulders. He knows where to draw the line... at least he better."

Erik's giving me that look—the one that says he's about to drop some philosophical bullshit about destiny. He starts in about this prophecy, how this random mortal's supposed to save our immortal asses. I drain my glass, wishing it would make this crap make more sense.

"Show some respect for what we don't understand," Erik lectures, formal as a funeral. "The prophecies have guided us through the darkness for centuries. Perhaps there are forces at work beyond our comprehension."

Hate to admit it, but the stoic bastard's got a point. Much as this feels like chasing smoke, I can't afford to ignore it. If there's even a snowball's chance in hell this 'awakening' is real, I've got to see it through.

"We shall seek out Lucian's counsel," Erik declares, like he's announcing the second coming or some shit.

After he finally leaves me in peace, I start throwing gear into a bag. With his web of secrets and lies, Seattle's waiting, and so is Lucian. Plus, this wannabe king needs a reality check—time to remind him who runs this show.

These doubts are eating at my gut like acid. A mortal savior? Sounds like something out of those trashy paranormal romances Lucian pretends he doesn't read. But fuck it - sometimes the craziest plans are the ones that work.

We're about to jump headfirst into this mess, ready to handle whatever shitstorm is brewing. Because when push comes to shove, we make the rules. Prophecy or no prophecy—let's see what destiny's got in store.

Time to raise some hell in Seattle.

DANICA

6

Curled on my couch with a scientific journal forgotten in my lap, I can't help but grin as Emily's voice explodes through my phone like a glitter bomb. "Let's shake things up tonight!" she announces with zero room for negotiation. "I'm *dying* to hit this new club, Karma!"

Saturday night freedom beckons, a welcome respite from the sterile confines of my lab. Karma isn't just any club—it's where supernatural and human worlds collide in a dance of danger and desire. The mere thought of being near vampires, perhaps even offering a vein to those fanged enigmas, sends an electric current through me that's equal parts scientific curiosity and primal fear.

The question keeps circling in my analytical brain—what drives humans to volunteer as living cocktails? What biological or psychological reward makes the risk worthwhile? The researcher in me itches to understand, even as my stomach knots at the prospect.

I've heard whispers that their bite is euphoric—that people actually get off on it. How the hell can a puncture wound feel good? It defies everything I know about biology and pain responses.

I'm a textbook introvert—give me a quiet lab bench over a pulsing nightclub any day of the week. This foray into Emily's world has my heart hammering against my ribs in protest. That nagging inner voice won't shut up, reminding me I'm infinitely more comfortable analyzing vampire blood samples under a microscope than swaying beside their original owners on a dance floor. What if my homebody tendencies embarrass us both?

Damn. Emily and I haven't hit the clubs since... hell, I can't even remember when. These days, our idea of a wild night is perching on barstools at the Playful Pint, sipping John's signature cocktails while he entertains us with his dad jokes and stories about rowdy customers. The thought of actual partying makes me feel like a retired socialite being dragged back into the scene.

Emily, reading my hesitation like it's written in neon, cranks her persuasion to maximum. "Don't you dare chicken out on me! I need my wingwoman, so get your ass in gear for a night that'll make your boring lab work look like a kindergarten science fair!"

I laugh nervously. "Are you sure this place is our scene?" But her enthusiasm is infectious, stirring the rebellious streak I usually suppress under lab coats and safety protocols.

To hell with caution—my life could use some chaos that isn't contained in a test tube!

"Fine, you win—I'm in!" I concede.

Emily's victory whoop nearly blows out my speaker. "That's my girl! Wear something that'll make those vampires question their immortality!"

I hang up laughing, though my racing pulse betrays me—beneath the nerves, I'm actually looking forward to this madness.

Tossing my phone aside, I feel anticipation flutter in my stomach as I prepare to trade microscopes for martini glasses. Who knows what revelations await beyond those velvet ropes?

Lately, I've become a total lab rat, married to my research and completely ghosting anything that looks like a dating life. Romance? Please.

That's like trying to solve a complex DNA sequence while blindfolded—way too many variables to figure out between running gels and analyzing blood samples. My most intimate relationship these days is with my vibrator, and it's starting to feel a bit pathetic.

With newfound determination, I squeeze into a black dress that hugs every curve. Emily arrives and circles me like a fashion predator. "Sex on Legs," she declares with scientific certainty. "If you don't get offered at least three eternal lifetimes tonight, I'll eat my favorite stilettos."

"You think?" I reply with a sly smile, soaking up her enthusiasm like a catalyst.

"Honey," Emily snorts, slathering on another coat of her signature blood-red lipstick, "with that body and that dress, those fanged fuckers won't know whether to bite you or worship you. Even the mortal boys will be on their knees begging for a taste. I give it twenty minutes before someone offers you immortality or their credit card—possibly both." She steps back to admire her handiwork in the mirror, completely unfazed by her own crudeness. "Trust me, your dry spell is about to get soaked."

I burst out laughing at her outrageous assessment, my cheeks burning. "Jesus Christ, Em! With that mouth, you should be writing vampire erotica, not working in biochem. And no one—" I emphasize with a pointed look, "—is getting their fangs anywhere near my jugular tonight. I'd rather not end up as some bloodsucker's midnight snack, thank you very much." Though even as I say it, a tiny thrill runs through me at the thought.

The drive to Karma pulses with Emily's running commentary on vampire club etiquette and which blood types make the best cocktails.

Then reality hits—the vampire doorman looks like he bench presses tombstones for fun, his expression suggesting we're interrupting something important. Emily and I exchange glances that speak volumes about our questionable life choices.

"Ready to make some bad decisions?" Emily whispers, her tone dancing between excitement and the first hint of genuine nervousness I've heard all night.

With a steadying breath, I nod like I'm agreeing to jump into the scientific unknown. Because at this point, backing out would be more terrifying than whatever waits inside.

RHYLAND

7

I push my Audi through Seattle's streets like I'm trying to outrun destiny itself. Erik's playing with the GPS like it holds the secrets of the universe, making sure we don't miss Lucian's den of sin downtown. This city has an energy that makes my fangs itch—equal parts temptation and trouble.

Lucian, that smooth bastard, has always known how to work a crowd. Seattle might as well have been built for him—a playground for mortals and immortals alike who get off on dancing with danger. He's carved out his own little empire here, and damn if he isn't proud of it.

The city's a fucking contradiction wrapped in neon and shadow. Every street feels like it's waiting for a showdown between good and evil, and there's Lucian, strutting around like the referee. Got to hand it to the cocky son of a bitch—he's got balls. Never met a situation he couldn't talk his way out of or a person he couldn't wrap around his finger. I'd rather get staked than admit it, but the way he owns this scene? It's impressive, even if it's wild as hell.

We thread through streets packed with humans living their best night lives, the air thick with different languages and bass lines. These mortals are out here acting like they're immortal themselves, drinking and dancing like tomorrow's never coming.

"Look at this shit," I growl to Erik, disgust dripping from every word. "These drunk idiots throwing their dignity in the gutter after a few shots."

Erik gives me that knowing look I fucking hate. "Something on your mind, brother? You seem particularly hostile toward these mortals' pursuit of pleasure."

"Just calling it like I see it," I snap back, already regretting starting this conversation.

"Of course," Erik says in that formal tone that means he's about to psychoanalyze my ass. "Though perhaps your reaction stems from a deeper concern..."

The steering wheel creaks under my grip as I catch his drift. Subtle as a sledgehammer, Erik.

"If you're about to start that destined mate bullshit again—" I snarl, fury and denial fighting for control of my voice.

"What's got you so twisted up about this?" Erik asks in that formal tone of his. "Yes, fated mates are rare—even unheard of these days, but the ancient texts mention them for a reason."

I level a murderous glare at Erik. "I've watched enough fucking lovers ripped to shreds over the centuries to last me an eternity. Now you're feeding me this destined mate bullshit?" The words burn like acid on my tongue.

These ancient prophecies about fated pairs—one soul completing another—won't leave me the hell alone. But I made a vow. My wife's blood stains centuries of memories, and since losing her, my heart's been a wasteland. No room for fairy tales about destiny.

Erik goes all philosophical on me. "Our past experiences have made us cynical, true. But these mate prophecies have survived millennia. There must be some truth buried in there."

I bark out a laugh that's about as warm as a gravestone, watching the parade of mortals stumbling down the sidewalk. Each one probably carrying their own sob story of love gone to shit, happiness ripped away like a band-aid off an open wound.

"Or maybe it's all premium grade bullshit," I snarl back. "Just another pretty lie we tell ourselves so we don't have to face how fucked up everything really is."

But Erik, stubborn bastard that he is, won't let it go. "We shouldn't dismiss it entirely. The universe might surprise you yet."

"Christ, Erik," I sigh, my mind at war with itself. "You might have a point," I admit. "I'm stuck between wanting to believe and knowing better."

Erik's hand lands on my shoulder, steady as always. "Keep faith, brother. Perhaps our destined ones are out there, waiting to be discovered."

His words punch through my armor, stirring up something that feels dangerously like hope. Maybe there's something to this destiny shit, even for cynical bastards like us. For one weak moment, I let myself imagine it—a world where love isn't just another way to get fucked over.

The bass from Lucian's club hits us before we even park, vibrating through the night like a heartbeat. Erik shoots me that 'let's raise some hell' look. We're dressed to intimidate, ready to own this night. Our brother's holding court somewhere in that maze of sin and sound. We share a look that says it all—time to crash Lucian's party.

Danica

8

Karma pulses as the city's supernatural hotspot, magnetically drawing in the living and undead alike. Its unremarkable exterior hides the sensory explosion waiting inside—the ultimate predator's camouflage.

Stepping through the entrance feels like crossing dimensions. The dance floor throbs like a massive heart, neon lights slicing through darkness in rhythmic patterns that match my quickening pulse. Bodies—warm and cold—converge in this melting pot of desire where species distinctions blur under the spell of music and alcohol. The energy is palpable, a living thing that wraps around newcomers and pulls them deeper.

Bartenders perform their choreographed dance, mixing colorful concoctions for humans and discreetly pouring rich crimson drinks for their fanged patrons. The bouncers—mostly vampires with muscles carved from marble—scan the crowd with predatory focus, ensuring the delicate ecosystem of pleasure remains balanced.

Emily and I navigate the sea of writhing bodies, the bass vibrating through my bones like a second heartbeat. The club doesn't just suggest sin—it demands it, every corner designed to lower inhibitions and heighten senses.

My gaze catches on a couple in a shadowy alcove, barely concealed from view. A vampire with midnight hair has a woman pressed against the wall, his hands gripping her hips with an intensity that should hurt but clearly doesn't, judging by her expression of rapture. His mouth hovers at her neck—not drinking, just teasing the possibility—while their bodies move together in a rhythm older than time. Her fingers clutch his shoulders, nails digging into pale skin as her head falls back in surrender. The raw intimacy makes my breath catch, a voyeuristic heat spreading through me that I haven't felt in too long.

I tear my eyes away, a painful reminder of my own drought. Scientific precision doesn't translate to bedroom prowess, apparently. My love life has flatlined so completely that my vibrator deserves hazard pay for overwork.

Emily catches my wrist, pulling me from my thoughts as she shouts over the music's thunderous pulse. "Stop analyzing everything and live a little, Dani! This isn't one of your experiments!" Her electric blue eyes dance with mischief as she tugs me toward the dance floor, red lips curved in a knowing smile that says she caught me staring.

I can't peel my eyes away from the entangled couple in the corner alcove. Their bodies move in perfect synchronicity, crossing boundaries of life and death with each sensual motion. I find myself nodding absently to Emily's words, my attention divided between her and this raw display of desire playing out like my own private show.

Laughter bubbles from my throat, surprising me—when was the last time I felt this alive outside my lab?

We claim a spot at the gleaming bar, a momentary sanctuary from the sensory overload. Bartenders in fitted black move quickly, creating liquid art for the thirsty masses. I lean against the cool counter, watching the rainbow of bottles glowing under strategic lighting.

"What're you having?" Emily shouts over the bass that vibrates through my ribcage. Her eyes scan the exotic menu, a smirk on her crimson lips.

We catch a bartender's attention, and he saunters over with confidence that borders on arrogance—but with a face carved by genetics that clearly favor him, he's earned it. "What can I get you ladies?" His voice carries despite the noise, practiced and smooth.

The bar is understaffed, just two mixologists handling the crowd's insatiable thirst. I decide quickly, leaning in slightly. "Something wickedly sweet," I request, my voice carrying a hint of challenge I rarely use outside negotiating research grants.

Emily interjects from behind me, "And throw in some shots! We're celebrating science girl's prison break from the lab!"

The bartender's lips curve appreciatively. "I know exactly what you need," he promises, eyes lingering a beat longer than necessary.

His hands become a blur of motion, ingredients combining in a dance as precise as any laboratory procedure. Within moments, he presents two electric—colored cocktails that glow under the blacklights, alongside shots of amber liquid that promises regret tomorrow.

Emily and I exchange a conspiratorial glance before clinking glasses. I knock back my shot with determination—and immediately question my life choices as liquid fire scorches down my throat. My face contorts involuntarily, triggering Emily's delighted cackle.

"Oh my god, your face!" she howls, utterly unfazed by her own shot. "You look like you just drank one of your lab specimens!"

The bartender doesn't bother hiding his amusement, shooting me a look that says he's seen this reaction a thousand times. I quickly chase the burning sensation with my actual drink—a perfect balance of sweet, tart, and just enough alcohol to make me forget I'm supposed to be the responsible one.

Emily grabs my hand, eyes wild with anticipation. "Let's show these immortals how the living do it!"

I return her grin, feeling something reckless awakening inside me. My lab coat persona is officially checked at the door—tonight, Dr. Pierce is taking a much-needed vacation.

RHYLAND

9

As Erik and I push through the club entrance, the bass pounds through my chest like a second heartbeat. This place is a writhing mass of bodies, all lost in whatever trance Lucian's created here. I scan the sea of faces, looking for my cocky little brother.

We purposely move through the crowd, avoiding the drunk idiots stumbling around. There's a magnetic pull toward the VIP section, and I spot him immediately—lounging like the king of this depraved castle.

Lucian is sprawled on what can only be described as a throne, some half-naked woman grinding on his lap while he feels her up without a care in the world. The air around him practically crackles with that charisma he's always had—the bastard could charm a snake into wearing boots.

Erik and I exchange a look that says everything without words as we approach. Lucian spots us, his face lighting up with that infuriating smirk of his.

"Well fuck me sideways! If it isn't my favorite brooding duo." he calls out, waving dramatically. "To what do I owe this unexpected pleasure?

Did someone die, or are you just here to ruin my perfectly good evening?"

"Good to see you too, asshole," I fire back with a reluctant grin, slapping his shoulder hard enough to make a normal man wince.

"Never thought I'd see you two slumming it with us peasants," he quips, dismissing his lap dancer with a pat on her ass. "Especially you, Erik—didn't they revoke your fun privileges in the 1800s?"

Erik's face remains stoic, but I catch the slight twitch at the corner of his mouth. Lucian always could get under his skin.

We take seats around his ridiculous throne, the music still vibrating through the floor. Lucian surveys his kingdom of debauchery with undisguised pride, looking like the cat that ate the canary and then fucked its way through the entire aviary.

"So what insane shit have you been up to, little brother?" I ask, eyeing the operation he's built here. Got to hand it to him—the place is impressive.

"Oh, you know, just providing a safe space for people to explore their deepest, darkest, kinkiest desires!" Lucian grins like a maniac. "This place is basically a confessional booth, except instead of forgiveness, you get orgasms and overpriced cocktails! I bought this little slice of heaven about a year ago, and business is booming!"

Erik leans forward, his silver eyes narrowing. "You always did excel at catering to mortals' baser instincts."

"What can I say? It's my superpower." Lucian laughs, spreading his arms wide. "These humans are just so adorably desperate for a good time. Flash a little fang, buy them a drink, and suddenly they're telling you their life story and begging to be your midnight snack."

I hate to admit it, but his shameless approach to life has always impressed me. The little shit knows exactly who he is and makes no apologies for it.

"Any other depraved ventures you've been diving into?" I ask, genuinely curious about what other trouble he's stirred up.

"Well, now that you mention it..." Lucian leans in conspiratorially, his eyes dancing with mischief. "I may or may not have started an underground fighting ring in the basement. And before you get your panties in a twist, Erik, it's totally consensual. Mostly! Okay, sometimes I have to convince people they want to fight, but hey—that's just good business!"

Erik's disapproving stare could freeze hell, but Lucian just winks at him.

"Relax, Silver Fox. Everyone walks away... eventually. Some just walk with a more interesting limp than others."

Despite myself, I bark out a laugh. This is why we need Lucian—he's chaos incarnate, but there's no one better at getting information or infiltrating the darker corners of both mortal and immortal society.

"What drags you two killjoys to my lair of hedonism? Gotta be some heavy shit."

I lock eyes with him, cutting through the bullshit. "The council's all worked up over the prophecy. Fate of the world crap."

Lucian's eyes sharpen with interest. "Which one? There's so many doomsday predictions these days, I've lost track."

"The one about some super-important human," I explain, keeping it blunt. "Word is they're the only one who can save all our asses from some unknown shit that's coming."

Lucian's face splits into a derisive grin. "A human savior? Oh, spare me the YA novel clichés! What, are they the 'chosen one' too? The special snowflake destined to rescue the world from ultimate evil?" His laugh is sharp and mocking.

"Don't tell me—this rando also just happens to be the key to preventing the apocalypse and holds the fate of all realms in their grubby little mortal hands. Ha!" He smacks his knee, thoroughly amused by the absurdity.

I fight back a smirk at his colorful assessment. "I agree. It sounds far-fetched as fuck. But the council is all in on this prophecy business."

"The council? Oh, please." Lucian scoffs, waving his hand dismissively. "Those doddering old relics wouldn't know their assholes from a hole in the ground. They're so senile, they probably think the skidmarks in their tighty-whities are divine omens!"

I can't help but crack up at that. Erik sighs, his face a mask of disapproval.

"Mind your tongue, Lucian," Erik warns, formal as ever. "The prophecies are not to be mocked, no matter how outlandish they may seem."

"Oh, God. Pull the stick outta your ass, Erik, before it takes root and sprouts leaves," Lucian retorts, rolling his eyes. "Honestly, those decrepit windbags are so gullible, they'd buy ocean-front property in Nebraska if you told 'em it was sacred ground!"

Lucian's unique brand of assholery should make me want to throttle him, but damn if the bastard doesn't have a way of making it almost charming. I gotta admit, he raises some valid points about this whole thing.

I mention the latest douchebag making waves in Seattle—some self-proclaimed "vampire king" stirring shit up on Lucian's turf.

Lucian's eyes gleam with malicious delight. "Oh, I've got plenty of dirt on that pathetic excuse for a vampire."

"Then spill it," I demand, not in the mood for his games.

"Azrael," he practically spits the name, "thinks he's the big bad wolf of Seattle's underbelly. In reality, he's just a bully with delusions of grandeur. He's built himself a little empire of ass-kissers through blackmail, threats, and good old-fashioned violence. The dickhead's getting bolder by the day."

I raise an eyebrow at his blatant hatred. "Not a fan, I take it?"

"Fuck no." Lucian explodes, his face twisted with disgust. "That bloated parasite's been pushing tainted blood, collecting humans like they're goddamn trading cards. He's got exploitation down to a science."

He downs his drink in one gulp, launching into a tirade that would make a sailor blush. "And this Azrael prick... sweet zombie Jesus, the ego on that asshat! Strutting around Seattle like he's vampire royalty. Mr. Look-At-My-Fancy-Fangs can go fuck himself sideways with a rusty stake."

I lean forward, cutting through his bullshit. "Where's this asshole operating from?"

"Oh man, wait till you see this place," Lucian perks up like a kid about to share gossip. "It's this massive, tacky monstrosity just outside city limits. Basically a giant middle finger to good taste and a shrine to his own ego."

Erik's silver eyes narrow dangerously. "His blatant disregard for our ancient codes cannot stand. We must intervene before irreparable damage is done."

"Chill your tits, Erik," Lucian waves dismissively. "I've got eyes and ears everywhere. Word on the street is Azrael's cooking up something major. But forewarned is forearmed, or however that saying goes."

His smug grin makes me want to punch him. "Then we need to figure out what he's planning and shut it down," I growl. "I won't let some wannabe king fuck up everything we've worked for."

Lucian sighs like we're ruining his night. "Fine, fine, we'll play detective. Christ, when did you two become such buzzkills?"

Erik's mouth twitches with the ghost of a smile. "When matters of grave importance arose, brother."

Lucian rolls his eyes, and mock salutes. "Aye aye, Captain Serious!"

After scanning the club briefly, Lucian turns back to me. "So this super-special mortal we're supposed to find... do they come with a tracking device? A glowing birthmark? Or are we just supposed to wander around hoping to bump into them?"

"I was hoping you might have some information," I reply flatly.

Lucian shrugs dramatically. "Sorry to disappoint, but I've got nothing. Nada. Zilch. Zero."

I suggest contacting Adrian for help—the bookworm's our best shot at deciphering this ancient prophecy bullshit.

"Let me guess," Lucian snorts, "he's still hanging with those creepy blood magic freaks at the Enclave? Jesus, when is he going to outgrow that goth phase?"

"We need answers, so we work with what we've got," I say firmly.

Lucian shakes his head, but there's a gleam of excitement in his eyes.

"Well, strap in, boys. This is gonna be one epic disaster."

I let the heavy conversation fade as we kick back, hammering out our next moves while the night's still young.

A server hustles over to take our orders, giving me a flirty wink. "Coming right up, handsome."

Lucian's already got his arm around some blonde. Erik scans the club with military precision, missing nothing. The minutes drag until our drinks finally arrive. I grab my scotch and toss the server a twenty before she can ask.

The club's bass hammers through the floor like a primal heartbeat, and I scan the sea of bodies, my mind still churning over our conversation. I catch Erik's eye and give him a quick nod—won't be long. I move toward the pillar that gives me a better vantage point over this den of sin.

Then I see her, and everything else turns to fucking static.

She commands the dance floor like she owns it, moving with an almost supernatural grace. Those curves could bring a dead man back to life—full, perfect tits straining against that excuse for a dress, cleavage deep enough to drown in. Her chocolate-brown hair whips around her face as she rolls those hips in ways that should be illegal, lips parted like she's already mid-orgasm. She wields her sexuality like a goddamn weapon, leaving a trail of broken hearts and hard cocks in her wake.

No mortal woman has *ever* hijacked my brain like this, short-circuiting centuries of self-control in seconds. She's got to be something more—some ancient goddess slumming it with these pathetic mortals. Those caramel eyes seem to look right through my bullshit as she twists and grinds to the music.

Inside, I'm at war with myself. The cold, calculating part of me is screaming to walk away, to lock this shit down tight. But in my core, where the raw, primal hunger lives, there's no denying what's happening. Not with her lighting fires in me that haven't burned for centuries.

Lust surges through my veins like liquid fire. I want to claim this divine creature completely, to taste every inch of her sweat-slicked skin.

To fuck her until she can't remember her own name—only mine as she screams it. To feel her nails drawing blood down my back as I pound into her with everything I've got.

Consequences be damned. Morality can go fuck itself. She's awakened the beast, the savage core beneath my civilized veneer. My cock is hard as steel, aching to take what it wants, by seduction or force. Her feminine power will be her undoing—nothing will stop me from having her.

I close my eyes, letting the fantasy take over. Pinning her against the wall in some dark corner, my fingers twisted in that wild hair, yanking her head back to expose her throat to my hungry mouth. Sinking my teeth into that tender flesh as she moans, our bodies grinding together frantically. Tasting her sweet juices as I devour her wet pussy until her legs shake and she begs for mercy. Filling her completely with my throbbing length until we both shatter in a blinding rush of pleasure.

The vivid scene overwhelms me, my body tense with need. This mortal temptress has stirred something dangerous in me. I will make her submit, certain that beneath her innocent exterior burns a desire as forbidden as my own.

Fuck me

Who is this beautiful angel sent to torment me?

Danica

10

A few shots in, and my analytical brain finally shuts up long enough to let my body flow with the music. That's when it hits me—a strange electric current crawling up my spine. The unmistakable sensation of being watched, studied, *hunted.*

The club's strategic darkness and writhing crowd make visual confirmation impossible, but my skin prickles with awareness. Someone's eyes are on me, consuming me with an intensity that triggers an inconvenient heat low in my belly. My heart accelerates beyond what the alcohol should cause, the air around me suddenly charged with potential energy. Despite my better judgment, curiosity takes over—the researcher in me needs to identify this unseen variable in my equation.

Emily's dancing in her own universe, completely oblivious to my sudden sensory overload. I scan the churning sea of bodies, seeking the source of this unsettling attraction. Without warning, a solid mass presses against my back, its unmistakable hardness grinding against me with clumsy intent. Hot breath, tainted with cheap liquor and bad decisions, washes over my neck.

"Hey sexy, wanna dance?" Beer breath and bad cologne assault my senses.

I spin to face the human equivalent of a failed experiment—some frat boy whose personality probably bench presses his IQ. Any arousal from earlier evaporates fast.

"I'll pass," I snap, extracting myself from his grip. His face twists with entitled rage, but I've faced scarier things in petri dishes. Emily catches my eye, ready for battle, but I wave her off.

Retreating toward the bar, that earlier magnetic pull returns with amplified force, drawing my gaze upward like a physical command. There, on the VIP balcony overlooking the dance floor, stands a figure partially concealed in strategic shadows—but his eyes, intense and predatory, burn through the darkness directly into mine. The connection hits with physical force, sending a current of awareness through every nerve ending.

Who is he, and why does it feel like he's been waiting for me?

We get seats at the packed bar. As I guzzle water, the pushy guy from earlier sidles up. "Let me buy you girls some drinks!"

Emily eagerly agrees. I decline, still creeped out by this dude.

"I'm Max," he says smoothly.

We exchange names. "Max, huh?" Emily cackles. "What are you, a golden retriever?"

I have to laugh, too, at the innocuous name.

He grins, taking our teasing in stride. "It's short for Maximus, actually."

I smile, but it feels forced. Emily happily chats him up, but my attention keeps drifting across the club, searching for him in the shadows. That mysterious watcher has awakened something in me I'd forgotten existed.

My skin feels too tight and sensitive under clothes, which suddenly seems restrictive.

Who are you, and why am I aching for a stranger I haven't even met?

Sensing he's losing me, Max touches my arm lightly. "So Danica, what brings you out tonight?"

I meet his pleasant gaze. *Get it together,* I tell myself. Just a regular guy. No need to be paranoid.

"Just blowing off some steam with my friend," I reply, willing myself to sound upbeat.

"I hear that!" Max says amiably. "Well, I'd love to buy you a drink if you change your mind." He lingers, hopeful.

I know I'm being unfair by letting my odd nerves ruin his night. With an effort, I smile more genuinely. "Sure, I'll take that drink now. Whiskey neat, please."

Max's face lights up. As he flags the bartender, I try to focus on him and not my irrational fears. I came here to have fun. What's the worst that could happen?

Max insists his friends join us. I'm too dazzled to object. We squeeze into a booth, and he introduces Samuel and Dakota.

"Pleasure," Samuel says smoothly as we shake hands. Dakota ogles Emily openly. Their relaxed vibe seems genuine, but something about them puts me on edge.

I try ignoring my doubts, determined to have fun. Throwing myself into lively banter, I push away the niggling voice urging caution. I'm being paranoid—it's time to cut loose!

But unseen eyes bore into me, sending a chill down my spine. I quickly scan the crowds but find nothing.

Max slides in close at the crowded booth, his thigh pressed to mine. I try ignoring my unease and chat brightly with him and his friends. But each time I sip my drink, nausea swirls in my gut.

Max's hand creeps onto my leg under the table. I shift away and pretend not to notice, laughing louder at Samuel's lame joke. But Max grows bolder, and his hand slithers up my inner thigh.

"So sexy," he murmurs in my ear. "I can't wait to have you alone." His hot breath makes my skin crawl.

I firmly remove his groping hand. "Keep dreaming, buddy." My sharp tone only seems to excite him.

"Don't play hard to get, babe," he goads. "I know you want it." His roving eyes undress me shamelessly.

Acidic bile rises in my throat. I need to shut this shit down now.

But as I open my mouth to tear into this creep, the room starts spinning. Sudden dizziness washes over me. Strange—I usually have a high tolerance. But my head spins, my limbs leaden. Escape seems impossible as I weakly call Emily's name.

Max seizes the chance to pull me closer to him. "Feeling alright?" He grins wolfishly as my head lolls. Emily seems equally out of it next to Dakota.

"Don't touch me—" I try to snarl, but I can barely form words. The world fades in and out. I am helpless against Max's roving hands.

Through the haze, he lifts and tugs me along. My leaden limbs won't cooperate. I want to scream, to rage against this violation, but only a feeble moan emerges.

This can't be happening. I have to fight! But my body fails me, leaving only frantic, unvoiced protests.

Max's grinning face blurs above me. "Let's have some real fun now." He guides me toward the exit, his grip viselike on my waist. I have never felt more trapped and terrified.

I should be throwing a fit, but all my energy has been completely zapped. My body is limp, and words are failing me; the only thing that comes out of my mouth is a quiet "Noo..."

I sink into a pit of despair as it dawns on me that Max has somehow managed to maneuver me into the back seat of his car. I swing my fists blindly, and there's a delicious crunch as I connect with Max's face.

He grunts in pain, "Fucking cunt."

But I know there is no time to lose. Summoning my strength, I push open the other door and stagger out on jelly-like legs.

The flickering neon lights of the club beckon me like a beacon as I stumble toward them, only to hear Max's voice echoing behind me, "Get back here, you fucking slut!"

My heart hammers within my chest as I painfully careen into an alleyway, searching for cover. I tumble onto the ground, feeling the sting of gravel shred my bare knees.

Max thunders up to me and snatches me off the ground. His rancid breath gags me as he screams, "You fucking bitch I was gonna go easy on you, but you had to piss me off!"

My head spins from a lack of oxygen, and my heart hammers in my chest; I can't even move. He flips me around like a discarded doll, yanking my dress so violently that it rips at the seams.

NO! Fear and pain wrack my body. His meaty hand clamps down over my mouth, dragging his rough hands over my skin as he savagely rips away my thong. I try to scream, but it only comes out as garbled nonsense.

My tears stream down my face; I feel helpless. With fear and rage coursing through my veins, I muster all of my strength and whip my elbow back into his face with a sickening crunch.

He kicks my legs out from underneath me and slams me against the unforgiving brick wall as I'm left immobilized, my knees scraping concrete as he prepares to make good on his threat and carry out the vilest act imaginable. The impact sends shards of pain radiating throughout my limbs.

"You fucking bitch, I'm gonna own this cunt. Then I will sell this slutty ass and let all kinds of guys take turns. You'd like that, wouldn't ya?"

My eyes squeeze shut in despair as I cannot muster an ounce of resistance. I hear the sound of his belt buckle being unfastened and the metallic rasp of his zipper lowering. No, this can't be happening! My heart races in fear.

Max's weight lifts off me instantly as I crumple to the unforgiving cold ground. Max is snatched from me on the opposite side of the back street. He's being restrained by a colossal silhouette concealed by darkness.

"What the fu—?" I hear Max attempt to say.

I stretch my eyes wide and blink rapidly, hoping to clear the fuzziness clouding my vision. I take a deep breath of the rancid alley air, hauling myself into a sitting position and tugging my dress over my exposed ass. After a few seconds of blurry-eyed squinting, my mind eventually shifts out of the fog.

Finally, I can make out the scene before me—Max pinned against the grimy wall by some sinister figure with their hands squeezing his throat. Max makes choking sounds as this giant stranger pins his body against the wall. My mouth goes dry with fear, and I cover my face with my hands in horror.

The behemoth of a man snarls in Max's face, "You filthy piece of shit. I'm only giving you one chance to get the fuck out of here. Or else."

Max's eyes bug out as the stranger clamps onto his throat. Clawing at his wrist, he tries everything to regain air in his lungs. He flails around like a fish out of water. Suddenly, he is thrown to the ground with enough force to send him skidding across it. Max lies there like a bug on its back, gasping for air while eyeing up his attacker in fear.

The stranger's menacing presence fills the alley as he glares at Max, his chest heaving so heavily it seems like he is about to explode.

"Who the *fuck* do you think you are?" he snarls through clenched teeth; the venom in his voice is like a knife slicing through the air. "Get the fuck out of here, or I swear to the GODS you'll regret it." says the dark stranger, his whole body trembling with rage.

Max bolts out of the alley faster than The Flash, leaving me alone with this unknown man whose fury still charges the air between us. His face remains hidden in shadow, but I feel his eyes devouring me, seeing straight through my brave façade to the trembling woman beneath.

I try to stand tall, to reclaim some dignity, but my legs betray me completely. They buckle like they're made of jelly, sending me unceremoniously onto my ass on the dirty alley ground.

"Sit down," he says menacingly.

My voice shakes, but I manage to ask him, "Who... Who are you?"

No explanation is offered; "You need to be more fucking careful about who you hang out with, woman."

He moves toward me with dangerous grace, each step deliberate as a predator stalking its meal. My stomach flips and twists, heart racing like I've just sprinted a mile. The alley's darkness swallows everything except his imposing silhouette, his oversized hoodie giving him an otherworldly appearance that belongs in midnight nightmares—or forbidden fantasies.

I scramble backward until my spine hits brick with a dull thud that knocks the wind from my lungs. He closes the distance with unhurried confidence—like time itself bends to his will—then drops to one knee, bringing us face to face. His arms cage me in, palms flat against the wall on either side of my head, creating a prison I'm not sure I want to escape.

I gulp down air, trying to steady myself. His scent engulfs me—crisp night air and raw masculinity—infiltrating my senses until my head spins with it. The heat of his want radiates between us, tangible as a physical touch. His gaze drops to my heaving chest, and the sound that rumbles from his throat isn't quite human—something between a growl and a purr that makes everything low in my body clench with answering need.

A wicked smile curves his lips, promising things that good girls like me aren't supposed to want.

"You are so incredibly delicious." His voice wraps around me like dark velvet as he draws deep breaths. "You smell so good I could eat you up right now." The words rumble from his chest, vibrating with raw hunger.

My heart hammers against my ribs while my skin prickles with awareness. I should be terrified—this stranger has me cornered in a dark alley—but instead, heat pools low in my belly, my body betraying my better judgment with an intensity that shocks me.

Words die in my throat as he leans closer, his sculpted jawline barely grazing my cheek. The veins in his neck stand prominent as he fixes me with that penetrating stare. There's some marking on his neck—a tattoo maybe—but in this light, it's just a tangle of dark lines against pale skin. His presence wraps around me like a physical force, drawing me toward him despite every warning bell in my head.

Something pulls at me from the inside, like we're connected by some invisible thread that's being slowly, deliberately tightened.

Heat radiates from him in waves, tingling my skin wherever we're close. A shiver runs through me when his lips hover near my ear, his breath caressing my skin as he murmurs, "You are an interesting little creature, aren't you?"

His mouth ghosts along my neck with deliberate slowness, and the sensation tears an involuntary moan from my lips. His tongue, hot and velvet-smooth, traces patterns that send electric currents straight to my core.

My head swims with a desire that defies all logic, my scientific mind struggling to understand what's happening to my body.

What the hell is wrong with me?

Fatigue suddenly crashes over me—a combination of the adrenaline crash, Max's attack, and too many shots. My vision blurs at the edges as my eyelids grow heavy. Through the haze, I feel strong arms gathering me close as his voice rumbles through my bones.

"I need you to invite me into your home. I promise no harm will come to you."

The realization clicks through my foggy brain: vampire. Only vampires need an invitation to enter a human dwelling.

Logic screams this is the stupidest decision possible, but he just saved me from a fate I don't want to contemplate. Against every rational thought, I hear myself mumble, "You're welcome in my home."

His response is a gentle whisper against my hair, "Let's get you home, Angel."

Darkness claims me before I wonder how I'll explain this to Emily.

DANICA

11

I snap awake, drenched in sweat, heart pounding. Disoriented, I scan my apartment, trying to ground myself. Everything looks normal, but that sixth sense you develop—the one that tells you when something is about to go wrong—is screaming at me.

Then I see him. A dark figure by my window, watching me.

Holy shit!

My muscles lock up, a silent scream building in my throat as he moves toward me with deliberate steps. "What the hell?! What do you want?" My voice sounds stronger than I feel.

He advances with predatory grace, a low chuckle rumbling from his chest. The sound wraps around me like a physical touch, both threatening and thrilling.

"Such a feisty little thing, aren't you?" His voice drips with dark promise. "You passed out cold, Angel. Had to make sure my new... investment was safe and sound."

Reality crashes down—I was nearly assaulted in an alley, and now this vampire-shadow-man has brought me home.

How does he know where I live?

The pieces click together with terrifying clarity. I invited him in. I literally invited a vampire into my home.

My eyes snap to my purse and phone on the counter, and ice floods my veins. He went through my things and found my address. This dangerous creature knows everything about me.

I leap up, ready to run, but suddenly he's there—moving faster than physically possible. His scent slams into me like a tidal wave—sandalwood, juniper, something wild and sweet I can't name, and beneath it all, the bite of ocean air.

He towers over me, his presence filling my apartment until there seems to be no room for oxygen. My pulse races with fear and something else I refuse to name. He leans down, his face mere inches from mine, close enough to feel his breath against my lips.

"Like what you see, Angel?" His voice is pure sin wrapped in velvet. "Because I'm *definitely* enjoying the view."

A shiver dances up my spine, but there's something else mixed in with the jolt of fear— a strange fascination that holds me captive. Running would be the smart move. Screaming? Even smarter. But, hello, legs? Any plans on working tonight, or are we just cemented to the floor here?

Those eyes, hidden yet burning with an intensity that could either be my undoing or the start of an insane story to tell at parties, seem to dive into mine. It's like he's not just seeing me but *reading* me—and I can't decide if I want to smack him or applaud his audacity.

The nerve of this man, playing hero one minute and home invader the next! He presents an unsolved riddle that tempts me with every silent step he takes. I might not know his endgame, but one thing's certain—he's stirring up a cocktail of thrills and annoyance that this 'damsel in distress' never ordered.

He looms over me, his massive frame stealing all my oxygen. "Look who's got her strength back," with a deep throaty rumble—his hot breath fanning across my skin.

My pulse races like a spooked rabbit, but it's not just fear making my blood sing. My traitorous body responds to his presence with a hunger that shocks me, every nerve ending sparking to life.

His mouth hovers at my neck, each exhale a silken promise that draws shameless shivers from my body. He's like a live current running straight to my core, lighting up parts of me I didn't know existed.

His scent surrounds me, overwhelming my senses until I'm drunk on it. Each breath brands him deeper into my memory, like he's claiming me through chemistry alone.

Then his lips touch my skin, trailing fire from my neck to jaw. Every kiss ignites another flame under my skin, building a bonfire of need I can't control. His touch is more addictive than any substance I've studied, each caress eroding my self-control.

"I can smell how badly you want this," he rumbles against my throat, "how your body's begging for my touch."

God help me, he's right.

My face burns at his words while my knees threaten to give out entirely. I should be terrified of this dangerous stranger, but instead, my body hums with a need that short-circuits all rational thought.

His rough hands map my neck like he's claiming territory, each touch sending sparks of pleasure straight to my core. I'm melting into a puddle of want, mentally cursing my treacherous body's response.

Being this close to him is pure electricity—thrilling and terrifying in equal measure.

"Fuck, you're gorgeous," he growls against my ear. "No one compares to you. Not a single person."

Heat blooms inside me like wildfire, and my legs become jelly as anticipation coils low in my belly.

What the actual hell is happening to me?

His teeth graze my neck, and I moan shamelessly. His tongue traces patterns that have me seeing stars, my skin blazing wherever he touches. I'm lost in a haze of desire, unable to think past the feel of his mouth on me.

"Fucking delicious," he rumbles, hands exploring every curve with devastating skill. "You taste like the sun."

I should stop this. Right now.

Instead, my fingers clutch his shoulders, tangling in his hoodie as my heart threatens to burst. "Wait... who are you?"

He nips my skin one last time before pulling back, suddenly all dark mystery again. "You should rest. You've had enough excitement for one night."

Then he's gone, leaving me collapsed on the couch, drunk on his touch. My mind spins while exhaustion creeps in, but the ghost of his lips still burns on my skin.

I'm terrified by how much I want him—this dangerous stranger who sets my body on fire. I don't know whether to hope he returns or pray he stays away.

As sleep claims me, I'm haunted by his scent, his touch, and the craving he's awakened in me. I'm drowning in something I can't explain, and worse—I'm not sure I want to be saved.

RHYLAND

12

I'm tearing down the street, my mind replaying the night over and over, each flash of memory stoking my rage like gasoline on a fire.

The moment she stepped onto that dance floor, it was like some invisible chain yanked me toward her, my body responding to a call I couldn't ignore or explain.

The predator in me was ready to claim her, mark her, make her understand she belonged to me and no one else. But something else was fighting against those savage impulses. I've always kept my shit together around mortals, but this woman nearly made me blow centuries of careful control in seconds.

From my spot in the shadows, I was fucking mesmerized, watching her body move like liquid sin. Then that piece of shit put his hands on her, shattering the spell and igniting a murderous rage in my veins. He had no right to touch what was already mine in my mind!

In that moment, I wanted to rip him apart, watch the light fade from his eyes as punishment for his audacity. The violent jealousy that surged through me was unlike anything I'd felt in centuries.

Watching them together felt like someone had shoved a white-hot blade between my ribs. My dead heart slammed against my chest, and it took every ounce of self-control not to end that fucker on the spot.

As they made their way to the bar, I tracked them like a shadow, my fury burning holes in my palms where my nails dug in. My rage reached a boiling point when I saw that lowlife spike their drinks, thinking he was being clever. That's when I knew I had to intervene to save her from his sick intentions. Never in my long existence had I felt this protective urge toward a female, but leaving her to fate wasn't an option.

Time to bring Erik into this mess. I caught his eye across the room and jerked my head toward the women, silently communicating that we had a situation that needed handling.

Erik slides up beside me, his silver eyes assessing the scene in seconds. "What's the play?" he asks, formal as ever even in this cesspool.

I bark at Erik to tail the blonde, make sure she gets home in one piece. He gives me a look, probably wondering why I'm ready to commit murder over some random mortal. Hell, I don't even understand it myself. Something about her—all I know is she's mine to protect.

I follow them outside, my blood boiling hotter with each step. Takes everything I've got not to turn that piece of shit into a red smear on the pavement. The law's the only thing holding me back, but every cell in my body is screaming for blood, for vengeance.

I rip him away from her before he can do real damage. Her safety is all that matters right now. Crushing that would-be rapist feels good, though I wish I could've ended his miserable existence right there. I'll deal with the fallout later.

Even drugged and scared, she's fucking stunning, her voice doing things to me I can't explain. I can barely string two words together while she's pressed against me, her scent driving me crazy.

She's got me ready to start a war just to keep her safe. I don't get why this mortal's got such a hold on me, but I know I'll tear apart anyone who tries to hurt her.

I'm pissed about how careless she was tonight, but damn if her spirit doesn't impress me. When she decked that bastard? Pure fucking poetry. Taking him down in that alley? She's got fire in her veins-precisely what I want in a woman.

She's beautiful even passed out. I grabbed her purse from the parking lot-that piece of shit Max probably tossed it to cover his tracks. Her ID tells me everything I need to know.

Danica Pierce. My angel has a name.

A doctor at GeneTech Institute. My angel's got brains to match that killer body. Too bad her street smarts need some serious work.

After getting her home safe, I stuck around to make sure she was okay after that shit show. At least that's what I told myself. Truth is, I couldn't tear myself away from her if I tried.

The second those eyes opened, my whole body went on high alert. Every step closer to her felt like walking through lightning. Her scent hit me like the finest drug, making me drunk on pure need. Nothing else existed but the urge to taste her, to claim her.

Her skin tastes like fucking sunlight. My cock's rock hard, and some primal force is hijacking my brain, burning through centuries of iron control like it's tissue paper.

Jesus, that body of hers is pure sin. My hands are itching to explore every inch, but I force myself to stay in check. No female's ever knocked me on my ass like this—she's something else entirely, and the thought of another man touching her makes me want to commit murder.

Trying to keep my shit together while she's asking innocent questions, with these wild fantasies ripping through my head? Pure fucking torture. When we finally broke apart, it felt like withdrawal—left me craving another fix.

I got the hell out of there fast. My need for her was about to steamroll right over my common sense. But this isn't over—not by a long shot.

Erik and I have talked about finding our true mates forever, but I always thought it was bullshit. Now I'm caught in a war with myself, trying to make sense of this obsession with Dani that's eating me alive.

These feelings are too intense to be normal. Part of me wants to believe fate brought us together. But the cynical bastard in me is suspicious, especially since my dick seems to be doing most of the thinking lately.

This is just the beginning. I'll take my time, watch her from the shadows, figure out what the fuck is happening to me.

No way in hell I'm walking away from this.

Danica

13

My skull feels like it's hosting a demolition derby as I pry my eyes open with a groan. Pushing myself up from the couch, I try to piece together the fog in my brain.

What the actual hell happened last night?

I stumble to the kitchen on unsteady legs, the cold tile sending shivers through me—or maybe that's just the memory of *him*. That dangerous stranger who saved me, then... Heat floods my cheeks at the fragments I remember.

Sunlight streams through my curtains, making me squint as I reach for a glass of water. The microwave clock catches my eye, and I freeze—noon? I never sleep this late. Then again, I never usually let mysterious men with wandering hands into my apartment either.

The memories hit me in waves—Max dragging me into the alley, the shadowy figure appearing like an avenging angel, those burning kisses that felt too real to be dreams. My mysterious savior has been in my home, knows where I live.

Why did everything feel so hazy? Like I was drunk on his presence alone.

My phone sits accusingly on the counter. I snatch it up and dial Emily, needing my best friend's reality check. The ring echoes through my pounding head until her groggy voice answers.

Time to find out if I've completely lost my mind.

"Yo—"

Relief floods through me at Emily's voice. "Oh, thank GOD. Are you okay?" My words tumble out, throat tight with worry.

"What's up with the panic attack?" Emily mumbles, clearly still half-asleep. "Weren't you the one to drive me home last night, genius? Because if not, I've got bigger problems than this hangover."

I exhale slowly, grateful she's safe but realizing she has no idea what happened after we separated. The memory of Max in that alley sends a chill down my spine.

"Wait a second," Emily cuts through my thoughts, suddenly sounding more alert. "What the hell happened? Are *YOU* okay?"

I spill everything about Max and admit I definitely wasn't the one who took her home.

"Holy fucking shit!" Emily explodes on the phone. "That creepy bastard! I will find him and set his balls on fire—literally."

"We need to meet," I suggest. "Gram's Diner? Greasy food might help knock some memories loose."

"Fine. See you there in thirty," Emily says with a dramatic sigh. "And you better bring details. All of them. Including why you sound like you just had the best sex of your life when you're talking about being attacked."

I hang up, wondering how my best friend can read me so well even through the phone. We've been out countless times, but never have gotten so shitfaced we couldn't function.

After a quick shower, I throw on jeans and a sweater. Stepping outside, the afternoon air seems to whisper secrets against my skin. Whatever happened last night was more than your typical Saturday night adventure.

And why can't I stop thinking about him?

I slide into the booth across from Emily, immediately scanning the menu for something to soak up last night's bad decisions. Em looks like she rolled straight out of bed, her rainbow hair piled on her head in what can only be described as an artistic disaster.

"I'm going all in," I announce, setting the menu down. "Eggs, bacon, biscuits drowning in gravy, a tower of pancakes, and enough coffee to jump-start a small country."

Emily eyes me over her sunglasses, which she dramatically pushes down her nose. "Jesus Christ, Dani. Want to trade bodies while you're at it? You can keep the metabolism, I'll take the food coma."

We share a knowing grin as the server raises an eyebrow at my order before scribbling it down. Emily orders her usual egg-white abomination while I silently thank my genetics.

Once we're alone with steaming mugs of coffee, Em leans forward. "So spill. What exactly happened last night?"

"What do you remember?" I counter.

She rubs her temples. "Fuzzy shit. Us at the table doing shots, then... nothing. Woke up feeling like roadkill marinated in tequila."

I take a deep breath and tell her about Max dragging me to the alley. Emily's eyes flash with that dangerous electric blue that appears when she's truly pissed.

"That fucking piece of shit!" she hisses, loud enough to turn heads. "We're reporting his ass to the cops!"

When I explain about my mysterious rescuer who brought me home after I passed out, she nearly spits out her coffee.

"Hold up," she slams her mug down. "Some random dude saved you, went through your purse, took you to your apartment, and what—tucked you in? If this isn't serial killer behavior, I don't know what is."

"Yeah, super weird," I mumble, shifting uncomfortably and hoping she can't see the heat rising in my cheeks.

If only she knew about the kissing part.

"Do you remember anything about Max's friends?" I ask, trying to determine if last night was some coordinated attack. "Were they acting weird before I left?"

Emily shakes her head, rainbow strands falling across her face. "Honestly, it's all a blur after the third shot. But forget those losers—tell me more about this mysterious savior of yours. What was he like?"

I hesitate, fidgeting with my coffee mug. "Well, for starters... I think he was a vampire."

Emily's coffee sprays across the table as she chokes. "I'm sorry—a *what?"*

"A vampire," I repeat, lower this time. "He asked me to invite him into my apartment. Only vampires need that, right?"

"You invited some random VAMPIRE into your APARTMENT?" she practically shrieks, drawing stares from nearby tables. "Have you completely lost your mind? That's like Horror Movie Survival 101—don't invite the creepy supernatural dude inside!"

I wince at her bluntness, but she's right. What was I thinking? My judgment was clearly compromised, but something else was at work too...

Heat creeps up my neck as forbidden memories surface—his towering frame, breath hot against my skin, those lips tracing fire along my throat. My body betrays me again, responding to just the memory of his touch.

I hide behind my coffee mug, avoiding Emily's too-perceptive gaze. I never imagined a stranger—vampire or not—could affect me so viscerally. Yet my treacherous body still hums with awareness, as if he marked me somehow.

No way am I telling Emily about that part. She'd think I've lost my mind, developing some twisted Stockholm syndrome for my dangerous savior.

Or worse, she'd be right.

There's no way I'm telling Emily how his hand cupped my neck, holding me captive as his lips branded my skin. Or how my body betrayed me, aching to surrender completely to his touch.

"I was compromised," I try to reason.

Our server arrives with food, saving me from Emily's scrutiny. I attack my pancakes like they personally offended me. "So, how *did* you get home? Because nothing about last night makes sense."

"Hell if I know," Emily snorts, stabbing her egg whites. "Complete blackout." She leans forward, eyes sparking with that dangerous curiosity. "Tell me more about this creepy vampire dude. Did you get a good look at your mysterious rescuer?"

I chase pancakes with coffee, trying to seem casual while my mind floods with images of his powerful frame pressed against me.

"It was dark, but he was huge—like six-foot-two minimum," I say, remembering how he dominated every inch of space around me.

"Jesus Christ," Emily mutters. "Serial killer much? Was he actually helping or just being a different kind of creepy?"

I sip my coffee slowly, fighting the heat spreading through me. "I was scared at first, but... he seemed genuine about helping." I carefully omit how his scent made me dizzy with want.

"He did save me from Max," I add casually, like this dark stranger hadn't turned my world upside down. "Who knows what would've happened otherwise?"

My pulse races remembering his strong arms, but I force the arousal down. "Anyway, weird night. Could've ended way worse."

"Damn," Emily shakes her head, her hair a rainbow tornado. "That's some grade-A fuckery right there."

If she only knew the half of it.

"It's like someone slipped us something," I say with a nervous laugh that doesn't entirely hide my seriousness.

Emily's eyes flash dangerously. "Wait—you think we were roofied?"

I wince as heads turn toward us. "Keep it down," I whisper. "I'm just thinking out loud—"

"No, listen," Emily leans in, all scientist mode now. "Date rape drugs cause confusion, memory loss, lack of coordination, unconsciousness..." She ticks off symptoms on her fingers.

I fall silent as the pieces click together with sickening clarity.

"It's quite obvious that we were drugged last night, which explains why my memories are zapped and why 'Captain Save A Ho' came to your aid."

"Shit..." The word escapes me like air from a punctured tire. Her theory makes disturbing sense of the night's chaos. Our eyes lock, the unspoken question hanging between us.

Emily inhales sharply.

I quickly intercept her distressing implication. "No, don't think that, Em! Let's go to the cops first, okay?"

I suggest checking Karma's security footage to see who Emily left with. If we can identify them, we can unravel this whole sick plan.

Emily's already diving into her phone, pulling up articles on date rape drugs. She shows me information about GHB that reads like a play-by-play of our experience.

Disgust rises in my throat at the calculated malice behind drugging us. Yet even as concern for Emily fills me, my mind betrays me by drifting back to my dark guardian.

The way he made me feel... Was he genuinely protecting me? Or did he have his own agenda?

Emily made it home safely without me. Was that his doing, too? If so, why would he care about both of us?

I'm disturbed by my fixation on him even as I try to focus on Emily's safety. I shouldn't crave the touch of someone so mysterious and potentially dangerous, yet desire burns inside me like a pilot light.

Is it just adrenaline and forbidden attraction? His enigmatic presence should terrify me, not excite me.

"It's fucking disgusting," Emily spits, jolting me back to our conversation. "Having no respect for consent."

"We'll figure this out," I promise Emily, though inside I'm confused. Those intense eyes that followed me through the club... the sweet drink that masked their vile intentions... how I grew sluggish and confused...

Emily and I sit in smoldering silence. One thing's certain—these predators messed with the wrong women. Once we have proof, there'll be hell to pay.

And maybe I'll find my dark guardian again in the process.

RHYLAND

14

I drop into a corner booth at Lucian's club like I own the place. Sun's up, so we've got the joint to ourselves. We're hunched over blueprints of Azrael's fortress, planning how to slip in and out without starting a war.

"Alright, my brooding brothers," Lucian quips, his finger tracing security points on the map. "This isn't exactly Ocean's Eleven here. That place has more security than my ex's phone after I texted her, 'we need to talk.'"

Erik's silver eyes scan the layout with military precision. "Discretion is essential. Detection would prove... problematic."

My fists are clenched so tight I can hear my knuckles crack, thinking about the innocent blood being spilled in that bastard's dungeon. "If that sadistic fuck catches wind of us, he'll slaughter everyone. We need to end him."

"Pump the brakes there, Captain Bloodlust!" Lucian throws up his hands. "This is reconnaissance, not The Expendables 4. Let's not go full Rambo just yet."

The rage is building in my chest like a storm. "Every second we waste playing it safe, that piece of shit's grabbing more victims. We need to move now."

"Listen, Mr. Growly," Lucian rolls his eyes, "I know you want to go full berserker on his ass, but that's a fantastic way to get everyone killed. We scout, we plan, then we rain hell on his parade. Got it?"

Fucking hate to admit it, but the smartass has a point. "Fine," I growl through clenched teeth. "What's your master plan?"

Lucian grins. "I'll hack their system here-child's play for someone of my talents. These tunnels are where our wannabe king keeps his blood bank buffet."

My hands are crushing each other, fury burning in my gut like acid. It's taking everything I've got not to flip this table and storm that fortress right now.

"We split up inside," I order, my voice rough as sandpaper. "Cover more ground that way."

"I'll take the creepy tunnels marked A and B," Lucian volunteers. "You take C and D. And Erik, buddy, you get to play lookout because someone needs to keep their silver hair clean!"

Erik nods, formal as ever. "Consider it done."

I drain my whiskey, already itching to get this show on the road. The sooner we shut down Azrael's operation, the better. That psychotic bastard's days are numbered, and I plan to be the one holding the stake when his time runs out.

"We get those people out, Lucian."

"Before you go nuclear on this place," Lucian cuts in with that smar-tass grin of his, "we need to scope it out properly. Get the lay of the land, figure out what kind of shit show we're walking into."

I exhale hard enough to fog glass, knowing this clown's right but hating every second we waste. My whole body's itching to tear that place apart, but rushing in like a bull in a china shop would just get people killed. Means I've got to swallow my pride and do this by the numbers, even while those innocent people suffer in that bastard's dungeon.

"Listen," Lucian smirks, gripping my shoulder, "we'll shut down this discount Dracula and free his blood bags. But we do it without getting our asses handed to us on silver platters."

I give him a grudging nod, though it feels like gargling broken glass. The council and their fucking red tape make me want to put my fist through concrete—I'm not built for this sitting around and talking shit to death. But one wrong move could blow the whole operation. Got to keep my head straight, even if it's killing me.

"We gather evidence," Erik states in a formal tone, " to build an airtight case for the council. They will authorize proper intervention."

"Fine," I growl through clenched teeth. "We stick to surveillance. But we take it the second we see an opening to get those people out. Clear?"

"Clear as your anger management issues!" Lucian chirps, that shit-eating grin plastered on his face. "We'll take down this asshat and free his juice boxes. Cross my dead heart and hope to die... again!"

I lock eyes with him, seeing the steel behind all his jokes, and give him a firm nod. Then the front door of the club rattles, followed by that unmistakable sound of hinges creaking.

I shoot Lucian my patented "what the fuck" glare, and the bastard just shrugs like we're not in the middle of planning a covert operation.

"Whoopsie! Guess I forgot to lock up!" he says with a wink. "My bad!"

Jesus Christ, I'm going to kill him myself one of these days.

The door swings open, and there she is—my angel with her friend in tow. Just the sight of her lights a fire in my blood—pure need mixed with possessive rage and a hint of wariness fighting for control. I keep my eyes on these damn blueprints, playing it cool, but I'm stealing glances at her every chance I get. Having her this close is testing every ounce of self—control I've got.

"Well, well, well! If it isn't two lost little lambs wandering into the big bad wolf's den!" Lucian announces with his typical smartass flair. "We're closed for business, but I might be persuaded to make an exception for you lovely ladies!" He throws them a wink that would make a stripper blush.

Danica shifts her weight nervously, those honey-gold eyes avoiding mine as she tucks back a stray piece of hair. "Um, hi... I'm Dani," she says softly. "This is Emily."

Dani. Her name echoes in my mind, sweet and dangerous all at once. Short, fierce, sexy as sin. Just like her.

She gestures to her friend, who's standing there like she's ready for war, arms crossed and looking like she wants to murder someone. Dani shoots her an apologetic look before turning back to face us.

Just hearing her voice sends molten lust coursing through my veins. Every instinct in my body is screaming to grab her, claim her, make her understand down to her bones that she's mine and mine alone.

It's fucking with my head—goes against every promise I made to keep women at arm's length. But here's this mortal, shattering those walls like they're made of glass. She calls to the darkness in me, the primal need to possess her so wholly she'd never even think about another man.

Keeping my distance is torture—the intensity of my need for her defies all logic. I've got to find a way to handle this before she becomes my weakness.

"We were here last night, and we think our drinks may have been spiked," Dani explains, looking uncomfortable as hell.

Emily jumps in, all piss and vinegar. "So we need to see your security footage from last night, figure out what dickhead slipped us something."

Dani nods, still playing peacemaker. "I know it's weird to ask, but we'd really appreciate the help. We're just trying to understand what happened."

Lucian's jaw tightens for a split second, but I catch the flash of concern in his eyes.

"Spiked, you say?" he asks, dropping the comedy routine for once. "That's serious business. But what makes you think it happened here in my establishment of ill repute."

Emily crosses her arms, glaring daggers at Lucian. "We're damn sure your bullshit club staff or one of your sleazebag patrons slipped something in our drinks," she snaps angrily. "Otherwise, we wouldn't have blacked the fuck out with almost no memory of last night."

Lucian flashes that shit-eating grin of his. "My, my! Aren't we just a ray of fucking sunshine wrapped in a thundercloud!" he quips, looking way too amused for his own good.

Emily's face could curdle milk. "Go fuck yourself," she snarls. "This isn't a joke."

"Whoa there, Angry Spice! Retract the claws!" Lucian throws his hands up in mock surrender, still wearing that insufferable smirk. "I'm just your friendly neighborhood club owner, here to help!"

Dani gives her friend a "please behave" look before turning those honey-gold eyes back to Lucian. "We just need to check the security footage from last night. Emily can't remember who she left with or what happened after she blacked out."

"Say no more, buttercup!" Lucian bows with exaggerated flourish. "Your wish is my command. Step into my office, ladies!"

I follow behind them, my eyes locked on how Dani's hips sway with each step. The attraction between us crackles like lightning, ready to strike. When she catches me looking, her breath catches in her throat. Her caramel eyes are full of shy curiosity, but I keep my face neutral even while my blood's on fire.

Jesus Christ, this woman's going to be the death of me. And I might just let her.

Lucian pulls up the security feeds while Dani breaks down last night's events like a seasoned detective. Her sharp mind catches every detail, focused on unraveling this clusterfuck. Our connection keeps pulling at her attention until Lucian's theatrical ass draws her back to the screens.

I hang back in the shadows, selfishly guarding my anonymity while I wrestle with the unwanted feelings she stirs up.

"Roll that beautiful bean footage!" Lucian announces, fingers flying over the keyboard. Then that piece of shit Max shows up on screen, slipping something in their drinks while Dani's distracted.

Her beautiful face twists with rage and disbelief. Emily goes nuclear, cursing a storm and practically putting her fist through Lucian's desk. "Mother-fucking piece of shit! I knew it!"

But Dani... she's processing it all with her brilliant scientific mind, analyzing every frame. Their reactions couldn't be more different.

Watching this shit replay feeds the murderous rage burning in my gut. Seeing her violated like this makes me want to hunt Max down and tear him apart with my bare hands. Yeah, I got her out safe, but the trauma's still there. And here I am, fighting these intense feelings for her like a goddamn coward.

"We need to take this to the police," Dani insists, her moral compass pointing due north.

"Whoa, whoa, whoa!" Lucian practically squeaks, panic creeping in. "Let's not go nuclear here! My baby doesn't deserve to get shut down over one bad apple!"

Dani's righteousness flares up like a torch, and suddenly the room's so tense you could cut it with a knife. "So what's your brilliant solution?" she demands. "We can't just let this go—one of those bastards tried to rape me in your fucking alley last night!"

Christ, every word she says makes me want to commit murder. But I keep my mouth shut, watching this trainwreck unfold.

Lucian's face twists into something deadly, real rage burning behind that smartass facade. I'm fighting my own murderous impulses, remembering that piece of shit putting his hands on what's mine.

"Listen up, ladies!" Lucian announces with forced cheer. "We'll amp up security, pat downs, the works. My bad for not catching this sooner. But trust me—those dickwads are gonna seriously regret their life choices."

"Oh really?" Emily scoffs. "And how exactly are you planning to serve up justice? That creep belongs in jail!"

"Sweet cheeks," Lucian's voice drops to arctic levels, "don't worry your pretty little head about the details. I said I'll handle it." His stare could freeze hell over, and Emily actually backs down, nodding like she finally gets it.

Trust that manipulative bastard Lucian to flex his compulsion powers, protecting his precious nightclub like it's the crown fucking jewels. Though I have to admit, when he wants to, my brother can bend minds like a master puppeteer. At least his talent for mental manipulation comes in handy when we need to clean up messes—even if half those messes are his own damn fault.

Dani's been quietly seething this whole time, but even she sees the writing on the wall. "We just don't want anyone else getting hurt," she says diplomatically.

"Trust me, sugar." Lucian's smile is all teeth. "It won't happen again. Now, if you'll excuse us..." He waves toward the door like the world's deadliest maitre d.

Emily starts to argue, but Dani shuts her down with a look. "Thanks for your help," she manages through gritted teeth as they head out.

"We can't seriously let him handle this!" Emily hisses once they're moving. "We need cops!"

"Trust me," Dani mutters, "I think his version of justice might be more... effective." She glances back at Lucian's predatory grin.

Her scent hits me like a drug, making my whole body ache with need.

I need to keep my shit together, take this slow, not let my dick do the thinking. But watching her walk away, I know one thing for sure-I'll be seeing my angel again soon.

Our paths are tangled now, whether we like it or not.

Game fucking on.

Danica

15

Emily tears out of the parking lot, her ancient Honda protesting as she pushes it beyond its limits. I sink into the passenger seat, watching buildings blur past while my thoughts tangle themselves into knots.

"Can you believe this shit?" Emily's voice cracks with rage barely contained. "I was—"

"Don't," I cut her off quickly. "We don't know for sure yet." The possibility makes my stomach turn to concrete.

She nods sharply, knuckles white on the steering wheel. "And this Lucian character—can we actually trust him?" Her eyes flash with suspicion.

It's a fair question—he's still a wild card. "What other option do we have? He's a vampire. They probably have their own justice system or something."

Rage burns through me like wildfire—the thought that Emily and I were targeted for date rape makes me want to scream and break things. Those predatory assholes deserve whatever nightmare Lucian's justice system throws at them.

But even with my anger blazing white-hot, I can't stop my mind from wandering back to *him*—my mysterious savior with those penetrating eyes. The way his presence filled the alley. The heat of his body against mine. The dangerous thrill when his lips brushed my neck.

What is wrong with me? I should be traumatized, not fantasizing about some dark stranger who appeared out of nowhere. Yet here I am, replaying those moments on loop like my favorite movie scene.

Maybe it's shock. Maybe it's my brain's way of coping with what almost happened. Or maybe there's something about him that calls to something in me—something I didn't even know existed until he stepped from the shadows.

Whatever it is, it's dangerous. And I can't seem to stop myself from wanting more.

My mind goes back to that guy in Lucian's office—the tall one with midnight hair and intense blue eyes who never said a word. He just stood in the corner, radiating danger and mystery.

He was gorgeous—the kind of beautiful that makes you forget how to breathe. I had to force myself not to stare at him instead of watching the security footage.

Could he be my dark knight?

Something about that silent, brooding presence set off fireworks in my belly— those ice-blue eyes seemed to look straight through me.

"Earth to Dani," Emily snaps, yanking me from my fantasy. "Who was that mountain-sized dude talking to Dakota in the footage? He looked like he eats people for breakfast."

I frown, wondering the same thing. Why did Lucian cut the video right then? The massive man with silver hair had approached Dakota just as Emily slumped unconscious in the booth.

My mysterious savior's warning echoes in my mind. Had he witnessed Max drugging us and followed?

"No clue," I tell Emily. "But Max and his crew deserve whatever nightmare comes their way."

Emily scoffs. "Damn right they do."

I squeeze her shoulder supportively. "Whatever happened, we'll deal with it together."

"I'm scheduling a doctor's appointment," Emily says quietly. "Just to be safe."

"Smart move," I agree, grateful she doesn't elaborate further.

We drive silently for several blocks, each processing our violated sense of security. I know Emily's mentally reviewing every fragment she can recall. Meanwhile, I can't stop obsessing over my dark guardian. What did he see in me that made him intervene? The questions multiply with each passing minute.

Emily finally breaks the silence. "Seriously, you can't remember anything else about your rescuer? Could be dangerous if he's fixated on you now."

I hesitate, debating how much to reveal about those heated moments. "It's all foggy," I lie. "I just remember, he was huge. Told me I should be more careful." The evasiveness in my voice is obvious even to me.

"Bullshit," Emily gives me her patented 'cut the crap' look. "There's more you're not telling me."

I squirm under her gaze. "Can we just focus on getting through today?" I plead softly. "Everything else can wait."

Including the fact that I can still feel his lips on my neck.

I don't understand why I'm reacting this way...there's this magnetic pull when I think about his shadowy features—a dangerous current that sparked to life when he stood close to me that night.

Something primal inside me recognizes something in him—a connection I feel but can't explain, like a half-remembered dream.

Who are you, and why can't I stop thinking about you?

Emily finally drops her interrogation, though her skeptical expression tells me this conversation isn't over. For now, I'll keep these dangerous thoughts to myself.

Some secrets are better left in the shadows.

"Let's watch something hot," Emily suggests. "Vampire Memoirs?

I laugh at the irony—those vampires are walking thirst traps—hotter than a jalapeño pepper on a summer's day. "Trading real vampires for fictional ones," I agree. "Perfect."

While microwave popcorn pops, Emily raids my linen closet for blankets, ready for some mindless escapism. I hit play and we burrow into the couch, eager to lose ourselves in ridiculous supernatural drama. The overwrought dialogue and smoldering stares never fail to entertain us, offering the perfect distraction from our real-life vampire encounter.

I glance over at Em, relieved to see her genuinely smiling again. For a few precious hours, we can pretend we're just two normal friends enjoying trashy TV instead of potential victims in some supernatural conspiracy.

Four episodes fly by in a blur of laughter and our usual commentary. The pizza delivery interrupts our vampire marathon, and we attack the hot slices like we haven't eaten in days, which isn't far from the truth considering we only had breakfast.

With the pizza demolished, Emily reluctantly announces she needs to head home. "Early lab tomorrow," she sighs, gathering her things. I nod in understanding, also facing morning responsibilities despite the surreal weekend.

After Emily leaves, I take a long, hot shower, letting the water wash away the lingering tension in my muscles.

The inviting sight of my bed pulls me in. Slipping between cool sheets, I exhale deeply, trying to quiet my racing thoughts. So much has changed in just twenty-four hours—my entire reality has shifted, filled with new questions and strange connections.

Exhaustion wins over curiosity as my eyelids grow heavy. As I drift toward sleep, my mind conjures tantalizing images of my dark guardian. Dream blurs into memory as phantom hands trace fire across my skin and hungry lips brand my neck. My mysterious protector's presence envelops me entirely in my dreams. Wrapped in his strong arms, I surrender to my most peaceful sleep in years.

In dreams, at least, I'm not afraid of what I want.

Danica

16

The lab hums with energy as I lean over an intriguing sample, my fingers tingling with anticipation. Something about this DNA calls to me—whispering secrets I can't hear yet.

Oddly comforted by its rhythmic whirring, I slide the vial into the centrifuge. What mysteries are encoded in those microscopic strands? My heart races with scientific thrill.

"Making any progress on those samples, Danica?" Dr. Hayes appears at my shoulder.

I rub my tired eyes, fighting a yawn. "The sequences are bizarre—not fully human. Some unclassified hybrid."

"Keep at it," he encourages. "We need answers sooner rather than later."

The pressure should intimidate me, but it only fuels my determination. My mind wanders to the origin of this strange bloodline, its history unwritten.

This sample is bizarre—not like the vampire DNA I've been secretly studying after hours when the lab is empty. Those forbidden samples are tucked away in the back of the freezer behind expired reagents where no one would think to look. I'm breaking every rule in both human and vampire society by even having those samples, let alone studying them. If either side discovered my secret research, the consequences would be severe. Career suicide would be the least of my worries.

"You've been glued to that microscope for hours," Sarah interrupts gently. "Maybe take five?"

I offer a tight smile without looking up from my notes. "I'm good, thanks. Need to keep going."

Sarah sighs. "At least eat something? You look half-dead." She squeezes my shoulder before walking away.

Hours blur together as frustration builds. Despite endless analysis, I'm no closer to understanding. My back aches from hunching over equipment while my colleagues filter out for the evening. I remain stubbornly in place.

"You'll burn yourself out at this rate," Simmons warns, his usually cheerful face serious. "Exhaustion won't help the research."

"Just a little longer," I plead, hearing the desperation in my voice. "This sample is different. I can crack it if I keep digging."

He studies me before relenting with a sigh. "Don't push too hard. We need your brain functioning tomorrow."

I promise to be reasonable, but we both know better. This work isn't just a job—it's my passion, and I won't stop until I solve the riddle.

My phone buzzes, yanking me from my concentration. It's John.

"Hey, Dani, I hate to ask on your night off, but it's my mom. Need to take her to the hospital and could really use backup. Any chance you could cover?"

Exhaustion pulls at me, but I can't say no. Family comes first. "Sure thing, John. I'll be there soon," I agree, injecting fake energy into my voice.

"You're a lifesaver, Dani. See you soon."

So much for that early night I promised myself.

After hanging up, I hurry out into the crisp night air, the cold shock jolting some life back into my tired body. A strange sensation crawls up my spine as I navigate through patches of darkness between streetlights—that feeling of being watched. I scan the empty sidewalks and shadowed doorways but see nothing unusual.

Get it together, Dani. It's just exhaustion making you paranoid.

Still, I quicken my pace, keys clutched tightly between my fingers as I make my way to my car.

As I push through the door, the bar's neon glow and pulsing music wash over me—my natural habitat after hours.

John's face melts with relief when he spots me. "Thanks for coming, Dani. Mom's in bad shape—gotta get her to the ER." Worry lines crease his usually smooth forehead.

I give his shoulder a reassuring squeeze. "Go. I've got this covered."

He snatches his keys and bolts, tossing a grateful "You're the best!" over his shoulder.

I slip into the familiar dance of bartending, mixing drinks for the Thursday night regulars. A tipsy businessman leans over, winking as he orders another round. I smile politely, my mind drifting back to those strange DNA samples while my hands automatically prep ingredients.

The bar thrums with energy—glasses clinking, laughter rising above the music. I absorb the vibe, swaying slightly as I banter with customers.

My thoughts keep circling back to one dark figure between serving drinks and taking orders. His urgent touches and heated whispers refuse to fade from memory. Even surrounded by people, I can almost feel his presence lingering just beyond sight.

As I work, I imagine his intense eyes following my movements. Ridiculous fantasy, but I still find myself scanning the shadowy corners, half-expecting to find him watching.

"Last call, folks!" I announce as the night winds down. The crowd gradually thins, stumbling out into the night. My real work begins—wiping down sticky tables, stacking chairs, and counting the register.

When the final patron leaves, I exhale heavily against the bar. The shadows seem to shift unnaturally in my peripheral vision. "Get a grip, Dani," I mutter, ignoring the prickle racing down my spine.

I rush through closing duties. Hauling trash bags outside, my heels click loudly in the deserted alley as I approach the dumpsters.

The flickering street lamp casts menacing shadows, raising goosebumps across my skin. The sensation of being watched intensifies.

"Just nerves," I whisper, trying to calm my racing heart.

Probably a stray cat. But as I turn toward the bins, a shadow detaches from the darkness. A tall figure stalks toward me with predatory grace, each step deliberate and decisive. Fear spikes through me, yet mingled with a strange thrill of recognition. I know that imposing silhouette...

"It's you," I breathe.

"You shouldn't be out here alone," he barks, his deep voice rumbling through the darkness. "Don't you know what kind of predators hunt at night?"

I step back, adrenaline surging through me. "Let me make something crystal clear," I snap. "I don't care who you think you are or why you're following me, but there's something seriously wrong with your brain."

He fixes me with a predatory stare, a low growl rumbling from his chest. "That's what I like to see. So much fire in you."

"Who the hell are you?" I demand, fighting to keep my voice steady.

I'm at war with myself. My brain screams danger while something primal within me responds to his raw power. My skin prickles with an electric awareness I can't deny.

"Tell me who you are and why you're stalking me." The slight tremor in my voice betrays my conflicted emotions.

He steps closer. "Has anyone ever told you how exquisite you look when you're angry?"

I clench my jaw. "You can't just follow people around like some creep-er! Who are you?"

"Someone who's been watching you," he replies.

"No shit, Sherlock. Why?"

"Because there's something different about you, Dani. Something... captivating."

"Look, I don't know what you're after, but I'm just a normal person," I insist, gripping the trash bags tighter. "Nothing special about me."

"Normal?" He laughs softly. "We both know that's far from true."

I swallow hard. His face remains hidden beneath his hood, but I feel the weight of his gaze. There's an undeniable connection between us—a magnetic pull drawing me toward him despite every warning bell.

"Stay away from me," I whisper, my voice shaking with fear and something else—desire.

"Is that really what you want, Angel?" he challenges, closing the distance between us.

He leans in, his breath hot against my ear. "If we keep meeting like this, I'm going to have to do something about it."

"What do you mean?" I whisper.

"Maybe I should find a more... suitable place for us to continue our little encounters."

"Us?" I snicker. "If by us, you mean 'you and me,' then there isn't one. You're just some weird stranger with a death wish."

"Am I a stranger, though? Or am I someone you've secretly longed to see again?"

"Longing?" I snort. "You must be mistaken. I'm not the type of girl who longs for anything."

"Am I mistaken?" He moves closer until our bodies are just a whisper away.

"Are you merely an echo of me, or do you *actually* have a purpose?" I quip.

His exotic scent surrounds me, clouding my judgment. "I have plenty to say," he states. "And your body is already answering."

"Oh yeah? You don't know anything about me, buddy!"

"I know everything about you. You crave the thrill of danger and forbidden pleasure. Don't bother denying it."

"I don't think so," I huff. "This isn't my scene."

Liar.

"Is that so? Then why haven't you run, Angel? Why do you let me get closer, even though I'm the predator and you're the prey? I can't resist solving the puzzle that is you."

Damn him for targeting my own curiosity! I want to scream at his arrogance, but find myself speechless. Despite every rational thought, part of me craves to unravel his mystery just as he seems determined to uncover mine.

My heart pounds against my ribs. "Let's cut the bullshit. I'm trying to figure out who the hell *you* are."

He advances with deliberate power, forcing me back until I hit the wall.

"What are you, Dani?" he demands.

"I don't know what you're talking about," I whisper—terror and desire wage war inside me.

"Your scent," he rumbles, inhaling deeply. "It's different. There's something about you."

The cold bricks dig into my back. Yet intense heat radiates from his body as he cages me.

"For the last time, I don't have a *clue* what you're talking about," I snap, frustration overtaking fear. "I'm just a normal human being, nothing more. So get over whatever fantasy you've created that I'm something special."

Even as I say it, I wonder if it's true.

I wrinkle my nose. "Actually, you may be sensing that I forgot to put on deodorant today. So if you're smelling something unusual, it's just me au naturel."

I give him an exaggerated stink-eye. "So sorry to be the human let-down when you were expecting some enchanting fairy creature. But I'm just ordinary me, reeking up the place in my natural, pitiful mortal state." He stands there, unmoving and staring at me. I wish I could see his face.

"So now that we've established I'm just an *ordinary* human, do you want to explain what you think you're sensing in me, Mr. Tall, Dark and Creepy?"

I fidget with my fingers impatiently. "Because I don't have all night to stand out here fielding wild accusations of being 'something more.' Honestly, I have a date with Netflix that's far more appealing than this pointless conversation."

He chuckles, the sound rich and deep. "Ordinary? Nothing is ordinary about how your blood calls to me. It sings to me as no other does. No mortal could ignite such an all-consuming thirst within me."

He presses closer to me, and I instinctively press back into the wall, my confidence faltering.

"From the moment I first saw you, I knew you were different. Your blood, your scent—it sings to me. I am powerless to resist."

My eyes widen in shock. He's a goddamn vampire, and now he's talking about my blood calling to him?

Any nerve I had goes out the window, replaced with mind-numbing terror. This bloodsucker knows things about me—hell, maybe can even smell something in my blood—that I sure as shit don't.

Because damn, shit just got real in the most petrifying way. This isn't some creepy fantasy—Dr. Fang over here looks ready to drain me dry.

"What the hell do you mean my blood 'sings' to you?" I choke out.

Maybe trying to sass a freakin' vampire wasn't my brightest move. Now, the only thought in my head is making a break for it before I end up this man's midnight snack.

"Please," I whisper. "You're scaring me. Just let me go."

"Scared? You should be. Tell me, Angel, what are you hiding? What secrets lie beneath that innocent façade?"

“I'm not hiding anything,” I insist, my voice barely audible as I fight back the tears. “I don't know what you want from me.”

"Perhaps not consciously," he muses. "But something tells me that there's more to you than meets the eye, and I intend to find out what that is."

"Are you trying to threaten me?" I ask, my voice shaking. "I don't take kindly to threats." I can feel helpless tears stinging at the corners of my eyes, but I refuse to let them fall.

"Let me tell you one thing," I continue with as much bravado as I can fake, "I don't take kindly to threats."

Even as my body responds to his.

My heart pounds wildly, and my instincts scream at me to run. This man—this vampire—terrifies me to my core. At the same time, part of me is perversely enthralled by his raw, dangerous energy.

I harden my expression, trying to appear more challenging than I feel.

He studies me for a long moment, then steps back. "Go. But know this, Dani, I will be watching you. And if I discover that you've been lying to me, there will be nowhere for you to hide."

He vanishes into the shadows, leaving me trembling.

Suddenly, I'm slammed back against the wall, a vise-like grip around my throat. I reach for his wrist, fear lacing through my veins.

"Did you think I would leave you so easily?" he whispers against my ear.

"Wh-what do you want from me?" I stammer.

"Right now, Angel, I want to see if your body is as responsive as your fear suggests."

"Please don't..." His hand slides under my shirt, tracing my waist before moving higher—fear and arousal war within me as his fingers graze my breast.

"Interesting. Your body reacts quite strongly. Tell me, how does this make you feel?"

"Terrified," I declare. "But..." My traitorous body responds.

"You are not immune to temptation after all."

"Stop it," I demand. "This isn't right."

"Isn't it? You can't deny the desire you have for me, Dani. I can smell it. Embrace it."

"I... I can't," I admit, my resolve wavering.

"Let me show you," he murmurs. Strong fingers work swiftly, unbuttoning my jeans. "Your body knows what it wants. Surrender to it."

"Oh God," I whimper as my legs turn to liquid. His lips trace a path down my neck. My fingers clench his shirt, trembling.

"You feel it too," he whispers against my skin. "There's no need for fear, Angel. Just let go."

And for one terrifying, electrifying moment, I do.

RHYLAND

17

I prowl through the darkness, tracking my prey with predatory focus. Can't shake this fucking pull toward her—this brunette-haired temptress moving through the city like she owns it. What kind of hold does this mortal have on me? I'm right there in the shadows, watching her every move, unable to break away.

"What the hell are you doing to me, angel?" I growl under my breath. Stealth isn't my style—I'm more of a tear-your-throat-out kind of guy. But spooking her isn't an option, not when she's got me by the balls without even knowing it.

Her laugh cuts through the bar's noise like a blade, hitting me right in the gut. My iron control is turning to shit around her—every smile, every swing of those hips chips away at centuries of discipline.

"Fuck this," I snarl, fighting the urge to step into her light. She's dangerous in ways that have nothing to do with fangs or claws, and it pisses me off. I don't do enchanted—I do death and destruction. But here I am, caught in her web.

"Get your shit together," I mutter, but my eyes never leave her. The night drags on, the crowd thins, but I'm still here, watching her like she's the center of the fucking universe.

Hidden beneath my hood, I'm invisible to her—a ghost with more power in one hand than her entire fragile body. Yet I'm the one circling her orbit, drawn by something I can't explain.

Logic says this has to be some kind of trap. No random human should have this kind of pull without some hidden agenda. If that's her game, I'll tear the truth from her, expose whatever lies behind those honey-gold eyes.

Every second near her is a battle with my darker nature—the beast inside that wants to drag her back to my territory and mark her as mine in every possible way.

The idea that she could be my mate after all this time is almost laughable. Part of me wants to believe it, but centuries of betrayal make me question every instinct.

I'm torn between keeping her at a distance and letting her breach walls no one has ever crossed. When I catch that look in her eyes—that flash of recognition—it's like fate's taunting me, daring me to take the risk.

I've survived this long by trusting no one, yet here I am, ready to throw it all away for a woman I barely know. My mind screams danger, but my body craves the fire only she seems to ignite.

The smart play is keeping her at arm's length, treating her like the threat she probably is. But when she looks my way, something in those eyes calls to me like a siren's song.

She disappears back into her bar, and the emptiness hits harder than a stake to the heart. I force myself to turn away, but every step feels like walking through holy water.

This woman is heaven and hell wrapped in curves that could kill, and I'm ready to burn just to taste paradise. Game on, little angel. This dance of ours is just getting started.

Danica

18

"Back at it already, Danica?" Dr. Hayes asks, peering over his glasses. "You look like you've seen a ghost."

"It's nothing," I lie, plastering on a fake smile as I slip into my lab coat. Work will distract my frazzled brain.

"Let me know if you need anything," Hayes offers before shuffling back to his station.

Try as I might, I can't stop replaying last night's alley encounter on mental repeat. The way he pressed me against the wall. His voice was like some hypnotic drug, and his touch? It was like he'd memorized a map of every sensitive spot on my body. I can't shake the feeling of his lips on my skin or his hands that practically screamed, "Mine!"

I should be freaking out about getting hot and heavy with Mr. Dangerous Stalker Guy, but instead, there's this traitorous little voice in my head whispering, "When's round two?"

It was like he hijacked my common sense without even trying. I barely know this man who somehow sees right through me—who's already left his fingerprints all over my psyche.

That alley is now burned into my memory, a forbidden territory I know I should avoid but can't stop wanting to revisit. To feel that dark thrill of surrendering to my mysterious seducer completely...

Focus, Dani. You have actual work to do.

The centrifuge hums to life as I carefully position the sample. Once processed, I slide it under the microscope with held breath. At first glance, it looks normal. But then I notice subtle anomalies in the DNA sequence—two distinct genetic codes intertwined, one clearly lupine.

"That's impossible," I whisper, staring in disbelief—my mind races, trying to process what I see. Unbidden images of my alley stalker flash through my thoughts. I clench my jaw, forcing him out.

My heart pounds as I study the impossible results glowing on my screen. But my concentration keeps slipping, drawn back to last night's encounter—

I push back from my desk abruptly, needing to move, to break this mental loop. *Get a grip, Danica,* I scold myself. But I can't seem to find my balance.

I sigh back into my chair, fighting for professional composure. But unease and longing churn inside me, irrational as it seems. I don't appreciate feeling this affected by some cryptic stranger's words and wandering hands.

But damn if I don't want to feel them again.

I inhale deeply, trying to calm my racing thoughts. But questions circle like hungry sharks in my mind. Why me? Why say I'm "different"? And most importantly—will I see him again?

In that alley, his touch awakened sensations I didn't know existed, drawing out responses both alien and terrifyingly natural. I shiver, remembering how easily my resistance crumbled, my body betraying me with its eager response. This absolutely cannot happen again. I need to build stronger walls against whatever this is.

"Dr. Hayes, could you look at this?" I call, fighting to keep my voice professional. He studies the screen, his eyebrows shooting upward. "Extraordinary..."

I explain the impossible fusion of lupine and human genetic markers, hoping for his perspective. Could this hybrid DNA be natural evolution or deliberate engineering?

Hayes's expression grows contemplative before he asks, "Have you considered something supernatural?" At my raised eyebrow, he continues, "There have always been stories about beings who exist between human and animal."

I scoff at the absurd suggestion of science and superstition mingling. "Werewolves, Doctor? Surely you don't give credence to folk tales?"

"The universe contains more mysteries than we can imagine, Danica," he replies with that infuriating wisdom. "Don't dismiss possibilities simply because they seem fantastic."

I nod politely, though skepticism clings to me like a lab coat.

Yet some rebellious part of me wonders—vampires just stepped out of the coffin and into reality. The world barely blinked before accepting their existence. So why is the concept of werewolves so far-fetched? If one mythological creature can walk among us, why not others?

The boundaries of "impossible" seem to shrink daily. Perhaps reality encompasses far more than our sterile science has acknowledged until now.

I refocus on my samples, methodically conducting every test to verify these impossible results. There's no denying the truth displayed on my screen. Logic stumbles where intuition whispers—wherever this leads, my life veers into unexplored territory. But the scientist in me can't resist diving into the unknown.

Even if it means diving into him again.

I enter the steam-filled bathroom and feel tension melt away in the hot, fragrant mist. Unbidden memories of last night flood back—my mystery man's skilled touch sending me spiraling into ecstasy I've never known before. Even now, my body hums with remembered pleasure.

I sway slightly under the shower spray, letting the warm water cascade over my skin. After indulging in the silky sensation of soap bubbles, I reluctantly prepare to return to reality.

Suddenly, the hairs on my neck stand at attention. My senses sharpen instantly. With unease, I yank the shower curtain aside and peer into the foggy bathroom. Nobody's there, yet something feels... off. A presence I can't see but somehow feel, sending ice down my spine despite the steam.

I hurriedly rinse the remaining suds from my hair, the water cooling as I speed through my routine. With growing apprehension, I shut off the shower and grab my towel, wrapping the plush cotton tightly around my dripping body. My heart hammers as I listen intently for any sound that doesn't belong.

I dry my hair quickly, every sense hyperalert. The apartment's silence feels wrong somehow, broken only by the air conditioner's steady hum. Taking a deep breath, I gather what courage I can and crack open the bathroom door, peering into my now-darkened bedroom.

Why are all the lights off? I definitely left them on.

As I cautiously enter the living room, the air feels charged with anticipation. I freeze mid-step, feeling the weight of someone's gaze on my skin.

It's him.

In the shadowy corner stands the figure haunting my thoughts. His presence bends reality, eyes roaming over me, sending electricity racing through my veins.

My heart pounds wildly. Fear, outrage, and something else I refuse to name radiate through me as he approaches.

Run? Scream? Confront him? My brain can't decide.

My pulse thunders. I try to back away, but remain rooted as his shadow approaches. I clutch my towel tighter, painfully aware of my exposure.

"What the hell do you think you're doing? How did you get in here?" My voice shakes despite my efforts.

Or how part of me was hoping to see him again.

His unique scent fills the space like an approaching storm. His breath fans across my skin, heat racing down my spine. His powerful frame makes my apartment feel tiny.

His fingers ghost along my arm, leaving fire in their wake.

Every instinct screams to run, yet I remain still, desperate to unravel his mystery.

His touch drifts to my throat, featherlight but commanding. From anyone else, this would be threatening. From him, it feels like awakening.

Finally, I bolt.

I make it three steps before he catches me, impossibly fast.

How did he move so quickly?

His grip closes around my throat. He pushes me against the wall with effortless strength. I can feel his hunger.

"Why are you here? What do you want from me?"

"You know exactly why I'm here," he purrs. "I can smell your desire, Angel. Your body betrays how badly you want this. Tell me you haven't been dreaming of my touch."

The urge to knee this arrogant bastard is overwhelming, but I can't deny the heat spreading through me.

Damn him. And damn me for wanting this.

His cockiness makes it unbearable as he revels in power over my chaotic mind.

Every thought of last night and the one before overwhelms me as his skilled touch lights my skin on fire, an unfamiliar sensation. I refuse to let my feelings get the better of me.

Steeling myself, I tell him boldly, “Nope, not at all. I kind of even forgot you existed.” I lie with a sarcastic tone.

I haven't been able to stop thinking about him. As soon as the words leave my lips, his demeanor changes into annoyance. Without backing down, I follow up with a challenge.

“What are you going to do?” He seems taken aback, and my courage rises.

A deep growl leaves his lips, sending pleasure through me. "You can't hide the truth from me. I'd be happy to illustrate just what I have planned for you," he murmurs into my neck.

His warm exhale intensifies the heat radiating from my core. I quiver as his lips ghost up my neck.

"You want this, don't you? My mouth on your skin, my hands all over you. I can smell your desire, feel your body screaming for my touch."

How does he know? Am I that obvious?

He nips my earlobe, making me gasp. Fear twists with arousal. My mind panics with questions.

Will this bloodsucking bastard drain me dry? Rip my throat out and leave me for dead? Or do something even more dangerous—fuck me senseless until I'm begging for more?

I curse as my core clenches with need. A treacherous part of me wishes for that last option.

"Tell me you want me," he commands, grinding against me.

I bite back a moan, hating my body for craving his touch despite the alarm bells.

"Go to hell," I fire back, even as my nails dig into his shoulders, pulling him closer.

"You're already there, Angel. Give in. I can make it heavenly for you."

I should run. But all I can think about is this dangerous stranger fucking me into oblivion.

I push against him, but it's useless—he's too powerful.

He grabs both wrists, slamming them against the wall above my head. His grip is iron-tight.

"Let me go!" I demand, trying fruitlessly to wrench my hands from his viselike hold. He only presses closer, using the weight of his body to pin me harder against the wall.

"Never," he growls.

Panic rises in my throat as I truly comprehend my helplessness. I'm trapped here with this all-consuming man whose true intentions remain unknown.

My mind screams to fight, but my limbs are leaden and weak with the bone-deep realization that I'm at his mercy now. His scent and heat envelop me as inescapably as the wall at my back.

As his thigh forces my legs apart, some primal part of me wants to surrender, to see how exquisite the darkness can be.

As I stand here, my heart pounds like a drum. I realize this moment is life-changing. He's not hurting me; his touch feels like I'm already climbing to an incredible peak, and it's taking over my body. His breath and facial hair tickle down my neck while he nibbles and kisses it with his lips. His hands are strong but gentle as they hold mine above my head, clasped at my wrist.

He's captured me with his gorgeous body, and there's no way I'm getting out of it anytime soon.

The towel grazing my skin is softly removed, leaving me bare and vulnerable to his passionate gaze. He leans back, admiring my curves, his gaze blazing and voice husky as he rasps, "Goddamn, you're so fucking beautiful."

I moan as his words sink into my skin. Hot arousal floods my core as his lips travel to my earlobe, sending intense shock waves down my spine. His gentle licks and nibbles make me quiver with pleasure. My nipples ache for more, begging to be touched by him while I'm trembling from the electrifying energy between us.

"Do you feel it, too?" he purrs huskily in my ear.

His muscular body presses against me, hard and unyielding—as his hips pin mine, I can feel his rock-hard desire demanding satisfaction, and my resistance crumbles. Despite myself, I crave the dangerous exhilaration of giving in to him completely.

The heat of his breath caresses my lips. I know I should fight, but my body has other desires I can't silence.

"Please...please," I plead, desperate for him to understand.

He stops and leans away from me, leaving a chill in the air where his warmth was once present.

He stares down at me. “Please, what?”

His voice is lost. I'm dumbstruck.

Do I want more of his touch?

For him to stay or go?

My mind is at war with itself. I'm both drawn to the mystery and scared of it. He's barged in on my home, followed me to work, and encroached on my space... but here I am, letting it all happen. Something inside of me demands his attention like a drug.

I've lost my mind.

Without an ounce of hesitation, his lips find my breast. His hand moves languidly, cocooning it before he latches his hungry lips to my sensitive nipple. His teeth graze and bite down, causing sparks of pain that vibrate through me as pleasure ignites in my being. The sensation is so intense I cry out spontaneously as I arch my back in response, pushing myself closer to him, begging for more.

His ironclad grip on my wrists traps me as his mouth explores my body. I want to soar, run my hands through his hair, and explore every inch of him. But all I can do is surrender with each moan that leaves my throat, which only incites a hungry growl from him.

He moves to the other breast, and I gasp as pleasure courses through me. “You keep making those delicious sounds, love, and it's going to get even better,” he murmurs.

My head reels from his touch, and I stammer in confusion, my breath coming in short gasps. “What...what are you doing to me?” I whisper, my voice trembling.

He groans, his stare molten. "Want me to stop?"

My heart races as I feel his desire burning, hoodie framing his face like a dark halo. Before I can answer, his mouth urgently crashes onto mine, and I let out a low moan.

Our tongues entwine deeply, exploring and tasting each other with an ever-intensifying hunger. His hands reach for me greedily, squeezing and grasping my curves as our moans echo together.

The power of our kiss heightens every sensation; our bodies are pressed tightly. His tongue flicks and dances with mine, finding a passionate rhythm that has me reeling.

This kiss...it's like nothing I've experienced before. It awakens something ravenous inside me, a primal craving for more of *him.* I cannot help but let out pleading little moans into his mouth as the kiss deepens further still.

He swallows my gasps of pleasure, claiming me. The world falls away until only him, his delicious scent enveloping me, and his talented mouth stealing my breath from my lungs.

I go pliant in his arms, my knees weakening, my core aching and ready. I have become liquid fire under his masterful kiss and touch, reduced to pure sensation and desire.

As his lips slant roughly over mine, again and again, I know I will never get enough of this exquisite torment. This kiss ignites an addiction deep in my cells and a gnawing need for more.

So much *passion.* My arousal drips down my thighs.

His hand snakes around the nape of my neck to hold me closer and, possessively, grabs a fistful of my hair, causing slight pricks to the base of my neck. With all the sensations coursing through me, I wrap one of my legs around his waist and moan into his mouth. His hand instantly releases my wrists and grips my thigh with immense power to massage up and cup my ass.

He pulls away from my lips, "Dani," he whispers into my mouth. "You're going to ruin me."

My mind spins in shock as my body coils, not from fear but anticipation.

Who the hell is this man?

My brain feels like it's been put in a blender and set to high power. I can't ignore the tingling feeling he's giving me, something I've never felt before. It's driving me mad!

Then suddenly, POOF! He disappears like magic. He's gone like a gust of wind, leaving me just a chaotic mess of hair.

My heart stops as a flood of pleasant confusion runs through my veins. My fingertips trace my lips, trying to understand the power of that kiss.

Did I allow this guy to rock my world with those delicious lips? How can something so wrong feel so right?

I pick up the towel off the floor and wrap it around me like a strait-jacket.

Was I dreaming?

No, way in hell—it was way too real. I try to assemble the pieces, but my mind and body are numb.

RHYLAND

19

Prowling through the silent city, my muscles still vibrate from our wild clash of skin on skin. Fuck, her taste—like some sweet, addictive poison—clings to my tongue, and the sound of her breathy moans haunts me. I was a damn hair's breadth from crossing a line I can't come back from.

With every goddamn step, flashes of her body writhing beneath me, yielding to my touch, hammer at my restraint. The night's cool air does shit all to extinguish what she's ignited within me tonight.

Centuries—fucking centuries—I've spent locked away in emotionless ice, and she's the detonator that's blown that to hell. But now, I'm warring with myself, fighting the impulse to tear down the walls I've spent lifetimes building.

I've laughed in the face of love, scorning anything permanent. Commitment? A leash I had no intention of ever wearing. And now? I'm fucking ensnared, battling to break free from the one woman who's restarted my dead man's heart—forced me to feel again after an eternity bathed in shadow.

This notion that she might be my destined mate sends a rush of both thrill and dread ripping through my gut. If I follow through with the old laws, if I bond our souls, it's irreversible. That shakes me to the bones. Accepting her as mine would mean shattering the goddamn fortress I've so meticulously erected.

But desiring her demands strategy—demands planning. This isn't some bullshit fling. This is chess with eternal stakes on the board.

When she looks at me with those deep, searching eyes, seeking answers from the mysterious man behind the shadows, it fucking guts me. Everything in me wants to rip off the guise, to come clean and offer her the assurance she doesn't even need to speak to ask for.

Yet, I bite back the truth, and that might cost me. She knows about the drugging and got the intel from Lucian when I stood silent as the grave. Will she get it when the truth comes out? Or will she see me as just another bastard who left her vulnerable?

She doesn't know the depth of it—how that whole fucked-up incident tore at me, given the shitstorm brew I'd stirred up, watching from the dark. Guilt eats at my gut like acid. Could she forgive this apparent negligence, a seemingly cold-hearted oversight?

Despite every damn effort to reset, to pull the old cool composure back into place, I can't stop the dread that claws at me. The fear that I'll lose her before we've even really started grips me and leaves me thinking of moving heaven and earth to keep her.

The more time I spend with Dani, the more I am drawn in, consumed by her light. If we're truly written in the stars to dance this dance, I'm not about to let it end before the music even fucking peaks.

I slam through the back door of Lucian's club, the music hitting like a sledgehammer. These oblivious humans grind away while I take the stairs to the office two at a time.

Erik and Lucian are glued to the monitors like they're watching porn.

"Our rats in the trap yet?" I growl.

"Just slithered in!" Lucian announces with theatrical flair. "Like cockroaches to a garbage buffet!"

After hearing what that piece of shit Max did to Dani, my brothers were ready for blood. Some things you can't leave to the law. I nod grimly. "Keep eyes on them."

Lucian's eyebrow shoots up, a smirk playing on his lips. "Did you get into a sexy alley fight, or is that the 'just got laid' look you're sporting?"

Erik's trying not to laugh. I shoot them both death glares. "The fuck are you talking about?"

"Oh, nothing," Lucian chirps, "you just look thoroughly debauched, darling! Like you've been rolling in some very pleasant hay!"

Christ. I check myself out—yeah, I'm a mess. "Got spare clothes?"

"Mi closet es su closet, Captain Rumpled!" Lucian winks like he knows exactly what I've been doing.

Part of me wants to tell them about Danica, but Lucian would never let me hear the end of it. Maybe Erik would understand. But tonight isn't about my feelings—it's about making that bastard pay for touching what's mine.

I head straight for the bar in Lucian's private office, pouring myself a double of aged whiskey. The burn steadies me for what's coming.

I rummage through Lucian's ridiculous designer wardrobe, settling on dark jeans and a black tee that won't restrict movement when I'm beating these assholes to a pulp.

Back upstairs, the playful mood's dead. "What's the status?"

Erik silently points to the screen. There they are—Max, Dakota, and Samuel—laughing like the sick fucks they are while scanning the crowd for their next victims. My vision goes red just looking at them.

"Our special guests have no idea they're about to star in 'When Vampires Attack: The Reckoning!'" Lucian's voice has lost its humor, replaced by something cold and vicious.

I grip Erik's shoulder, keeping him steady. "We do this clean and quiet. Get them alone, handle it, no witnesses. Clear?"

Erik nods, ice in his veins. On screen, those pieces of shit are eyeing women like they're picking out meat. My fists clench tight enough to draw blood.

"Ready to take out the garbage?" Lucian asks with deadly cheer.

"Let's hunt," I growl.

We move in like a pack of wolves. The scumbags are chatting up three girls, probably already working their sick game. They look up as we approach, confusion on their stupid faces.

Lucian's voice is sharp and menacing as he speaks. "Hey motherfuckers, I think it's time we have a little talk. You'll come with us quietly if you know what's good for you."

Max sneers like the cocky bastard he is. "The fuck's your problem, Lucian? We're just having fun."

Lucian's voice becomes sinister and threatening. "You're fuckin' with the wrong crowd, Max. You don't play games in my joint." Lucian points at his chest.

Max throws his hands up in defeat, "Fine, I'm coming with you."

"You two walking cum stains," Lucian points at Dakota and Samuel, "up and at 'em! Family meeting time!"

We herd them through the crowd like cattle to slaughter. My blood's on fire, Erik's watching our backs, and Lucian's practically skipping ahead.

In the office, we've got them surrounded. Lucian drops the act: "You think you can drug and rape girls in my fucking club?"

Max is shaking. "Come on, man, it was just for fun..."

I snap, grabbing his throat. "Fun? You call drugging *my* woman fun, you worthless fuck? Who were you selling her to?"

Erik and Lucian exchange looks at my possessive outburst.

"You enjoy destroying lives?" Erik asks, voice like arctic ice.

I'm barely holding back from ripping his head off. "I'll tear you apart for thinking you could touch what's mine!"

Max looks ready to piss himself. "Oh god," he whimpers.

Stupid fuck thought he'd gotten away with it. He had no idea who was hunting him.

"I didn't know she was yours!" Max whimpers, his face drained of color. "It was nothing, I swear! I-I work for Azrael. He pays me to find girls. Please, I'll never do it again!"

Samuel and Dakota look like they're about to shit bricks. Dakota's voice breaks as he tries to save his worthless skin.

"I swear I didn't know—" he stammers out.

"SHUT UP!" Max screams, panic in his eyes.

"Well, looks like we've got ourselves a confession!" Lucian announces with deadly cheer. "Time to check out permanently, boys!"

I don't hesitate. My fangs tear into Max's throat, his blood flooding my mouth with the taste of fear and weakness. Power surges through me as I drain the life from this pathetic excuse for a human. His pulse stutters and stops against my lips, and I drop his empty shell to the floor.

Erik moves with cold precision, ripping Samuel's throat out in one clean motion. The light leaves his eyes before he can even scream.

Lucian attacks Dakota with theatrical flair, drinking deeply from his neck while making exaggerated sounds of satisfaction.

Three bodies hit the floor in rapid succession. I wipe blood from my mouth, a dark satisfaction settling in my chest.

The stench in the air is nauseatingly pungent.

"Goddamn, that hit the spot. There's nothing quite like devouring a piece of shit for dinner." Lucian exclaims, kicking Dakota's lifeless body. "Though this one tasted like day-old garbage."

I chuckle darkly. Erik asks about the bodies. Lucian texts his cleanup crew—problem solved.

A few minutes later, there's a knock on the door. Lucian answers it and instructs three men to come in and take care of the bodies. With the sweet taste of revenge in my mouth, I feel a rush that lifts the weight off my shoulders. That fucker had it coming. Drugging women just to get laid? It made me want to puke. And when he did it to *my* girl, that was the end of his sorry ass. He fucked up big time.

But Max's words continue nagging at me—his boss, Azrael. My suspicions regarding Azrael's activities involving humans only deepen. Trafficking them, or something even more insidious...

I voice my most chilling thought out loud. "Azrael," I growl, the name like poison on my tongue. "So the bastard's expanding his operation. Do you think he's working for Moretemis?"

Lucian's face goes white at that name. "We are well and truly, royally, mega-fucked if that's the case." Lucian throws his hands up dramatically. "That freak's been jonesing to bust through the realms and go full Anakin-kills-younglings for ages now. If he's got Azrael on the payroll, brothers...it's lights out, game over."

Erik's face goes grim. "We must locate the prophesied mortal. Our time grows short."

Guilt hits me like a sledgehammer. I've been so wrapped up in Dani that I've neglected our most sacred mission.

"You're right," I concede. "We need to speak with Adrian immediately."

"Hold your horses, Captain Impulsive!" Lucian interrupts. "We stick to the plan. Azrael first, prophecy later."

My jaw clenches at being contradicted, but he's right. Finding hard evidence of Azrael's betrayal takes priority over chasing legends. The clock's ticking on finding our savior, but Lucian's strategic mind is sharper than mine right now.

After the cleanup crew handles our mess, Lucian drops a bombshell in the office.

"Azrael's throwing his annual look-at-how-rich-I-am masquerade ball," he announces. "Perfect cover to sneak in and do some snooping."

My mind immediately goes to Dani in a ball gown, and Lucian catches my look.

"Two weeks, Romeo! Plenty of time to coordinate your couple's costumes!"

I ignore his bullshit. "Where do we get what we need?"

"Leave it to your friendly neighborhood party planner! I'll handle everything."

I nod, already planning how we'll slip away from the party and find proof of Azrael's deal with Moretemis. Maybe free some prisoners while we're at it.

"I'll dig deeper into his operation," Lucian promises, "get us some fancy dress that'll let us blend right in with all the other snakes."

Erik gives a rare smile. "An excellent strategy."

The plan's set. In two weeks, we start dismantling Azrael's empire. And if I happen to run into my angel there... well, that's just a bonus.

DANICA

20

What am I doing, letting this dark and dangerous stranger seduce me night after night? I know I should resist his tantalizing touch, but my desires betray me.

Who does this shady weirdo think he is, sneaking into my apartment uninvited like a damn ninja? I don't care how ripped his abs are or how good he makes this kitty purr. It stops now.

This guy has more red flags than a game of Minesweeper. Stalking me at work? Yeah, that's not suspect AT ALL. And what kind of kinky Fifty Shades crap is he into with the dark hoodie and keeping his face hidden? Some vampire asshole who gets off on control.

Well, I'm nobody's plaything. Next time tall, dark, and shady shows up, I will tell that fine piece of man meat to kick rocks.

My heart pounds as I try desperately to think straight. I need answers.

I begin to feel a strange warmth radiating through my hands. I lay frozen on the bed, my eyes fixed on my open palms, watching in stunned disbelief as a spark of glimmering white fire explodes from my skin.

Bright flames erupt from my palms—not ordinary fire but something like liquid starlight. Heat radiates outward as mystical energy hums beneath my skin. My heart hammers against my ribs as terrifying realization dawns: this power comes from *inside me.*

I stare dumbfounded at my glowing hands. Hallucination? Mental breakdown? The rational scientist in me scrambles for explanations while evidence of the impossible pulses between my fingers.

Have I finally lost my damn mind?

Furiously, I flail my arms as if shaking an Etch-A-Sketch could erase the supernatural shimmer enveloping my extremities. But the spooky glow persists, twinkling mockingly like glow-in-the-dark stars.

Yup, I've gone nuts. Somebody call the funny farm 'cause I need to be checked in, STAT.

I squeeze my eyes shut, desperately clinging to fraying threads of reality and reason. Maybe the madness will pass if I don't look for a minute.

But even with eyes closed, the otherworldly radiance pierces through.

Keep it together, girl. Breathe. You're not possessed or radioactive. This is just a momentary lapse of mental cohesion.

But then I catch sight of my disco ball hands again—reason flees, shrieking into oblivion.

Who am I kidding? The loony bin awaits!

As I stare at my burning hands, visions flash through my mind—strange lands and creatures I've never seen. A voice whispers in my head, urging me toward a shimmering doorway that's somehow opened.

I sense this portal calling me into the unknown. The flames brighten with my thoughts, responding like they're part of me. Something has awakened inside, tearing open connections to other places, unlocking powers I never knew existed. I gulp air, dizzy with possibilities.

Desperate for control, I thrust my hands under running water. The glow fades gradually, leaving me breathless and confused as droplets catch the last traces of that otherworldly light.

I stumble backward, heart pounding against my ribs.

What in the actual fuck?

There is no denying it—my hands glow and radiate blistering heat! I make a silent vow: I'd dive deeper and uncover the truth, no matter what. Once I get my hands under control, I slip into a form-fitting pencil skirt that hugs me in all the right places. On top is a soft, flowing blouse with a delicate floral pattern.

I gape at my reflection, glowing like a human nightlight suddenly switched on.

What sorcery is this? Did I stick my finger into a nuclear-powered outlet? Fall into a vat of radium like some ray gun-wielding superhero?

I breathe deep. Maybe I'm the victim of cosmic pranksters. Aliens experimenting on unwitting humans. Or maybe just be a healthy glow, and my makeup mirror lighting is playing tricks.

But my skeptical brain whispers, "*Girl, your highlight did NOT just kick into intergalactic overdrive.*"

I beeline for the kitchen to mainline some caffeine. Whatever weirdness is happening to me, coffee will help. The rich aroma fills my apartment, kickstarting my foggy brain. I'm completely freaking out, but trying to hold it together. Part of me is dying to call Emily and word-vomit about Stalker McCreepy's second appearance and how my fingers decided to go full Christmas lights for no reason. But the other part wants to figure out what the hell is happening before I sound like I've lost my marbles.

My finger hovers over Emily's contact, debating. In the end, I keep my mouth shut, secretly replaying both the encounter and my impromptu finger light show in my head like some twisted highlight reel.

Instead, I distract myself with mindless social media scrolling. As I swipe through photos of people pretending their lives are perfect, an event catches my eye—the Twisted Masquerade Ball.

Emily and I have our dress fitting today.

Azrael Blackwood, the host, is basically the definition of "filthy rich." His company, Nightfall Industries, has its fingers in every pie imaginable, making him practically untouchable in business circles.

The ball is supposedly this super fancy fundraiser, but there are always rumors swirling about what really goes down behind those masks. Still, as a respected doctor (go me!), I scored an invitation along with the city's other important people. It's a chance to network with bigwigs and maybe do some good—assuming the rumors are just jealous gossip.

The coffee maker beeps like it's judging my procrastination. Time's ticking, so I gulp down what's in my mug and pour the rest into my travel cup for the road.

I grab my bag, do the mental checklist dance (keys, phone, wallet, sanity—three out of four ain't bad), and head out the door, trying to psych myself up for whatever fresh hell today might bring.

Just another day in the life of Dr. Danica Pierce, possible genetic freak and professional stalker magnet

I pull into my designated parking spot, morning sun glinting off my car's black paint. Those white letters spelling "Dr. Pierce" still give me a little thrill—they represent years of busting my ass to get here. I fish out my phone to text Emily about our dress fitting for the hospital's fancy-pants masquerade fundraiser.

Emily replies instantly with her signature dancing lady emoji. I send back a kiss emoji, grateful for my bestie's enthusiasm.

Climbing out, I smooth my pencil skirt (which makes my butt look amazing, thank you very much) and strut into the building.

Tony, our security guard, greets me with his usual warmth. "Good morning, Dr. Pierce! Looking lovely as always."

"Thanks, Tony! How's the fam?" I genuinely like hearing about his life.

"Great! My little girl started kindergarten—loves it," he beams.

After our quick chat, I click-clack my way to the elevator in my power heels. The familiar antiseptic smell hits me as I reach the research wing—time to science the hell out of this day.

I burst into my private lab like I own the place (which, technically, I kind of do). But underneath my confident strut, anxiety churns. That weird tingling in my fingers, that ghostly glow I swear I saw... Sleep deprivation or something bigger?

Get it together, Dani. You're a woman of science.

I prep my equipment with practiced precision. The routine helps quiet my racing thoughts. When everything's ready, I tie the tourniquet around my arm. I've done this a million times, but today feels different. Watching my blood fill the vial, I can't help wondering what secrets it might spill.

The PCR machine hums away, copying DNA fragments while I document everything meticulously. Soon, the gel is ready for electrophoresis—science's version of sorting laundry by size.

My heart pounds as the viewing box lights up, revealing fluorescent bands that raise more questions than answers. I photograph everything before prepping samples for sequencing. Now comes the fun part—waiting while the machine reads my genetic code like some biological fortune teller.

Please don't let me be a freak.

Hours later, the results pop up and... holy shit. The DNA pattern on my screen looks like two drunk snakes got frisky with the double helix. It's definitely not normal human DNA, and it's sure as hell not werewolf either.

What the actual hell am I?

Glancing at the clock, I realize it's lunchtime. My heels echo down the empty hall as I head to the cafeteria, mind spinning faster than a centrifuge.

I grab food on autopilot, barely registering what lands on my tray. The cafeteria buzz fades to white noise as I stare into space, trying to process everything.

A shiver runs down my spine. Has some dormant X-Men gene

suddenly decided to wake up? Am I still me, or am I about to go full superhero origin story?

I want so badly to call Emily and spill everything, but I should probably wait until I have actual answers instead of wild theories.

My sandwich tastes like cardboard as I force it down. I feel like Alice tumbling down the scientific rabbit hole, except this Wonderland involves genetic mutations and possibly supernatural DNA.

My phone buzzes, displaying an unknown number.

Unknown:

Are you still thinking about last night? I'm sure I can make tonight even better.

Who's this?

His audacity astounds me.

Angel, you know exactly who this is. I'm the one you can't resist—Rhyland.

Angel? Who the hell does this man think he is? Telling me *I'm* the one who can't resist when he's the one stalking me like some leather-clad shadow? The balls of this man is truly next-level.

But damn it all—he's not entirely wrong. Something about him pulls at me in ways I can't explain or defend. My body betrays my brain every time I think about his encounters.

I hate that he knows it too.

Time to flip it.

Angel? Give me a damn break. Do you think a lame pet name makes this better?

I roll my eyes, seething as I hit send. The nerve of this guy! His immediate reply pops up.

I'll call you whatever I want, Angel. You're mine.

His cockiness fuels my anger. How dare he act so possessive over me!

I'm nobody's property.

Listen up, asshole. I don't belong to anyone, got it? Now tell me how the hell you got my number before I call the cops.

The bubbles taunt me as I await his response. He's hesitating, considering his options. My threat of police action must have given him pause.

Finally, his message appears.

I have my ways, Angel. But we both know you won't turn me in. We both have an interest in one another.

Damn him and his cocky assumptions! I should report his stalking ass immediately. But something holds me back...a dangerous curiosity I can't seem to shake.

You're right about one thing—you do seem to know a scary amount about me. Care to share how?

I must know more about this mysterious man who easily gets under my skin. My phone pings.

All in due time, Angel. For now, just know I'll always be close by.

Cryptic bastard. I huff in frustration.

Yeah, 'cause that's not creepy at all. Leave me the hell alone already!

I scowl at the screen, hoping he will stop pursuing me. Yet, a part of me hopes for another message. My reaction disgusts me—why does he captivate me so? My phone obliges, lighting up once more.

You're even more alluring when you're fiery. I'm not going anywhere. You didn't seem to mind my attention last night.

Arrogant ass! He needs to get a clue that this sick game of his won't work on me.

Look, dickwad. I'm NOT your damn "Angel." Stop harassing me, or I WILL call the cops on your pathetic stalking ass. Got it?

I seethe as I hit send, imagining my fingers wrapping around his throat. The nerve of this presumptuous prick! Assuming I'm his possession, that I won't fight back. Ha! Last night was an accident, and I don't plan on repeating it. My phone vibrates with his irritating response.

Your passion is admirable. But we both know there are more constructive ways to channel your fiery spirit.

Oh, I'll show him passion and fire, alright! I'll kick his ass six ways to Sunday and throttle him with his own intestines!

Here's an idea, jackass—take your deranged delusions, shove them up your ass, and lose my number while you're at it. We clear?

My chest heaves, adrenaline surging. I relish the thought of him sputtering over my text, realizing I'm not some meek victim he can intimidate. But the three bouncing dots appear, mocking me.

Crystal clear, Angel. I admire your strength. But you won't deter me so easily. I know you feel something, though you fight it. Give this a chance. You won't regret it.

Give this a chance? Is he out of his goddamn mind?! There's no way I'd ever willingly let this stalker-vampire slither into my life.

Let me make this real simple—fuck off and die, you deranged dipshit! Oh, wait... you did that already. I'd rather swallow acid than "give this a chance." Lose my number and get a fucking life!

I stab the send button like I'm trying to impale his ego through the screen. My hands are shaking—half fury, half that annoying little zing I get when I think about him.

Nope. Not going there. I silence my phone with a vengeance, swearing to ignore his texts even if my life depends on it.

But as I stomp to my lab, doubts start circling like vultures. *What if this creep doesn't take the hint?* Should I call the cops? My anxiety is having a cage match with my anger, and that stupid sliver of curiosity keeps trying to referee.

I take a deep breath that does absolutely nothing to calm me down. Focus, Dani. I'll deal with Mr. Stalker McHottie later. Right now, I need answers that aren't going to appear while I'm having a mental meltdown magically.

I ignore my phone (which feels like it's burning a hole in my pocket) and dive back into research, scrolling through sketchy forums where internet "experts" share conspiracy theories about genetic anomalies. For every semi-promising lead, I hit ten ridiculous dead ends. This shadow-lurking weirdo has my brain so scrambled I can't concentrate on saving my own DNA.

Finally, I throw in the towel. I'm too frazzled for science right now. I grab my purse and head out to meet Emily, hoping some bestie time will reset my brain. But with every step, my phone feels heavier, those unread messages practically screaming for attention.

I can't fully relax knowing they're sitting there, waiting. His grip on my thoughts is still iron-tight despite my best efforts to pry it loose.

This little war between us is just getting started.

And part of me is looking forward to the next battle.

Rhyland

21

I punch Dani's number into my phone, a predatory grin spreading across my face. She can play hard to get all she wants, but it only took one word in Lucian's ear to get her digits.

Breaking through that stubborn wall she's built is precisely the challenge I need. That firecracker temper of hers promises it won't be easy, and I wouldn't have it any other fucking way. It'll take every trick in my ancient playbook to seduce her properly, but victory tastes that much sweeter when the chase is this good.

I can already picture those golden eyes flashing with anger, her brilliant mind working overtime to shut me down. But every sharp comeback is just foreplay. She can deny this electricity between us all she wants, but her body betrays her whenever I get close. I'll fan those flames until she's burning for me, until those smart lips scream my name and only mine.

I pocket the phone, smirking at her fiery texts lighting up the screen. Her rejections don't discourage me—they're just gasoline on the fire—a teasing preview of the heat to come when she finally surrenders.

We roll up to Dapper Affairs, a high-end suit shop that screams money and taste. It's perfect for finding gear for Azrael's party, and their late hours are ideal for our kind.

Inside, we're greeted by rows of tailored perfection. We dive in, each gravitating to our style. Lucian, dramatic as always, zeroes in on a blood-red suit with black lace detailing.

"Behold, my fellow fashion victims." Lucian announces, spinning like he's on a runway. "I call this look 'Satan's Sexy Accountant'—guaranteed to make the angels fall."

Erik goes for understated power—a classic black tux, crisp white shirt, and a silver mask that screams mystery. "This will serve adequately for the mission," he states, ever the minimalist.

I'm drawn to a midnight blue suit that catches the light like the ocean at night. It's the perfect blend of power and style paired with a black shirt and matching mask.

"Holy mother of fashion!" Lucian fans himself theatrically. "You look like sex on a stick dipped in midnight. The ladies will be dropping panties faster than I drop bad guys."

I roll my eyes at his bullshit as we head back to the car.

"We need better accommodations than your club," I tell him. "Somewhere with actual security."

Lucian's grin turns devious. "Well, I've got my little love nest outside town, but there's a five-star paradise nearby that'll make your balls tingle with luxury. Straight outta LA!"

Intrigued, I nod. "Take us there."

Lucian paints a picture of luxury that even impresses me. We pull up to the hotel—all sleek modern lines and imposing grandeur. As we enter, the uniformed staff snap to attention, their practiced smiles firmly in place.

I stride across the polished marble floor like I own the place, past chandeliers that probably cost more than some countries' GDPs. The lobby screams old money and power—exactly my kind of playground.

At the front desk, I don't bother with the fake charm. "Your finest suite," I state, not asking. The clerk picks up on my tone immediately, his eyes catching my tailored clothes and the confidence that comes from centuries of command.

"Of course, sir. May I have a card for the room?" His voice is perfectly calibrated between respect and professionalism.

I slide my black card across the counter, watching his eyes widen slightly. He processes it quickly and hands me the key card with a deferential nod.

"Thank you for choosing us, Mr. Erikkson. Enjoy your stay." Without another word, I give him a curt nod and head for the elevators.

The suite is a masterpiece of luxury—floor-to-ceiling windows showcase the city lights, plush furniture, and every amenity imaginable.

"Welcome to paradise, gentlemen." Lucian announces, spreading his arms like he's introducing a game show prize. "Where the minibar is stocked, the beds are bouncy, and the neighbors can't hear you scream... with pleasure."

We each claim our territory within the suite. My room is exactly what I need—understated opulence with a king bed that looks like it could handle my bulky ass and then some. The bathroom's bigger than most apartments, with a tub I could swim laps in.

I join the others at the bar, pouring a generous scotch before we get down to business. The blueprints are spread out on the table as I turn to Lucian.

"What's the play?"

"Here's the master plan." Lucian taps the blueprint with theatrical precision. "While the rich assholes are busy comparing yacht sizes, we slip in through this service entrance. It's like the back door to heaven—rarely used and poorly guarded."

I nod approvingly. "Perfect. Quick and quiet."

"Now, gentlemen," Lucian raises his glass with a wicked grin, "everything is in motion—two weeks from now, get ready for a night of sinful indulgence."

I smirk, thinking of Dani. "Got my own plans for that."

Erik downs his drink, shaking his head. "Lucian, you're a horny little shit."

I watch them bicker, but heavier thoughts are weighing on me—time to come clean about Dani.

"I need to talk about that brunette from the club," I say finally. "There's something... different happening."

"Oh, you mean Miss Mortal Hottie?" Lucian laughs. "Buddy, you've got better odds of winning the lottery while getting struck by lightning and being abducted by aliens simultaneously than finding your mate in a human."

I exhale heavily. "You think I don't fucking know that, asshole?"

"Hey, if you want to buy a ticket on the Heartbreak Express, be my guest." He slaps my shoulder. "Just don't come crying when it derails spectacularly into Dumpsville, population: you."

I arch an eyebrow at Lucian's bullshit, but he doubles down with that shit-eating grin.

"What? Too real for you?" He clutches invisible pearls. "I'm just saying you might as well try riding a unicorn into battle. But hey, if you're determined to play with dynamite while smoking..." He throws his hands up dramatically. "Who am I to stop you? I'll just grab some popcorn and watch the Rhyland Gets His Heart Stomped Show. I'll even bring the tissues for the series finale—' Immortal Falls for Mortal: What Could Possibly Go Wrong?'"

He slaps my shoulder like we're in some buddy comedy. "Buckle up, Romeo! You're in for one hell of a ride with absolutely no happy ending in sight."

I shoot him a death glare. "Your support is overwhelming. Remind me why I don't rip your tongue out?"

"Because I'm the only one with the balls to tell you the truth." Lucian cackles. "And you'd miss my charming personality."

Erik looks genuinely shocked. "A human mate? That's unprecedented. You know our laws—if one dies, so does the other. Have you bound her yet?"

I meet his silver eyes. "No. She doesn't know anything."

"Well, well, well!" Lucian rubs his hands together gleefully. "Mr. 'No Relationships Ever' has finally caught feelings. Alert the media. Grab the smelling salts. The apocalypse is upon us!"

Erik takes a measured breath, ignoring Lucian's shit. "If you believe she's your mate, I stand with you. Your instincts have never led us astray."

My mind's a fucking hurricane of thoughts about Dani—those golden eyes that see right through me, that sun-kissed skin I want to taste. Desire burns through me, but doubt's right there with it. Can a mortal even handle what this means? Am I seeing something that isn't there?

Erik reads me like a book. "Trust your gut. If the bond feels real, it is."

I nod, grateful for his support. Having my brothers behind me steadies me, even with all these questions swirling. But one thing's crystal clear—I need to see Dani tonight.

A few hours later, we've nailed down our strategy for infiltrating those tunnels during the ball. I head back to my room, surrounded by luxury that means nothing compared to the thought of my fierce little angel.

DANICA

22

I wrap up at the lab and head to meet Emily for our fancy dress adventure. We're hitting up Enchanted Elegance, which is basically Disney princess heaven for grown-ups who need ball gowns and masks.

The second I walk in, I'm hit with classical music and enough tulle to suffocate an army. Mannequins draped in sequins and silk stand around like frozen supermodels. It's like stepping into a fashion fever dream.

Victoria, our fairy godmother for the evening, whisks us off to a private fitting room that's bigger than my first apartment. Emily and I turn into giggling teenagers as we try on dress after dress. Somehow, they fit like they were made for us.

Victoria works her magic with pins and measuring tape, suggesting accessories that'll make us look even more fabulous. When we finally face the mirrors, I almost don't recognize myself. These dresses aren't just pretty—they're straight-up transformative.

While Victoria does her ninja seamstress thing, Emily and I can't stop staring at our reflections. These gowns make us look like we should be running kingdoms or breaking hearts.

Then comes the pièce de résistance—Victoria presents two gorgeous masks like she's offering crown jewels. "These will add that perfect touch of mystery, ladies." She says it like she's blessing us for battle.

We practically float out of the store, wrapped dresses in hand, still riding the high of feeling like fairy tale royalty.

Emily suddenly clutches her stomach like she's been shot. "Oh. My. God. I'm dying here! I haven't eaten all day, and my stomach is staging a revolt!"

She gives me her best puppy dog eyes. "Please tell me you know somewhere nearby we can stuff our faces. I need food, stat!"

I laugh as my stomach lets out a growl worthy of a monster movie. "Girl, same. After today's lunch disaster, I'm ready to eat my arm."

I snap my fingers as inspiration hits. "Oh! There's this adorable French place around the corner—LaBelle something. You in?"

"YES!" Emily practically screams, latching onto my arm like a lifeline. "Move it or lose it, sister! I'm so hungry, I'll even let you order dessert first!"

We snag a table at La Belle Epoque and immediately order wine because, hello, priorities. We dive into the menus like we're studying for finals.

Emily's eyes go comically wide. "Holy mother of food porn! How am I supposed to choose? I want to eat literally everything!"

Same, girl. My eyes bounce between French onion soup that probably tastes like heaven, snails swimming in garlic butter (fancy escargot my ass), crepes stuffed with everything imaginable, and seafood that costs more than my car payment. It's like food paradise threw up on these pages.

After grilling our poor server about every dish, we finally decide. Emily goes for the fancy-pants sea bass, while I play it safe with coq au vin because sometimes you just need chicken drowning in wine sauce.

We sip our wine and gossip like teenagers, momentarily forgetting about my X-Men situation and other life dramas. Tonight is strictly BFF territory.

Our food arrives looking like it belongs in a magazine spread. The smell alone makes my stomach growl.

I take a bite of chicken so tender it practically melts, while Emily makes sounds that should probably be illegal in public over her fish.

Halfway through demolishing our meals, I take a deep breath and decide to spill about Mr. Tall-Dark-and-Stalkerish, who keeps popping up like a creepy jack-in-the-box.

My hands shake a little as I describe our latest encounter outside the bar—you know, the one where he went full dominant alpha male and pinned me to the wall while spouting cryptic warnings like some sexy fortune cookie.

Emily freezes mid-bite, fork hanging in the air like she's forgotten how arms work. I can see her brain short-circuiting as she processes this Grade-A crazy.

I tell her everything—how he makes my heart do gymnastics from both terror and... something else. How I'm becoming borderline obsessed with figuring out who he is. I've been keeping all the secrets while trying to solve this mystery solo.

I admit that keeping quiet has been driving me nuts. Part of me gets a twisted thrill from whatever power he has over me, even while my common sense screams to run far away.

Emily's face goes through about twelve expressions before settling on pure outrage. "What the actual fuck, Dani? Call the goddamn police! This isn't some romance novel—this is serial killer origin story territory!"

If she only knew about the glowing fingers...

I shift in my seat, unsettled by her outrage and my lack of fear. "I know, I should be freaked out. But every time I think about reporting him, something stops me."

Emily gapes in disbelief. "Uh, it's called common fucking sense! Get a restraining order on this weirdo stalker now."

I bite my lip, hating my own chaotic emotions. "You're completely right; it makes no logical sense. I just...I need to understand who he is first."

"Screw that psychoanalysis crap! Have you forgotten he's also a vampire? Stay away from this whack job and let the cops deal with him." Emily points her fork at me sternly. "Do not try to get inside your stalker's head, you idiot. That's how people end up dead in a ditch!"

I rake my hands through my hair in overwhelmed turmoil. "Trust me, I know it's insane. He just...he draws me in somehow, like an obsession. I can't explain it."

Emily throws her hands up dramatically. "This is some screwed-up fatal attraction fairy-tale bullshit! *Fatal Attraction* meets *Twilight* on crack!"

I cringe, destroying my napkin. "I know, I sound like a complete nutjob getting turned on by this whole seduction-slash-terrorism thing."

Groaning, I face-plant into my hands. "I've lost my damn mind..."

I hesitate, knowing the next part will make her explode. "Also... he broke into my apartment again, got all sexy-times on me, and somehow got my number. He's been texting."

Emily's eyes blow up as big as dinner plates, looking like she's about to go full mama bear.

"WHAT?" Emily practically shouts, making me jump. Other customers glance over curiously.

I throw my napkin at her. "Shhh! Inside voices." But Emily is not having it.

"Girl, you gotta change your name, dye your hair, and flee the country! First, Tall Dark and Stalks-A-Lot is creeping outside your work like a discount Jason Voorhees. Now he's breaking into your apartment? Hard pass."

I chew my lip. I know she's right, but my curiosity has already won.

Emily grabs my hands, staring daggers. "You deserve someone who understands boundaries. This dude would absolutely boil your pet rabbit if you broke up."

I nod, wincing.

Emily's eyes narrow, her expression turning devious. She leans across the table with a salacious smirk. "Okay, real talk—is it his massive meat stick reeling you in? This freak packing serious heat down below?"

Wine goes down the wrong pipe as I sputter and turn tomato red. Leave it to Emily to ask about dick size! "Jesus Christ, filter much?" I wheeze, dying inside.

She cackles like a witch. "What? Inquiring minds need to know! And that blush is telling me everything."

I desperately try changing subjects, but Emily's like a dog with a bone. I can already tell she'll be speculating about my stalker's dick size for the rest of forever. So much for having a normal dinner conversation!

Our drinks arrive looking radioactive purple, thank god for small mercies. But after ordering enough sugar to put us in a diabetic coma, Emily goes full serious mode and grabs my arm.

"For real though, Dani, I'm scared shitless about this situation. You need to be careful with Count Dick-ula," she says, genuine worry creasing her forehead.

Despite my recent terrible life choices, I nod, grateful for my ride-or-die bestie. She's right—time to woman up and deal with this vampire stalker situation before I end up as a cautionary tale.

We finish our drinks with lighter topics, the cozy vibe and sugar high improving my mood. By the time we're ready to leave, I'm feeling determined to take back control and kick this dark obsession to the curb.

Emily plays bodyguard until my car arrives, refusing to let me stand alone. She crushes me in a hug that threatens to crack ribs.

"Text me the second you're home safe, bitch. I mean it!"

I promise Emily I'll text. I'm touched that my bestie's gone full mama bear mode. Climbing into my car, I feel stronger knowing I've got backup in this crazy situation. It's time to break free from Mr.

Tall-Dark-and-Boundary-Issues and reclaim my sanity.

Tomorrow morning, I'm marching into the police station and spilling everything. No more playing vampire bait.

But even as I'm planning my escape from this mess, there's this annoying little voice in my head—the one that gets a twisted thrill from being his obsession. And god help me, part of me wants to dive deeper into whatever this is...

No. Bad Dani. I shut down that train wreck of a thought. I'm not some swooning romance novel heroine. I need to woman up and end this supernatural stalker situation.

Even if the way he looks at me makes my knees weak...

Even if his touch sets my skin on fire...

Even if—NOPE. Stopping right there. Tomorrow. Police station. End of story.

...probably.

Hot water pounds my back, but does nothing to quiet my chaotic mind.

So much for trying to purge him from my thoughts.

This arrogant bastard thinks I'm his personal plaything, available whenever he snaps his fingers. Hell no! If he shows his perfectly chiseled face tonight, I'll give him a peace of my mind. Though part of me hopes he does show up, which is all kinds of messed up.

Get it together, Dani!

That kiss keeps replaying in my head. I want to kiss him again and maybe whack him with my heaviest frying pan! I'm definitely losing it, caught between wanting to jump his bones and kick his ass. What is wrong with me?

Wrapping up in my fluffiest towel, I eye my reflection. Talk about baggage—stalker drama, finger fireworks, and my DNA doing weird shit. I attack my wet hair with a comb, mind spinning with possibilities.

I slip into my fancy midnight blue chemise because sometimes a girl needs silk against her skin. The fabric clings in all the right places, my nipples perking up like they're hoping for company. My jewelry catches the light as I sprawl across my bed.

Glancing at the clock—shit, when did it get so late? I'm exhausted, but my brain won't shut up. Like an idiot, I check my phone, hoping for his message.

Nothing. Typical. What's a vampire stalker do on his nights off? My curiosity is seriously becoming a problem.

Note to self: Google "How do you get a vampire-proof apartment after a stupid invite?"

Do I even want to uninvite him, though?

I drift off and suddenly I'm in some gothic wet dream—stone walls, candles, me in a see-through dress like some discount fantasy heroine. My heart's doing gymnastics. Where the hell am I?

A door creaks (because, of course, it does) and in walks Tall-Dark-and-Mysterious. Can't see his face but I'd know that cocky walk anywhere. Fear and... something else... make my stomach flip as he takes his sweet time approaching.

"What do you want?" I demand, proud, my voice only shakes a little.

He stops just shy of the light, still playing up the mystery.

"Isn't it obvious, my spirited one?" His voice should be illegal. "I want you."

Before I can tell him where to shove that line, he yanks me against his chest. My breathing goes haywire as his fingers trail down my neck like he owns it. I'm frozen...

"We've only scratched the surface," he purrs in my ear like some sexy fortune teller. "What we could unleash together..."

His lips brush my neck, and I embarrass myself with a gasp. The smug bastard chuckles, clearly feeling my pulse race.

"Stop fighting our connection."

Then he's kissing me like he wants to devour my soul, and I'm not putting up much of a fight...

I jolt awake, sweating and wound tighter than a spring. It's 2 AM—I've been asleep for like an hour.

Growling in frustration, I assault my innocent pillows. Damn him for hijacking my dreams too!

I try forcing myself back to sleep without thoughts of him. Yeah, right.

Finally giving up, I flip on the light. The shadows make me jumpy, half-expecting him to materialize.

But I'm alone with my disaster of a brain. I rake my hands through my sex-hair (from sleeping! Just sleeping!), trying to shake off that dream.

He's just a man. A stupid, hot, supernatural man, but still.

I stumble to the kitchen for water, gulping it down. Gripping the counter, I try getting my hormones under control.

You're in charge here. Don't let this twisted attraction win. Time to end this before it ends you.

Back in bed, I'm feeling stronger. No more sexy vampire dreams tonight. I'm taking my life back.

Let him prowl around in the dark. Tomorrow I'm calling the cops and ending this supernatural soap opera.

Tomorrow, I reclaim my sanity. Tonight, I sleep.

...unless he shows up.

Rhyland

23

I swirl the scotch in my glass, barely tasting it as I piece together the disturbing pattern. Another disappearance—the third this fucking week. Has to be Azrael. My gut churns at the thought of him joining forces with Moretemis. That unholy alliance could bring down everything we've built.

I punch in the council's number, ready to lay out my suspicions—Killian answers, his voice tight with tension.

"You're certain about this?" he demands.

"Not concrete proof yet, but my instincts are screaming," I growl back. We need hard evidence to take down someone of Azrael's standing. Killian's pushing for immediate action and constant updates.

Then Eva brings up the mortal savior, and Dani floods my mind. I can't tell them how deep she's gotten under my skin. "I'm handling it," I snap, irritation masking my turmoil.

"You've accomplished nothing!" Killian's frustration buzzes through the phone. "Time is running out, Rhyland."

"I'll get your proof on Azrael," I snarl through clenched teeth. "Then you'll hear from me." I stab the end call button like I'm putting a knife through someone's heart.

Alone with my scotch and rage, Dani's image refuses to fade. Respected scientist, brilliant mind, curves that could bring a man to his knees—the whole package is fucking intoxicating. The more I learn about her achievements, especially at her young age, the deeper she digs into my soul.

I'm a man torn in half—starving to uncover every layer of this woman while terrified of what that means.

I pace the room like a caged predator. Dani's mix of defiance and surrender is driving me insane. The uncertainty, the hot-cold signals—it's enough to make me want to put my fist through a wall. I don't do chaos. I don't do uncertainty, not like this.

Tonight, I end this game—no more chasing shadows or dancing around what's happening. Dani will give me answers, even if I have to rip them from her.

She thinks she can handle me? Play me like I'm some rookie?

Fuck this.

I'll break through that stubborn wall she's built, strip away her defenses piece by piece. I'll make her understand that defiance has consequences and that we play by my rules now. I'll uncover the truth behind her hold on me, even if it means shattering her resistance because losing myself to whatever spell she's cast isn't an option.

I take the steps to her building two at a time, blood pumping with anticipation. Moving like a shadow through the hallway, I use my telekinesis to unlock her door with a flick of my mind. Slipping inside like I own the place, I find her bedroom bathed in the soft glow of city lights.

There she is—my prey, my obsession—sprawled across her bed like a goddamn fantasy come to life.

Her chest rises and falls with each breath, utterly unaware of the predator at her bedside. My eyes devour every inch of her—those slightly parted lips begging to be claimed, those long lashes resting against sun-kissed cheeks. That flimsy excuse for a nightgown hugs every curve like a second skin, the neckline dipping just low enough to make my mouth water.

Did she wear this thinking of me?

My gaze trails hungrily over her body. That chocolate hair spilling across her pillow, those soft curves that my hands itch to possess. Each breath she takes stokes the fire burning inside me.

What version of Dani will I get tonight?

The spitfire who challenges me at every turn, or the woman who melts under my touch?

What boundaries will we push together?

And how long can this dangerous game continue?

I trace one finger lightly across her cheek, tucking a stray strand of hair behind her ear.

Without hesitation, I yank the blankets off her body, exposing those toned legs that I'm dying to taste. I slide my palm up her inner thigh, savoring the heat radiating from her skin.

She moans in her sleep, her body already responding to my touch. I palm her flat stomach, drowning in her softness. I can't hold back anymore.

My hands glide down those silky legs, and I smirk as she shivers beneath my touch. Her eyes flutter open, confusion turning to shock when she realizes I'm between her thighs. She gasps, her back arching as she scrambles away.

I move faster, grabbing her throat with one hand and spinning her around to face the wall. I pin her there, applying just enough pressure to remind her who's in control.

She whimpers as I tighten my grip on that delicate neck, feeling her pulse race against my palm. My smile grows predatory as I listen to her ragged breathing, each desperate inhale fueling my hunger.

My hard cock presses against her perfect ass, sending fire through my veins.

I pull her hair back, exposing her neck, and she *groans*—not in fear, but pleasure. I wrap my free arm around that tiny waist and grind against her, letting her feel exactly what she does to me.

Her body trembles against mine, and I savor every second of her surrender.

"Hi, Angel," I whisper against her ear, my voice rough with desire. "Did you miss me today?"

"Rhyland?" Her voice is barely a whisper, but it hits me—making my cock heavy.

I ease my grip on her throat, stroking the delicate skin with my thumb. She trembles under my touch, and the sound of my name on her lips does things to me no woman ever has.

"That's right, baby," I growl against her throat, my lips brushing her pulse point.

She can't hide it from me—she fucking loves this. Every second of me taking control makes her wet. I can smell her arousal like a drug in the air.

The scent drives my cock painfully hard, my balls tight with need. I want to taste every inch of her smooth skin and claim what's mine. But beneath the lust, my gut churns with confusion. These walls I've built over centuries feel impenetrable, trapping me between being just a body for pleasure or something more. I don't know how to bridge that gap—how to make her see the man beneath the monster.

I'm set in my ways, hardened by time and blood. I know damn well I'm not the gentle soul she deserves, yet I can't stay away. My mind is a battlefield, my heart a war zone.

How can I want someone so badly when everything about me is wrong for her?

Fear transforms into rage, a fucking hurricane inside my chest. She blindsided me with those sunkissed eyes and that fierce spirit, jump-starting something in me I thought died centuries ago. How does this one woman have such power? Furious at feeling exposed, at the cracks she's put in my armor, I spin her around to face me.

Those eyes capture me instantly. Dark amber with swirling gold flecks that seem to glow from within—not fully human, not entirely natural. In all my centuries, I've never seen eyes like hers. They pull me in like a gravitational force, and I willingly surrender to their power. I could drown in that gaze for eternity and never want to surface.

I press her harder against the wall, my body flush against hers, unable to look away. I see the intoxicating mix of fear and desire in her stare. She's trembling but holds my gaze, just as trapped as I am.

"Little Angel," my voice is rough with need, "I'm losing my fucking mind over you. You're consuming me. No more games—what have you done to me?"

She whimpers, tears gathering in those mesmerizing eyes. "What do you mean? How do you keep getting in here? I don't know what you're talking about."

Her confusion feels genuine, like she doesn't understand the power of what's between us. My mouth waters with hunger for her, her scent filling my nostrils with the unmistakable aroma of desire.

I see the fear in her eyes, and I understand it. This pull between us is primal, untamed, and dangerous. Part of me wants to surrender to it completely, but doubts claw at my mind—this could be the biggest mistake of my immortal life.

I try to tell myself she has free will and can choose her own path. But who the fuck am I kidding? I've already marked her as mine in my mind. The possessive rage that rips through me when I imagine her with anyone else is like a knife to the gut. It's undeniable—a voice roaring that she belongs to me and no one else.

I growl low in my throat, licking my lips. "I'm going to find out what the hell is happening between us. Since the moment I saw you, this fire's been burning through my veins—and it's not fucking coincidence, Angel. Tell me the truth."

She must be working some spell, or there's something darker at play.

She's a puzzle I can't solve, a lock I can't pick. As she struggles against my grip, I know in my bones there's more to this. She feels it too—I can see it in those magical eyes. Her denial only feeds my anger.

"STOP!" she suddenly screams, raw fury in her voice. "Get the fuck off me, you bastard!" She fights like a wildcat, her body twisting and writhing against mine. That tight little body squirms beneath my hands as she tries to break free. "You don't get to do this!" she rages, eyes flashing fire. "I won't let you just take whatever you want!" She bucks her hips, trying to throw me off.

I can't help the predatory smile that spreads across my face. Her small fists pound against my chest, ineffective as a kitten's claws. I capture both wrists in one hand, pinning them above her head against the wall.

"But you want this, Angel," I purr, watching outrage flash in her eyes. "You're just too scared to admit it."

She tosses her head wildly, hair clinging to her flushed face. "Go to hell, you sick freak!" she hisses. "I'll kill you, I swear."

Her threats only fuel my desire. I lean in close, my lips brushing her ear. "There's my feisty little Angel," I murmur. "I love watching you burn."

She screams in frustration, renewing her struggles with everything she has. I groan as her movements press her body against my hardness. Yes, I'm going to enjoy breaking through that defiance—watching her inevitable surrender when she finally admits what we both know.

Her sharp words hang between us, but they only feed the dark amusement growing inside me. Her futile attempts to seize control are laughable.

I smirk and let out a low, dangerous chuckle. "Oh, sweet girl, we both know you don't want me to leave," I say with absolute certainty.

Those mesmerizing gold eyes bore into mine with defiance. I can smell the war inside her—desire fighting confusion, anger wrestling with need. I meet her gaze unflinchingly, enjoying her internal struggle.

I can't hold back anymore. Her closeness, intoxicating scent, and those curves pressed against me are driving me to the edge of sanity. I'm ready to risk everything I've protected for centuries just to lose myself in her for one night. I need her with a desperation that borders on madness.

I grind my rock-hard cock against her stomach, savoring her sharp intake of breath. I wrap both arms around that luscious waist, then sweep my hands down to grab her perfect ass, squeezing hard enough to make her gasp.

I yank her off the wall, and she clings to me like she's drowning. My dick strains painfully against my jeans as I crush my mouth to hers, my tongue invading every corner. She gasps between our savage kisses, her hips grinding against me with a need that matches my own.

I carry her to the kitchen, her body writhing against mine as I devour her mouth and swallow her desperate little sounds.

Fuck my misery and inner conflict. I need to feel her come apart in my hands, need to hear her scream my name. It's crystal clear she burns for me as fiercely as I burn for her, and that knowledge only makes me hungrier. Gripping her ass firmly, I set her down hard on the kitchen island, spreading those toned legs wide as I position myself between them. With one savage tug, I rip her flimsy nightgown, exposing those perfect breasts to my hungry gaze. I attack her mouth again, devouring her lips with desperate need as she responds to every kiss with equal fervor.

"Rhyland," she whimpers, her breath tickling my lips.

I grab the back of my hoodie and shirt, yanking them over my head in one fluid motion. Her eyes widen at the sight of my muscled torso, her breath catching as her delicate hands explore every ridge and plane of my chest.

I seize her by the throat, and she moans as I crash my lips down on hers. Her body quivers against mine as I growl deep in my chest and pull her closer. The heat radiating from her skin sends lightning through my veins. Her hands trace my chest hungrily before sliding up to my neck, her fingers threading through my short hair and tugging just enough to make me suck in a sharp breath. My hands roam up those smooth thighs, heading straight for the prize when my fingers find her soaked.

"Fuck, baby," I groan, my voice thick with need. "Already this wet for me?"

Her answering moan tells me everything I need to know. Our power struggle turned her on as much as it did me. I cup those perfect breasts in my hands—they fit like they were made for my palms. Taking a hardened nipple into my mouth, I suck and bite until she's arching off the counter, her hands clawing through my hair as she pulls me closer. I slam my free hand down on the countertop to steady myself as she writhes beneath me.

I smirk against her heated skin. "You're so fucking needy," I growl, enjoying the way she responds to my words.

I move to her other breast, sinking my teeth into the soft flesh with just enough pressure to make her gasp. Her panting fills the kitchen as I hook my fingers into her soaked panties and yank them aside. My fingertips glide through her slick petals, finding her dripping and ready.

She moans louder as I rub her clit in frantic circles. "Is this what you need, Angel? Do you need me right here?"

"Yes...please," she whispers, her voice breaking with desire.

I work her slick clit with practiced precision, my fingers exploring every inch of her soft pussy. I find every spot that makes her gasp, memorizing what drives her wild.

God, she's so soft—so wet.

Our tongues battle for dominance as I thrust against hers. A feral groan tears from my chest as I stroke and toy with her clit, making her shudder.

She gasps, her body trembling against mine. I grab her breast roughly with my free hand, tugging on her hardened nipple with just enough force to walk the line between pleasure and pain. "You taste like fucking heaven, Angel."

My head spins with lust as I spread her open, sliding one thick finger inside her, then adding a second, stretching her tight channel.

Christ, she's tight as sin!

I have to work my fingers in slowly, her pussy gripping me like a vise. I can only imagine how those walls will feel squeezing my throbbing cock.

I can't wait to bury myself in that perfect wetness. A raw, animal sound escapes her as pleasure overtakes her.

"Rhyland!" My name on her lips is the sweetest sound I've ever heard.

I lock my eyes on hers, my gaze intense enough to make her tremble. "Say it again when you come on my fingers, Angel."

My mouth attacks her perfect nipples with hungry desperation. I bite down hard before soothing the sting with my tongue. Her moans drive me wild as I pump two fingers deep inside her, my thumb circling her clit with relentless pressure.

"Come for me, Angel. Let me hear those dirty screams. You know I'm the only one who can take you there."

Her inner walls clamp down on my fingers, and the sensation sends fire racing through my veins.

She's panting now, barely able to form words. "Rhy...OH, god." Her voice echoes through the apartment, a sound I want to hear every night for eternity.

"That's right, baby. Let go for me."

She screams my name as her pussy clenches around my fingers in violent spasms. Her orgasm crashes through her like a tidal wave while I thrust deeper, pushing her higher than she's ever been.

"Goddamn," I growl through clenched teeth, nearly blowing in my jeans from the sight alone. She clamps down harder, her inner walls milking my fingers as pleasure wracks her body. Her cream coats my hand, dripping down onto the counter below.

My god, she's fucking transcendent. "Perfect," I tell her, my voice rough with need.

As her cries fade to whimpers and her body still trembles with aftershocks, I slowly withdraw my fingers from her soaked heat. I bring them to my mouth, sucking her essence from each digit, savoring her taste like the finest whiskey. The flavor hits me like a supernova, sending a jolt straight to my cock that makes me grunt and spill in my pants like a teenager.

Her taste is unlike anything I've experienced in my lifetimes—like the sweetest cotton candy, flooding my senses. Every inch of her is absolute perfection.

I want to bend her over this counter and fuck her until she can't remember her own name. I need to get a grip. I fist her hair in my hand, forcing her to look up at me. I claim her mouth in a savage kiss, my tongue invading the warm cavern of her mouth. She tastes like sugar and sin—a combination more addictive than blood.

I break the kiss long enough to growl against her lips, "Taste yourself, Angel. You taste like pure fucking sin."

She whimpers against my mouth, pressing herself against me like I'm oxygen and she's drowning. I love the desperate way she needs me and silently begs for what only I can give her. But I'm not ready to give her everything. Not yet.

I want to make her ache for me, make her beg. I pull back from her mouth, whispering wickedly, "Don't rush it, baby. I want you desperate and begging for this hard cock."

Her breath catches, her body trembling as she inhales sharply.

Is it fear making her shake? Guilt? The aftershocks of her orgasm? I can't read what's happening behind those golden eyes, but something's shifted. My heart sinks as I lock my gaze with hers, searching for answers. A cold feeling spreads through my chest as I catch a flicker of wariness that wasn't there before. She breaks the heavy silence by nervously biting her lip. The tension thickens around us, and my gut twists with foreboding.

What the fuck have I gotten myself into?

I whisper against her lips, demanding, "Tell me."

She flinches at my intensity, but holds her ground. Her voice comes out husky and raw. "I can't separate the physical from the emotional with you. You overwhelm every sense I have." She takes a trembling breath, her eyes trying to focus on mine. "I can't deny there's something between us, as terrifying as that is."

The sincerity in her words hits me like a punch to the gut. But what if this is all some elaborate trap? The dangerous spark of hope battles with centuries of ingrained suspicion.

I search those eyes, fighting against the fortress I've built around my heart. I can't ignore the possibility that whatever this is between us is real and destined. For both our sakes, I need to believe we were meant to collide.

"Help me believe this is real," I rasp, surprised by the raw vulnerability in my voice.

I move closer, hesitantly wrapping my hand around her neck, our foreheads touching lightly. My thumb traces her jawline as I meet her gaze with uncharacteristic uncertainty, nearly drowning in the moment's intensity.

"Angel...I feel it too," I murmur, my fingers caressing her lips before I breathe against her ear. "Let me take you to bed."

I grip her hips and pull her against me. She clings to me desperately, wrapping those perfect legs around my waist, burying her face in my neck. The feeling of her pressed against me sends waves of pleasure through my body. She feels so fragile in my arms, like something precious I never want to release. I lay her down gently on the bed, savoring the softness of her body.

"Why do you hide your face?" she asks, her eyes piercing through the darkness as if she can see straight into my soul.

I give her a predatory smile. "Soon, Angel." But doubt still gnaws at me.

She laughs softly. "You think you can just have me whenever you want—?"

"You're mine," I cut her off. "There's no fighting what's between us." I inhale deeply, trying to control the possessive surge that threatens to overwhelm me.

I want to tell her everything I'm feeling, but my thoughts are a fucking hurricane. Despite the chaos, I need to choose a path. Before she can respond, I turn and leave, more conflicted than when I arrived.

My mind races as I exit her apartment. Our connection is undeniable, yet I still fight against it.

I have two choices: surrender to whatever spell she's cast on me and embrace the unknown, or find a way to break these chains and reclaim my sanity. But which leads to freedom, and which to deeper bondage?

I walk alone through the night, wrestling with my demons. But deep down, I know the answer will only come when I'm with my angel again...

Danica

24

So much for my iron will—it crumbled faster than a cookie in milk when he showed up.

Mr. Tall-Dark-and-Dangerous hit me like catnip hits a cat! That masculine scent, his rock-hard body pressed against mine, the way he whispered filthy promises... I had zero defense against this sensory ambush!

Now I sit here, questioning my life choices while certain parts of me tingle. It's like he marked me with his vampire voodoo, and now my brain's forgotten how logic works.

Who does Mr. Magic Fingers think he is, reading my vulnerabilities like a steamy paperback? I should've been freaked, but nope! This thirsty gal was gulping down everything he served.

I trace my fingers over my neck, remembering his hot breath, those soft lips... Girl, get it together! My body betrays me, aching for more of his sweet lovin'.

Everything about him pulls me in like gravity, even though he's clearly trouble wrapped in a sexy package. I barely know him, yet feel like we've been doing this dance for centuries. It makes zero sense!

Why can't I get him out of my system?

I gulp my scorching coffee, trying to shock some sense back into myself and my rebellious lady bits.

My rational side is screaming to end this—call the cops, get that restraining order, install better locks. Take control before I'm in too deep.

But even thinking about cutting him off makes my chest hurt. As crazy as this obsession is, I need it like air.

I used to think I knew myself. Now everything's sideways. All my ideas about relationships and attraction have gone out the window.

This vampire has demolished my walls, leaving me raw and exposed in ways that terrify and excite me. He sees straight through to parts of me I didn't know existed.

I should run screaming from this threat to my sanity, but every cell in my body gravitates toward him. My heart, body, and mind are all betraying me, desperate to see where this dangerous path leads. I'm teetering on the edge of something wild, and I can't stop myself...

He ignites something in me hotter than anything I've ever felt. And those arrogant words of his!

"I want you aching and begging for this cock."

That made me want to yell out loud, begging him to fuck me senseless. His energy is overwhelming, and I still haven't seen his face!

But when that hoodie came off... Sweet baby Jesus! Even with his face hidden, his pure masculine presence is burned into my brain forever.

I am so screwed. Possibly literally.

I recall the feel of him under my fingertips—hard slabs of muscle as my hands explored his chest. Those shoulders, impossibly broad, seemed to block out the world around us. His massive arms could easily crush or protect with equal measure.

His hair—cropped short on the sides, almost military-precise, with just enough length on top to be appealingly disheveled. That perfect stubble, rough against my skin.

He must stand at least six-foot-four, every inch of him radiating raw, primal physicality.

"Damn..." I breathe, the memory alone making my pulse quicken.

I mean, what chance did I have against this behemoth beefcake? Resistance was futile against that sculpted physique. I was powerless not to be overpowered. My only choice was to be swept away in his strong arms like a dainty doll.

I could feel the scorching desire in his eyes raking over me. It sent a traitorous dart of heat through my core that I still despise.

Everything about him is hard edges, rough, and demanding. He is built for claiming, forcing surrender, and taking without mercy. I hate that part of me still craves to feel that raw physicality against me again. When I felt the hard, pulsing monster in his pants pressed against me, it was a shock that ran through my entire body and made my eyes widen in surprise.

The man is packing.

It's pathetic, but some twisted part hopes we cross paths again. He remains burned into my senses for now—a dangerous enigma I can't stop thinking about.

I am definitely going to hell for these thoughts...

My core clenches with need, mouth watering at the thought of his massive length stretching my throat. Would he be rough, slamming into me until I choke? Or torturously slow, letting me savor every thick inch? God, I want him to wreck me until I'm a drooling, begging mess.

Just the thought has my pussy throbbing, embarrassingly wet.

I drag myself back to reality and head for the bathroom, pushing the door open with a yawn. I crank the shower on high, letting steam and lavender scents wrap around me like a hug. My bare feet flinch against the chilly tiles as I catch my reflection in the fogged-up mirror—my chestnut hair looking like I stuck my finger in an electrical socket, wild strands framing my sleepy face.

I rake my fingers through the tangled mess, trying to detangle the worst knots. As I massage my scalp, my traitorous brain flashes back to last night—to Rhyland's strong hands fisting through these same locks, tugging just hard enough to make me gasp—heat pools between my legs at the X-rated memory.

Focus, Dani!

I grab my brush and attack the tangles properly, starting at the ends like a responsible adult. No matter how much I spend on fancy products, my thick hair turns into a rat's nest overnight. It's hopeless, but I'm stubborn.

While I brush, my mind wanders to the lab tests waiting for me today—more bloodwork to figure out what the hell is happening with my mutant DNA situation. I'm equal parts thrilled and terrified. But science will give me answers eventually. That's the one thing I can count on.

After a quick shower, I make a beeline for the kitchen, stomach growling like an angry bear. I fling open the fridge door and stare at the contents like they might rearrange themselves into something amazing.

I grab eggs and bread, popping the slices into the toaster. When they pop up golden-brown, I slather them with butter and jam. I scramble the eggs until they're fluffy perfection, then plate everything up. Nothing fancy, but it'll keep me from eating my coworkers later.

Sitting at my table, I savor the creamy eggs and crunchy toast while scrolling through my phone. I mindlessly flip through social media until a memory photo stops me cold.

It's from our family vacation in Italy years ago. My seventeen-year-old self stands between my parents, all of us grinning like idiots under the Italian sun. We look so happy, so normal.

Before I knew I was a freak of nature. Before vampire stalkers. Before glowing fingers.

For a moment, I miss that simple life with an ache that takes my breath away.

But as I stare at the image, a wave of emotions crashes over me, and a vivid flashback consumes my mind. It's a memory I have buried deep within that has haunted me ever since.

I'm transported to our old house outside my parents' bedroom door.

Their hushed voices pique my curiosity, and against my better judgment, I press my ear against the wooden surface, desperate to catch their conversation.

"We can't keep this from her forever, Martha. She deserves to know the truth."

"I know, but she's so happy and doesn't need the burden of her past right now."

"She's not a child anymore, Martha. She deserves the chance to discover her roots and understand her origins."

My heart pounds in my chest as their words sink in. My mind races to make sense of what they're saying. The realization hits me like a freight train. The ground beneath me feels unsteady as my world tilts on its axis.

I whisper to myself, "No... I'm... adopted?"

The weight of this revelation crashes down on me, suffocating me with its enormity.

My childhood memories reflect a new light, casting shadows of doubt and uncertainty. Every moment shared with my parents now feels tainted, as though a secret lurks beneath the surface, hidden from my knowledge.

I barge in. How could they keep this from me? Why didn't they tell me? The realization stings, leaving me feeling betrayed and adrift in a sea of unanswered questions. I struggle to make sense of my identity, to reconcile the person I thought I was with this newfound truth.

I shout, "I'm adopted?!"

My father says, "Dani, my dear, we didn't keep it from you out of malice or deception. We wanted to protect you, to ensure you had a happy and stable childhood."

My mother offers, "You were left at the hospital when you were just a few days old. We had been on a waiting list to adopt, and when the call came, it felt like a miracle. We were overjoyed to welcome you into our lives, Danica."

My voice shakes. "But why didn't you tell me? Why keep it a secret?"

My father looks at me with a pained expression. "We feared it would change how you saw yourself and us as your parents. We didn't want you to feel any different or less loved."

My mother grabs my shoulders, teary-eyed, "Danica, you are our daughter in every way that matters. Biology doesn't define a family; love and care do. We chose you, and you chose us."

My heart aches as I grapple with conflicting emotions. The truth of my adoption feels like a double-edged sword, both a revelation and a wound. I try to process the love and intention behind my parents' decision, but the sense of betrayal lingers.

I cry, tears streaking my face, "I wish you had trusted me enough to share this with me. I feel like a part of me has been hidden for so long."

The DNA test after finding out I was adopted? Total bust. Zero info about my bio parents—figures! I've run so many blood tests on myself over the years, but nothing weird has shown up. But now this freaky double helix appears in my genes like "Surprise, bitch!" and I'm questioning my entire existence.

I wipe away tears, giving myself a mental pep talk. This bombshell might knock me sideways, but I'm not staying down. Still, my hands are now putting on their own little light show, and my need to understand what the hell is happening has reached desperate levels.

I wolf down the rest of my breakfast, grab my stuff, and head out. My stomach's doing nervous gymnastics about what today might bring. The morning air hits my face like a wake-up slap.

The lab welcomes me with its familiar chemical cocktail smell and soul-sucking fluorescent lighting. I claim my usual computer in the back corner, settling in for another marathon session of "Who the Hell Am I?" For hours, I click through databases and scroll through articles until my eyeballs threaten to revolt. As usual, big fat nothing.

When the lab techs start flipping off lights, the crushing weight of another failed search settles on my chest. My mysterious past remains locked up tight as I trudge out to my car.

Streetlights flicker ominously as I slide behind the wheel, catching my defeated expression in the mirror.

Why did my parents ditch me? Is this glowing-hands business a cool superpower or some genetic curse?

As I unlock my apartment and step into the silent darkness, these questions keep taunting me.

My brain's spinning like a hamster wheel. Am I the only freak with this ability? Or are there others out there? Fear and confusion are having a cage match in my stomach.

I thought I knew who I was. Now everything's sideways. I stare at my hands—they look normal but are strangers to me now. What other surprises are hiding in my DNA, waiting to jump out and yell "Boo!"?

I need Emily—her no-nonsense reality check would be a lifeline right now. I grab my phone and text her to meet me for drinks.

Because nothing says "I might be a mutant" like tequila shots with your bestie.

I park on the street and hustle inside Karma, boots echoing on the floor. Emily waves me over, already ordering drinks.

"Holy hell, you look like something the cat dragged in, chewed on, and spit back out," she declares, eyeing my disaster-zone appearance. I groan, shoving my hair back as the bartender delivers our liquid therapy.

"So what catastrophe has you double-fisting drinks before saying hello?" Emily asks, one perfectly arched eyebrow raised.

I make her swear on her collection of vintage band tees not to freak out before unloading everything—the weird DNA, my impromptu finger light show. Her eyes nearly pop out of her head.

"Shit, you're a freakin' circus sideshow lately!" At my solemn expression, she adds gently, "Kidding. But seriously, weird stuff is happening to you."

I cling to her hands desperately. "It's like some fucked-up conspiracy—my stalker, my weird-ass DNA results, now these random mutant powers?" I slam my drink and continue my rant. "This shit's dredging up everything about my adoption, living down that bullshit memory—not knowing who the hell my real parents are. My entire life feels like it's gone completely batshit!"

Emily's face turns serious when she realizes this is reopening all my abandonment wounds about my bio parents. "I get it, sweetie. This is a lot." She wraps me in a hug that smells like expensive perfume and tequila. "But we're in this shit show together, got it? Team Dani all the way."

Behind her snark, I know Emily's ride-or-die. Her unwavering friendship is my anchor in this storm of weirdness.

Emily gives me that look—the one that says she's about to call me on my bullshit. "Sooooo... have you reported Captain Creepy to the authorities yet? Like you promised your very concerned best friend, you would?"

I suddenly find the ice in my drink fascinating. Emily sighs like she's dealing with a stubborn child. "Dani, you cannot keep letting Dracula's hotter cousin lurk around your apartment. What's the latest with Mr. Tall, Dark, and Restraining-Order-Worthy?"

I mumble into my drink, "He might have made another house call last night."

Cue Emily's head explosion in 3...2...1..

"He did what now?!" Emily shouts, making me wince. "Please tell me you sprayed him with pepper spray and slammed the door on that psycho!"

"Well, no, I didn't exactly do that..."

Emily drags both hands down her face. "You've got to be kidding me! What the hell happened?"

I take a deep breath. "He sort of just let himself in. I probably should've thrown him out, but..."

Emily's eyes go wide. "Oh my god, you didn't! Girl, tell me you did NOT have sex with Sir Stalks-a-Lot himself!"

I give her an exasperated eye roll. "Give me some credit! Of course not." Maybe she doesn't need to know all the details.

Emily shakes her head in disbelief. "Look, I know it's been approximately a million years since you got some action. But letting your unhinged admirer become a booty call? That's a hard pass."

I let out an embarrassed groan but can't help an amused snort. "You literally have no filter, you know that?"

Emily waggles her eyebrows. "Nope, it's a part of my charm! But seriously, phone 911 next time that whack job shows up."

I know she means well under all the snark. With Emily's help, I'll find the courage to take control of this insane situation.

As Emily and I chat, a tall figure detaches from the shadows. My heart seizes as he comes into the light—head shaved bare, and every visible patch of skin is etched with spidery black tattoos. I smell the reek of death clinging to him even before he stops inches away.

"Well, well...aren't you a sweet little treat," he rasps. I recoil as he leans in, inhaling deeply with a grotesque grin. "Mmm...never smelled anything so delic—"

"Get away from me, you freak!" I yell, visceral anger overriding my fear. Emily shifts closer, ready to defend me.

The vampire's grin widens, sending prickles of dread down my spine. "Such fire in this one! I think I'll take just a little nibble—"

He reaches for me. My heart plummets. I shove him back with all my strength. "What the fuck?—Back off, asshole!" I spit, hands trembling despite my bravado. "I'm not in the mood for your bullshit tonight."

He slams me against the bar. Granite crashes into my spine. Air explodes from my lungs as I'm pinned, his face inches from mine.

"Don't you dare tell me no, bitch!" Spittle flies. I wince from his rancid breath.

Emily screams. He whips around, backhanding her viciously. She crashes into a table. Glass shatters.

"Emily!" Tears blur my vision as she collapses.

His grip becomes iron shackles on my arms. I struggle wildly—digging heels in, pulling with everything I have—but it's useless.

I stop thinking. Clench my fist. Rear back with pure rage. Suddenly, warmth floods my veins. Flickering flames lick over my knuckles. Adrenaline overrides shock and I follow through.

Pain explodes as my flaming fist connects with his face. He stumbles back bellowing, blood gushing from his shattered nose. The flames vanish instantly.

I brace for retaliation, blood roaring for justice.

He looks momentarily confused before pulling back his fist. Time slows as I watch it come toward my face.

A deep growl sounds beside me. A dark blur intercepts the blow midair.

The vampire howls as he's wrenched backward and lifted off his feet. His body soars, crashing down feet away.

My heart ricochets as I recognize my rescuer—piercing blue eyes, thick black hair cropped short on the sides. His muscular frame stretches a tight black t-shirt, tattoos coating his arms from shoulder to wrist. His imposing height and powerful build dominate the room.

This is a man built for war.

Recognition floods through me—it's the sexy man from Lucian's office.

"Back. Off." His voice is a low, dangerous rumble that bypasses my ears and vibrates straight through my body. "She's protected."

Power emanates from him in waves. The room seems to shrink in his presence.

"Who the fuck do you think you are?" the vampire snarls, though fear edges his voice.

My protector's lips curl into a predatory smile that promises violence. "Your worst fucking nightmare." His eyes never blink. "Leave before I tear your spine out through your throat."

The vampire scrambles away, not daring to look back.

When he turns to me, his expression shifts—still intense but now possessive, concerned. "Are you hurt?" he demands, eyes scanning every inch of me. His hand reaches out, fingers brushing my cheek with surprising gentleness that contradicts the raw power still emanating from him.

Emily's fingers dig into my shoulder. "What the hell...? Are you alright?"

I stare blankly, thoughts disjointed. "Yeah...I'm okay. Just freaked out."

Emily peers at me critically. I snap back to reality—"Shit, your face! That bastard hit you. Are *you* okay?"

She touches her swelling bruise, forcing a pained smile. "Yeah, just fucking peachy. I'll live."

I look back where my rescuer stood; he's gone.

We sink onto bar stools, sipping replacement drinks.

"Jesus, this place is cursed," she mutters. "Time we find a new hangout."

I nod vaguely, fixated on my mysterious savior. We'd only met once before, yet he protected me with shocking ferocity.

"Earth to Danica!" Emily's voice jerks me back. I've been silent for minutes.

"Sorry, just...processing everything."

I examine my hands, half-expecting to see mystical flames. Nothing—just ordinary flesh.

Emily reaches over, stilling my fidgeting. "That asshole really rattled you, huh?" I nod.

I try to focus on Emily's lighthearted chatter as we finish our drinks, but my attention keeps straying. A prickle on my neck makes me turn frequently, and I irrationally expect to see *him* linger nearby, watching me.

Later, arm-in-arm with Emily in the shadowy parking lot, apprehension and anticipation war within me.

Something about my savior's intervention reminds me of another—my cryptic "dark guardian angel." Could tonight's confrontation reveal Rhyland's true identity?

I don't have enough pieces yet. But my instincts whisper I haven't seen the last of either shadow.

Danica

25

Rain hammers the window like it's trying to break in as I white-knuckle the kitchen table, willing my trembling hands to get their act together. This supernatural shit show has officially exceeded my ability to cope alone.

One week of my hands glowing at random, endless lab tests leading nowhere, and Rhyland keeping his physical distance while bombarding me with texts day and night to "check in." The questions keep multiplying, and his magnetic pull threatens to drag me into his dangerous orbit.

I'm drowning in secrets and starting to question my own sanity. I need a life preserver before I go completely under.

My panic-scrambled brain runs through escape options before landing on an obvious one—my parents. Their boring, normal world is exactly the reality check I need right now. Sure, I'm still pissed about the whole "surprise, you're adopted" bombshell, but they're still my rock.

Before I can talk myself out of it, I grab my phone, fingers fumbling like I've had three too many cocktails. But even as I start dialing, doubt slithers down my spine like ice water. Can I really outrun whatever freakshow my life has become? Or will this supernatural circus follow me like a bad reputation?

I shove those thoughts into the "deal with later" file and focus on my escape plan. I just need a timeout to get my head straight. My parents' mind-numbingly normal suburban existence sounds like paradise compared to my current "flame hands, and vampire stalker" situation.

I grip the phone like it's a lifeline, clinging to this temporary escape route. I just need to catch my breath before diving back into whatever mystical mess is waiting for me.

Please let this work, I silently beg the universe. *Just give me five minutes of normal before the next supernatural curveball.*

Mom answers warmly, lifting my spirits instantly.

"Hi, sweetheart! How are you?"

"Hey, Mom," I reply, smiling genuinely. "Hanging in there. Any chance I could visit this weekend? I need a break."

"Yes. Please," Mom exclaims. "Your father is boring me to death with his endless fishing stories. I could use some girl time!"

I smile, picturing Dad gesturing wildly as he recounts the epic battle with "the one that got away"—complete with sound effects and the inevitable expansion of the fish's size with each retelling. Some things never change, and I wouldn't have it any other way.

I hang up with my Mom and just stand there for a minute, emotionally drained. My suitcase sits by the door, taunting me. This whole freaky supernatural situation has me tied up in knots.

What the hell do I even tell my folks? "Surprise, I'm a mutant now?" They'd have me committed. No, I'll have to figure out this weirdness on my own.

The lights in my apartment suddenly flicker, making me jump. I guess my powers don't like being ignored.

A trip out of town might help me sort through this madness. I desperately need the comfort of familiar surroundings. But a voice in my head whispers I can't run forever. This is just a temporary break from the crazy.

I find myself rubbing my neck. Lately, it tingles whenever I think about Rhyland. His mysterious vampire voodoo pull won't just disappear.

With a sigh, I shut down the anxious thoughts for now. I need this time-out, even if the shadows creep back soon. Zipping my suitcase angrily, I head out the door before I overthink this.

The answers to this insanity are waiting here for when I'm ready. But for now, I'm gonna take a breather in a place where magic doesn't exist. Here's hoping for a little peace and quiet, at least for a while.

The lush green wonderland of the Pacific Northwest whizzes past my window as I drive toward Leavenworth, all those rolling hills and massive trees working their therapeutic magic on my disaster of a nervous system. I flex my fingers on the steering wheel, trying not to think about how they were recently doing their best lightsaber impression. Nope—focusing only on the peaceful scenery ahead, mentally slamming the door on thoughts of supernatural shenanigans. This weekend is strictly for family reconnection time.

As if the universe is eavesdropping on my thoughts—the rain suddenly quits, and the sun bursts through the clouds like it's making a dramatic entrance, transforming the gloomy downpour into postcard-perfect sunshine.

Even the weather's trying to improve my mood. Too bad it can't fix my vampire problem.

Catching my reflection in the rearview mirror is a mistake—I look like I've been hit by a truck, then backed over for good measure. I blink hard and roll down the window, letting the cold air slap me awake. Just need to keep it together a little longer before I can collapse at my parents.

As I turn onto their street, my heart does a little happy dance at the sight of their stone cottage tucked among towering pines like something from a fairy tale. My tires crunch satisfyingly over the gravel driveway bordered by rhododendrons showing off their purple blooms. Before I can even put the car in park, the front door flies open, and my parents come charging out like I'm returning from war.

Home. Finally, somewhere vampire-free.

...I hope.

Their smiling faces lift my spirits like sunshine breaking through clouds.

"Hey, sweetheart!" Mom says against my hair, her arms wrapped around me.

"Mom," I breathe, feeling tears prick at the corners of my eyes as I wrap my arms around her. Mom's silver hair tickles my nose. She smells of lavender and home-cooked meals, and the last of my defenses crumbles.

"Hey, Kiddo," Dad chimes in, pulling me into a bear hug once Mom has released me. Dad's plaid shirt is soft under my cheek. "We missed you." Their arms feel like a bulwark, keeping the shadows and mysteries at bay for now. I inhale deeply, comforting nostalgia washing over me.

"I missed you, too, Dad." I sniff, wiping away tears before they can fall. "Both of you."

"Come on, let's get you inside," Mom says gently, guiding me toward the house. "You must be tired from the drive."

"Actually, I feel better now that I'm here," I admit with a small smile. "Just being with you guys makes everything else seem less... overwhelming."

"Let us take care of you this weekend," Dad suggests as we step into the familiar warmth of their home. "We'll help you forget everything weighing you down."

The soft glow of the evening sun filters through the windows, casting a warm light on the walls.

"Thanks, Dad," I reply, stepping into the cozy room that has always been my sanctuary during visits. The quilted bedspread and lace curtains are unchanged, as comforting as ever. Setting my bags down, I take a deep breath, feeling a weight lift from my shoulders.

“Take your time settling in, Dani,” Mom tells me, reassuringly squeezing my hand. “Dinner will be ready soon.”

“Okay.” I nod, smiling at her before she leaves the room.

I unpack my clothes into the antique wooden dresser, its flowered wallpaper peeling slightly at the edges. While not my childhood home, I've come to know every corner of this cozy house since my parents retired here three years ago.

It's become a sanctuary I visit to escape the pressures of daily life. Now, I need its comforting familiarity more than ever—a temporary refuge from the chaotic supernatural entanglements I left behind in Seattle.

My thoughts drift back to the mysteries awaiting me—the lab’s sterile halls, the bar’s smoky corners...and Rhyland. Unbidden, my skin tingles, recalling his strong hands exploring my body, his earthy scent enveloping my senses...

The vivid memory of the vampire attack at the bar flashes again. My fury and fear as clenched fists began to glow, heat building. The panic rose as this deadly new power threatened to erupt, nearly exposing my terrifying secret...

I rush to open the window, gulping the crisp autumn air to calm down. Breathe. Think. But there are too many mysteries, too much I still don't understand. I shake my head, redirecting my thoughts. I came here to get distance, to clear my cluttered mind. But Rhyland's dark allure still lingers, casting its shadow over this peaceful place. And I know soon I must return and confront the secrets that await me back home. But for now, I will seek comfort in the tranquility of this haven, however fleeting it may prove.

As I step into the kitchen, the mouthwatering smell of Mom's lasagna hits me like a comfort bomb. Golden-hour sunlight pours through the windows, making everything look like an Instagram filter come to life.

"Just in time for the feeding frenzy, kiddo. Park it," Dad says with his trademark grin, plopping down a salad bowl. I slide into my usual spot, the chair that's practically molded to my butt after years of family dinners. For a blissful few minutes, we chat about gloriously mundane things—Dad's golf score, Mom's book club drama, the neighbor's scandalous fence paint choice. It's wonderfully, boringly normal.

"So what's cooking in that fancy lab of yours?" Dad asks through a mouthful of garlic bread. "Curing cancer yet?"

I set down my fork, suddenly animated. "I found something crazy weird in my blood work..." I launch into science-speak about the bizarre double helix, not missing the look my parents exchange, like they just spotted a ghost.

Mom recovers first, concern wrinkling her forehead. "How strange, honey. Any theories about what it means?"

I swirl my wine like I'm in a dramatic movie scene. "Not yet. But it feels... significant. Like it might connect to my biological parents." I take a deep breath. "I was hoping you might have some adoption paperwork tucked away somewhere that could give me clues..."

The parental eye-exchange happens again. Dad clears his throat in a way that suggests I'm not getting what I want. "Sweetheart, we've been over this. The adoption was closed—no identifying information. Your DNA doesn't define who you are."

I nod while internally rolling my eyes. They're in full protection mode, as usual. Outside, the sun disappears like my hopes for answers. The temperature seems to drop ten degrees in seconds, matching my mood.

Mom swoops in with a subject change. "How's that bartending job treating you? Meeting any interesting people?"

My mind flashes to Rhyland pinning me against walls and doing things that would make my mother faint. "It's... um... educational. The clientele is definitely... memorable."

Understatement of the century.

I take a long sip of wine, buying time. My heart does a little tap dance thinking about Rhyland's intoxicating scent and that voice that could melt butter. My emotions are doing the world's most confusing conga line—yearning, doubt, and that dangerous little thrill.

Dad throws me a knowing look. "So... any special someone in the picture?"

I consider dodging, but finally cave. "There's this guy..." I trail off, wondering how to explain my complicated situation with Seattle's hottest vampire.

Mom and Dad perk up like meerkats spotting prey. "Tell us about him!"

"I'll... fill you in later," I mumble, suddenly fascinated by my lasagna. They exchange one of those telepathic parent looks but mercifully drop it. "Let's just enjoy dinner," I add, desperate to escape the Rhyland inquisition.

My parents practically fled to Leavenworth to get away from the "vampire infestation" in major cities. If I told them the undead is basically courting me, they'd need defibrillators.

"Whatever you say, pumpkin," Dad agrees, and we spend the rest of dinner trading stories about family vacations and embarrassing memories. The kitchen is filled with laughter that almost drowns out my internal chaos.

But even surrounded by their warmth, I can't fully banish thoughts of Rhyland and his magnetic pull. He's like a song stuck in my head, impossible to silence. Meanwhile, my parents' protective secrecy about my adoption hangs over me like a storm cloud.

"Think I'll head to bed," I announce, standing up.

"Sleep well, honey," Mom says with that look that makes me feel five years old again.

"Night, kiddo," Dad adds, squeezing my shoulder as I pass.

"Night," I echo, already halfway gone.

My parents want to shield me from life's darker corners—they always have. But my weird DNA and glowing-hand situation can't stay hidden forever. I want to tell them everything, but fear stops me cold. Will they still look at me the same way once they know what I might become?

Under the vast starry sky, I feel torn in half—one part craving family's safety, the other being pulled toward the unknown. I don't know how to exist in both worlds simultaneously.

For now, I'm stuck in limbo between two families—one by birth, one by choice. But eventually, I'll need to merge these fractured pieces of myself.

I step onto the back porch, tilting my face to the stars and finding comfort in their ancient light. My breath clouds in the cold air as I whisper, "I wish you'd trust me with the truth." My questions hang unanswered in the night. But I won't quit searching.

Back inside, I retreat to my bedroom. The scent of fabric softener and Mom's lavender sachets welcomes me as I push open the door. I'm drawn to the window like a magnet. The moon looms large, bathing my parents' property in silver light. Despite the peaceful scene, goosebumps rise on my arms. Thoughts of Rhyland's intense gaze follow me even here, hundreds of miles from Seattle.

I shake it off and change into pajamas, sliding between sheets that smell like home. This isn't the time for vampire-related existential crises.

Sleep calls to me, promising a few hours' escape from my increasingly bizarre reality.

If only my dreams would cooperate and not feature a certain sexy vampire...

RHYLAND

26

I watch Danica through the curtains, my chest clenching like a fucking vise. She's all innocence and light, untouched by the darkness that's been my constant companion for centuries.

The night air carries whispers as the pines sway, promising rain before dawn. I blend into the shadows like I was born from them, watching Dani's parents' house with its windows glowing like nosy eyes cutting through the blackness.

When she moves to her bedroom, the moonlight bathes her in silver, making her look like something not quite human. I watch her as she settles into bed. My body tenses with the need to go to her. With her parents knocked out for the night, nothing stands between us.

I type out a message, my thumb hovering just a second before hitting send. There is no turning back now.

Alone at last?

I add a devil emoji and watch her face in the dim light as she reads my message. The way her body tenses up, those amber-colored eyes scanning the darkness for me—it's fucking intoxicating. I can't help the low laugh that escapes me, though she can't hear it from this distance.

"Thought you could slip away from me, Angel?" I mutter to the shadows, playing this little game primarily for my own amusement.

Her flustered defiance is the sweetest kind of tease. Nothing gets me harder than drawing out that fire in her. It's all foreplay leading to the main event—all the more satisfying when I let the heat build between us.

Just a little longer

Her fingers fly across her phone screen, and I can practically feel the heat of her irritation from here. My phone buzzes with her response:

Did you seriously follow me here? Stalking is illegal in all 50 states!

I can almost hear the piss and vinegar in her voice.

Bring your sexy ass outside.

I stand there, soaking in the symphony of the night and the low hum of the sleeping town bathed in moonlight. There's a primal beat thumping inside me, a surge of raw fucking power. I squash that shit down hard. This is about who rules the roost, about pure, unadulterated control.

She belongs to me—to drive insane until she's panting and pleading. With the night honing my edges, I'm primed for this showdown of might and ravenous want.

Then my phone goes off—she's taken the bait.

Fine.

That angry-faced emoji she sends makes me smirk like a predator.

I melt back into the darkness as her door swings open. There she stands like a warrior queen, arms crossed over her chest, ready for battle.

"What the actual fuck are you doing here?" she hisses, voice sharp enough to cut glass. Before I can answer, she's right in my face, jabbing her finger into my chest. "You think stalking is sexy? Newsflash, Count Creepy—I'm not some helpless bunny for you to hunt down!"

Her rage is like foreplay—every word, every flash of those golden eyes gets me harder. I can't help but laugh. "Count Creepy? That's the best you've got, Angel? You're way off base." I close the distance between us, drawn to her fire like a moth to flame. "Admit it—part of you loves that I came for you."

She scoffs, but her feet stay rooted to the spot—like my gravity won't let her escape. Moonlight catches her face, revealing the war in her eyes. My darkness calls to something inside her, even as she fights against it.

"You need to leave," she says, but there's no conviction behind it. Every inch of her body betrays what she really wants—the danger I bring, the shadows I offer. No more games, no more pretending.

As she turns to walk away, something snaps inside me. Before she can take a step, I grab her from behind, one hand clamping over her mouth to silence her shocked cry. Adrenaline surges through me even as my rational mind screams this is fucking insane. Too late—I've already crossed the line.

I feel Dani's heart hammering against my arm locked around her waist. I kick into vampire speed, the world blurring around us into streaks of twisted branches and flying leaves. She struggles against my iron grip, her muffled curses hot against my palm.

But there's no escape as I race deeper into the dark forest.

What the fuck have I done?

Some wild, desperate part of me needed to take her away, to have her to myself even for a few stolen moments...

I finally stop in a clearing deep among the towering pines, my supernatural speed fading. Moonlight filters through the canopy above us. Dani gasps for air in my unyielding embrace, her hair tangled with pine needles.

I should let her go, but some irrational fear keeps my arms locked around her. What will I see when she turns to face me? The hatred and fear I deserve?

I force myself to release her mouth, bracing for the explosion. She sucks in a sharp breath, disoriented. I expect screaming, clawing—but she freezes, momentarily stunned.

The silence hangs heavy between us. Then she erupts—"Let me GO!" She shoves against my chest, her strength nothing against mine. "What the hell is this? Take me back RIGHT NOW."

She glares daggers as I let out a low chuckle. Her jaw clenches so tight I can hear her teeth grinding as she visibly swallows back a torrent of curses. "Not until you calm down, Angel. We don't want to attract anything that might be hunting in these woods."

"Fine," she spits venom dripping from that single word. The fury rolling off her could set the forest ablaze.

I loosen my grip. She stumbles backward, rubbing her arms where I held her, and eyes me like a rabid animal. The woods around us seem to hold their breath, waiting.

Despite her fury, Danica takes in the tranquil brook shining in the moonlight, oak branches etched in silvery relief. Admiring the beauty even now betrays her tender heart.

Our eyes lock silently across the small distance. Hers are fiery with outrage and hurt. Mine are pleading for a chance to explain unforgivable actions.

This stunning forest scene framed by darkness reflects our situation perfectly. Where do we go from here?

"What the hell, Rhyland?" she shouts, eyes blazing. "Kidnapping is your idea of courtship? What century are you living in?"

I meet her fiery gaze unflinchingly. In those golden eyes, wariness and mistrust swirl—but also a flicker of something more vulnerable.

I've kept my distance, fought against every primal instinct screaming at me to claim what's mine. This past week has been pure fucking torture—trying to focus on anything besides breaking down her door and taking what belongs to me. But now she's here, hiding away like wounded prey. My beast stirs, sensing something's wrong. No more playing nice. No more waiting. Time to find out what's got my mate running scared.

"I needed to see you, Angel." My voice is a growl, the ownership ringing loud and clear even to my own ears. "You belong to me now, Danica," I declare bluntly. This goddamn enigmatic woman has ensnared me in ways she hasn't even begun to comprehend. "Why the hell are you hiding up here? Are you running from me? You're mine—we have a connection that must be discussed."

Her eyes, they spark with fury...and something else, something softer, like a goddamn plea. She's cornered against a tree, scouting an exit. "Yours?" she spits back, pure venom. "I don't belong to anyone! Whatever 'connection' you think we got is a fuckin' farce — torqued up without my say in it!"

Yeah, I know I come off like some beast. But after centuries of loss, I grip onto the chance that she's rightfully mine like a damn lifeline. "There's something fierce and raw between us, Dani," I admit, struggling to keep my passion under wraps. "This isn't some petty bullshit. We're connected on a deeper level, you and I."

The forest holds its breath, our standoff stretching taut. Dani snorts. "You've lost it. The only thing 'between us' is you trying to box me in."

I search her eyes, wondering if she can sense the truth. She says nothing, but her body responds to my words, belying her feigned indifference.

I invade her space. "You can't bury it; this connection's deeper than simple lust, more binding than any command. Old magic — it's real, and it's us."

"You've gone off the deep end," she hisses, but there's this glimmer of doubt, a tiny crack in her armor. "The only 'magic' is the crap you've conjured up in your messed-up head."

But as I close the gap, the moonlight casting us in silver and shadow, her sharp intake of breath speaks volumes.

"Keep feeding yourself those lies, Angel." My finger traces her throat, and she quivers. "You can't help it—your body's hungry for mine, just as I'm fuckin' starved for yours."

She tilts her head away but doesn't retreat from my lingering caress.

"You don't affect me," she denies weakly. But we both know it's a lie.

She might turn her head and play it off, but she's not fooling anyone.

I bite back the full truth to avoid scaring her further. Patience is a virtue, I guess. Our destiny isn't going anywhere.

"Own up to it. There's fear in those beautiful eyes, but desire, too, itching under your skin. Our fate begins now."

I know it's there, deeper than the raw hunger between us. The way she came undone on my fingers, her body surrendering to mine. The way my body reacts to hers—this is more than just lust.

Her internal war is almost goddamn palpable — her body's yielding, but her mind's in full retreat. She's not quite there yet. But give it time. She'll be all in.

"Our fate?" She throws back, in disbelief, painting her scowl. "You sound like a lunatic, like some kinda creep, showing up here! This isn't normal, Rhyland!"

"No shit, it ain't normal," I shoot back. "But when the hell have we ever been just 'normal'?"

She's a mess of conflict, arms wrapped around herself. She bites her lip, clearly torn up inside. "I... I need some space to wrap my head around this."

I close in, the crackle between us charged enough to light up the night. "I hear you, Angel. But it's like my soul's been hardwired to yours. There's no turning back from whatever the hell this is."

Her eyes flick to the shadows that cloak me. "Why keep yourself hidden, Rhyland?" There's a desperate edge to her demand.

My hood's my disguise, shrouding most of my face, no need for more. A simple shift of my head, and she's kept from the full picture.

I avert my gaze, struggling for the right way to put this. How do I tell her that dropping the truth now might shatter what we're building?

"There are... complications. I want you to get it, but fuck if I can spell it all out right now," I admit. She can sense I'm pulling punches, and she's not backing down.

"I think I deserve some answers after everything," she fires back, arms crossed.

The truth hangs poised on my tongue, but instinct stays my reckless impulse. Patience and trust must come first. I will unravel our tangled story slowly and gently. When the time is right, she will know me fully.

"Have you even tried?" Danica demands in frustration. She thinks I'm toying with her.

"Yes, Angel. In the only way I know how," I rasp. Before she can react, I crush her fiercely against me, revealing my desperate longing through action, not inadequate words.

Danica inhales sharply, startled. Her palms press against my chest as if to push away, but she hesitates, pulse racing under my hands.

My body trembles with restrained need. I know I should release her, but I can't let go. I groan deeply, her intoxicating scent stealing my breath. Having her pressed against me ignites a visceral craving.

The wind swirls ominously through the trees, portending dangerous temptations if my fragile control slips. No matter how powerfully this girl calls to my darkest desires, I vow to take things slow. "For now, just feel," I whisper, drawing her body close to mine. "Feel this connection between us, this power that transcends human bonds. You were meant for me, Dani." I capture her mouth in a searing kiss. "And I will have you completely."

She tries to pull away, but I feel her melt into my kiss despite herself. Her defenses are crumbling. She is mine.

"Let me show you what I can't express in words," I murmur heatedly before claiming her mouth again.

She opens to me with a hunger matching mine, our tongues dancing as we cling desperately. As my mouth claims hers, a spark ignites within me. Her lips are impossibly soft and warm, melding to mine with a rightness that steals my breath. I kiss her deeply, trying to express what I cannot say.

A slight sound of pleasure escapes her, kindling my longing. I cradle her cheek gently, even as passion threatens to consume us. The kiss deepens, speaking of yearning and mystery.

Reluctantly, I release her, holding on a moment longer than I should. Her eyes remain closed, emotions simmering beneath the surface.

I trail my fingers across her cheek. "If you need time for yourself, I understand. I'm sorry for intruding..."

I am not one to sugarcoat the goddamn truth. She's mine, and there ain't a fucking thing to apologize for. Dani might be playing this little game, thinking she's pushing back and reclaiming some ground. But deep down, she can't deny what's firing up inside her—it's me she's aching for.

The more she's away, the hotter that flame's gonna burn. Every second apart is just cranking up the heat. By the time she's back in my arms, she'll be so damn hungry it'll match my ravenous desire.

I'm the one calling the shots here. I'll decide when she's ripe for the taking. For now, I'll back off and just watch her beautiful defiance crumble to the raw need I've awakened. She'll come crawling back, make no mistake. Her submission? That's gonna taste oh so fucking sweet after this little chase.

So no, I am not sorry. I'm playing this dangerous game like a master, pulling the strings to that sweet ending where she comes to me, all fired up and surrendering herself completely.

Dani's breath hitches in her throat, her eyes slamming shut as she tries to sort the whirlwind I've stirred in her. A storm brews in those eyes when she finally looks at me again. She touches her lips, as if feeling them might give her some answers.

"This—what you're doing, Rhyland," she says, barely above a scandalized whisper. "It's like nothing I've ever felt. It fucking terrifies me."

I nod, keeping my face as still as stone. I know what's happening here. Our worlds are colliding, shattering any barriers we thought we had.

And then she's pacing, frustrated as all hell. "This is insane. You bust into my life, rock my world with your...your kisses." Her fingers tangle in her hair like she can squeeze some sense back into her head. "I can't make heads or tails of this!"

Her panic lights a fire in me. Without thinking, I'm on her, hands on her waist, soft. "Angel, look at me." She hesitates, but her gaze eventually finds mine. "I get it, you're freaking out. But what we have started? Don't run from it."

She's searching my face like she will find some roadmap to navigate her confusion. "Just...I need time. To figure this out. Please."

I let her go slowly, already regretting pushing her too far tonight.

She moves to leave, then throws me a look over her shoulder. "Will I—will I see you again?" She's surprising herself with that one.

"Do you want to?" My voice is a razor's edge, ready to slice through whatever she decides.

"I...I don't know what I want," she admits, biting her lip like it's the source of all her mixed feelings.

With a heavy sigh, I nod, watching her retreat. The harsh truth is setting in—I am no longer the sole owner of my heart. Dani sparked something fierce inside me, and it's a threat, dangerous and wild. But goddamn, if I don't want to chase that danger as far as it'll go.

A chilling howl echoes through the moonlit forest. Before we react, a branch cracks behind us, and a menacing growl interrupts me. Spinning around, we face the monstrous beast, slavering before us, yellow eyes gleaming with evil intent.

Danica stumbles back with a scream, clutching my arm desperately. My muscles coil, ready to rip the vile creature apart. But with a sickening crunch of bones, it shifts into the form of Marcus Welsch, Cascade Pack leader, sneering cruelly.

"Rhyland Eriksson. It's been a while."

Burying my violent urges, I demand through clenched teeth, "Not nearly long enough, asshole. The fuck do you want?"

Marcus's laughter is hellish. Danica grips my arm, trembling. "I caught a strange scent. These are my woods, after all. Had to investigate."

My mind races for a solution as he scans Danica hungrily. Her aura attracts predators—even the wolves drool for her.

Feigning nonchalance, I snort. "No idea what you mean. All I smell is your nasty ass fouling my air."

Marcus takes another step, pine needles crunching underfoot. Behind me, Danica grips my arm tightly, barely peeking out. His tongue flicks over his lips lecherously. "Oh, I know exactly what I mean," he grumbles, stepping closer. "A new toy for me, Rhyland?"

"Back off, you mangy fuck," Danica shouts. "Touch me, and I'll neuter your ass!"

Marcus cackles as I plant myself firmly between them. "Got yourself a wildcat, eh, Rhyland?" His smirk promises cruelty.

Red creeps into my vision. One wrong move from this bastard and my restraint will snap.

"Get lost before I beat your sorry ass, Marcus," I spit, barely containing my rage.

The motherfucker just laughs bitterly, knowing he's outmatched if I fully unleash. "Watch yourself, Rhyland."

His bones snap and contort sickeningly, and his pale skin erupts in dark fur. Muscles ripple and reform as the hulking beast emerges. Deadly claws gouge the dirt, and drool drips from gleaming fangs.

With an ear-splitting howl, the wolf bounds away, dirt and leaves spraying in its wake.

Beside me, Danica spews out stunned curses. "What the hell?! Did...he...was that a goddamn wolf?!"

I crush her shaking form against me, wishing I could keep her innocent from this shitstorm a bit longer. In the distance, the wolf's mournful cry echoes through the trees like an omen. Our troubles have only just begun.

The whisper of leaves is the only sound in this loaded hush. Danica tries to find her words, mouth opening then snapping shut like she's wrestling with some fucked up puzzle. Finally, she spits out the bombshell—her lab tests—showing an intertwined wolf gene.

My hands clench around her like a vise. "Let's get back to the house." I snatch up her hand, pulling her with a fierce grip. Every shadow in the woods seems like it's hiding some threat, lurking, waiting.

Danica matches my pace and pins me with that searching stare. "So what's the beef with you and Marcus?"

The truth feels like a goddamn boulder in my throat, but I spit it out. "That son of a bitch laid waste to my turf centuries ago. I had the bastard under my boot, and I let him slide. He's on my shit list for good."

She nods, her head spinning from the load of crap I've dropped on her. "Werewolves," she mutters like the word tastes weird on her tongue. "Just when I thought I'd seen it all." She huffs out a breath like she's been sucker-punched. "Everything's turned to chaos, and I'm here wondering why the hell my life's the punchline!"

It's gotta be her scent, whipping up a shitstorm and calling every freaky thing with fangs or fur right to our damn doorstep.

Our hands locked, we beeline for the house. Danica sneaks peeks at me, like she's stealing herself to spill her guts. She's twitchy as hell, her shoulders rigid, and her breaths coming too quickly. Her face gets flushed, and she's playing some mute game, her mouth flipping open and shut without spitting out a word. I ride it out, silent as the grave, until we hit her doorstep.

Then she loses it. "Okay, what the hell?!" she explodes. "Werewolves, vampires — what are we ticking off some monster bingo card here? Zombies up next?!" She's chucking her hands around like grenades, vibrating with the insane shit we're living.

I mull over Dani's off-the-charts flip-out about Marcus. Even after she explained her wolf DNA findings. Now, Marcus's show-and-tell turns her world upside down?

I expected nerves, maybe curiosity—not finding her on the edge of a fucking meltdown.

Something's off, scratching at my instincts like a warning bell. She's holding back, playing defense. Can't blame her—trust between us is as stable as nitro in an earthquake. Hell, I'm sitting on my own mountain of secrets. Part of me wants to shake the truth out of her, force those walls down. But we're both dug into our trenches, neither willing to show our hand first.

I let her rip into her panic until the storm burns itself out. Then I'm closing in, fingers tipping her chin up to meet my burning stare. "You're scared, you're confused—I get it. But you're mine to protect now. That means you're not alone in this shit."

Dani's eyes search mine desperately, like I hold the fucking answers she's dying for. "I just need to understand what's happening—why I'm—" She catches herself, biting back whatever secret she's keeping.

The abrupt silence hits me like a punch to the gut. There's more to this than just supernatural shit throwing her world off its axis. Something deeper, darker. The way she cut herself off, swallowing back her words—my instincts scream that she's hiding something major.

What the fuck is my little angel not telling me?

I've been missing the plot, overlooking some heavy burden she's lugging around. Dani damn near faced a horror show not long ago, with the asshole at Karma, nearly biting her, and now she's like a beacon for trouble of the hellish kind. But her pleas hint at some deep-seated chaos I've been blind to, or just plain ignored.

My mental gears kick into overdrive—I gotta step up to be the rock she can crash against with all her darkest demons and fears.

I thread my fingers through her hair, hoping it's a whisper of comfort. "You'll get your answers, baby. I'll tear apart heaven and hell to find them if I have to. But first—" My tone brooks no argument. "Stay inside tonight. No exceptions."

She nods weakly, the razor edge of her panic finally dulling. I watch until she's locked safely away before tearing back to the cesspool of Seattle.

Time to hunt for some answers.

DANICA

27

My trip to Leavenworth zipped by way too fast. I'm already missing my parents' bubble of normality. But I can't hide in their guest room forever. Real life awaits me—terrifying and unpredictable, but mine to deal with.

My heart's still pounding, replaying that werewolf encounter that basically shattered my entire worldview. I'd convinced myself those weird DNA results were just a lab error. But watching a man literally transform into a furry nightmare right in front of me? Kind of hard to explain that away with "equipment malfunction."

I ran those tests over and over, desperate to prove it was contamination or faulty equipment or maybe that I was hallucinating from too much caffeine.

But nope! Every single test confirmed the impossible—wolf DNA braided through human genetic code like some science fiction nightmare. It's like finding a unicorn in your backyard and admitting magic might be real.

So down the research rabbit hole I went, diving into werewolf lore—the whole magical human-to-beast transformation thing.

Reading about their bone-cracking changes, super-senses, and supernatural strength hooked me. I've been dragged into this Twilight Zone where science fiction is suddenly my new reality.

Apparently, these furry friends can wolf-out whenever they want, courtesy of their special genetic lottery win. They're not immortal, but they're definitely working with an upgraded human model. I've got so many questions keeping me up at night, my brain spinning like a hamster wheel.

I rub my wrist nervously, thinking about my own magical light show episodes. When Rhyland and I were alone under that moonlight, I nearly blurted out my terrifying secret—that I can somehow conjure fire from my hands like a walking lighter.

The confession was right there, dancing on my tongue as he stared into my eyes. Part of me desperately wanted to spill everything and beg this mysterious man for answers, or at least a hug and an "it's gonna be okay."

But fear locked my lips. What if he saw me as some freak once he knew? Some unnatural anomaly that shouldn't exist? Would my weird fire-starter abilities destroy whatever this thing is between us?

Or worse—what if he wanted to use my freaky new powers for his own agenda? I barely know the real Rhyland beneath all that brooding hotness—his true motives, his past, whether he's actually one of the good guys or just really good at pretending.

And why does that uncertainty make him even more attractive? I need serious therapy.

So I choked down my confession like a bitter pill. Until I know for sure he's in my corner, this whole "surprise, I'm a human sparkler" situation stays my private nightmare to deal with at 3 AM when I'm staring at the ceiling.

Questions keep bubbling up like a pot about to boil over. How much crazier can my life get? I get the feeling Rhyland's sitting on his own bombshell confession but can't quite spit it out.

Another Rhyland-free week was supposed to be my chance to focus on work and untangle my mental spaghetti. Yet here I am, thinking about him constantly for reasons my brain can't explain. It's completely baffling how I'm drawn to this walking enigma wrapped in muscle—my body and heart staging a mutiny against common sense.

The distance from him is starting to bother me. I don't do longing, I don't dwell on guys—it's not my style. But Rhyland is different. He's gotten under my skin in ways I never anticipated, and that terrifies me more than any supernatural weirdness ever could.

Apparently, my type is "dangerous and mysterious" with a side of "probably hiding something major." Great job, self.

Evening light streams through my windows while Emily and I prep for tonight, our dresses sprawled across my bed like fancy corpses.

Steam fogs up the mirrors as I hop in the shower, hot water working its magic. I inhale my lavender body wash like it's aromatherapy. Lathering up my hair, my mind wanders to tonight's possibilities—some fancy-pants mansion all lit up like Christmas, orchestra music floating through the air. And maybe, just maybe, a certain vampire making an appearance...

"Hey! You grow gills in there or what?" Emily's voice shatters my daydream.

"Jeez, I'm coming!" I laugh, shutting off the water.

I'm barely toweled off when Emily bulldozes into the bathroom.

"Enough shower daydreaming, we've got a ball to crush!" she announces. "Tonight's mission: Get you some grade-A man candy!"

My face goes nuclear as Rhyland pops into my head uninvited. He's the only candy I'm craving.

"Time to transform you into a certified man-trap!" Emily winks, brandishing my blow dryer like a weapon.

"Yeah... not really looking to meet anyone," I mumble, fiddling with the cord. "Just want to hang with you and see what happens."

Emily serves me her patented "bitch, please" look. "Uh-huh. By 'what happens' you mean running into Mr. Stalker McHottie, right?"

I drop my hairbrush with soap opera levels of drama. "Oh my god, shut up!" My face could fry an egg.

"Your tomato face tells me everything!"

My stomach's doing backflips thinking about seeing Rhyland, but I'm not giving Emily more ammunition. I hit her with my best "knock it off" glare.

"You're impossible," I groan, rolling my eyes to the ceiling. "Now hand over that brush before my hair becomes its own ecosystem."

Emily grabs my hands, suddenly serious. "Listen up, babe—Rhyland's gonna short-circuit when he sees you, because you're already a whole meal. But if you wanna destroy him..."

She whips out her makeup bag like it's Mary Poppins' carpet bag. "Let your fairy godmother work her magic. We're going for 'goddess walks among mortals' vibes. By the time I'm done, his fangs will pop out involuntarily. Now sit your cute butt down!"

Emily attacks my face with brushes and powders, creating some serious smoky eye action and rose-tinted lips. When she's done, I barely recognize my reflection—in a good way.

Maria shows up hauling enough styling tools to open a salon. Our resident hair wizard has arrived.

Operation Vampire Bait is officially underway.

Our girl-talk soundtrack fills the room while Maria circles me like a hair artist stalking her canvas. I zone out watching her in the mirror, finding zen in the gentle tugs on my scalp. The hairspray cloud threatens to make me sneeze.

With dramatic flair, Maria spins my chair around. My jaw drops—my usual bird's nest is transformed into something out of a fantasy movie, with perfect curls framing my face like I'm about to meet Prince Charming.

Emily goes full paparazzi, phone clicking away. "Holy shit, you look like a freaking goddess!"

I imagine Rhyland seeing me like this, his eyes burning with that intense look that melts my insides. My heart does the rumba, butterflies throwing a rave in my stomach. Tonight feels electric with possibilities.

As we add our final touches, the sunset paints the sky in cotton candy colors. I'm practically vibrating with anticipation for whatever magic this night might bring.

Squeezed into our gowns and masked like sexy mystery women, Emily and I slide into the waiting limo, our excitement cranked to eleven.

I grab Emily's hand like it's a lifeline, trying to calm the cocktail of thrill and panic bubbling inside me. Tonight could be amazing if I'd just chill out and stop trying to micromanage every second. Easier said than done for a control freak like me who breaks out in hives facing the unknown.

My brain's working overtime, crafting elaborate scenarios for my perfect fairy tale evening. But Emily's champagne-bubble energy yanks me back to reality. She squeals like a teenager when the mansion appears, lit up like something from a Disney movie.

Emily squeezes my hand, reminding me to actually breathe and just enjoy hanging with her. As we adjust our masks and step into the grand entrance, I make myself shut down the worry machine and actually notice what's happening around me. The music, the colors, the buzz of excitement—it's intoxicating.

I don't need some perfect storybook night—just the ability to actually experience each messy, real moment as it happens.

The magic isn't in some perfect future scenario—it's right here if I'd just pay attention. For now, being with my best friend is enough. Sometimes you just need to trust the universe's playlist instead of trying to skip to the next track.

But if a certain vampire shows up, I definitely won't complain.

Rhyland

28

I step into Azrael's grandiose hellhole, the place dripping in riches but marinated in menace. Drenched in shadows and barely-there lights, the place reeks of a charm laced with doom. The main event, the ballroom, hits me like a beast, with chandeliers casting a spell over the masked freaks below. I stride through the crowd, magnetic and menacing, snagging every damn stare.

These masked assholes prance around in their fancy-ass disguises, hiding behind some high-end craftwork that costs more than most people make in a year. Dresses in every sinful shade imaginable catch the light, a twisted kaleidoscope of wealth and power.

The orchestra's playing some haunting shit that floats through the air like dark magic. Couples spinning across the floor like they're practicing for their own funeral dance.

Waiters weave through the crowd with enough champagne to float a fucking battleship. I stalk through this circus of excess, feeling the raw power crackling just beneath the surface of all this bullshit.

Then there's Blackwood, playing king of the castle in his designer suit. Got these sheep eating right out of his blood-stained hands, hanging on every poisoned word. But underneath that smooth exterior, there's a darkness that makes my skin crawl. The bastard's a fucking plague—power-hungry piece of shit who'd step over his own mother's corpse to get ahead. Watching him work the room makes my blood boil.

And what the actual fuck? Marcus Welch slithering between the suits like he belongs here. Wolves are everywhere I look. Has Azrael made a deal with those mangy fuckers now? The question clouds my head like smoke.

Focus on the mission—tear down Azrael's façade of lies and keep the humans breathing. It's gonna be a bloody mess, but we're seeing this through.

Up on the stairs, Lucian and Erik own their space like the ancient lords they are. Lucian's wrapped around some woman in red, whispering god knows what in her ear. Erik's nursing a glass of O-positive like it's thousand-year-old scotch. I join them, and Erik acknowledges me with a slight nod. "Evening," he says, cool as frozen steel.

"Gentlemen," I say.

Erik leans in close. "We're ready when you are."

I take a breath before dropping the bomb. "Change of plans. You two scout below while I stay topside."

Erik looks astonished. Lucian gapes. "What the hell? Why bail suddenly?"

I turn away, steadying myself. Danica must be here. Leaving her alone with prowling wolves and vampires isn't an option. Before I can explain, Lucian cuts in snidely.

"Let me guess—it's about that hot piece you're panting after, right?"

I spin sharply, grabbing a fistful of his shirt. "Watch yourself," I warn through clenched teeth. Lucian puts his hands up in mock surrender.

"Touchy!" He smirks infuriatingly. "We get it, loverboy."

I release him roughly, still seething—Erik's voice reassures me in my mind. *"We understand, brother. The girl complicates things, but we'll adapt. Just be vigilant."*

Gratitude swells within me. "Thank you. I'll join you soon." They know what's at stake for us both now.

I'm chewing over the clusterfuck of stuff that's gone down. Just last week, I tracked down the vampire scum who laid hands on Danica. I ran on pure rage—beat him into the ground until his teeth rattled, and he coughed up the truth about her scent being some kind of heavenly drug. Then it clicks—that sweet fragrance of hers that damn near envelops me, clouding my senses. No wonder Marcus is practically a dog with a bone over her.

The need to claim her, mark her as mine—it's pounding through my veins like liquid fire. The beast inside me is clawing to get out, and I'm losing the fight to cage it. Then she walks in, and holy fuck—the whole room stops breathing. She's ethereal in that dress that hugs every perfect curve like it was painted on. That slit up her thigh—Jesus Christ—shows just enough skin to make me want to tear the whole thing off.

That azure mask with its teasing feathers makes her look like some dangerous angel. She's glowing under these lights like a goddamn fantasy. I blink hard, thinking my mind's fucking with me, but when I catch those honey-gold eyes—there's no doubt. It's my Angel. Costumes and bullshit can't hide the woman I'd spot in a blackout.

Some worthless asshole approaches her for a dance, and my fangs drop instantly. Every cock in the room is mentally stripping what belongs to me. The beast roars, demanding blood—she's claimed, she's MINE! But I reign it in, for now. Soon enough, she'll be back where she belongs—underneath me, screaming my name.

A growl rips from my chest, deep enough to shake the fucking foundations. These moths can flutter around her flame all they want, but they'll never touch her. She's mine to possess, mine to devour.

Her eyes scan the crowd until they lock with mine, and everything else disappears. Time stops. Even across the room, I can hear her heart racing, smell her arousal. Pure fucking proof that what's between us is more than physical—it's primal, eternal.

I'm trapped in her gaze, hypnotized by those fierce eyes and the thunder of her pulse. This connection between us is older than time—raw and absolute. We're two storms destined to collide and consume everything in our path.

Only my Angel can tame the monster inside me, make me feel something close to human again. Before this night ends, I swear to every god listening—she'll be writhing beneath me, marking her as mine forever.

A part of me recoils from that tenderness—I am the beast, the demon, meant to instill fear, not love. But under her gentle gaze, my walls begin to crack, light seeping into the dark recesses where my battered soul hides.

No one else could evoke such conflict in me, this simultaneous yearning for her affection and disgust at my own weakness. She is my strength and my undoing. My angel of mercy.

No more resisting our twisted bond. She will give herself to the shadows willingly, irrevocably. I will show her the bleak poetry we can create together from my darkness and her light.

Our fates are bound as one. I am the beast; she is my beauty—two halves of a whole.

DANICA

29

Crystal chandeliers drip light over the packed ballroom where designer-clad guests sway to orchestral music. A hundred curious stares suddenly turn my way, making my stomach plummet like an elevator with cut cables. My hands fidget with my dress, palms embarrassingly sweaty under this unexpected spotlight.

Emily leans in, voice panicky. "Why's everyone eyeballing us? Did I flash nipple or something?" I just shake my head, wondering the same thing.

Then my wandering gaze crashes into *his*—I'd know that cocky stance anywhere. We're locked in visual combat, the air between us practically crackling. My brain short-circuits even as my racing heart confirms it's definitely *him*.

I square my shoulders, march forward, and snatch champagne for liquid courage. I down it like water after a desert hike.

Needing breathing room, I retreat to a less crowded corner. I grab another bubbly and chug it. Emily materializes with a raised eyebrow.

"This place is crawling with hot guys," she announces. "I'm off to hunt for premium penis!" Then she twirls away, leaving me choking on my drink.

I roll my eyes, laughing at her zero-filter approach to life. But I can't shake the tension, even with the party swirling around me.

Because Azrael Blackwood is heading straight for me, wearing that plastic smile that makes my skin crawl. His reputation as Seattle's shadiest businessman has me instantly on guard.

"Good evening," he purrs like a predator. "That gown complements you beautifully. May I know your name?"

I force my face into polite-stranger mode. "Thank you, Mr. Blackwood. Lovely event. I'm Dr. Danica Pierce."

His eyes lock onto mine like targeting lasers. "Indeed. But you stand out remarkably. Something about you fascinates me, Dr. Pierce. I find myself quite drawn to you."

Ew. Hard pass.

I step back instinctively. "That's very kind, but I'm here with my friend." I try changing the subject to his company and the charity event.

He smiles like he knows a secret. "But I simply can't look away. Your scent is... extraordinary. Unlike anything I've encountered."

Oh shit. Can he smell whatever supernatural weirdness is happening with me?

Another strategic retreat. "How flattering," I manage, scanning for escape routes.

He grabs my hand before I can bolt. "Don't rush off. I'd love to know you better. You intrigue me. I've heard about your scientific work. Tell me more."

Someone please save me from Creepy McCreeperson before I "accidentally" spill champagne on his perfect suit.

I yank my hand back like it touched a hot stove. "Thanks for the interest, Mr. Blackwood, but I'm here for the party, not networking."

He smirks, enjoying my discomfort. "My offer remains open when you reconsider."

When hell freezes over and Satan starts a snowball fight. I force a smile as he slinks away.

Taking a deep breath, I scan the crowd for Emily, my skin still crawling from Blackwood's creepy attention. I need to keep that snake at a safe distance.

Before I can spot my friend, another predator locks onto me—a hulking figure in an ominous mask, mentally undressing me with his stare. My stomach knots as he struts over like he owns the place.

Jesus, what is this—Creep Convention 2023? All these bloodsucking pervs can apparently smell whatever supernatural weirdness is happening with me, and they're circling like sharks.

"You're breathtaking," he says with a smile that screams "serial killer vibes."

I force my face into something resembling politeness. "Thanks."

As he invades my personal space, I retreat strategically. "Care to dance?" he pushes.

I shake my head quickly. "No thanks, just arrived..." I gesture at my drink like it's fascinating evidence in a crime scene.

He stares at me like I'm an all-you-can-eat buffet. I feel naked under his invasive gaze.

"All alone tonight?" he asks in that sugar-coated predator voice.

Before I can tell him where to shove his question, warm breath tickles my neck, and a solid wall of muscle presses against my back—*Rhyland.* Relief and tension hit me simultaneously.

Rhyland's arms snake around my waist possessively. "She's taken," he growls, his eyes promising violence if challenged. I practically melt into a puddle. His intoxicating scent short-circuits my brain cells.

My scary vampire just became my knight in brooding armor.

Creepy dude backs off with fake surrender. "My bad," he says smoothly before melting into the crowd.

I break free from Rhyland's grip, shooting daggers at him. "I don't need a supernatural bodyguard."

He stalks closer, caging me against a pillar. "Clearly you do, Angel. This place is crawling with predators dying for a taste."

His overprotective alpha male act pisses me off. "I can fight my own battles, thanks."

Rhyland captures my chin in his steel grip. "Really? Because Blackwood and that wolf were about to make you their midnight snack."

Those ocean-blue eyes hit me like a tidal wave. I swallow hard, really seeing them for the first time. I yank away, channeling my attraction into anger. "Stop hovering! I'm not some helpless princess."

His eyes flash dangerously, something wild lurking behind them. "I won't apologize for protecting what's mine. Anyone who threatens you is dead."

"Yours?! I'm not property, especially not belonging to some stalker with control issues."

Rhyland crowds me, his body a wall of heat against mine. "Keep lying to yourself, Angel. But we both know the truth."

His lips brush my ear, sending tingles down my spine. "You were made for me. No one else gets to have you."

His possessive declaration should infuriate me, but my traitorous body says, "Yes, please."

His dark chuckle raises goosebumps everywhere, and my brain starts fantasy-casting our future together. The muscles in his neck flex as he laughs, and my inner hussy wants to trace those veins with my tongue.

Rhyland's knowing smile says he can smell my arousal through my anger. "Dance with me, Danica," he purrs. "Let's show these fuckers exactly who you belong to."

He's sex on legs in that midnight-blue tux that matches my dress like it was planned. Those ocean eyes pierce through his mask like lasers, pulling me in like a riptide. His stubbled jaw could cut glass, and I want to lick it.

He radiates pure alpha energy, danger wrapped in desire. Under that scorching stare, my heart is doing gymnastics. Being near him is like standing next to a lightning storm—terrifying, thrilling, and addictive.

Why does he have to be so goddamn hot when he's being possessive?

No guy has ever made me feel this alive with just a look. My brooding vampire promises the kind of adventure romance novels wish they could deliver. His pull is stronger than my common sense.

Fire races through me as Rhyland's lips brush my hand like a whispered promise. "I've missed you, Angel. Tell me you missed me, too," he whispers, his breath setting my skin ablaze.

My body screams "yes" while my brain waves red flags. I hate how he can turn me into a hormonal mess with zero effort.

"I..." My snark factory is temporarily closed for maintenance. My traitorous body's writing checks my attitude can't cash. I'm caught between wanting to punch him and climb him like a tree.

The music swells around us as we stand frozen in our own little bubble of sexual tension. No matter how far I run, I keep boomeranging back to him. My survival instincts are getting drowned out by my libido's cheerleading squad.

This will probably end in disaster, but holy hell, what a way to go.

He captures my hand in his iron grip and yanks me close. His breath teases my ear as he rumbles, "Let's show them how it's done, Angel."

He spins me like a pro and pulls me against his wall of muscle. His moves are making my knees weak and other parts decidedly not weak. His hands find their targets like heat-seeking missiles—one claiming my waist, the other threading through my fingers. Under the ballroom lights, I finally get the full HD view—that marble skin decorated with black ink that disappears temptingly under his collar. My imagination goes into overdrive wondering just how far those tattoos go. *Please let them go everywhere.*

The electricity between us could power Seattle as I feel his hard body and gentle touch combine, holding me like I'm something precious yet dangerous. We start moving in perfect sync, and I've never felt more *right.* His hand slides dangerously south, nearly crossing into X-rated territory. I'm burning alive and loving every second. No point fighting it now—I'm already addicted to his flame. He leads with pure alpha confidence, and I actually let him.

We flow with the music like we've danced together forever. "You're stunning, Angel. Everything I knew you'd be."

I look up at him—way up. He's a mountain of sexy in a tux, making me feel deliciously tiny.

I smirk. "You clean up nice yourself! Finally seeing my favorite stalker in proper lighting."

Note to self: Tall, dark, and dangerous is even hotter up close. I am so screwed. Hopefully literally.

He laughs, but there's a shadow behind it that tugs at my heart. "Not all of me... yet." He taps his mask, and my chest tightens.

I'm playing along with his masked mystery man routine, but damn if I don't want to know what he's hiding. The curiosity is killing me, but the answer might be worse.

His electric touch sends my nerve endings into party mode as we escape the dance floor. We weave through the fancy crowd like we're in our own music video, orchestra sounds bouncing off the walls.

We hit the bar, and he hands me champagne in a glass worth more than my rent. His fingers "accidentally" brush mine during the handoff. That tiny touch feels like a lightning strike, and the look he gives me could melt steel.

Our glasses clink while my emotions play ping-pong—want versus worry, thirst versus terror. He downs his drink like a boss, and I'm hypnotized by his throat working. My eyes crawl up to find him watching me like I'm dessert.

His voice drops to sex-on-wheels level: "Keep eye-fucking me like that, beautiful, and I'm gonna have to find us a private corner."

My eyebrows shoot for the ceiling as I channel my inner flirt. "Oh really? And what exactly are you planning to do with me?"

He grabs my hand across the bar, squeezing just enough to make promises. That smirk should be illegal in all fifty states. My eyes do another full-body scan as he purrs, "I think you've got some ideas."

My brain misfires while every cell in my body screams, "Yes!" The room suddenly feels like a sauna, and oxygen becomes optional. Just imagining what those hands could do is making me dizzy.

He clears his throat, trying to dial down the sexual tension that could power a small city. "So—" he lounges against the bar like sex in a tux, "what did Blackwood want?"

Like always, he's watching me with those predator eyes, and I should be running for the hills from his possessive ass. Instead, I'm diving deeper into whatever dangerous game we're playing, addicted to the thrill.

Why do I always fall for the complicated ones? Couldn't I just crush on a nice accountant?

I drop the bomb, ready for his jealous explosion. "He said I was impossible to resist, that I smelled amazing, and he wanted to get *personal.*"

Rhyland's eyes flash like blue fire as he snorts, "That bastard *had* good taste. But his little obsession ends now. You're fucking breathtaking, and your scent? Pure addiction. I could get drunk on it for days."

He rises and invades my space, his hot breath setting my neck ablaze as he inhales me like I'm the finest vintage in his collection.

A moan escapes before I can catch it, my body going nuclear under his attention. His voice rumbles through me like a seismic event, making everything quake. Each word is foreplay, lighting up my nerve endings like Times Square.

I channel my inner vixen: "So tell me, what exactly do I smell like?"

Rhyland locks me in his iron grip and yanks me against his chest. Sitting back down, he cages me between those tree-trunk thighs, my back pressed to his marble abs. His lips tease my ear as he purrs, "Like cotton candy wrapped in sin. Like the sweetest forbidden fruit. Like a siren's song made flesh."

My breath catches as his lips ghost my skin. "Keep making those little noises, Angel, and I'll show you exactly what I mean."

The party fades to background noise as I'm practically in his lap. Candlelight dances across his jaw as he leans in closer, his hot breath on my exposed skin raising an army of goosebumps while my brain drowns in hormones. This is probably the dumbest game of chicken ever, but I'm already addicted—this sexy vampire has unleashed my inner wild child, and she's not going back in her cage.

"Prove it," I challenge.

The air crackles between us like a storm about to break. Time stops. He springs up and grabs my hand, dragging me away while my heart tries to escape my chest. I'm terrified and thrilled and completely lost.

I stumble after his giant steps, lungs burning, no clue what's coming next. Where is this man taking me, and what deliciously dangerous things has he planned? The music dies as we vanish down a marble hallway. My nerves dance as we take turn after turn, the shadows growing deeper. I strain for party sounds but find only silence.

I'm lost in this mansion maze, getting more anxious with each step. He moves like he knows this place by heart, while I wonder if we'll need breadcrumbs to find our way back. Everything's gone cemetery-quiet, like we've stepped into our own private dimension.

This will either be the hottest thing ever or the start of a horror movie. Maybe both?

My heart's doing parkour as Rhyland feels along the wall like a sexy secret agent until something clicks. He swings open a hidden door with that "I'm about to ruin you" grin.

The second we're inside, he pins me against the door like I'm his favorite prey. The impact knocks the air from my lungs in the best way, trapped between wood and wall of muscle. Our eyes lock, and my knees forget how knees work.

He leans in until his breath teases my lips. "Careful with those dares, Angel," he purrs. "Sure you want to see what I've got planned?"

His words melt my brain. My eyes close as my resistance waves the white flag. "Yes... please," I breathe.

Heat pools low in my belly at my surrender. My body betrays me, arching toward him like a magnet.

His kiss hits like a hurricane, and I moan shamelessly as he devours me. He fists my hair, sending lightning down my spine. He yanks me closer as our tongues tangle. My hands find his hair, giving as good as I get. He tastes like sin and salvation rolled into one delicious package.

He grabs my waist like he owns it, crushing me against him. I moan as his tongue does wicked things to mine.

He nips my bottom lip and growls against my mouth, "Fucking missed you, Angel." I grab his lapels, desperate for more.

God, I missed him, too. So much for playing hard to get.

His hand finds bare skin through my dress slit, cupping my ass. His groan of approval vibrates through me as he squeezes. He presses his impressive length against me, showing exactly what I do to him. My gasp gets swallowed by his hungry kiss. I surrender to our connection. Fighting this is like trying to stop a tsunami with an umbrella.

He lifts me like I weigh nothing, depositing me on a desk. Our kisses turn feral as need takes over. His mouth blazes down my neck, his breath raising goosebumps. I tangle my fingers in his hair, loving the contrast of silk and stubble. His teeth graze my ear, and my back arches. The desk edge digs in, but I'm lost in his touch, his heat. He's pure alpha male, and I'm drunk on it.

I want him desperately. *When did I become this addicted?*

He's invaded every part of me. My sanity's on vacation, and I can't process these feelings.

His touch leaves me aching for more.

Am I in too deep?

Spoiler alert—Yes. Yes, I am.

RHYLAND

30

I need Danica like a dying man needs air. Her scent drives me to the edge of sanity, making my fangs ache and my cock throb. Every fiber of my being screams to claim her, to sink my teeth into that soft flesh and taste the sweet nectar pumping through her veins.

Her intoxicating aroma has become a fucking beacon, drawing every supernatural predator within miles. The thought of Azrael's eyes on her makes my blood boil with murderous rage. That bastard's hungry gaze is fixed on what's mine, and she's not safe from him or any other piece of shit who thinks they can take her.

"I need to taste you," I growl against her throat, my voice rough with need.

She tenses, assuming I mean blood. I let out a dark laugh at her innocence. "Not like that... *yet,* Angel. Unless you want me to bite right here?" I slide my hand between her thighs, finding her pussy already soaked through her panties. I press my finger against her clit, making her gasp.

She arches into my touch, a ragged moan escaping her lips. "Yesss..."

"Pull up that dress and lie back," I command, my voice pure gravel. She obeys, the fabric bunching at her waist. I smirk as I rip off her drenched panties and pocket them like a trophy.

She won't be needing these when I'm done with her.

Her arousal is undeniable—her pussy glistening in the dim light, begging for my touch. I lock eyes with her as I drop to my knees. "Show me what paradise tastes like, Angel. I'll show you what it feels like to be claimed by a real fucking man."

She's spread out before me like a feast—wet, pink, and desperate for my tongue. My mouth waters at the sight of her perfect cunt.

I bury my face in her dripping pussy, dragging my tongue up her swollen clit before circling it with devastating precision. I attack that sensitive bud, pulling desperate moans from her trembling body. I increase the pressure as she quivers beneath me, drinking down her sweet nectar like a man starved. Pure animal hunger rises in me as I devour her. Her intoxicating scent makes my cock throb painfully against my zipper. I growl against her flesh—her taste is fucking paradise.

She writhes in ecstasy, her delicate pussy quivering under my savage mouth. I feast on her like a starving beast, sucking her dripping cunt with primal need. Her arousal floods my senses, driving me mad with lust. I lap up every drop of her honey like it's my last meal, gripping her lush curves as she trembles.

Her desperate cries of pleasure vibrate through me as I yank down the top of her dress, filling my hands with those perfect tits. The sight of them makes me fucking feral—I can't wait to mark them with my teeth. I pinch and twist her hard nipples while my tongue plunges deep into her soaked core.

"Fuck—your mouth..." she pants like a bitch in heat.

I grin against her dripping pussy. "Is this what you need, Angel?" Her gasping moan is all the answer I need.

Feeling her edge approaching, I force those thighs up, exposing her completely. I thrust two fingers into her scorching cunt. "Come for me, Angel," I growl. "Soak my fucking face. I want to taste every drop."

She screams my name as her body convulses, her sweet cream flooding around my pumping fingers. The obscene sounds of my feasting echo through the room as I devour her. My cock leaks precum, her taste driving me to the edge of control.

She tries closing her shaking legs, but I force them wider. Our eyes lock, raw fucking hunger burning between us. I see fresh desire igniting in her gaze.

"Too much..." she gasps brokenly. I pin her thighs down, keeping her spread wide and vulnerable as I latch onto her swollen clit, working it mercilessly with my tongue.

"Keep those legs spread, Angel, or I'll bind you down and force every orgasm from this sweet body," I growl, my voice dark with promise.

She moans my name like a prayer, pleading for more. My tongue ravages her mercilessly, drawing out her honey like the sweetest fucking poison.

Her pleasure spirals higher as I assault her with fingers and mouth. She's lost to primitive sounds and desperate writhing. The sight of her coming undone triggers my own release—I groan savagely as I come hard in my pants for the second fucking time.

She screams as another orgasm rips through her, her pussy clenching around my fingers. I plunge them deeper into her spasming cunt, coating them in her slick arousal.

"Open that pretty mouth," I command roughly, pulling out my drenched fingers. She eagerly sucks them clean, her body still trembling from the aftershocks.

In a flash, my hand is around her throat as I crash our mouths together. Our tongues wage war while I feast on the taste of her desire.

My cock throbs painfully, far from satisfied. Dominating her awakens something primal in me—a desperate need to fuck her until she's raw and hoarse from screaming my name. She's mine now, marked and claimed.

I pin her against the desk, grinding my hard length against her soaked core as we kiss like savage beasts. She clings to me, wordlessly begging for more.

I'll give this little vixen more than she ever dreamed possible.

DANICA

31

We remain in our position, gasping for breath and feeling the warmth that radiates from each other in the muted light of the room. I draw away from the kiss only to remove his mask, wanting to see who this man is behind the shadows and the mind-blowing orgasms he gives me. He stops me by grasping my wrists tightly, anxiety or confusion playing across his features. With trembling fingers, he lifts the mask away and reveals himself.

All thoughts escape me as I look at the enticing figure before me. He stands tall and muscular, with chiseled features reminding me of an ancient Norse God. His ice-blue eyes pierce into mine, framed by silken, dark lashes.

It's him.

Everything about him radiates raw masculine sensuality. My pulse quickens as I look over his ruggedly handsome face—the scar above his brow somehow enhancing his magnetism, his full lips curved in a subtle, knowing smirk.

It's him.

I inhale sharply, my mind spinning like a runaway carousel. I know those ice-blue eyes and that chiseled jawline.

It's him—the silent watcher from Lucian's office, my dark guardian, and the one who intervened at the club. Emotions war within me.

I freaking knew it!

I try to speak, but my voice takes a vacation. My thoughts are like hyperactive puppies, running in every direction. This is way too much to process.

He waits while I do my best goldfish impression, the air between us practically crackling.

I stare in shock as the fancy room comes into focus. He was right there, watching silently while Emily and I went through the security tapes. Anger bubbles up inside me as puzzle pieces start clicking together.

My heart's trying to escape my chest as he slowly removes my mask, that smirk triggering a tornado of emotions. Questions explode in my brain—why didn't he say anything during the security footage review? Why the secret identity? Why stay silent about Max drugging me? My body tenses as suspicion floods in. Has this all been some elaborate game?

Just once, couldn't I meet a hot guy who isn't hiding massive secrets? Is that too much to ask?

I need answers.

"It's you," I breathe, like the world's dumbest detective finally solving the obvious case.

The air between us could power a small city as I search those ocean eyes for some explanation that doesn't make me want to kick him in his perfectly sculpted nuts.

He nods and reaches for me, but I jump back like he's radioactive. "Was this whole thing just some fucked up game?" I shove his rock-hard chest, needing space to breathe before I explode. "What the actual hell is this?"

He freezes, those blue eyes locked on mine while I try to remember how lungs work. My brain's running like a hamster on Red Bull. I watch his throat work as he swallows hard.

"Why did you just creep in the shadows that morning during the security footage review? You knew exactly what happened, but you played mute?!" I push him again, channeling my inner Hulk. My rage and confusion are having a party. "What kind of twisted bullshit are you pulling, Rhyland? What happened to Max and his douchebag squad? Don't you dare lie to me, or I swear to god!" I'm practically breathing fire. Lies piss me off worse than abandonment, courtesy of people who were supposed to be trustworthy.

He backs up, running fingers through that unfairly perfect hair. "It's complicated," he mutters.

I cross my arms, rage level reaching critical. "*Un*-complicate it," I snap.

If his explanation isn't Nobel Prize worthy, I'm going to introduce his balls to my knee.

He lets out a heavy breath, "The moment I saw you, something inside me shattered, and all these buried emotions came flooding back."

I watch him, remembering that same gut-punch feeling when we first met. I wait for more.

"Where I come from, vampires aren't supposed to feel this intensely—we keep everything locked down until..." He trails off, looking lost in thought.

"Until what?" I push. He's struggling like a guy trying to explain quantum physics to a fish.

"Until one person can rise and enlighten us."

Confused, I crease my eyebrows. "What are you talking about, Rhyland?" I say with a tinge of annoyance in my voice.

"I'm scared to tell you. You won't understand," he says. "But I can tell you Erik ensured Emily got home safely that night. He drove her back when he saw Dakota's intentions."

My rage explodes like a nuclear bomb. "You kept that from us?!" I'm practically breathing fire. "Emily's been torturing herself thinking she was drugged and raped! Did your vampire brain think maybe we needed to know that?!" I glare daggers at him, demanding answers. "Why hide it if you knew? And what about Max and his creep squad? Lucian said—"

He slams his hands down beside me, trapping me against the desk. We're nose to nose as he snarls his confession like an angry wolf: "I fucking killed them! That piece of shit deserved everything he got—and I'd do it again!"

I shrink back, shock hitting me like a taser. "You... killed them?" My voice shakes like a leaf. "You're a lying murderer!" I scream, my voice bouncing off the walls like a pinball.

A killer who's been playing me. Emotions hit me like a tsunami, confusion riding the wave. Part of me wants to rip his perfect face off for the lies, but another part feels weirdly responsible. Even through my rage, I know murder's not okay—guilt and anger having a cage match in my gut.

I've spent my whole life chasing truth, and now this walking sex god with fangs is feeding me more lies. My chest aches as tears blur my vision. Way to go, Dani—falling for another grade-A liar.

He stalks behind the desk like he owns the place, ignoring my emotional meltdown. He's ransacking drawers like a burglar on crack, treating expensive furniture like it personally offended him. I back away, anxiety climbing. We're definitely not supposed to be here, but Mr. Silent Treatment keeps destroying property.

Finally, he pockets something and turns back.

Oh hell no. I slam my hands down, making everything shake. "Now you're stealing?! Lies, murder, theft—what's next on your crime spree?!"

Rhyland's eyes bug out at the desk. "How are you doing that?"

I look down. *Well, shit.* My hands are doing their best nightlight impression again! Stupid mood ring hands. I yank them back, but it's too late.

"What the actual fuck was that?" He prowls around the desk like a predator, his massive frame boxing me in. His hand grabs my neck, fingers tangling in my hair as he forces me to meet his gaze.

Great. Now we both have some explaining to do.

His eyes are a tornado of emotions as he searches my face. "Because you're my mate," he finally drops like it's a normal thing to say.

I blink like I've been slapped. "Your *what* now?" He leans in for a kiss, but I shove him back hard. "No. We're done here."

Suddenly, we hear the door handle rattle loudly. "Someone in there?!" a frantic voice from beyond asks.

Rhyland steps away from me and curses under his breath, “Fuck.”

My eyes go wide as flying saucers. I scramble away from him, scanning for another exit, but we're trapped. "Now what?" I hiss.

He grabs my face between his hands like he's trying to telepathically download instructions. "Walk out that door and tell the guy you needed a moment alone because your boyfriend upset you."

Well, that's not exactly a lie.

I'm nuclear-level pissed!

This fanged felon wants me to be his accomplice now? I want to slap that perfect face into next week. But I also want to escape this mess. I need to get as far from him as possible.

Rhyland crouches in the corner shadows as I stomp over, fists clenched. I shoot him a death glare that could pulverize diamonds. "Give me back my underwear," I demand icily. He stares at me like I'm speaking Klingon until I snap my fingers twice. "Panties. Now."

He fishes them from his pocket. I wiggle into them awkwardly, ignoring the continued banging.

Showtime.

I arrange my face into a mask of distress and fling open the door. Time for an Oscar-worthy performance...

"What's happening in here?" the security guy demands. "This area's off-limits."

I dab at fake tears. "I'm so sorry, I just... needed to escape my... boyfriend..." I sniffle pathetically.

His suspicion visibly deflates. "There are proper facilities near the ballroom, miss."

I look up with puppy-dog eyes. "I got lost... I was upset..."

Satisfied with my performance, he steps aside, motioning me out. As he leads me back toward the party, I spot Rhyland slithering away down the corridor.

Lying, murdering, panty-stealing asshole.

RHYLAND

32

Guilt's eating me alive after dropping that bomb on Danica. Stalking through this fucking circus of a Ball, every step feels like walking through quicksand. My gut's twisted in knots, wondering if telling her the raw truth was worth watching her heart shatter.

These regrets are like poison in my blood. I prowl past these clueless party sheep, my mind screaming with the death sentence hanging over their heads. Can't shake the look on Dani's face—that pain, that betrayal. Fuck, it guts me like a blade.

And what the hell was that light show with her hands? Like watching lightning get bottled up in human skin.

Her questions are driving me fucking insane. Should've grown a pair and told her everything when she first walked into Lucian's club asking about the spiked drinks. Why'd I have to drop the mate bomb and drag Max's corpse into this mess?

That murder weighs on me like concrete shoes. She thinks she's just another piece on my chessboard. The need to hunt her down and lay everything bare claws at my chest—but how the fuck can she process any of this supernatural shit?

A mate from different worlds wasn't even in the playbook. Then she lights up like a damn supernova, proving Dani's anything but ordinary. She's got power that makes humans look like ants, and it's got me spinning.

Fae blood? Something older? Whatever Dani is, she's beyond anything I've seen in centuries.

I find a dark corner in this oversized dollhouse, my heart hammering like war drums. Try to steady my breathing, but rage and confusion are setting my blood on fire.

Fuck! How do I explain this to Dani when I can't even read the goddamn map? We're in uncharted territory, and her power display has us both stumbling in the dark.

She must be scared shitless, dealing with abilities that shouldn't exist. And in her eyes, I'm just the lying bastard who played her!

Pure fury burns in my veins at this fucked-up situation. I should be with her, fighting through this storm together. Instead, I'm backed into a corner by my own stupid choices.

Then Azrael fucking Blackwood saunters up, darkness crackling around him like a storm. Our eyes lock, and I can see that manipulative fuck's mind working overtime. Every instinct screams danger—Azrael's earned his reputation as a master puppet master, a vampire who turns lives into his personal playground.

"I didn't catch your name..." he purrs with that snake-oil smoothness. "Where did our lovely doctor disappear to? Are you two...togeth er?"

He says the last word with a smirk that makes me want to rip his fucking throat out. I swallow the rage, barely keeping it in check.

"I didn't offer it," I cut back coldly. "And Danica's whereabouts aren't your goddamn concern."

Azrael's eyebrow arches. "So protective, aren't we? I simply wish to become better acquainted with her..."

"Yeah? Well, you can go fuck yourself sideways." The words rip from my chest like a growl. "Stay the hell away from her, you sick piece of shit."

The bastard doesn't even flinch at my threat, looking almost amused. "Such hostility is unnecessary," he replies with oily calm. "I understand if you're...territorial about the young woman. She's clearly gotten under your skin."

My hands curl into fists, knuckles white with restraint. "You don't know a fucking thing," I snarl.

"Oh, but I believe I do," Azrael says, voice dripping with calculated malice. "There's something extraordinary about her, isn't there? Something that's caught more than just your eye..."

"Enough!" I bark, shoving into his space. "I'm not fucking around—Danica is off limits. She's too pure for your filthy world, so keep your goddamn hands off her, or I'll tear you apart and feed you your own entrails."

Azrael chuckles, clearly getting off on my rage. "Such passion," he muses. "One might suspect you harbor...deeper feelings for the girl."

"Fuck you." The words shoot out like venom. "She's under my protection, and if you or any of your lackeys so much as breathe near her, I'll paint this whole fucking place with what's left of you."

My body vibrates with barely leashed violence, every instinct screaming to end this monster here and now. But I can't reveal my true power in this pit of vipers.

Azrael's eyes gleam with predatory interest. "Well, this has been most illuminating," he says silkily. "I can see Danica is in very...possessive hands. Do give her my warmest regards."

He slinks away, and I stand there burning with murderous rage. That bloodsucking parasite dared speak of Danica like she's a toy for his amusement! I should have crushed his skull when I had the chance.

But finding her comes first, ensuring Azrael's claws haven't already sunk into her. She needs to know I'll destroy anything that threatens her. No one touches what's mine if they want to keep breathing. Danica belongs to me, and I'll annihilate anyone who tries to come between us!

Still seething, I stalk off to track Danica's scent. That manipulative fucker will rue the day he crossed my path. I swear his miserable existence ends by my hand.

My thoughts burn with fury as I slam into Erik and Lucian's minds.

"Any luck?" I growl.

Lucian's reply hits like a gut punch, *"Oh shit yeah! We found a whole fucking slave camp in this hellhole!"*

I clench my jaw so hard my teeth might crack. This twisted bastard needs to die for what he's done. My mental voice shakes with rage as I demand their location, desperate to get the fuck out of this cesspool.

"We're heading back to the car topside," Erik reports.

The need to find Dani is like physical pain. Would she even look at me after all this?

I grit my teeth and reach out one final time to Erik, *"On my fucking way."*

DANICA

33

My hands ball into fists as I bolt for the bathroom, my brain on fire. This can't be happening—he's been lying to my face this whole time? What's this "mate" bullshit? It's not just unbelievable—it's next-level insanity!

He stood there like a statue, keeping his mouth shut while we reviewed the security footage. Meanwhile, Emily's been having panic attacks, not knowing if she was assaulted. Rhyland knew everything and decided to play judge, jury, and executioner with Max and his cronies like some vampire vigilante. And he manipulated me into stealing documents for him! Rage bubbles up as I grab the bathroom door. I glance down to see my hands doing their best flamethrower impression again—I need to get a grip.

Why didn't he tell me he already knew what happened that night? That I was just a convenient pawn in his twisted game?

Who the hell is this guy really?

My hands tremble and glow with fury and frustration. I hate feeling this out of control. I race to the sink and thrust my hands under cold water, creating a mini sauna as steam rises. I breathe deeply, fighting back angry tears. No way am I crying over this lying bloodsucker. Rhyland will regret thinking he could manipulate me like some disposable chess piece.

Once I've downgraded from nuclear meltdown to regular pissed off, I'm determined to find Emily and get the hell out. I scan the packed ballroom, the upbeat music and laughter a slap in the face compared to my internal screaming. Through the sea of masks and designer gowns, I spot Emily's rainbow hair. Relief hits me like a tidal wave as I rush over. One look at my face and she knows something's wrong.

"Holy shit, you look like you've seen a ghost! What happened?" I tell her we need to bail ASAP. She nods and makes quick excuses before linking arms with me. "Let's go."

But as we head for freedom, my stomach drops—Azrael Blackwood's blocking our exit like the final boss in a video game. His tall frame and slick, dark features scream "danger." Something about him sets off all my alarm bells, and I instinctively back up. His reputation for being Seattle's most ruthless businessman isn't just talk.

Can this night get any worse?

"Leaving so soon?" he purrs with forced charm. "The night's just begun. I'd love for you to stay."

I strain to keep my tone light. "Thank you, but we should be off."

Azrael moves closer, undeterred. "Come now, indulge a little longer," he presses.

My unease grows, but I stand firm. "I appreciate the offer, but we have plans."

Azrael's intense gaze bores into me. "You have a remarkable aura, Danica," he says cryptically. "Something different, something intriguing."

My nerves spike at his scrutiny, but I repeat my refusal.

At last, he steps aside. "I'll see you very soon," he warns with a hint of irritation as we depart. His words linger like a chill.

Emily looks at me sharply as we leave the ballroom. "What the hell was that about?"

I rush downstairs, gagging like I just ate month-old sushi. "Azrael's pathetic flirting attempts. I need a shower in bleach." I keep quiet about my apparent new supernatural man-magnet scent—Emily has enough to worry about.

Back at my apartment, I spill everything about Rhyland's confession. Emily's face turns volcanic when she learns they knew what happened with Dakota all along.

"What's this 'mate' garbage?" she snorts. "What are you, his Labrador retriever?"

I laugh without humor. "Your guess is as good as mine—we got interrupted before Vampire Encyclopedia could define it."

I explain about the stolen documents and feeling manipulated. "You know how I am with liars, Em. It's just like..." My voice cracks.

Emily squeezes my hand. "I know, babe. Bringing up all that old shit, isn't it?"

I nod, feeling those familiar scars reopening. Emily's the only one who knows the full story of my past trauma. The web of lies that still gives me nightmares. Rhyland's secretive bullshit feels like déjà vu.

"Talk to me, honey. Verbal vomit it all out so we can start the healing process." Emily's voice is warm but no-nonsense.

"Where do I even start?" I sigh. "I really thought Mr. Tall-Dark-and-Fangy was different, you know? Our connection was off the charts. I actually trusted him, Em."

Tears spill over. Emily hands me a tissue, her eyes soft despite her sharp tongue.

"I know, sweetie. It's absolute bullshit that he tap-danced all over your heart like that." Emily shoots me her signature "told you so" smirk. "Not to be that bitch, but I knew something was sketchy when you said you were into Secret Agent Creepshow. What did you expect from a dude who lurks in shadows?"

"Yes, yes, you're psychic, we get it," I roll my eyes.

"Just remember who called it when the next hot mysterious asshole starts orbiting you," Emily fires back with raised eyebrows.

"I was so stupid!" I explode. "Thinking someone actually gave a damn about the real me. What a joke!"

Emily grabs my shoulders like she's about to perform an exorcism. "Listen up, because I'm only saying this once. You are NOT stupid for believing in someone. That makes you brave as hell, Danica. Don't you dare beat yourself up."

I wipe my raccoon eyes, her words hitting home. "You're right. I thought I was over this—that I wouldn't fall for lies again. But the second he started hiding things, it felt like being gutted."

Emily nods knowingly. "Because it triggered all that ancient history. But you survived that nightmare, and you'll survive Vampire McDreamy, too. You've got more power than you realize!" She snickers, "And I don't mean your new disco ball hands."

Something fierce rekindles inside me. "You're absolutely right. No more excuses for his behavior. I deserve someone who tells me the truth, and if Rhyland can't manage that basic human decency, he can fuck all the way off."

Emily grins. "There's my badass bitch! Now, prescription for tonight—wine, terrible movies, and creative insults about men."

I laugh through my tears. "God, I'd be lost without you. Thanks for always being in my corner."

"That's what ride-or-dies are for! I'll verbally castrate anyone who hurts you." We clink glasses and settle in for emergency emotional triage. My heart's still raw from Rhyland's betrayal, but Emily's right—I've rebuilt myself before.

After Emily leaves, my phone buzzes with a message from 'Agent Stalker.' I snort and send back a middle finger emoji.

Wine-wobbly, I double-check the locks and even shut my bedroom door like that would stop a determined vampire. "Ha! Figure that out, asshole!" I yell at the empty apartment. Of course, a locked door means nothing to him.

I face-plant into bed, wondering if Rhyland will show up tonight. Part of me wants to tear him a new one, while another part wants to tell him to get lost forever. I don't need this supernatural drama...yet the chemistry between us is nuclear, and my body doesn't care about his lies.

But can I trust him after this? His secrets dug up painful memories I've tried desperately to bury. What else is hiding behind those perfect blue eyes if he lied about this?

Why do the hot ones always come with so much baggage?

RHYLAND

34

We storm back into the hotel, my blood still boiling with murderous rage. Erik and Lucian bombard me with the sick details from those tunnels, confirming our worst fears. Those fucking mortals are being treated like livestock, used and traded like goddamn blood bags.

I slam the documents I ripped from Azrael's desk onto the table, the evidence of his depravity laid bare. I'd already burned every detail into my memory about that secret room marked on Lucian's maps—unintentionally getting Dani involved.

These papers prove that snake is balls-deep in human trafficking. Raw fury surges through me; part of me wants to tear his spine out through his throat and watch him die screaming. Every page reeks of corruption—offshore accounts and transactions designed to sell dark blood and innocent lives. His complete disregard for human life radiates from each line, showcasing the massive reach of his twisted empire.

My urgent texts to Danica will probably go unanswered. That lewd emoji she sent earlier flashes in my mind.

"I fucking knew that psychotic prick was neck-deep in this shit," Lucian snarls as I down a hefty shot of scotch, embracing the burn.

Lucian describes people crammed into rusted cages lining the chamber walls. Chained, gagged, their faces contorted with pure terror.

"Why is Azrael locking up random humans like animals?" I ask, baffled.

"They might be for Moretemis," Erik suggests grimly, pouring himself a drink. Lucian's eyes go wide at our ancient enemy's name.

Goddamn right—it all clicks into place with brutal clarity. Moretemis feeds on his victims' terror, paralyzing them with dread. Azrael has to be working for him, trafficking these terrified souls to feed Moretemis' insatiable hunger in exchange for dark power. That's the fucking heart of the prophecy—the spreading darkness Moretemis will unleash.

My mind instantly transports me back to that day—the Battle of York in 867. I was a young Viking warrior hungry for glory in the chaos of battle. An unnatural darkness hung over the land like a shroud. The air reeked of doom. We all sensed it—that stench of fear, like the gods themselves were about to wage war, but we had no idea about the true nightmare waiting to descend.

In the end, we were fucking swallowed alive as that tide of darkness crashed down. I lay gutted and dying in the mud and gore as an unnatural night smothered everything. Then, just before the shadows could drag me under, they pulled back like a retreating beast, leaving behind that bone-chilling silence. I sensed some massive seal had blocked the dark forces, though I had no clue how or why.

Half-dead and delirious, I watched a figure approach through the carnage, offering me another shot at life—a chance to keep fighting when everyone else had fallen. With blood bubbling in my throat, I took that deal and felt fangs pierce my flesh as my fate was forever changed.

Nothing was the same after that day. I rose as something new—unnaturally powerful, beyond the reach of death. Only as years turned to decades did I fully understand what I had become...and the shadow world I now walked in.

Centuries rolled by, but that battle never left me. Years later, I learned the brutal truth—that malevolent darkness that nearly devoured my soul was none other than that ancient bastard Moretemis himself.

Though the shadows retreated before they could finish me, I came to see that Moretemis's corrupting influence was everywhere, threatening to tip the scales between darkness and light. My second chance at existence came with a price—to stand against the same shadows and destructive powers that still threaten to consume everything.

Lucian goes pale as death, dragging his hand through his hair. "If this shit is true..."

I down another burning shot, bracing myself. "What's our next fucking move with this intel?"

Erik suggests going to the authorities, but Lucian shoots back that they're probably already in Azrael's pocket.

I turn to him, confusion etched on my face. Lucian exhales heavily. "That snake has connections everywhere. High-level government puppets." His voice drips with pure disgust. "Nothing this massive operates without someone on the inside greasing wheels."

I know the bastard's right. We need more dirt before we make our move. "Can you crack those accounts and pull names?" I demand.

Lucian's mouth curls into that predatory smirk. "Fuck yes. Give me a day to tear it all open."

I nod sharply. "Good. Keep me updated on whatever you find. I'll reach out to the council soon."

With that business handled, my thoughts crash back to Danica. The thought of telling her everything twists my gut—I'm terrified she'll run and never look back. But she deserves the whole truth, no matter how ugly. Erik watches me, his silver eyes filled with doubt.

"You still haven't claimed her properly?"

I shake my head, trying to sort through the chaos in my mind. "No, it's more complicated than I thought."

Erik sighs, fixing me with that ancient stare. "If you're serious about keeping her, you need to move fast. True mates are rarer than dragon's teeth. I wouldn't fucking hesitate if I were you."

After centuries of immortal existence, I've grown cynical—yet something deep in my soul whispers that she might be the one exception, the missing piece I've searched for across endless lifetimes.

I need to know if my fierce angel holds the key to a destiny greater than either of us can comprehend. No matter how hard she fights against the truth burning between us, I'm determined to find out.

"I can't force the bond, not when she's this raw," I growl. The thought of imposing my will on her makes me sick to my stomach. "She needs to come to me willingly. To understand our connection runs deeper than just lust."

Erik shakes his head but backs off. I dismiss him with a nod, my thoughts a violent storm.

I strip off the tux and pull on jeans and a shirt. Dread wars with desperate need. Even if it drives her further away, she deserves the whole brutal truth. I have to approach this carefully.

But if she rejects me as just another monster, it'll gut me like nothing else could. Because somehow, against all fucking reason, I need her light to balance my darkness. I steel myself as I head out into the night. This is the moment of truth—can Danica ever truly accept what I am, with all my shadows? Her reaction will reveal if this connection runs as deep as I feel it burning in my immortal soul.

I slip into her apartment, heading straight for her bedroom. She tried locking every entrance, but locks are just suggestions to me. She has no fucking clue what I'm capable of. I reach her bedroom door—closed tight. Her anger doesn't concern me.

She's passed out on her stomach, one arm stretched above her head, the other tucked beneath her. My eyes lock onto that perfect ass barely covered by those tiny cotton shorts. I try to resist grabbing it, but my control snaps like a twig.

I slide my hand up her silky thigh, her skin burning hot under my touch. I squeeze that delicious ass before trailing down to the inside of her thigh. She stirs, groaning into her pillow. My fingers find the dampness soaking through her shorts, and I stroke her gently.

Is she wet dreaming about me?

I kneel between her legs and grip both cheeks firmly.

She begins to wake, whispering in that sleepy, husky voice, "Rhyland?"

Even half-conscious, she knows exactly who's touching her. "Hi, Angel," I say, my voice dark with hunger.

She bolts from the bed like she's been shocked, darts into the bathroom, and slams the door, locking it behind her. I sigh deeply. She's going to listen to what I have to say tonight—one way or another.

I knock on the door firmly. "Danica...give me a chance to explain." Silence. I pound harder, calling her name again. Nothing. My patience thins with each passing second until I'm hammering the door with my fist.

She finally erupts from inside. "Go away, Rhyland! I don't want to hear your bullshit. Haven't you fucked with my head enough for one day?"

I exhale sharply. "If you don't open this goddamn door right now, I'm going to reduce it to splinters!"

She shrieks back, "You wouldn't dare, asshole!"

Perfect. Now I'm an asshole.

I take one steadying breath. "You have until three before I tear this thing off its hinges, Dani."

I hear her frustrated huff. "Give me one reason I should believe anything that comes out of your mouth."

"One..." I begin counting.

"Just leave, Rhyland," she pleads.

"Two..." I continue relentlessly.

"This isn't funny, Rhyland..." Fear edges into her voice.

"Three... I warned you, Angel. Step back from the door."

Without hesitation, I slam my boot into the door. It explodes inward with a satisfying crack, showering the bathroom with wooden shards. She scrambles backward until she hits the far wall.

"How fucking dare you! Who do you think you are?"

I stalk toward her like a predator, pinning her hard against the wall with my body. She's trapped. She pushes against my chest futilely, her voice cracking with anger.

"Rhyland, what the hell? Just go away!" I capture both wrists in one hand and force them above her head, immobilizing her.

"Not a chance, sweetheart. I'm not going anywhere until you hear every word I have to say."

My cock throbs painfully against my jeans as she stands there defiant, spitting fire at me. Her ferocity fucking ignites something in me, and I can't get enough of it. I grind my hardness against her, making damn sure she feels exactly what her attitude does to me. Her arousal hits my senses like a drug, and I breathe it in deeply, savoring that intoxicating scent of her need. My fierce little Angel might fight me with words, but her body betrays her—she craves when I take control, when I force her to surrender to every dark desire I have for her.

Her face scrunches up in annoyance as I gently tilt her chin up. “Well, go on then," she grumbles. "This should be interesting.”

I inhale her scent, hearing her breath hitch. “In my past, there were tales of destined mates—two people who complete each other. We haven't seen this in centuries...until I met you."

Her eyes widen. "What does that even mean...soulmates?"

I take a deep breath. "Sort of. There's a ritual I must perform to claim you as mine fully."

Her brows furrow. "Claim me? What ritual?" Curiosity tinges on her confusion.

I smile wryly. "It involves drinking your blood."

She inhales sharply. "You can't bite me! That's...that's..." Her protest trails off, eyes flickering with intrigue.

I brush my lips against her ear. "You'll beg for more when I sink my teeth in, quivering with desire."

Her breathing quickens, soft breasts grazing my chest. She whispers, "I...please. Don't..."

I cling to her waist, aching as she trembles. "Shh, I won't until you ask. I promise."

She exhales, body relaxing before tensing again. This storm of fear and longing intrigues me.

Does she crave my bite?

I trail my thumb over her parted lips. "This is new, I know. We have time to understand it together."

She gasps sharply, those honey eyes locked on mine. For one perfect moment, she yields, pressing into my touch. Then doubt clouds her gaze again. She turns away, her emotions warring beneath the surface. I want to crush every fear that keeps her from surrendering to me completely. But I know better—the mating bond pulls us together like gravity, but it can't be forced.

"Talk to me, Angel," I command, my voice softening. "Let me destroy whatever's holding you back."

She wavers, caught between desire and distrust. In this razor's edge moment, I see the struggle raging inside her. And I see my opening. I lean in and drag my tongue along her neck. She trembles against me. "I won't bite, I promise. Not unless you beg me to. And trust me, baby...you *will* beg for it." I growl as my tongue traces her collarbone, savoring her addictive taste.

Fuck, she tastes incredible. I'm so worked up from before that my cock is painfully hard; my balls ache with a savage need for her that's driving me to the brink of madness.

She whimpers, finally melting into me. I move lower, giving her flesh a gentle bite before swirling my tongue across her heated skin. I lock eyes with her, watching her anger transform into raw curiosity. "I was scared," I admit, my voice rough with honesty.

She wrinkles her brow. “Scared of what?”

I shake with raw emotion, my throat tight as I force out words I've never spoken aloud. "When I lost my wife, something fucking died inside me. I turned my heart to stone, swearing no one would ever touch it again. Convinced myself love was for the weak, and built walls so high no one could scale them."

I meet Dani's eyes apprehensively. "For decades, I kept my promise, remaining cold and detached. Then I met you. From the first moment, something stirred in me—an ember thought long dead. Your inner light called to me, coaxing me back toward life." I rake my fingers through my hair in frustration. "I tried desperately to resist it. I couldn't acknowledge these feelings after swearing them off for eternity. But you eroded my defenses, opening my heart when I thought it closed forever." My voice cracks with emotion. "Dani, you brought color back into my world of gray. Being with you makes me feel truly alive for the first time since my loss. I was too afraid to accept that something so beautiful could be real again."

I reach for her cheek, stroking it gently. "I know I don't deserve your forgiveness. But you broke down all the walls I hid behind. You reopened my heart despite my efforts to freeze it out. With you, I remembered what it was to feel joy, passion...love. You gave me back life when I condemned myself to an eternity of emptiness."

I meet her eyes beseechingly, praying she understands the full impact she's had on my barren soul.

"So you thought following me around obsessively and imposing yourself into my life against my will would help you understand your 'feelings'?" Sarcasm bites her tone.

I nod, ashamed under her glare. "I used it as a twisted way to make sense of my reaction to you. I couldn't overlook or explain it."

Her eyes soften with sorrow. "I'm sorry for your loss."

I bristle at the sympathy. This isn't about my past—it's about comprehending this foreign eruption of passion.

"You unlocked something in me, Danica. Like a dormant volcano, frozen for centuries, that now has molten lava churning uncontrollably."

She digests my words, tentative understanding dawning. "I'm trying to grasp how one look from you shattered every barrier I built. Your light pierced my darkness instantly." I rake my hands through my hair, vulnerable and exposed. "I don't know how else to describe it. The intensity terrifies me even as it compels me beyond reason."

She arches her body closer to me. "I can't pretend to understand what you're experiencing. But I know what it's like to feel your heart come alive and the fear it brings."

Her compassion stimulates long-forgotten stirrings within me. The icy walls inside start to thaw. This is uncharted territory, but the unknown seems less threatening with her by my side.

Danica

35

His emotional confession hits me like a Mac truck, nearly knocking the wind out of me. My knees go weak, and my heart does this pathetic little flutter thing. Words this deep, this earth-shattering—no one's ever dropped a bomb like this on me before. I'm stumbling through his confessions like I'm drunk on feelings.

Finding out he's been in self-imposed emotional lockdown since his wife died centuries ago casts a shadow over his intensity. It's tragically noble and completely heartbreaking. How does he even function, carrying that kind of baggage? His unleashed passion is like catnip to my hormones. Yet he's built himself into this emotional fortress, rejecting even the idea of love after lifetimes of isolation.

After taking a deep breath, I challenge him, "To claim me as your soulmate, you must bite me and exchange blood. And not telling me about the drugged drinks wasn't technically lying—just 'withholding information' while you sorted your feelings? And I'm supposed to nod and smile?"

My anger bubbles up like lava. "You murdered people, Rhyland! And

I helped you steal documents without knowing what the hell was going on. Were you just using me as your personal assistant? Yet here you are, expecting me to swallow all this supernatural crap without choking?"

The hurt cuts through my rage. His decisions affect me, whether he wants to admit it or not. He stares at me with eyes that burn with longing.

This would be so much easier if he weren't looking at me like I'm the air he needs to breathe.

"No, Dani, I'm not expecting you to get it all at once. I'm trying to be honest with you—show you what you've done to me—something I haven't done with anyone. I wasn't using you—I never meant for you to get tangled in my war with Azrael. It just happened that way."

His commanding tone sends heat through me, even as some invisible force keeps me rooted to the spot. Fear and desire are having a cage match inside me, while my trust issues are waving red flags and setting off air raid sirens. He releases my wrists, and I flex them to get feeling back. Before I can retreat, his arm snakes around my waist, yanking me against him while his other hand fists my hair, forcing my head back to meet his scorching gaze.

Through teeth that could crush diamonds, he growls, "And those bastards deserved every second of pain I gave them. I don't regret avenging what almost happened to you, or what Max did to those other women. I will always protect what's mine, even if I have to paint the walls with blood."

My face flushes as I remember teasing him at the ball, daring him to back up his seductive threats. I get his vendetta against Azrael's shady empire. But the casual way he talks about murder terrifies me—even as it sends a forbidden thrill through places it absolutely shouldn't.

What the hell is wrong with me?

Feeling my internal struggle, he softens his iron grip, gently smoothing my hair like I'm something precious. "I know it's overwhelming, Angel. But you wanted the truth, all of it. There's an ocean of darkness inside me, but none of it would ever touch you."

His gentle tone contrasts starkly with his savage words. I'm horrified, captivated, and alarmed by how much I want him despite everything.

"You make me feel things I don't understand," I whisper, vulnerability cracking my voice. "Every instinct says run, but I'm drawn to you like a moth to flame."

His thumb traces my cheekbone with surprising tenderness. "Then stop thinking and just feel. What's between us doesn't follow normal rules."

Is this really some supernatural bond? Or has his mysterious intensity warped my judgment? I search those ocean eyes for clarity, but only find more mysteries.

For now, I lean into his touch, allowing myself this moment of comfort. But inside, I'm a hurricane of conflicting emotions. I'm drawn to his darkness even as I crave the light.

My heart and head speak different languages, and I no longer know which one to trust.

I'm drowning in those beautiful blue eyes, blazing with hunger. His powerful body presses against mine, his arousal unmistakable through his jeans. His embrace feels like a fortress around me, while his words promise eternal devotion. The passion in his voice sets every nerve ending on fire. I want to surrender completely to this magnetic pull between us.

"Angel, you're mine now, and I'll destroy anyone who tries to hurt you. I belong only to you, and I don't give a damn who knows it."

My pulse thunders like a stampede as his sapphire gaze penetrates my soul. My body aches for his touch, and the anticipation makes me tremble.

"Why?" I whisper. His brows furrows in confusion. "Why choose me?"

That devastating smile curves his lips, and as if reading my thoughts, he captures my mouth in a gentle kiss that quickly turns hungry. His teeth tug at my bottom lip before releasing it with a soft pop. "Because you were created for me, Angel."

His gaze holds mine captive as my eyes drift to his tempting mouth before meeting his stare again, silently permitting him to cross this final boundary.

His arm tightens around my waist as he claims my mouth, overwhelming my senses with his demanding kiss. His powerful hands roam possessively over my curves, squeezing and caressing my ass before traveling upward toward my breasts. Electric pleasure shoots through me at his touch, drawing an involuntary moan from my lips as I surrender to the moment.

"Christ, Dani, I need you so fucking badly. You push me to the edge of sanity every time." Rhyland's raw confession ignites a wildfire in my veins. He tears my shirt open, exposing my chest to his hungry eyes. "So goddamn beautiful," he purrs, taking one nipple into his mouth while roughly palming the other. Scorching pleasure cascades through every inch of me.

I reach down boldly and grasp his impressive length through his pants, feeling it throb against my palm.

Holy hell. This man is packing a cobra...

This is probably a terrible idea, but right now, it seems like the only sensible thing in this crazy world.

I gasp eagerly at the rigid girth awaiting me. He hisses and quivers from my exploring touch. His heated hand slides between my thighs, delving under my shorts to find my drenched, aching pussy.

"Shit, baby—so wet," he mutters, thick fingers massaging my aching slit. I tremble and groan as he firmly cups my throbbing sex.

He tears off my shorts in one smooth motion, leaving just my panties, barely concealing my slick need. He rips those aside and strokes my swollen clit while thrusting a thick digit inside me. Waves of scorching pleasure flood my veins. Rhyland knows precisely how to play my body. I cry his name ecstatically as he finger-fucks me.

"Tell me what you want, baby," he demands.

My willpower crumbles under his commanding presence and relentless passion. No man has made me feel so desired yet protected. My body screams to be possessed by him. "Fuck me...Please," I finally beg. "I need you inside me."

He rips open his jeans with a wicked grin. "Music to my ears. I love hearing you beg."

He's lifting me and pressing me against the wall in a blur, his rigid length nudging my soaked entrance. I cling to his shoulders, dizzy with anticipation.

He holds maddeningly still, letting me feel his heat but denying penetration. The rough lace of my panties cuts into my skin—the fabric merely pushed aside rather than removed—this urgent need too powerful to waste time on complete undressing, as I try rubbing myself against his swollen head. I've never needed to be filled this badly.

"Want it, Angel? Tell me how much you ache for me," he orders roughly, fingers lightly stroking my pulsing clit.

"Please, Rhyland..." I moan desperately. "Fuck me. I ache so bad for you." Vulgarity flows freely in my arousal.

His thick head presses against my entrance, making me gasp at the sheer size. "Relax for me, Angel," he pants, his voice strained with restraint. "You're so fucking tight."

I whimper as he eases forward, the stretch almost overwhelming. My body resists the intrusion even as it craves more.

"Oh god," I pant, clinging to his shoulders. "Too big..."

"Breathe," he commands softly, pressing deeper with agonizing slowness. "Let me in, baby."

The burn is exquisite as he works his massive tool inside, inch by torturous inch. My walls clench and flutter around him, trying to adjust.

"Fuck, you're tight," he groans against my neck. "Like a vice around my cock."

When he finally bottoms out, we both freeze, panting. I've never felt so utterly filled, so completely possessed.

"Move," I beg breathlessly. "Please..."

His first slow thrust has me crying out, pleasure bordering on pain. But my body eagerly accepts him now, growing slicker with each careful stroke.

"Goddamn. Been aching for this pussy," he pants against my throat, his grip crushing my thighs. I can only whimper and nod drunkenly, barely comprehending speech. He withdraws slowly before pounding back in bruisingly deep. "Killing me, Angel... feels too fucking good."

Rhyland ravages me relentlessly, my back slamming the wall with each devastating thrust. I'm mindless, reduced to a well-fucked rag doll impaled on his pistoning cock. He hits untouched depths within me, wringing screams from my raw throat.

"Oh god, too much," I gasp raggedly, but my traitorous body clutches him tighter, hungry for more.

He fists my hair painfully, growling, "You begged for this cock. Now you're going to take it all, sweetheart."

I dissolve into whimpering euphoria, dripping wet and quaking around him. He fucks me with savage force until the sharp edge of pain gives way to blistering pleasure. I never want this to end.

He hitches my legs up with an iron grip, splaying me helplessly against the wall. Now he can drive even deeper, reaching my core and grinding my swollen clit.

The relentless pounding pulls shrieks from me. My wailing cries fill the room, barely muffled by his devouring mouth. His animal ferocity pushes me toward a mind-shattering climax.

"Harder..." I plead shamelessly, drunk on him.

With a sexy grunt, he complies, cock pummeling inside me brutally. My ass slaps the cold wall, the shock heightening everything—reduced to primal moans.

His swollen head hits my cervix now on every stroke, stealing my breath. I'm balanced on a knife's edge, right at the brink...

"Give me what's mine, Angel. Let me feel you come apart," he commands roughly. His words trigger my orgasm instantly.

I detonate around his pistoning cock, vision whiting out as I gush down his length. He fucks me through every powerful convulsion as I scream his name.

"That's it, baby. There's my good girl," he groans approvingly. I clench desperately to keep him lodged inside, never wanting this ecstasy to end.

His words of ownership should offend me, but right now they feel like the most natural thing in the world.

Soon, he swells impossibly thicker. With a bellow, he slams home, flooding me with cum. The scalding heat pushes me into another dizzying orgasm. He continues pounding every drop into me. The echo of his guttural roars mingles with my ragged cries, composing the filthiest duet.

Finally spent, he pins me to the wall as we tremble through the aftershocks. Our mingled arousal paints my thighs. The electrified air crackles between our sweat-slick forms. Gently, he tilts my head back, kissing me passionately until my legs liquefy. Scooping me up easily, he carries me to the bed, desires already rekindling in his eyes.

We fall onto the mattress together, his lips trailing fire across my skin. I sink into his encompassing warmth, feeling utterly safe and claimed. Our kisses turn lazy and deep as exploring hands map new territory, our bodies finding each other again. My heart pounds as I breathe in his intoxicating scent of sandalwood and ocean breeze, marveling at our overwhelming connection.

"I'll never get enough of you," he murmurs tenderly against my ear.

I look up into those intense blue eyes that seem to see straight into my soul. "Tell me more about this mate bond you mentioned." I need to understand what this powerful pull between us means.

Something tells me this is just the beginning of a highly complex situation.

Rhyland strokes my hair gently. "For my kind, when we find our true mate, it creates an unbreakable soul tie. I can sense your essence, your spirit, as if it's a part of me. Your joy and your pain—I feel it too." He kisses my forehead sweetly. "Our bond, once forged, lasts for eternity."

My brows knit together. "Eternity? But how, when I'm mortal?"

He nods thoughtfully. "I don't know, honestly. But your soul calls to mine, Dani."

His conviction resonates through our point of contact. This transcends human comprehension.

"Is that why I constantly crave your touch?" I ask. "It's like an almost painful yearning in my core when we're apart."

"Yes," Rhyland murmurs. "Our souls call out for one another. Being together satisfies something deep within us both."

I close my eyes, focusing on the thrum of energy flowing between us. This bond transcends the physical—it's like we share one spirit. I understand now why it feels impossible to pull away despite the complications threatening us. We are two halves of one whole. This connection goes beyond conscious thought or choice. I finally understand why I feel so powerfully and inexorably drawn to him.

"Have you ever felt something so deep?" he asks intently.

I shake my head, thinking of my past failed relationships. "Never anything close to this." I cup his cheek tenderly. "The way you make me feel—there are no words. You undo me completely, Rhyland."

He smiles joyously at my admission, the warmth reaching his vivid eyes. "We don't need words," he murmurs. "Through our bond, I will feel everything within you—your highest peaks of joy and your lowest moments of despair. Your sadness resonates in my heart as if it were my own. When you feel fear, I sense it creeping through my veins, too."

He brushes his fingers along my cheek tenderly. "But also your passion and your desire," he continues, his voice low. "The quickening of your pulse, the heat rising within you...it also echoes through me. Your longing and sensuality mingle with mine until they are one."

He leans in closer, his nose nuzzling against my neck as he inhales my scent. "This bond allows me to experience your emotions, pleasures, and pains as if they live inside me, too. It connects us at the deepest levels." He captures my lips in a searing kiss, conveying all his joy, passion, and devotion through the caress of his mouth on mine.

After long, blissful moments, he shifts slightly, grave purpose entering his face. "What was that light show shit from your hands earlier?"

I cringe internally. I can't avoid this conversation now. Haltingly, I explain how I discovered my abnormal test results and strange abilities manifesting. He listens intently to every detail.

Propping up on an elbow, I finish my account. "So I still have no clue who my biological parents are. I was adopted."

In a flash, he pins me under his powerful frame. I gasp, then moan as his mouth blazes a trail down my throat. My hips buck instinctively, desperate for more contact.

"When did these powers first appear?" he rumbles against my ear, his hips rolling torturously slow against mine.

"After meeting you," I manage between ragged breaths, his teasing movements scrambling my thoughts. He makes a thoughtful sound before capturing my mouth again. I sense he knows more than he's saying, but I just want to drown in sensation right now.

Breaking another scorching kiss, he suddenly pulls me upright, wicked promise in his eyes. "Time to get you cleaned up, Angel."

I follow him eagerly toward the shower, anticipating getting deliciously dirty all over again.

Something tells me he knows exactly what's happening to me, but right now, I'm too intoxicated by his touch to care

RHYLAND

36

I stalk after Danica into the bathroom, her words hammering through my skull. Half human, half something else—what the fuck could it mean? She spoke of power awakening inside her. Could she be the one from the ancient prophecy? The mate destined to unlock abilities that will save us all? The light bursting from her hands confirms what should be impossible. Everything fits.

Fear and disbelief crash through me. I crank on the shower and strip down as she steps in ahead of me. I wrap my arms around her waist, pulling her against my chest as water pours over our bodies.

She leans into me. "If you need to tell me something, just say it," she urges.

Of course, she senses my hesitation. I take a moment to contemplate what I should reveal. I've never shied from speaking my truth…until her. "There's more I must tell you," I confess slowly.

She inhales deeply. "Oh?"

I choose my words carefully. "There's a prophecy about a mortal savior who will gain great power once awakened to save the realms."

Her body tenses. She turns to face me, her honey eyes burning with questions. “What? Realms? What are you saying?”

I exhale heavily. "There are things in this world beyond your imagination."

She narrows her eyes. "Then explain it. I show you my 'powers,' and now you're suggesting what, exactly?"

Her razor-sharp mind hungers for understanding, demanding answers. I fucking love her fierce curiosity. I tangle my fingers in her wet hair, gripping tight as desire roars through me. I'm completely obsessed with her.

I crush my mouth to hers, claiming her lips with desperate hunger. My hands ravage her body, greedy for every inch of her. In this moment, I'm entirely at her mercy. My heart, my soul, my entire existence belong to her now. I've fallen harder than I ever thought possible. Every defense I built has been obliterated, all pretenses incinerated by the wildfire she ignites in my core. I stand before her stripped bare, every carefully guarded vulnerability exposed.

As she returns my kiss with equal fervor, I know I will do anything for this woman who holds the fractured pieces of my heart. She can nurture me to wholeness or destroy what remains. My fate is in her hands now. All I know is that I cannot live without her. She is the air in my lungs, the blood in my veins. For the first time in a millenia, I have found something worth the ultimate risk—love powerful enough to save or ruin me.

I reluctantly pull back, “I came here to find the foretold mortal as the leader of the council. It’s my duty to locate them for the good of all.”

Her eyes widen as she traces my tattoos, each one marking a battle fought and survived. Our gazes lock, raw emotion crackling between us.

"Seriously? I mean, vampires and werewolves were one thing," she scoffs, "but this is just going from ridiculous to full-on batshit crazy town."

I exhale heavily. She can't possibly grasp the magnitude of this yet. I'm fucking terrified to tell her she might be *the* prophesied mate...that our union could trigger events that will shake worlds to their foundations. The weight of these revelations is already crushing her. I need more answers before I heap this cosmic burden onto her shoulders. For now, I pull her against me, hoping my touch might ease her chaos. But those perceptive eyes see right through my hesitation.

"There's something you're not saying," she accuses, eyes flashing. "You promised to be truthful, Rhyland. Whatever it is, I can handle it."

I freeze, warring with myself. Do I shield her or lay my suspicions bare? She deserves honesty, yet this could push her away for good.

"I..." My voice fails. Her eyes cloud with doubt and hurt.

She steps back out of my arms, leaving me cold and empty. "When you're ready to be fully open, we'll talk. But I can't do secrets anymore." Her words slash through me.

We finish showering in silence so thick you could cut it with a fucking blade. The tension claws at my insides because I'm holding back when every instinct screams to lay everything bare. But the stakes? It's life or death...

My gut demands I tell Dani everything, but I can't unleash that kind of hell on her without warning. She's already been dragged through fire. I need to get some goddamn answers first and make sense of this twisted prophecy before I shatter her world again.

I'm worried about what this will do to her mind with all this supernatural shit crashing down. Dani's strong as steel, but everyone has a breaking point. I've been walking that razor's edge for years. The last thing I want is to be the bastard who pushes her over it. I'm supposed to protect that light inside her, not extinguish it.

For now, I cling to the hope that her brilliance will cut through this darkness—one bloody step at a time. She's the only thing keeping me anchored, illuminating the shadows I've been drowning in. Our fates are intertwined now, and I'm praying to gods I stopped believing in that we're not too late.

I can't—and won't—lose her. Not now, not fucking ever. Her heart, her soul—she's become my entire existence.

DANICA

37

I step out, wrapping one towel around my body while using another to dry my dripping hair.

Is this some cosmic joke?

How am I supposed to process being part of some ancient prophecy? It's hard enough wrapping my head around vampires being real, let alone my new party trick of human glow stick fingers. I barely accepted that werewolves aren't just Halloween costumes, and now the universe is dumping more supernatural drama in my lap.

What else is hiding in the shadows of what I thought was reality? Am I ready to face whatever's lurking beyond my comfortable little bubble of science and logic?

Knowing Rhyland might have answers about my weird light show is somewhat comforting. The possibility of other supernatural elements existing both terrifies and fascinates my inner scientist. This could be my chance to understand what's happening to me, even if my world is spinning like a crazy carnival ride.

What's next?

Then suddenly, like storm clouds parting, Rhyland's explanation of our bond clicks into place. It explains why his presence feels like gravity—why being apart from him physically hurts.

He's become my ultimate weakness and greatest strength rolled into one devastating package, a force field that draws me back even when my brain screams to run. When we touch, warmth spreads under my skin, awakening parts of me I didn't know existed.

Those beautiful blue eyes strip me bare with just a look, leaving me defenseless against this pull between us. I'm desperate to lose myself in whatever this is, to let our destinies tangle until they're inseparable.

I can't ignore how my pulse races when he talks about sharing blood in some intimate vampire ritual. Fear mingles with burning curiosity about what new heights such a connection might reach.

He's lit a fire in me that burns away rational thought, leaving only raw need in its wake. This obsession goes deeper than physical attraction—it's like he's branded my very soul.

His cryptic hints about this prophecy send chills down my spine, but beneath the fear, there's an insatiable need to uncover the truth.

I'm either falling into the greatest adventure of my life or the biggest trap ever set. Maybe both

Rhyland stands behind me and reaches for the edges of the towel; it falls away, revealing my sun-kissed skin glistening with water droplets. Through the mirror, my eyes rove over his smooth, toned chest and corded arms. The intricate tattoos that decorate every inch of his massive body make him even more seductive. I want nothing more than to trace each ink design with my tongue and find out what they mean in a much more intimate way.

He lowers his head to nuzzle my neck, and I shiver delicately against him. He traces his fingertips along my tight stomach and then up to my ample breasts. He's gauging my reaction in the mirror—a soft sigh escapes my lips. My body melts into his with every kiss and nibble on my neck.

We'd just finished our frenzied lovemaking, and my body already aches for more of him, desperate to feel his warmth pressing against me and inside me. The man is large and imposing, like a sturdy stallion. His thickness alone made me scream out in ecstasy. My craving for him starts to rise again. I want him more than before, and my body burns with desire.

I meet his gaze in the mirror, my breath hitching at the intensity of his stare. He towers above me, making me feel minuscule and vulnerable. His height is intimidating as he has to stoop to reach my neck. I can almost taste the fire of his mouth against my skin—a sensation that sends a heated shudder through me.

Memories of our discussion about biting surface, raising questions I never thought I'd consider. What would it feel like? Could something supposedly painful bring pleasure? How has something forbidden become so tempting?

His breath caresses my ear as he whispers, "One taste isn't enough—I'm addicted to every inch of you." His lips tease my neck, igniting sparks of pleasure.

With trembling lips, I whisper, “Rhyland...”

Do I want this?

"Yes, Angel?" he purrs, his voice pure seduction.

Moistening my lips, I gather my courage and speak the words that will change everything: "Bite me."

There's no going back now.

His fierce azure eyes hold me captive in their gaze as we peer into the looking glass. My nipples harden to two diamond-like points, aching for more of his touch. His tall, muscular frame embraces me from behind, caressing my body and igniting my passions with his lips and hands.

“Dani...I...” He begins, but I know what I want.

Before he can even finish his words, I beg, “Bite me...Please,” I crave the feeling of him consuming me whole.

Without hesitation, he plants soft kisses along my neck until his teeth pierce my skin. A sharp gasp escapes me as pleasure and a hint of fear flood my veins when his bite grazes against my carotid artery. He pulls me closer in response to my gasp as he moans against my neck. His powerful hands caress my breasts, each squeeze escalating the waves of pleasure that surge through me.

I am transfixed, unable to look away as I watch him consume me. His hands lovingly cradle me against him while his lips greedily absorb my life force from my neck.

Scarlet droplets cascade down my skin like a trickle of fire, staining my breasts. Each drop of blood he takes into his body causes me to moan with pleasure until I am lost in an ocean of ecstasy. His lips suck hungrily on my neck, igniting an inferno within me that threatens to consume us both. Each touch is like a symphony of sensations I never want to end.

His hand slides farther south, finding its way to my aching, pulsing clit where he toys with it expertly while simultaneously taking life from my neck. I lean back into him with abandon, offering up my throat, giving him total access to take what he desires.

As he drinks deeply, euphoria spreads through my veins. Our moans mingle, our bodies becoming one in this intimate act.

This is more intimate than anything I've ever experienced—I'm giving him my essence, and he's taking it with reverence.

When he finally withdraws his fangs, his eyes blaze with possessive hunger. He runs his hand down my torso, coating his fingers in the blood still dripping from my neck. Gazing intensely into my eyes, he trails his bloody fingers down my bare skin, leaving glistening red smears across my breasts and stomach.

"So beautiful," he rasps.

Still dizzy with pleasure, his hands grip my waist from behind, our gazes locked on each other in the glass. I don't recognize myself in this feral, sexual creature I've become. But I can't look away, intoxicated by the raw carnal energy flowing between us. Rhyland has awakened my inner darkness, and I crave more.

"Do you see how exquisite you are?" he murmurs hotly in my ear. "And...mmm...you taste like the sweetest honey." He says, licking his lips, before going back for more.

I'm drenched with wanton desire. His finger delves in and out of me as his lips and teeth suck on my neck. The sheer eroticism of the moment is indescribable, like nothing I have ever known before. All my worries, anxieties, and fears course through me like a river and cascade into him. He drinks from me so carefully and with care, his eyes never leaving mine. I feel relieved yet vulnerable, as if my soul is bare before him.

He forcibly pulls away from my neck; his heated gaze devours me. His hard body presses against me as he pushes me down onto the countertop, whispering guttural demands as I submit to him. He forcefully spreads my legs with his knee, trapping my feet between his own and spreading me wide.

His hard cock presses close to my dripping opening. My head is forcefully jerked back—a handful of hair from the base of my neck is grabbed. Each sting of pain brings forth a moan from within me.

"I want you to watch me fuck your tight, heavenly hole," he commands lewdly.

Our eyes meet in the mirror's reflection, my breath fogging its surface. He seems more visceral and ungovernable.

Did my blood do that?

I know his bite has me going completely crazy with desire and craving.

Fuck, this is insane.

My lips part, my gaze never straying from his. He stands there, leering at me with carnal desire. His hard cock pressing against my entrance, anxious to be buried inside my warmth. He nudges the tip in as if testing the waters. He's savoring every moment, wanting me to beg for it.

Oh, how his ego swells with every passionate plea and beg. "Rhyland...please."

His darkness thrives on my supplications. He tightens his grip on my hair, a reminder of who has the control here, and demands, "Please, what?"

I moan in surrender and whisper breathlessly, "Please...fuck me."

His fiery hand burns my hip, squeezing it tight. His voice is husky and powerful, "God, I fucking *live* for it when you beg me, baby."

His thick cock slams into me, and I scream out in pleasure. I've never felt something as big as him inside me before, and it's still a tight fit despite the initial pain wearing off. He's not gentle by any means, but that's what I love—feeling every single thrust, writhing, and moaning in hopeless bliss. His muscles ripple from the effort as he pounds me from behind.

He leans over my back and whispers savagely in my ear, "Look how fucking sexy you are when I fuck you."

My moans grow louder as I watch us in the mirror, my hips slamming against the cold, hard marble counter as Rhyland thrusts himself inside me from behind. The marble feels like ice against my skin compared to the furnace of his hard, muscular body.

I will be sore and bruised after this ferocious pounding against the unforgiving marble surface. My breasts bounce and smack against the slick stone, my tight nipples rubbing almost painfully with each jagged thrust. The pleasure sears through me like a wave of boiling fire. My lungs gasp and struggle for air as exquisite pain and intense gratification entwine in an intoxicating and punishing yet rewarding concoction.

Rhyland grips my hips brutally, pulling me back onto him as he slams home to the hilt again and again.

The mingled sensations overload my senses until I'm mindless, reduced to a screaming mess of raw, sensual sensation. Rhyland conquers my body utterly with overwhelming thrill and agony.

His bite has sent pure ecstasy through my body, and he's right—I'm already craving more.

I moan and grit my teeth in filthy delight as he slams into me, his tight balls smacking against my clit with each thrust. How he has me positioned—wide open, neck craned, and back arched—drives me wild. I bite down hard on my lip to keep from screaming out the pleasure ripping through every inch of me, unable to suppress the carnal utterances that bubble up from inside me.

He stares hungrily at our entwined bodies, grunting with desire. "God...I'm drowning in your juices. You're so fucking sexy with how slick and wet you are around my cock."

Rhyland grabs my arms and seizes them behind my back, entwining his arm through them, locking me in place, and still clasping a fistful of my hair with his other hand at the base of my neck. He yanks me back forcefully, smashing his chest into me as he rams me into a new position. My tits bounce as he holds my arms captive, and my neck cranes backward as he savagely fucks me with animalistic hunger.

My breathing is labored as I moan, "Fuck... yes.....more..." I can't get enough.

I'm held in a way that puts me entirely at his mercy. "You're so fucking greedy, baby. I love how you take my dick." He's thrusting harder and faster, our bodies smacking audibly, his balls hitting me as he slams himself against me. "Come on my cock, Angel. I love hearing you scream."

His command sends me an electric jolt, and I let go completely. My pussy clamps down tight around his raging cock, and I let out an earth-shattering cry as pleasure washes over me. Hot liquid pours from my soaked slit, sending juices dripping down my thigh.

"Good girl. That's...it. There's my dirty little Angel," he grunts into my ear.

His movements become choppy; his breaths quicken. His cock swells, giving way to more intense delight in my slippery depths. With a roar, he floods me, and I cannot help but melt in sheer ecstasy. His expletives make me even hotter.

We stand there, panting and out of breath. I've never experienced such arousal before, nor climaxed so hard in the presence of anyone else. He's trapped me for sure—there's no denying that. He gently runs his fingers down my jaw before turning my head to meet him. His kiss is passionate, deep, and penetrating, so powerful it feels like he's reaching inside me.

Exhausted. Rhyland insists on staying with me until I fall asleep. I don't protest, although I've never slept alongside someone before. He pulls me close, embracing my body in his strong arms. I can't help but let myself be immersed in his presence, like a protective shield. His scent is intoxicating as I take a deep breath, and my eyes instinctively shut.

Before I realize it, I drift off into a peaceful sleep.

RHYLAND

38

I wrench myself away from her heat, knowing dawn approaches and I need to go. My mind races with her fucking mind-blowing revelations. I need to get this information to my brothers immediately.

We have to track down Adrian fast to decode these mysteries and what the prophecy really means. I stalk through the darkness, haunted by visions of her perfect body. The way she shuddered and screamed my name as I dominated her pleasure, driving her to the edge and beyond. Just thinking about it has my cock hard and throbbing again.

Will this savage hunger for her ever be satisfied? I'd forgotten what this kind of raw need felt like until I found someone I craved down to my bones. Her passion ignites mine, leaving me desperate and starving for more.

And her blood...holy fuck. It was pure and untainted, like drinking from the gods themselves. In all my centuries of darkness, I've never tasted anything so divine, so perfect. She tastes like bottled sunlight, sweet and addictive as sin.

She wasn't ready to complete our bond yet, but she trusted me enough to taste her—that's all I can demand right now. Soon though, I'll seal that connection and claim her completely as mine.

The prophecy claims our bond unlocks her power. But how the fuck does it happen? Has it already begun? Questions pound through my skull like a battering ram.

Dani said she first noticed her light shortly after we connected. Have I already triggered something inside her? Could she be immortal?

I need answers now...preferably without getting us both killed. If I've set ancient powers in motion by claiming her, the fallout could be catastrophic. And if others discover Danica's role before we're ready, they'll hunt her down.

I'll keep her safe, even if she hates the monster lurking beneath my skin. By uncovering the prophecy's truth, I hope to finally give her the answers she deserves.

I stride into Lucian's club, the familiar bass vibrating through my bones. I find him in his office, drowning in paperwork. Erik sits nearby, nursing what looks like top-shelf whiskey.

"Lucian, Erik," I announce, my voice tight with urgency. Both snap to attention, their expressions shifting from boredom to alert concern. "We need to talk. It's about Dani."

Lucian drops his pen dramatically and leans back, interlocking his fingers behind his head with that shit-eating grin of his. "Finally get to play hide the vampire sausage with Miss Hottie McHotpants?" he cackles, wiggling his eyebrows like a cartoon villain.

I growl, shooting him a death glare. "It's fucking bigger than that."

Erik straightens in his chair, eyes narrowing with interest. A storm of emotions—frustration, determination, fear—churns inside me as I lay out everything.

Erik's eyes widen. "Let me get this straight. You're saying Danica conjured white flames from her bare hands?"

I rake my fingers through my hair, stalking across the office like a caged predator. "Yes. It sounds impossible, but I watched it happen. One second, nothing—the next, her hands erupted with some kind of mystical fire."

"Extraordinary," Erik murmurs, leaning forward intently. "What else did you observe?"

I exhale harshly, stopping at the desk. "That's just it—I don't know what the fuck to make of it. The fire doesn't burn her. Where it comes from is a complete mystery."

Erik taps his chin thoughtfully. "This changes everything. We need to investigate these abilities immediately. The archives might contain references to similar magical manifestations..."

I nod sharply. "We need answers fast. Whatever's happening with Danica could have massive implications for her safety—and for all of us, if she is who I think she is."

Erik meets my gaze with steel in his eyes. "Then our path is clear."

Erik's body goes rigid as realization hits him. "Rhyland, the prophecy speaks of a mate who will awaken—"

I thrust my hand up, cutting him off before he can finish the thought we're both having. He stops, releasing a heavy breath.

Lucian's face scrunches in confusion before his eyes suddenly go dinner-plate wide. "Hooooly shit-tickets, Batman! Are you saying your sexy-time mission is to wake up Sleeping Beauty's magical mojo? Talk about performance pressure!" He mimes an explosion from his crotch.

I growl in frustration, pacing the room like I might wear a hole through the floor.

Lucian lets out a long, low whistle. "That's one hell of a cosmic cock-block. You sure your vampire mojo can handle that kind of responsibility? I mean, most guys just worry about finding the clitoris, not unlocking ancient prophecies with their dick."

I exhale heavily. "We need to contact Adrian immediately. He knows all this mystical bullshit—legends, prophecies, ancient lore. I can't leave Dani unprotected, so I need you both to track him down."

Lucian throws his hands up dramatically. "Fuck to the no! What are you smoking? I love you like the broody brother from another mother that you are, but I've got a nightclub full of horny humans and thirsty vampires to babysit. We can't just drop everything for some magical mystery tour to Creepy Scrolls-ville!"

Reality hits me hard—I shouldn't burden my brothers with my problems. This is my responsibility to figure out how to protect Dani. "Fine," I growl. "I'll go myself."

Erik rises to his feet, his silver eyes hardened with resolve. "I'm coming with you. This isn't something you should face alone."

Every primal instinct in my body screams to stay and guard her, but I need those answers. I turn to Lucian, my expression deadly serious. "Watch over her. If she shows up here, keep her safe. She's emitting some kind of scent that attracts the wrong kind of attention. Including that piece of shit Azrael."

Lucian's smirk vanishes, replaced by rare seriousness as he nods. "Don't worry, Captain Broody-pants. I'll keep Miss Glowy-hands safe from all the fangy perverts. Scout's honor!" He makes an exaggerated salute.

We plan to complete our mission within two days. I decide against telling Dani about my departure yet—she doesn't need more complications right now.

Erik and I pack our gear with military precision and board my private jet, ready to conquer whatever lies ahead. We're heading straight for the Obsidian Enclave—the legendary Veil of Arcane Society—carved into the remote Appalachian peaks of Nova Scotia. This hidden fortress is where our vampire ancestors stockpiled their most dangerous knowledge, a sanctuary accessible only to those with enough power or bloodline to demand entry. We're about to rip open those ancient secrets, and nothing's going to fucking stop us.

Nine hours later, we land. The moment we cross the threshold, the air shifts. Everything darkens, like reality itself is being compressed and twisted. A primal energy pulses through the shadows, charging the atmosphere with ancient power. The hair on my neck rises in primal warning.

Massive obsidian pillars tower around us, their mirror-black surfaces reflecting distorted images of vampire history. The chamber vibrates with raw mystical energy as if the knowledge contained here could rewrite the fate of worlds. Erik and I move with predatory caution through the Enclave's labyrinthine corridors and forbidden chambers. Our mission is clear: find Adrian, the keeper of this sacred knowledge, and extract whatever information we need to decode this prophecy—by force if necessary.

We prowl down a pitch-black corridor barely illuminated by guttering torches that cast more shadows than light. The passageway terminates at massive double doors, nearly invisible in the oppressive darkness. Beneath our boots, an intricate marble mosaic pattern struggles to show itself through centuries of accumulated grime, our footfalls echoing like gunshots in the dead silence. We pass chambers with decaying wooden doors that gape at us like the hollow eye sockets of ancient skulls. The air hangs thick and suffocating—a miasma of decay and forgotten power. Dust with the texture of pulverized bone crunches beneath our steps, marking our passage through this tomb of knowledge. A sickly yellow candlelight flickers from one doorway down the hall, drawing us like moths past the other chambers into a vast stone room. At its far end, another doorway stands open—black as the void, ready to devour anything that dares enter.

Erik freezes beside me. "Adrian is this way," he murmurs, his silver eyes narrowing. "I can feel his presence."

As we stalk into the chamber, the atmosphere shifts—heavy with the weight of forbidden knowledge. A fireplace dominates one corner, the wood hissing and popping as flames devour it, casting dancing shadows across the stone walls. The scent of ancient parchment, leather bindings, and dust saturates every breath. Adrian hunches at his desk, surrounded by towering stacks of crumbling tomes and yellowed scrolls, his dark eyes racing across text no mortal has seen in decades. He radiates an aura of ancient wisdom and solemn purpose; his gaze is piercing and distant.

As I approach my brother, suspicion and unease burn through my veins like acid. Adrian's head snaps up from his research, his eyes widening with shock and disbelief.

"What the hell? Am I hallucinating, or have my brothers actually descended into this pit of forgotten lore?"

I grab him in a crushing embrace before he can react, holding on like he might disappear if I loosen my grip. Adrian's penetrating gaze cuts through us both, that serious expression barely concealing the brilliant mind we all respect. His command of prophecies and ancient lore is unmatched, and his grasp of dark magic is beyond anyone living.

I clamp my hand on his shoulder, my grip intense enough to convey how much I've missed him. "Goddamn good to see you. How you holding up, little brother?"

He shrugs casually. "Can't complain. Livin' the dream."

Erik steps forward, extending his hand. "Brother. Good to see you."

Adrian takes it with a firm grip. "You too, Erik."

Slumping back in his chair, Adrian radiates exhaustion beneath a veneer of self-assured confidence. "What brings my brothers to this forgotten hellhole?"

Relief floods me, seeing Adrian untouched by this place's malevolent energy. I cut straight to it: "You know about the Dark prophecy?"

Adrian's eyes sharpen with interest. "Of course. But refresh my memory—what's happening?"

I stalk across the room, inhaling deeply. "What exactly do you know about it?"

Without hesitation, Adrian moves to a towering bookshelf, fingers dancing over ancient spines until he extracts a worn leather volume. He cracks it open, releasing the scent of centuries, studying the cryptic symbols and illustrations with practiced ease.

"The text states the mortal savior must find their true mate to awaken dormant power. Their full strength emerges only when a genuine bond forms between them, hearts completely pledged to one another."

I lean forward intently. "Any clues about this individual?"

Adrian shakes his head. "No physical description." His eyes narrow, studying my face. "What have you found? Is it the one we've been looking for?"

I hesitate before answering. "Possibly." I detail everything about Danica—her mysterious heritage, her strange energy. Adrian listens with scholarly focus until I describe the white flames erupting from her hands.

He jolts upright. "What color did you say?" When I repeat the ethereal white glow, Adrian's eyes widen dramatically. He grabs his hair, struck speechless. I've never seen my unshakable brother so fucking stunned.

"What is it?" I demand.

Adrian shifts nervously, visibly processing. "It sounds like... but no, they haven't been seen..." He trails off cryptically.

My patience snaps. "Tell me. Now."

He laughs—a tense, disbelieving sound. "Ancient myths speak of celestial beings with that exact radiant power. But it's been eons."

My jaw clenches in shock. I press Adrian for every scrap of information about these legendary creatures. He explains they supposedly wielded purifying light energy and possessed extraordinary abilities. But most knowledge has been lost to time.

Erik can't contain himself. "Incredible!"

Adrian's expression darkens. "The prophecy never suggested anything of this magnitude. For Danica to be celestial is virtually impossible."

Impossible or not, her glowing hands and delicious smell suddenly make perfect fucking sense. This revelation hits me like a physical blow. Too many questions swarm my mind, making it hard to focus. I need clarity.

"What exactly would that make her?" I ask Adrian.

He hesitates, deep in thought. "The possibilities are endless—angel, deity, demigod. The only certainty is such a mating bond would be catastrophically powerful, elemental in nature."

My mind detonates with possibilities. "How the fuck am I supposed to help her when I don't even know what she is?"

Adrian's gaze cuts through me like a blade. "You believe it's your responsibility to guide her?" Before I can answer, realization crashes across his face. "She's your mate," he declares, not a question but a verdict.

Adrian looks as thunderstruck as I felt when first confronted with this inexplicable connection. "We haven't completed the ritual," I admit, "but she is unquestionably mine."

Adrian stares at me with bone-chilling gravity. "This bond you describe between you and Danica is completely unprecedented, Rhyland. Never in our bloody history has one of our kind joined with a celestial being."

He stalks across the study like a caged predator, hands locked behind his back. "We know nothing of the true extent of Danica's powers nor the ancient bloodline from which they originate. To bind yourself eternally to something so unknown...it will have cataclysmic consequences." Adrian whips around to face me. "There are cosmic forces at play beyond our comprehension. Your union could trigger events that will spiral completely beyond your control." His eyes burn into mine with frightening intensity. "Danica's destiny, our future...everything we know may be obliterated because of your bond."

I rake my hand through my hair, fury and frustration boiling over. "I fucking know the risks, Adrian, but I can't fight what fate has branded into my soul."

"No," he concedes. "But you must proceed with extreme caution, brother. Danica's gifts are awakening, and with them, your intertwined destiny. But this journey into uncharted territory will be savage and merciless." His expression softens slightly with genuine fear. "Swear to me you'll protect her, even from herself if necessary. The powers her abilities summon may prove too devastating, too chaotic for any mortal vessel to contain."

I meet his stare unflinchingly. "You have my blood oath. Nothing will harm Danica while I still draw breath. Whatever hellstorm comes, we face it together."

His grave warning slams into me, striking a raw nerve. I understand his skepticism given my history of cauterizing all emotion. But this connection feels primal and absolute, as if etched into the fabric of existence itself. Yet Adrian is right to demand caution with forces that could rip reality apart. If Danica truly carries celestial blood, our union could transform everything, for salvation or damnation. The prophecy's ambiguity haunts me like a fucking specter.

Adrian grips my shoulder, his gaze burning with urgency. "There are treacherous waters ahead, shrouded in impenetrable darkness. But remember, brother—this burden isn't yours alone to shoulder. You need not face the void without light to guide your way."

DANICA

39

The music thumps through the floorboards while drunken whoops create the soundtrack to my Friday night shift. I mix drinks on autopilot, my mind stuck on Rhyland's disappearing act. He's been radio silent for days—no steamy late-night visits, no texts that make me blush in public places. Pretty weird behavior from Mr. Control-Freak-Sex-God, who usually can't go twenty-four hours without checking I'm still breathing.

I catch myself glancing at my phone for the millionth time.

Pathetic.

Even hearing that growly voice would make my day, but I'll be damned if I'm chasing after him like some lovesick teenager even if this silence is slowly driving me up the wall.

The heavy door swings open, and the rowdy laughter cuts off like someone hit mute. An eerie quiet blankets the bar as heads swivel toward the entrance. Azrael Blackwood glides in wearing a black suit. His tall frame moves with malicious intent as those ice-chip eyes scan the room. My stomach drops to my toes while goosebumps pepper my arms. He looks like GQ material, but my internal alarm system blares like a five-alarm fire. This guy is bad news with a capital DANGER.

Of all the joints in this town...

Azrael slides onto the empty stool directly across from me, pinning me with those unnerving blue eyes. His gaze does a slow crawl down my body that makes me feel like I need a shower, even as my traitorous face flushes. His lips curve upward, but the smile is as warm as an Arctic winter.

"Whiskey. Your finest label."

His voice is silk wrapped around a razor blade. I turn to grab the Glenfiddich 1934, grateful for the momentary escape from that predatory stare. My hands threaten to betray me with a tremor, but I force them steady as I pour the amber liquid.

Azrael takes a deliberate sip. Those winter eyes lock onto mine again as he sets the glass down with a click that sounds like a gun being cocked.

"I must say, you intrigue me. You smell nothing like the sheep surrounding us." His tone feigns interest while barely concealed hunger darkens his gaze. "Tell me...what exactly are you?"

Ice water floods my veins even as anger bubbles up. I scan the crowded bar desperately for Rhyland's tall frame. Nothing. I'm on my own with this snake coiling around me.

"Wow, that's your pickup line? I'm just your average bartender trying to make rent," I quip, forcing a casual eye-roll while my heart hammers against my ribs. "Nothing special about this girl, sorry to disappoint."

Where the hell are you, Rhyland?

His eyes narrow to icy slits. The cruel twist of his perfect lips can hardly be called a smile—it's more like watching a shark bare its teeth before the feeding frenzy. The refined façade slips, revealing something ancient and malevolent beneath. He leans closer, his voice dropping to a silky purr.

"Oh, I very much doubt that, my dear. Your scent has become... intoxicating. And something decidedly *un*-human now stirs within you."

His tongue flicks over a pointed fang. "Won't you tell me what it is? I've developed a, shall we say... special interest in your case."

Each word oozes false concern while his stare dissects me like a lab specimen. My heart does a flip against my ribs.

How the hell can he sense what's happening to me?

Before I can cobble together a witty deflection, Azrael leans closer, invading my personal bubble. "Tread carefully, little one. You seem to forget it's unwise to make enemies of those in power." His voice drops to a menacing whisper. "Especially when one harbors such dangerous secrets..."

His fingers suddenly clamp around my wrist like an iron shackle. Disgust and fury surge through me like wildfire. "Get your hand off me. Now." I wrench myself free, trying to hide my trembling while meeting his predatory stare with all the defiance I can muster. "Back off before you find out exactly how 'special' I can be," I growl.

His dark chuckle crawls down my spine like a spider, the air practically crackling with menace. I desperately scan the room for Rhyland's familiar figure, but Azrael's imposing form blocks my view. *Trapped like a rat.* Then suddenly, he turns and leaves, the bar door jingling cheerfully behind him as stunned silence blankets the room.

"You okay there, Dani?"

I jump at John's question. Noticing several nosy patrons quickly looking away, I force my trembling lips into what I hope passes for a casual smile. "Yeah, just some pushy drunk. No biggie."

John's forehead wrinkles with concern. He leans closer, lowering his voice. "Dani, I know difficult customers. But that guy looked ready to have you for dinner." I attempt a carefree laugh that sounds more like a strangled cat. My skin still crawls from Azrael's hungry stare.

"Really. I'm good," I insist, wiping the already spotless bar with my shaking hands. "Just another creep who can't take no for an answer."

John frowns, his kind eyes full of worry. His gentle touch on my shoulder sends warmth through my thin shirt. "Something's wrong. You know you can talk to me, right? I've got your back."

My throat tightens at sweet, protective John, always looking out for me. Part of me wants to spill everything... but I shake my head with forced confidence. "Thanks, but I'm fine. Just another weirdo at the bar. Nothing this girl can't handle."

Though right now, I'd kill for Rhyland to show up and go all possessive vampire on Azrael's creepy ass.

The bustling bar can't drown out Azrael's threatening words echoing in my mind. Even surrounded by people, I feel watched, hunted. Every shadow seems to hide predatory eyes tracking my movements.

I need answers about these "changes" he sensed in me. Desperately.

My trembling fingers dial Rhyland's number the moment my shift ends. Straight to voicemail. *Perfect.* Looks like I'm flying solo tonight.

The empty parking lot stretches before me as I lock up Playful Pint, my car sitting alone under the single working light. My steps quicken as shadows writhe at the edges of my vision. Key poised at the lock, I scan the darkness.

"Rhyland?" My voice breaks the silence—only rustling leaves answer.

Stop being paranoid, I scold myself. But every sound makes me jump, every shadow seems alive. I scramble into my car, frantically hitting the lock button.

A dark figure materializes beside my window. Before I can scream, glass explodes inward, razor shards slicing my cheek and shoulder. Strong hands drag me through the jagged opening, my skin tearing as I'm wrenched from safety. A palm clamps over my mouth, crushing my lips against my teeth until I taste blood.

"Miss me, little Dani?" Azrael's voice slithers against my ear. My stomach plummets.

He slams me against the car, pain shooting through my spine as metal bites into my back. I fight uselessly against his grip while his massive frame pins me in place, his weight crushing the air from my lungs.

"Thought your precious *Rhyland* would save you?" His mocking laugh chills my blood. "You belong to me now."

I bite his restraining hand until I feel flesh give way. He snarls, fingers digging into my scalp as he yanks my head back. Those icy eyes have turned to bottomless black pools—lethal fangs gleam in the dim light, already dripping with anticipation.

"I warned you about defiance." His words drip venom. "Time to test my theory about you."

His fangs pierce my throat without warning. White-hot agony explodes as he tears into my flesh, the sickening sound of gulping filling my ears as he drinks deeply. Each pull draws life from my veins, my vision spotting as he groans with dark pleasure against my ravaged skin.

Warm liquid seeps down my neck, soaking my collar as the parking lot tilts and spins around me.

"Exquisite! I've never tasted anything so divine." Azrael's voice reaches me through a fog, his words slurring together as my consciousness ebbs.

Something ignites deep within me—a spark of defiance flaring into rage—heat pools in my trapped palms, building pressure like magma beneath the earth's crust. The sensation spreads up my arms, my skin glowing from within as white-hot energy surges through my veins. With a primal scream, light explodes from my hands, blasting Azrael backward.

I collapse onto the rough asphalt, tiny stones biting into my palms. The coppery tang of blood fills my mouth as darkness threatens to claim me.

Azrael's maniacal laughter cuts through the night. "My, my. What have we here? Such raw power hidden inside that delicious body." His eyes gleam with unholy fascination, like a collector who's found a rare specimen.

I stare at my trembling hands, still pulsing with fading golden light.

What the hell just happened?

Before I can struggle to my feet, Azrael stalks toward me, lips pulled back from bloodstained teeth. "We're only getting started, my pet."

"Stay the hell back!" I thrust my hands forward, desperately willing that power to return.

As he advances, something ancient awakens inside me. I gather every scrap of terror and fury, compressing it into a sphere of pulsating energy between my palms. The light burns my retinas, casting Azrael's face in stark relief—hunger mixed with caution. With a guttural cry, I hurl it directly at his chest.

His scream pierces the night as flames engulf him. The stench of burning flesh and hair fills the air, making bile rise in my throat. Azrael claws at his smoldering shirt, his skin blistering and bubbling beneath. Those black eyes lock onto mine, promising retribution beyond imagination.

"You'll suffer for this, bitch," he hisses through charred lips, voice distorted with pain.

His form dissolves into writhing shadow and smoke, leaving nothing but the lingering smell of burnt flesh. My legs give way as I slump against my car's cold metal, heart hammering against my ribs. The puncture wounds on my neck throb in time with my pulse, each beat pushing more warmth down my skin.

I peel myself from the ground and stumble into my damaged car, glass crunching beneath my shoes. Every shadow on the drive home seems to reach for me, every flicker of movement in my peripheral vision sending fresh adrenaline coursing through me.

Inside my apartment, I slam the door and engage every lock, knowing even as I do that such barriers mean nothing to creatures like Azrael. My phone shakes in my blood-smeared hand as I leave message after desperate message for Rhyland.

"Where are you? He's after me—Azrael. He... he attacked me. Something's happening to me. Please... I need you."

Only silence answers. The bitter taste of abandonment mingles with the iron tang of blood in my mouth. Tears sting my eyes as I sink to the floor, back pressed against the door.

So much for vampire protectors and destiny.

But as I sit in the darkness, something shifts inside me. The same power that saved me tonight still hums beneath my skin, waiting. I may be alone, but I'm far from helpless.

If Rhyland won't be here to fight my battles, I'll have to learn to fight them myself.

RHYLAND

40

Dread crawls up my spine as Erik and I exit the Enclave, Adrian's warnings still ringing in my ears. The area outside radiates an unnatural stillness, like the suspended moment before a predator strikes.

Erik and I lock eyes, both sensing the malevolent presence surrounding us. This place isn't fucking empty.

"We've got company," Erik murmurs.

I nod sharply, every muscle tensing for combat, adrenaline flooding my system. We edge forward through the oppressive silence. Just as we near escape, faint shuffling breaks the quiet. Stealthy footsteps approach through the encroaching darkness.

We freeze in unison, hyper-aware of the threat. Seconds drag by, loaded with menace, as massive silhouettes materialize from the shadows, blocking our exit. Their black cloaks bear the emblem I've hoped never to see again—the Brotherhood of Shadows. Corrupted by ancient evil, these ruthless fanatics serve only their depraved master. Surrounded and vulnerable, we're in deep shit.

Their massive leader, Cade, steps forward, surrounded by a visible black aura that presses down on us like a physical weight. My blood runs cold at his sadistic smile.

"Rhyland," he barks, voice like gravel. "What brings you trespassing on our territory?"

My fists clench, rage burning through my veins. Our secret mission was compromised—someone betrayed us.

"Our business here doesn't concern you," I spit back through gritted teeth.

Cade's grin widens, chilling me to the core. "Oh, I think it is. Lord Azrael wants your human pet eliminated. Permanently."

Fury explodes inside me at the threat against Danica. The Brotherhood has become Azrael's attack dogs. The danger to Danica just escalated beyond measure.

"You sick bastards won't lay a goddamn finger on her head." Erik snarls back vehemently.

Seven against two, but we share an unspoken vow—Danica's survival hangs in the balance now. And failure is not an option.

Cade's guttural cackle echoes mockingly through the empty stone corridors. "You pussy-ass weaklings think you can take on the Brotherhood's elite? In our stronghold?" His pale eyes glint with cruel amusement. "You must have a goddamn death wish."

Primal fury ignites within every cell as I stalk forward, my blazing stare locked intensely on his sneering face. "No one—and I mean NO ONE—will lay a finger on my destined mate!" I snarl through bared fangs.

The amused glint in Cade's eyes chills to ruthless intent. "The mortal belongs to Lord Azrael now. She's his pet project." A sadistic grin twists his mouth. "So do yourself a favor and back the hell off before you seriously regret it."

Murderous rage ignites in my veins, my vision bleeding red at the thought of that sadistic fuck anywhere near Danica. My fangs descend, beast howling for blood. Touch what's mine, Azrael, and I'll make you pray for death's mercy.

Cade hawks and spits near my boots, his face twisting with hatred. "That bitch is gonna get what's coming to her. For the last fucking time, stand down!" His laughter grates like nails on my soul. "You arrogant prick—you can't beat someone as powerful as him!"

My mind races, spiraling into darkness. Has Danica already fallen into that psychopath's hands? Without completing our mating bond, I can't sense her safety. We're surrounded, outnumbered, with no clear path to reach her.

Fuck this.

With a savage roar tearing from my throat, I unleash a devastating telekinetic blast at Cade. His body flies backward like a broken toy, slamming against the jagged stone wall. His skull connects with a sickening wet crack, blood spattering across the ancient rock as his body crumples to the floor.

Panic and rage claw through my chest, strangling me from within. I need to escape this fucking stone labyrinth and reach Danica before Azrael's sick obsession destroys her. The primal urge to protect my mate hammers like a battle drum through my blood.

Something snaps inside me as I stalk toward Cade's crumpled form. My fingers curl into lethal weapons, fangs extending past my lips, eyes burning with hellfire crimson. "I'll slaughter every last motherfucker who stands in my way!" The words tear from my throat, veins bulging at my neck.

Rational thought evaporates like mist. Only Danica matters now. I'll rip through anything—mortal, vampire, or demon—that blocks my path to her. She needs me, and I'll carve a bloody trail through these bastards if that's what it takes.

I twist violently away from a jagged blade aimed at my throat, feeling the wind of its passing against my skin. With a feral roar, I seize the attacker with my mind and slam him against the stone. His spine shatters with a wet crack, and his body goes limp like a broken puppet.

Ducking beneath another wild swing, I channel my fury into a telekinetic blast that crushes my attacker against the wall. Dark satisfaction floods me as blood sprays across ancient stone, even as two more shadows rush to replace him.

Erik becomes a silver blur of death, his blade carving crimson arcs through flesh and bone. But they keep coming, ancient darkness fueling their relentless assault.

As I crush another skull against cold stone, white-hot pain stabs into my neck—a needle. I whirl with murderous intent, ready to rip out this fuckers throat with my bare hands.

Cade's blood-smeared face swims before me, the drugs already working into my system—his broken grin widening as my limbs begin to betray me, paralysis spreading like poison fire through my veins...

My body slams against the stone floor, blood spraying from my mouth on impact. The metallic scent of carnage fills my nostrils as Cade's massive boot crushes against my face, grinding my cheekbone until something cracks beneath the pressure.

"Told you, you worthless piece of shit, you can't beat us." His putrid breath scalds my skin as he leans down, voice dripping with sadistic pleasure. "Now the real fun begins..."

Through the haze of agony, Erik's tortured howls echo down the corridor. My mind teeters between blinding pain and frantic thoughts of Danica. What unspeakable horrors might Azrael be inflicting on her while I lie here, helpless and broken?

Agony rips through me as Cade's blade carves into my back, steel biting deep. "We'll ship you to Lord Azrael in bloody fucking chunks. But not before I've had my entertainment." His voice vibrates with sick anticipation.

Darkness pulls at me, offering escape from this hell. But through the pain, my rage burns brighter—these fuckers will pay for every wound. Erik and I will break free. We'll find Danica.

As consciousness fades, I memorize their smirking faces. Each cut, each break will be repaid tenfold. They think this is victory. No—it's just the start of their nightmare.

Danica

41

I storm through Club Karma's pounding chaos, the throbbing beats drowning out my whirling thoughts. It's been seven fucking days since Rhyland ditched without a word, ignoring all my pleas for help, and now he's ignoring all my pissed-off messages demanding answers.

The absolute nerve of that tattooed asshole! Feeding me all that destiny crap, getting me hooked on his touch, then vanishing? Was I just another notch on his immortal bedpost?

I know venturing out with Creepy McFangs on the prowl is playing Russian roulette, but I need answers more than safety. Besides, my new glow-stick hands can handle themselves if needed.

I scan the writhing crowd for Lucian, fury propelling me forward. The second he spots me, his usual smirk vanishes. He seizes my arm, dragging me away from the dance floor.

"Let go of me!" I struggle against his vise-grip, confusion mixing with anger as curious onlookers stare. "I just want to know where—"

Lucian spins around, getting right in my face. "I know exactly why you're here. My office. Now." His harsh tone catches me completely off-guard.

Despite every instinct screaming to bolt, I follow him downstairs. My heart hammers against my ribs as questions multiply. Why is Mr. Sarcasm suddenly Mr. Serious? I need to understand why Rhyland abandoned me before I lose my mind completely.

Inside his dimly lit office, Lucian jabs toward a chair. I perch on the edge like it might bite me, twisting my fingers nervously.

"Start talking," I demand, fighting to keep my voice steady. "Where the hell is Rhyland?"

Lucian's jaw tightens as he downs a shot of amber liquid. Whatever comes next might shatter me completely.

"Rhyland ordered me to protect you *if* you showed up here," he finally says, watching me carefully.

If? Like he knew he wouldn't be around? My stomach drops to my toes.

My forehead creases in confusion. "Wait—he left instructions about me? Why would he do that?"

Lucian's gaze locks onto my neck where Azrael's bite marks still linger. "You're emitting a scent lately...like vampire catnip." His lips twist into a crude smirk. "Got them all hot and bothered for a taste."

I swallow hard, bile rising in my throat. *Fantastic.* "So I'm basically supernatural crack now. That's just fucking perfect," I snap.

"Like moths to a flame, sweetheart." Lucian pours himself another drink. "Rhyland told me to watch for you showing up."

My temper flares. "Then where the hell is he? Why ghost me for over a week?"

A muscle jumps in Lucian's jaw, but he remains frustratingly silent. My desperation finally trumps my pride. "Just tell me if he's okay! Did he bail on me?"

Instead of answering, Lucian grips my elbow, steering me firmly toward the exit while I pepper him with increasingly frantic questions. By the time we reach my car, my dignity is in shreds.

"Did he leave for good?" My voice sounds pathetically small even to my own ears.

Lucian exhales sharply, yanking open my car door. "Look, I honestly don't know, okay? I'm keeping my promise by getting you out of my club. Go home and lock your doors."

His words hit like a sucker punch. I peel out of the parking lot, hot tears blurring the neon signs as they streak past. Maybe I never really knew Rhyland at all. Maybe I just imagined that connection between us...

I drive in stunned silence, Lucian's cryptic non-answers bouncing around my skull. That smug jerk told me absolutely nothing useful about Rhyland's disappearance, only making everything more confusing and infuriating.

But I refuse to shed tears over some guy who couldn't even bother with a goodbye text. If Rhyland wants to vanish without explanation after all that mate-bond talk, I'll force myself to move on.

Even as questions torment me, I cling to my last scraps of pride. I've never needed a man's validation before, and I'm not about to start now.

I merge onto the freeway, pressing the accelerator harder than necessary. Rhyland walking out is his choice—his loss. I don't have time to waste on someone who whispers sweet nothings about destiny one minute and disappears the next.

So much for forever. So much for fate.

Wind whips through my shattered window, drying the tear tracks on my cheeks like some cosmic wake-up call. City lights smear into watercolor streaks as I furiously wipe my eyes. I'm nobody's victim, nobody's plaything in some supernatural chess match. And I definitely don't need Mr. Hot-Stalker or his destiny garbage.

Still...something sharp twists beneath my ribs. What we shared felt genuine, electric, raw, and real. So why throw me away like yesterday's trash?

Fresh tears burn behind my eyelids. I crank the stereo until the bass vibrates through my bones, drowning out the pathetic thoughts swirling in my head. I cruise aimlessly through empty streets, desperate to fill this gaping hole where my heart used to be...

Screw destiny. Screw prophecies. And screw Rhyland and his lying blue eyes.

I screech to a stop outside my building, tires protesting against the pavement.

I kill the engine and unleash a torrent of curses, pounding the steering wheel until my palms sting. The car door receives my next assault as I kick it open, the metallic bang echoing through the empty parking lot.

I storm inside, vision blurred with tears. My keys clatter across the counter as I hurl them down, momentarily fantasizing about the satisfying crash of hurling something breakable against the wall.

Then it hits me—that familiar knife-twist of abandonment, reopening old wounds I thought had scarred over. Why does this keep happening? Some cosmic prank on my expense?

I let myself believe in something with Rhyland, allowed myself to imagine a future that wasn't just me against the world. Only to have the universe yank away the first man who made me feel truly seen. The unfairness of it all splinters something vital inside me.

Without warning, blazing heat erupts from my palms—ivory flames dancing over my skin without burning. I stare in horrified fascination as this strange fire mirrors the chaos raging inside me...

Get a grip, Dani! This freaky light show only happens when I'm emotional about...him.

Great. Even my weird new superpowers are obsessed with that blue-eyed jerk.

I lunge for the sink, cranking the faucet to full blast. Eyes squeezed shut, I force deep breaths. *In through the nose, out through the mouth. Just breathe, dammit...*

The flames gradually retreat as I wrangle my emotions back into their cage. But in the aftermath, questions bombard me like machine-gun fire. What in the ever-loving hell is happening to me? What freakish thing am I turning into? I'm drowning in this supernatural tsunami with no lifeline! And with Rhyland pulling his disappearing act, I've got no one left to help me understand these terrifying new abilities. No one I'd trust, anyway.

Terror claws deeper as I imagine myself strapped to some sterile table, government scientists poking and prodding while I'm reduced to "Subject D" in their classified reports.

Hell no! Whatever this glowy hand business is, it needs to stay my little secret.

My mind drifts back to that day, when I finally confronted my adoptive parents about my mysterious origins. My need for identity had simmered for years before finally boiling over, too ravenous to ignore any longer...

Their evasive non-answers and hollow reassurances only confirmed what I'd always suspected—dark secrets lurked beneath their careful omissions. I remember that same cocktail of rebellion, hurt, and anger swirling out of control, just like tonight...

"We've told you everything we know, Dani," Dad says gently, though regret tinges his words. "You were left at the hospital just days old. There was a note left with your name."

Mixed emotions swirl within—surprise, curiosity, and a glimmer of long-sought connection. A note, a thread binding me to unknown origins!

"Was there anything else written?" I ask, voice trembling with fragile hope.

My mother hesitates. "Yes," she finally says softly. "One other word remained. D'larayn."

"D'larayn?" I echo. "What does it mean?" But their tense silence only amplified the denial plaguing me.

I snap back to reality, skin still steaming where ivory flames had danced moments before. How long had I been standing here, lost in the past? Water continues gushing down the drain, wasting gallons.

I twist the faucet off and grab a towel, drying my tingling hands. D'larayn... that strange word suddenly pulses with significance, just beyond my mental grasp. I kick myself for not digging deeper when I first heard it during my identity crisis. My adoptive parents had dismissed it as meaningless in their desperation for a child.

A complicated mix of irritation and understanding washes over me. I know exactly how badly someone can want family. But at what price comes willful ignorance? What uncomfortable truths have I been avoiding that might now explain what's happening to me?

I snatch my laptop with trembling fingers, anticipation twisting my insides into knots. I type the strange syllables into the search bar, pulse hammering in my throat. Results populate instantly, making my heart skip several beats.

D'larayn (dee-luh-rayn)—an ethereal figure prophesied to bring salvation and retribution—to bestow protection by delivering the wicked to justice while lifting up the persecuted...a savior.

I freeze, stunned into silence as puzzle pieces click into place. Rhyland's cryptic prophecy talk, my weird new glow-stick hands—

It all connects back to my mysterious origins, shrouded in secrecy, back to this single word scrawled on paper beside my hospital bassinet. It was a message spanning decades, waiting for me to finally understand when the time was right.

I inhale slowly, standing at the crossroads of past and future as everything converges on this bombshell revelation. The salvation bringer...a savior... D'larayn. This isn't coincidence—the universe is screaming my true identity, apparently destined for something way bigger than DNA research and lousy dating choices.

Great. Just what I needed—a cosmic job description I never applied for.

Rhyland

42

The harsh light stabs my eyes as consciousness returns, revealing a hellscape carved from nightmares—walls scarred with ancient symbols and dried blood, telling stories of decades of torment. Rusted chains dangle from the ceiling like metal serpents, hungry for flesh. In the corner, a decaying desk and chair rot in the filth, forgotten relics of humanity.

Sickly yellow bulbs flicker overhead, barely pushing back the suffocating darkness. Our chains bite deep into already mangled flesh, suspending us with arms stretched high, wounds never given a chance to heal. My feet have gone numb against the ice-cold concrete that leaches whatever warmth remains in my body.

Erik hangs beside me in this godforsaken pit, beaten to a bloody pulp. The constant rattle of our chains creates a twisted rhythm, marking time in this forgotten hell. Days? Weeks? I've lost all fucking track of how long we've been buried alive down here.

These Brotherhood bastards are relentless, breaking bones and tearing flesh to crush our will, beating us unconscious, then starving us until hallucinations dance at the edges of our vision. But we're not giving these fuckers the satisfaction. We cling to sanity with bloody fingernails, memories of better times keeping the madness at bay.

Thoughts of Danica burn through the darkness like a beacon—her silky chestnut hair, that intoxicating honey-spice scent, those golden eyes that see straight through to my soul. I replay every moment with her, a lifeline when the darkness threatens to swallow me whole.

For her, I'll endure this fucking nightmare. Once we break free, we're bringing unholy vengeance down on the Brotherhood and their psychotic leader—no mercy, no survivors.

Our incomplete bond tortures me, keeping her voice just beyond my reach—I strain against the void, desperate to touch her soul, to let my angel know we'll make this right.

Weakened in this hellhole, I've been fighting to shatter the psychic barrier containing us, to send a desperate SOS to Adrian that we're still breathing. I dig deep into my reserves, channeling everything I have left into breaking through. Adrian is our only shot at salvation before we're completely fucked.

Then, in the pitch blackness, a flicker. Subtle but unmistakable, the ancient blood connection between us pulses to life. For just a heartbeat, it's there—my signal punching through the void. Hope hits me like a shot of pure adrenaline, more intoxicating than the richest blood.

The connection to Adrian snaps like a frayed thread, leaving me hollow and adrift. Stranded without my mate's touch—it's a gut punch of pure agony, rage and desperation clawing through me at this fucking helplessness. Every second without her is torture worse than anything these sadistic bastards could inflict. Powerless to shield her from death, circling like a vulture.

Does she feel me fighting to get back to her? Or is she cursing my name, believing I abandoned her by choice? That thought cuts deeper than any blade they've carved into my flesh.

Soon, though, angel, I'll feel your soft skin trembling beneath me again. Not a goddamn chance—not even an army of demons will keep us apart! And when I return to you and drown in those golden eyes, we're sealing our fate forever.

My resolve hardens like forged steel, my purpose crystallizing through the pain. Whether I have to tear this place apart with my bare hands or burn it to fucking ashes, we're claiming our vengeance and seizing our destiny!

In the crushing darkness, I call Dani's name silently, a desperate prayer for her to stay strong and survive.

Consciousness flickers like a dying flame, coming and going in waves of agony. But I know enough to realize Erik and I have been rotting in this hellhole far too long. I turn to my brother, barely clinging to life, and rasp, "Erik... say something, goddamn it!"

He strains against his chains. "Still breathing, brother."

Every attempt to shift even an inch against these restraints sends fresh fire through my ravaged muscles. "I tried reaching Adrian," I force through gritted teeth, "but I'm running on empty."

He nods grimly, confirming he hit the same impenetrable wall.

Gunfire explodes through the silence without warning, ricocheting off stone walls like thunder. Harsh voices cut through the chaos as blinding light stabs into our darkness. The heavy iron door groans open, and like a vision from delirium, a familiar silhouette materializes—Lucian.

I squint against the blinding light, my ravaged eyes burning after weeks in darkness. "Lucian?" My voice emerges as a ragged growl, throat cracked and bleeding. Is this real, or just another hallucination before they kill us?

Lucian slashes through our chains with brutal efficiency, severing the iron that's become one with our flesh. As the final shackle breaks, I crash to the filthy floor, the chains hitting stone with a deafening clang. A surge of savage hope floods my system—our odds of survival just skyrocketed.

Lucian stares down at my broken body, whistling low. "Well, well, well! If it isn't the Torture Tourism Package's most valued customers! Heard you dipshits got yourselves gift-wrapped for the bad guys. Had to play Rescue Ranger Extreme!" He snorts dramatically. "Adrian sent out his magical vampire Morse code—which, by the way, super annoying at 3 AM—so I've been combing through every blood-soaked villain lair in a hundred-mile radius looking for you sorry sacks of shit."

My gut twists when I realize I've been wasting critical energy on failed telepathic distress calls when Adrian had already alerted Lucian. The sounds of battle rage outside—metal clashing against metal, punctuated by agonized screams. Adrian must be tearing through the compound guards.

Erik collapses against his restraints, a rasping sound of relief escaping his throat as Lucian grabs his mangled arm to haul him upright. Fresh adrenaline floods my system when Lucian extends his hand to me next—our fucking salvation has arrived.

I struggle to my feet, swaying but fueled by pure vengeance. "Ambushed and dumped in this fucking hellhole." My fists clench until blood seeps between my fingers, rage overpowering pain.

"Time to make like my ex-girlfriend's vibrator and buzz the fuck outta here," Lucian announces, glancing nervously over his shoulder. "Those Brotherhood cock-waffles will be swarming back any second." His face contorts with disgust. "So move those tortured asses unless you want to be their personal fuck-piñatas for another week."

We emerge into hell itself. The night air thick with burnt flesh and dark magic. Adrian stands like an avenging demon at the epicenter, ancient power crackling blue through his hands. His words split reality itself.

Brotherhood fodder collapse into smoldering husks around him. Black smoke spirals skyward from their corpses. His eyes blaze with murderous intent, face carved from marble.

His roar shatters the night. Magic tears through armor and bone, painting the ground red. Heads explode in fountains of gore. The stench is overwhelming, but survival doesn't wait for weak stomachs.

"MOVE!" Adrian's voice booms through the chaos. "CAR! NOW!"

His magic rages around us like a shield of death as we fight toward freedom.

Two more robed zealots spot us and charge, blades raised for blood.

Lucian's gun barks twice, sharp and decisive. "Sorry boys, but this ain't your lucky day! Consider this your severance package—emphasis on sever!" The rounds punch through their skulls with wet cracks, adding fresh corpses to the collection.

Lucian grabs me, practically carrying my broken body toward our getaway vehicle. Just as escape seems within reach, thundering footsteps announce a horde of pissed-off reinforcements closing in.

I collapse into the backseat, lungs on fire. Erik crashes beside me as Adrian launches himself into the passenger seat. Lucian hurries into the driver seat, as he slams the accelerator.

The car launches forward like a missile, leaving broken bodies and furious screams in our wake. One glance back reveals the shit-storm we've unleashed—a pack of Brotherhood zealots charging after us, weapons glinting in the darkness as they scramble for their vehicles like rabid dogs...

Tires howling, Lucian tears onto the mountain road, engine roaring like a beast from hell. The side mirror shows two black SUVs ripping around the compound's curve, headlights piercing the night like demon eyes.

"Well fuck me sideways, these persistent pricks are gaining!" Lucian stomps the gas pedal through the floor.

We surge ahead, but my tortured body can barely process the chaos. One SUV weaves alongside us, armed bastards aiming.

"Nuh-uh, not in my movie, assholes!" Lucian cranks the wheel hard, ramming our pursuer's vehicle.

Metal shrieks as both cars slam together. Lucian wrestles the wheel one-handed while drawing his Glock. "Time for some extreme driver's ed!" Through open windows, he pumps three rounds point-blank into the driver's skull.

The SUV spins out, flipping in a shower of sparks. "That's one for Team Awesome! How's that for a driver's test, dickwads?" Lucian howls.

But more circle us like wolves. Fury ignites in my veins, burning away weakness. My eyes blaze as I channel raw power, telekinetically hurling another SUV off the cliff. Their screams fade into the abyss.

"Hot damn! The torture-spa treatment didn't dull your edge!" Lucian cackles.

We dodge flaming wreckage, freedom just across the old stone bridge. Suddenly, the lead vehicle pulls even with us. Through its window, a rifle barrel aims straight at Lucian's face...

"Not today, assholes." Eyes burning, I unleash a devastating blast as gunfire erupts...The SUV disintegrates, cartwheeling through the air in an explosion of twisted metal before plummeting into the darkness below.

Lucian whoops loudly, swerving us clear of the plummeting wreckage. His laughter rings with unleashed chaos while I slump back, the brief burst of power fading. Up ahead, the tarmac finally comes into view, my sleek jet awaiting, its lines silvered alluringly by moonlight—a sanctuary worth fighting through hell to reach.

With a ragged shout of relief, Lucian spins us into a smoking drift onto the open runway. We barrel from the bullet-riddled sedan just as the remaining Brotherhood vehicles scream around the final bend. Lucian shouts furious threats while hustling us toward the lowered entry plank, where the pilot gestures wildly.

As the hatch seals close with a bone-deep hiss, euphoric relief crashes over me. Now safely inside, the jet engines ignite in sequence as we stagger into the plush cabin on unsteady legs.

Lucian's eyes burn with savage intensity as he screams at the terrified pilot, "Get this metal bird flying before those psychotic cocksuckers turn us into their personal leather collection! Move it or I swear I'll fly this thing myself—and trust me, nobody wants that!"

The engines unleash hell's fury, G-forces crushing me back into expensive leather as we thunder down the runway. The jet claws for altitude with desperate speed, finally putting those murderous bastards in our rearview for good.

The adrenaline crash hits, leaving me fucking drained. I look at Lucian and Adrian, my voice raw with emotion. "Thanks for pulling our asses out of that hellhole. You both walked straight into the fire for us."

Lucian smirks, tossing me a blood bag like a twisted party favor. "Thought you drama queens might need a pick-me-up! Got a whole vampire juice bar back there when you're ready for seconds!" His smartass comment pulls a weary grin from my battered face.

I drink deeply, dark power seeping into my ravaged muscles. As strength trickles back, I grill Lucian about Danica with desperate intensity.

He confirms she's safe, showed up at Karma looking for me three weeks ago. I collapse back, relief flooding my system like a drug. But we're still trapped in this metal tube for ten more fucking hours—an eternity when my mate faces danger without me.

I need to get to Danica to ensure her safety and explain why I disappeared like a ghost. To salvage our future before it shatters beyond saving.

My body aches to hold her, to beg forgiveness and taste the sweetness of her once more. Instead, I stare through the window, willing this damn jet to tear through time and space keeping us apart.

Soon, angel, I swear viciously. Hold on just a little longer...I'm coming to claim what's mine.

Danica

43

Three fucking weeks without a word from Rhyland. That gutless coward bailed, leaving me to sweep up my shattered heart alone. I let him see parts of me nobody else has ever glimpsed. Our connection was raw, visceral, unexplainable.

Now I'm suffocating. He fed me that soulmate bullshit about withering without each other. Is this what he meant—this slow death as half of me turns into a ghost?

I hate myself for swallowing his intoxicating lies, for falling under his spell. Disgusted that I let his body bring me to heights I never knew existed. With every passing minute, I loathe myself more for surrendering my independence to his toxic version of love.

Somehow, I peel myself off the kitchen floor, desperate to numb these raw, bleeding thoughts. I can't keep spiraling in this black hole forever. I can practically hear Emily's disapproving voice, horrified at how quickly I turned into just another Rhyland junkie, desperate for my next fix...

My treacherous body still responds to memories of him—his commanding presence, that wicked mouth. Even now, remembering his whispered filth makes heat flood my face.

How do you move on when someone's carved out a chunk of your soul?

As brutal as this withdrawal is, I have to power through it. Because with Rhyland gone, I'm facing whatever's hunting me completely alone. Whatever triggered these freaky powers has painted a target on my back.

Some destiny this turned out to be.

Scalding shower water stings my skin but fails to wash away the dread of this strange power brewing inside me. I dress quickly and down bitter coffee, hoping routine might calm my frayed nerves. It doesn't.

I've become a hermit, hiding from Azrael while inventing excuses to avoid Playful Pint, where supernatural eyes might detect what I'm becoming. At least I can still function at the lab.

My research has uncovered ancient languages connected to celestial beings with script similar to my mysterious note, but translations remain elusive. Do angels actually exist, or are they elaborate myths? As a scientist, I should demand evidence, but this mystery challenges everything I thought I knew.

I chase answers in endless circles, unable to crack this supernatural code. What am I transforming into? How do I control powers I don't understand? My logical mind rebels against this bizarre reality upending my existence.

Thoughts of Rhyland haunt me constantly. His face appears whenever I close my eyes, and memories trigger that now-familiar burning energy. My hands glow white-hot as heartache pulses through me in relentless waves.

Desperate, I call my parents again, hoping they might finally explain the cryptic note left with me. They remain as clueless as ever.

"We wish we knew more, honey," Dad says helplessly.

"Why not visit this weekend?" Mom suggests. "Might clear your hea d..."

"Extra night shifts," I lie, unwilling to burden them with supernatural dangers.

"The invitation is open if you change your mind," Mom says gently. "We're here if you need anything."

I end the call no closer to understanding my origins.

Emily's loud knock announces her arrival. I greet her with overwhelming gratitude for enduring my pathetic Rhyland obsession—every embarrassing detail of my emotional rollercoaster.

At least someone hasn't abandoned me.

When I show Em the mysterious note again, she rolls her eyes dramatically. "Girl, you need to drop this obsession. Whatever cryptic bullshit this note's trying to say, it doesn't change who you are."

I sigh heavily. She just doesn't get it. This burning need to understand what's happening to me. "I just want answers, Em."

"And you know what they say about curiosity..." she prompts with that signature devilish grin of hers, already trying to steer us away from dangerous territory.

I stare blankly. "What?"

Em snorts, her eyes gleaming with wicked humor. "Best way to get over one man is to get under another!" She tosses her rainbow hair. "Screw that disappearing dick-wad out of your system with some fresh meat! Nothing clears emotional constipation like a good orgasm from someone new."

I can't help but smile despite myself. If only it were that simple—just hop on some random dude and magically forget the man who turned my world upside down.

"That easy, huh?" I sigh. "After what we had, casual hookups seem kinda...bland."

Emily makes a gagging sound. "Oh, please! Because he's got some enchanted cock that makes you see Jesus? Ejaculates liquid enlightenment?" She jabs a finger at me. "Don't let some ghosting asshole become your sexual benchmark! You're too badass for that crap."

I appreciate Em's colorful pep talk, even if we're opposites in handling heartbreak. She can disconnect emotions like flipping a switch. Meanwhile, I'm drowning in feelings I can't escape. Letting go of Rhyland seems impossible—he's my lifeline in this supernatural storm.

Seeing the worry beneath Em's snarky exterior, I force a casual tone. "You're right. He's not worth the mental real estate—"

My hollow words don't fool either of us. Em yanks me into a fierce hug with an exasperated groan.

"Enough moping!" she declares, pulling back. "We're hitting the town tonight, and I'm finding you a rebound so hot he'll burn that man-shaped hole right out of your vagina. Time to party like we used to, bitch!"

Her crude enthusiasm coaxes a reluctant smile from me, though anxiety spikes at the thought. Lucian's warnings about staying hidden echo in my mind. He made it crystal clear nowhere was safe right now, especially after Azrael's attack...

But part of me is desperate to break free from this self-imposed prison. I refuse to let fear control my entire existence. I want my damn life back!

What's the worst that could happen? Besides death, kidnapping, or accidentally setting the club on fire with my new jazz hands..

Sensing my wavering resolve, Emily softens her approach. "Look, it's fine if you're not ready to bang your way to freedom yet. But sometimes you gotta swagger with fake big-dick energy until it becomes real. Get me? And I'll be right there to crush any creep's balls if they try anything sketchy!"

Her crude encouragement fans my dying ember of defiance. I'm so damn tired of cowering in this apartment. I need to reclaim my life on my terms instead of letting darkness beat me into submission.

Emily's right—I have to claw my way out of this pit before it swallows what's left of my spirit. I can't stay locked away, merely existing in this frozen state. Fuck that, and fuck him! Whatever lurks in the darkness, I'm done passively waiting for answers that might never come. Tonight, I'll hit the town with Em and find distraction, however temporary. Rhyland ghosted me without explanation, but I refuse to do the same to myself.

I square my shoulders and meet Emily's hopeful gaze. "Let's fuck this town up tonight." Her answering grin melts the last of my hesitation. Tonight, I'm channeling that fearless woman who commands every room she enters.

It's time I reclaim my light, mysterious powers be damned.

If Azrael shows his face, maybe I'll just barbecue his ass and call it a night.

DANICA

44

After five shots and three rum and Cokes, I'm feeling fan-fucking-tastic. Instead of sulking at home like a wounded animal, I embraced Emily's eloquent life advice—get absolutely shit-faced!

We avoided Karma's cursed ass and hit up the cozier Playful Pint instead—John's behind the bar, which calms my jittery nerves. A quick rundown about Azrael's attack, and he immediately had my back.

This place feels like home—familiar faces getting sloppy, awkward couples grinding on the dance floor. Weekend karaoke is always a beautiful disaster. Right now, some wasted blonde is murdering "Heart of Glass," missing every note but living her best tone-deaf life. You've gotta respect that level of delusion!

The bar's small enough that I can easily keep tabs on Emily once she inevitably commandeers the mic. She'll be screeching 80's power ballads within the hour, guaranteed to be the messiest bitch here by midnight. But her relentless push to get me out was exactly the kick in the ass I needed to break my Rhyland-obsession cycle. Time to get wrecked and stop overthinking every damn thing!

Emily giggles beside me, thrilled to be my drunk spirit guide. "Isn't this, like, way better than rotting in your apartment like a sad corpse?" she slurs, spilling half her drink.

"Abso-fuckin-lutely!" I agree, downing my cocktail. Just saying out loud that I refuse to keep pining over that man feels like removing a fifty-pound weight.

Emily howls with laughter. "That's my girl! Plenty of dick in the sea!" She makes an obscene jerking motion, eyebrows dancing suggestively.

I scan the bar through watery eyes—the usual mix of sad old drunks hypnotized by sports and antisocial twenty-somethings treating their phones like oxygen tanks.

"Not sure Magic Mike is hiding among this collection of future liver transplant candidates," I snort as Emily nearly shoots tequila through her nose.

"We can polish these turds!" she insists.

For once, I genuinely don't give a single fuck...I'm just blissfully, stupidly free.

After Emily traumatizes everyone with her banshee rendition of Broadway classics, I reluctantly call it a night before we're too hammered to function. I wave goodbye to John as we stumble, cackling, into the cool night air.

Maybe normal life isn't completely out of reach after all.

"Let me drive you two disasters home. You shouldn't be wandering around wasted," John calls after us, concern etched on his face.

"Aww, you're such a mother hen!" Emily slurs, blowing him a sloppy kiss. "We're fine! Gonna dance with the stars all the way home!" She demonstrates by attempting—and failing—at some TikTok dance move right there on the sidewalk.

I shoot John an apologetic grin through my drunken giggles. "Thanks, but we need the fresh air. It's just a few blocks."

He reluctantly nods. We turn and continue our intoxicated pilgrimage under the full moon's glow.

His worry is sweet, but tonight is my middle finger to caution.

Arm-in-arm, Em and I zigzag through shadowy side streets, howling with laughter at our uncoordinated stumbling.

The cold night air clears my head slightly, but we're still a hot mess. Given the recent supernatural fuckery in my life, this probably isn't my most brilliant move. But I'm done hiding in my apartment! Emily whoops loudly beside me, the perfect soundtrack to my rebellion.

Yet even liquid courage can't fully silence my paranoia as we weave forward. That prickling sensation of being watched... Could it be Rhyland? That's definitely the tequila talking—or worse, Azrael hunting me again?

I stop abruptly, the air suddenly feeling electric. "Em, hold up..."

She crashes into me with a drunk snort but sobers at my tone. I scan the darkness, fear crawling up my spine. Friend or foe watching from the shadows? I clench my fists, ready to face whatever's out there instead of running...

The silence stretches endlessly as I wait for something to emerge. Nothing does. With a frustrated sigh, I force myself forward, supporting Em's increasingly boneless form.

I can't keep jumping at shadows or hoping Rhyland will swoop in to save me. The hard truth is I'm on my own now, for better or worse—time to step out from his shadow and reclaim my life.

Maybe I'm not ready to "hop on fresh dick" as Emily so eloquently suggested. But tonight's escape from isolation feels like progress—my first wobbly step toward rediscovering myself. I chose life over hiding.

I might be drunk, but I'm done being afraid.

Finally, Emily and I squeeze into the elevator, its walls seemingly closing in on my spinning head. I slump against the cool metal for support. At my door, I fumble drunkenly with the keys, missing the lock repeatedly.

Emily cackles at my pathetic attempts, slurring something about "hole finding skills." After what feels like years, the lock finally clicks. I drag Emily's limp form inside, keys clattering across the counter.

"Bedtime, you boozy bitch!" I announce, hauling her fully clothed to the guest room. I flip off the light and shut the door on her incoherent mumbling.

Alone at last, I stumble toward the harsh kitchen light. My stomach feels like a hollow pit, gnawing itself from the inside. Need to sober up before I paint my bathroom with vomit. The microwave clock blurs sickeningly—shit, it's already 2 AM? How long were we out destroying our livers?

I chug water straight from the tap, then raid the fridge for anything remotely edible. Three-day-old Chinese takeout passes inspection. I shove it in the microwave as punishment for my excessive drinking, tapping impatiently while it rotates.

As sobriety creeps in like an unwelcome guest, doubts follow close behind. Was it wise to wander around at night, given everything that's happened? I angrily silence that voice. I refuse to question my independence or let supernatural assholes dictate my choices anymore!

A sudden chill creeps up my spine as I lean against the counter. Before I can process the feeling, I sense a presence lurking in the shadows. My heart stutters as I slowly turn.

I gasp as Rhyland materializes before me, his powerful arms wrapping possessively around my waist with familiar heat. Shock and rage explode through me simultaneously. I struggle against his iron grip, fighting to form words.

"What the fu—?"

His hand cups my face with impossible tenderness while self-loathing darkens his features. "Gods, I've missed you... I'm so sor—"

White-hot fury consumes me. My palm connects with his cheek in a resounding crack that echoes through the apartment. He growls low, but I strike again before he can recover. My handprint blazes red on his skin, my own pain irrelevant.

I step back, shaking with rage, and scream, "How fucking dare you just show up here!"

Three weeks of silence, and he thinks he can waltz back in like noth-

ing happened? Not in this lifetime.

Rhyland remains silent as I raise my hand for a third slap. With supernatural speed, he catches my wrist mid-air, his grip an unbreakable steel trap. He yanks me against his hard body, my thundering heartbeat the only barrier between us.

A dark chuckle vibrates through his chest. "Still my feisty angel..." His voice drops to that hypnotic rumble as he demands, "Just listen for a moment—"

"Fuck your explanations, Rhyland! You disappear for weeks, then materialize, expecting me to heel?" I spit, rage pouring out unchecked.

He forces my arms behind my back, pinning me against the counter with effortless strength. I struggle against his immovable frame but can't break free.

"I'm not leaving again, baby," his arousal already pressing insistently against me. His large hand tangles in my hair, yanking my head back to meet his electric gaze.

"You will submit, Angel...one way or another." His hard body grinds against me, trapping me between his unmistakable desire and the cold marble. Fury battles with unwanted need as he lowers those perfect lips toward mine.

His skilled tongue teases my clenched mouth relentlessly, triggering muscle memory of far more intimate connections. My treacherous body ignites, liquid heat pooling between my thighs despite my anger. How I've missed his taste, his possessive worship of my body...

Unable to fight both him and myself, I part my lips with a desperate moan. His answering growl reverberates through me as his tongue claims mine in a sensual dance. My mind short-circuits under the assault...rational thought, righteous anger, everything dissolves in the inferno between us.

I hate him. I want him. I hate that I want him.

RHYLAND

45

Her lips taste just as I remembered—sweet like the angel she is. Danica is a drug I can never get enough of. Knowing she would be furious, her anger only arouses me more.

My angelic beauty fears abandonment—trauma that surfaces from her past. Vanishing without explanation reawakened those wounds. But her intensity confirms how deeply she feels for me.

Watching her unleash that feisty spirit, slapping me with wild abandon, sets my blood on fire. Raw need surges through my veins. I want to devour her whole.

The moment we landed in Seattle, I tracked her scent to Playful Pint. Like a predator, I watched from the shadows as she and Emily stumbled out. I followed at a distance while she weaved her way home.

Now I'm desperate to claim every inch of her again. I'll overwhelm her with pleasure until she's writhing and begging for me. No part of her will go untouched or unsatisfied.

I ravage her mouth, feeling her heart thunder against my chest. She pulls back, breathing hard, skin flushed with arousal.

Those golden eyes flash as she whispers, "I hate you..." But her body tells a different story.

I know it's not real hate—only pain from my absence. I laugh darkly and capture her lips again."Hate me then, baby," I purr, "while I worship your body."

She fights it at first, but soon her mouth moves desperately with mine, weeks of need pouring out.

I thrust my tongue deep, swallowing her moan like the sweetest blood. My hands roam her curves, grabbing that perfect ass and kneading until she whimpers against my mouth. She clings to me like I'm her oxygen. Every sound she makes as I stoke her desire drives me wild. Her body awakens under my touch, begging for more.

Then I see it—an ugly purple wound on her throat, like some beast tried to mark what's mine. Rage explodes at the thought of another's touch on my mate.

I struggle to control my voice as I demand, "What. Happened."

Her chest heaves against mine as she breathes out one word—"Azrael."

Red rage explodes behind my eyes. I force down a snarl, trying to maintain control as she looks up at me, fear flickering in those golden eyes. I lean in, running my tongue over the wound. The flesh still burns with hellfire's taint—that unmistakable dark power that corrupts everything it touches. Azrael's growing stronger, becoming a threat I can't fucking ignore.

I lap at the mark gently, feeling her flinch then melt as pleasure overtakes pain. Her body surrenders to my touch, accepting the mix of agony and ecstasy.

"It hurts...hurts so bad," she whimpers, vulnerable yet unafraid of my savage need. "Won't stop burning."

"I know, Angel," I breathe against her throat, "I'll make it stop. No one marks what's mine. You'll only wear mine."

My fingers dig possessively into her neck as I claim her mouth. I drag my tongue down, tasting every inch of her sweet skin.

"I never abandoned you," I admit against her ear before nipping it. "Those Brotherhood fuckers trapped me in the Appalachians while I hunted for answers."

My hand works urgently at her shorts, yanking down the zipper. I hook my thumbs in the waistband and panties, slowly dragging them down those perfect curves until they pool at her feet.

She arches that delicate throat against my mouth with a moan. "Trapped? What happened in the mountains?" Her breathless voice makes my cock throb harder.

Lust radiates off her alcohol-loosened body in waves. I need her to understand I never chose to leave—that I'm here now, desperate to claim every inch of her. I want to fuck her so deep she forgets every name but mine.

I trace my tongue down her throat, savoring her taste before reaching her ear.

"Should've warned you before I left. Got ambushed and taken hostage, couldn't get back to you. I was trying to decode the prophecy, Angel. To understand what you're facing."

Her body trembles against mine, breath catching as her fingers tangle in my hair, those full lips demanding more. I rip her shirt off in one savage motion, revealing perfect tits barely contained by black lace. Her raw beauty hits me like a physical force. She's a fucking masterpiece, proof that divine power exists.

I may not know what darkness stalks her future, but I swear to guard her with my life, cherish her soul like the treasure it is, and stand between her and any threat until my final breath.

A growl rumbles from my chest at the sight of those curves. Her delicate hands slide under my shirt, and I tear it off, desperate for her touch. She explores every inch of my tattooed muscles, those golden eyes devouring my body before fixing hungrily between my legs. Pride surges through me—this goddess is mine alone. No other man will ever taste this pleasure.

How the fuck did I get this lucky?

My cock strains painfully against denim at her teasing touch. She attacks my zipper while I unhook her bra, our tongues battling for dominance as we devour each other's taste.

Her bra falls away, those perfect tits bouncing free. I grab them roughly, possessively, working her nipples until they peak under my fingers. Her whimpers of pleasure driving me wild.

She stares into my eyes, biting that tempting lip as her heart races. "I'm such an idiot," she whispers, voice like silk against my skin.

I capture her gaze, pouring every ounce of intensity into my words. "No, baby. Don't ever say that. You couldn't have known."

I grip her chin, "Listen to me, Angel—I'll never walk away from you willingly. No force in hell or heaven can keep me from coming back to you."

If her heart stops beating, mine dies with it. Without her, I have no reason to draw breath, no thoughts beyond the need to possess her completely. Her beauty consumes me like a fever, the mere thought of her touch driving me fucking wild. Those scars from her past may run deep, but I swear to spend eternity healing them with my love until death takes us both.

I crush my mouth to hers, pouring every ounce of pent-up need into the kiss. My tongue claims her thoroughly, marking her with passion that's been burning me alive. She feels my desperate hunger as I pour weeks of separation into this moment. Her body trembles against mine, telling me she's ached for this as badly as I have.

My pants hit the floor with a heavy thud. Her hands slide into my boxers, wrapping around my rock-hard cock with delicious pressure. I pull her closer, fingers tangling in that silky hair.

A growl rumbles from my chest as she explores lower, cupping my balls until I'm shaking with savage need.

She tastes like fucking paradise until she suddenly pulls back, those golden eyes swimming with doubt.

"I thought..." she pants, tears threatening to spill, "I thought you'd abandoned me for good."

The pain in her voice cuts like a blade, raw with fear and old wounds I never meant to reopen.

I cradle her face in my hands, stroking that soft skin. "Dani, I'm sorry I ever made you doubt us," I say as our eyes lock, regret burning in my chest. "You're my whole fucking world now," I breathe against her lips, claiming her with words and touch. "You're mine and only mine, just like I belong to you. Nothing in any realm will tear us apart again."

My gaze devours her lips before drowning in those golden eyes. She's fucking perfection incarnate, a divine gift I don't deserve.

"Dani...I need you," I whisper roughly. "I will always need you, baby."

Since that first night at Karma, she's consumed me like a fever—this primal hunger mixed with soul-deep love that threatens to devour us both.

Her love blazes through me as I claim those sweet lips. Her delicate fingers tear at my briefs, dragging them down my legs. I kick them away with a groan as our bare skin finally meets.

She grips my cock *hard*, and my hands slam against the counter, caging her between my arms as she works me. Every stroke of her hand sends lightning through my veins. Each kiss brings me closer to unleashing weeks of pent-up need.

"Let me pleasure you, please?"

Holy fuck. Her sexy voice begging to taste me sets my blood on fire. Raw desire surges through me like a tidal wave, my cock hardening painfully.

"Begging for it, Angel?" I growl darkly. "Want me to fill that pretty mouth?"

She knows exactly what her pleading does to me. Just hearing her beg ignites a hunger I can barely control. The urge to give her exactly what she wants sends un-checked desire through my veins. She smirks wickedly before pressing those perfect lips to my chest, marking me with scorching kisses and teasing licks.

Her mouth burns like fire against my skin. I stand transfixed as she works her way down my body, exploring every inch at an agonizing pace that has me ready to explode.

My cock aches with need at what's coming.

My breathing turns ragged with mounting desire. "On your knees. Now," I command.

She drops to her knees before me like a supplicant, back pressed against the kitchen island while my hands brace on the counter above her head. Those golden eyes worship me like a dark god. My cock stands massive and proud between us, harder than forged steel and weeping. Pre-cum drips heavily to the floor, marking my territory.

"See what you do to me, angel?" I growl as her eyes devour every inch.

That pink tongue darts out to wet her lips before she wraps both hands around my base, guiding me toward her waiting mouth. Her eyes widen at my size, that tiny hand struggling to circle my thick girth. She gasps as she explores me, making my grin grow wider. I'm far beyond average, and her reaction feeds my primal pride. Every stroke of those delicate fingers drives me fucking wild.

A feral groan tears from my chest as her lips brush my cock before taking me in. That hot tongue exploring me forces me to grip the counter for control. I tangle my fingers in her hair, desperate for more as she sucks me deeper into paradise.

"Fuck... baby." I pant as her silky mouth engulfs my cock. I tighten my grip and thrust deeper, feeling her gag around me.

She starts to pull back, but I hold her firm, demanding, "Relax that throat, Angel. Breathe through your nose. You'll take every inch like the good girl you begged to be."

Her throat relaxes, and I'm gasping, moaning as she swallows me deeper. "That's it... good fucking girl," I choke out.

I gather her silky hair into a makeshift handle, gripping tight as I thrust harder into that wet heat.

I watch entranced as she takes me. "Look at me while you choke on my cock." I yank her head back with her hair.

Those honey eyes lock onto mine, blazing with desperate desire. Tears stream down her face as I pound her throat raw, drool dripping from those stretched lips.

Her perfect tits bounce with each thrust as I lose myself to pure fucking ecstasy.

"That's it, baby. Take it like the good girl you are," I growl.

I catch her hand sneaking between her legs. "Don't you dare, sweetheart," I snarl. "Your pleasure belongs to me alone."

I unleash my full power, my heavy balls slapping her chin as I ravage that hot throat. Her desperate gags and moans drive me to pound her face harder, faster. I brutally fuck her mouth, drawing out those sweet choking sounds as she struggles to handle my savage pace.

The pressure builds until I can't hold back. Every muscle locks as my cock pulses.

"Fuck!" Her throat will be wrecked when I'm done using that pretty mouth.

She surrenders entirely. My head falls back with a roar. I hold her still, refusing to let her escape even when she fights against the intensity. She chokes and gags as I pour down her throat, making sure she takes every last drop.

She collapses back gasping for air, my cum and her spit dripping onto marble as she trembles. My cock throbs with renewed hunger, desperate to claim her deeper.

My beautiful angel's torment is far from over. Soon she'll feel me claiming every inch of her body.

Danica

46

I gag and choke on my knees, gasping for air as Rhyland leveled my face with his thick dick. His cum has seeped deep down, and the evidence of it drips down my chin. My pussy pulses and is drenched with desire as every inch of his hard, veiny cock rubbed my throat and the thrill of being so degraded.

No man has ever filled me like this before, and although I couldn't open my jaw wide enough to take him entirely, it only made the experience more erotic. I want him inside me, feeling every inch of him within me. He isn't done yet—still rock hard and poised for another round of relentless roughness.

I hastily try to wipe away the evidence of his orgasm off my lips, but he quickly grabs my hand and stops me.

His breath is heavy as he leans in close. "No, no, Angel. Every last drop."

He shoves my cum-coated fingers into my mouth, and I instinctively suck off the evidence. The bittersweetness of his taste sends a wave of arousal through me.

His hand wraps around my face, squeezing my cheeks so hard that my lips pucker. His other hand moves to the back of my head, bringing my face forward to meet his. His lips crash upon mine, penetrating deeper into my mouth as his molten, hot tongue explores his taste. I moan loudly onto his lips, savoring the taste of his arousal and desire.

Oh.

My.

God.

This man is pure filth!

I'm overcome with disgrace yet aching for more. His fierce dominance makes me so aroused, the evidence dripping down my inner thighs. He's like no one I've ever experienced, commanding and enticing all at once.

I moan in pleasure, my body trembling as his wicked kisses leave me desperate for more. His large, rough hand reaches the apex of my thigh, and he growls in appreciation when he feels how wet I am for him.

"Fuck..." His passionate voice ignites an even brighter flame inside me.

Two expert fingers go down to my slick desire and swirl around my swollen clit relentlessly, taking me ever closer to the edge of rapture.

I gasp loudly, feeling even more aroused with every passing second.

He moves his lips to my ear and whispers filthy words of promises, "Do you want me to fuck those naughty desires away? To fuck every filthy thought from that pretty head of yours?"

His words shoot straight to my core, making me shudder with need as I nod frantically.

"By the time I'm done, you'll forget everything but the feel of my cock stretching you open."

I'm beyond speech, trembling from the sheer force of his presence. My resistance crumbles like sand. He's lit a fire in me that threatens to consume everything—anger, pride, common sense. His absence nearly broke me, but I never realized how deep he'd gotten under my skin until now. Is this overwhelming magnetic pull between us... love?

Three weeks of silence and one touch reduces me to a quivering mess.

I'm so screwed. Literally and figuratively.

Every heartbeat syncs with his, as if he alone can resurrect my deadened spirit. These weeks without him have been hell, leaving me a hollow shell. Now his return floods life back into my veins. No other man could ever compare. I can't deny it anymore—this is love, transcending mere fate or coincidence. He owns every piece of me—mind, body, soul—and I never want this connection severed again.

His thick finger plunges into me, making me cry out. I'm helpless on the floor, back pressed against the cabinet, trembling thighs spread wide for his predatory gaze. My pussy pulses desperately, slick and swollen under his intense scrutiny. The vulnerability of my position—exposed and wanting—only heightens my arousal.

He kneels before me, one hand gripping my throat possessively while the other works me into a frenzy. His demanding lips crash into mine with raw hunger. My body coils tighter with each expert stroke.

"You want it rough, Angel?" He drives two fingers deep before withdrawing to tease my swollen clit. I writhe beneath him, climbing toward explosive release.

His grip on my throat tightens, making stars dance behind my eyes as my breath comes in gasps. He keeps thrusting his fingers with devastating precision, burying them to the knuckle before withdrawing with agonizing slowness.

He finds that perfect spot repeatedly, reducing me to desperate whimpers—keeping me balanced on the edge. I'm seconds from shattering, his intensity driving me toward sweet insanity. I need him to claim me completely until I scream my surrender.

"You're absolutely filthy, baby. I fucking love it when you fall apart like this."

This is definitely not how I expected this confrontation to go.

His skilled fingers dance along the edge of release I've been denied for weeks. His eyes burn with dangerous hunger as he watches me writhe helplessly beneath his touch, my control slipping away with each stroke.

My body winds impossibly tighter as I gasp for breath.

"So wet and tight for me. This pussy belongs to me alone."

His relentless teasing pushes me toward sweet oblivion until I can only whimper between thrusts, "Please..."

His eyes flash as his fingers plunge deeper. He pumps them with torturous slowness, wringing every drop of pleasure from my trembling body.

His wicked smile widens as that deep voice rumbles, "I love hearing you beg." He leans close, breath hot against my lips. "Make a filthy fucking mess on this floor."

He drives in harder and faster until I shatter completely, consumed by ecstasy. My eyes roll back as his fingers curl perfectly inside me, hitting that spot that makes me lose all control. I clench around him violently as a hot rush of liquid gushes from me, splashing onto the floor between us. The powerful jets pulse with each wave of pleasure, soaking us both as my release literally floods out of me. The orgasmic tsunami crashes through me endlessly until all I can do is moan brokenly in surrender, my thighs trembling uncontrollably in the growing puddle beneath us.

Holy shit. Who the hell knew I could come that hard? I've never squirted before in my life. So much for my righteous anger—it's currently pooling on my kitchen floor.

"Good girl," he pants, clearly pleased by the evidence of my complete undoing. Those two words, marking me as his willing pet, make me flush with renewed heat. His burning gaze devours the sight of my release spread across the kitchen floor.

A satisfied smirk curves his lips as he brings his glistening fingers to his mouth. He groans around them before claiming my lips in a possessive kiss.

His tongue claims my mouth thoroughly, making me taste myself on him. His grip tightens possessively as he speaks against my lips, "Sweet fucking hell, Angel. You taste like everything I've been starving for." The raw hunger in his voice makes me whimper.

Who the hell needs dignity when you can have mind-blowing orgasms instead?

Rhyland yanks me off the floor in one powerful motion. His muscular arms hoist me up as I lock my legs around his waist, clinging to him. His hand grips my bare ass while the other tangles in my hair, roughly pulling me against his solid chest. His demanding mouth claims mine as he carries me effortlessly toward the couch, our bodies fused. His hard length presses insistently against my stomach while my arousal slicks his abs. I'm desperate for him, addicted to his touch, and powerless against the raw magnetism of this man.

Will I ever get enough?

We crash onto the white couch as I straddle his powerful frame. His ravenous mouth devours me as his tongue invades mine. His hands find my aching nipples, giving them the attention they're screaming for. I arch into his touch as he sucks and tugs each sensitive peak, sending electric currents straight to my core.

This man knows my body better than I do, every secret spot that makes me tremble with need. He ignites fires within me that only he can extinguish, leaving me wetter than I thought possible. He grips my waist then seizes my ass with rough hands, kneading the flesh almost painfully as I moan shamelessly. He continues his assault on my breast, whispering filthy promises that only heighten my frenzy.

"You're gonna slide that greedy cunt onto my cock and ride it like the fucking goddess you are," he grumbles, his voice thick with lust. "Let me hear you scream while I ruin what's mine."

God, his words. His filthy, degrading talk sends shivers down my spine. I know I shouldn't crave it, but I can't help myself. I need more. He takes me with such primal intensity that I feel both utterly free and wholly owned as he ravages me.

He makes me feel worshipped and possessed, like his most precious treasure. His possessiveness ignites something primitive in me that can't be tamed.

Three weeks of righteous anger dissolved by his touch. I'm pathetic. Gloriously, blissfully pathetic.

My pussy throbs for him as I rock against the swollen head of his thick cock. His incredible size left me sore for days after our last encounter. But I don't care. I need his brutality. His savage thrusts take me so deep I'm physically rearranged by it. That's what I crave—not gentle lovemaking but wild, animalistic fucking that leaves me shattered and reborn.

I roughly seize his hair, yanking him closer as I grind against him. I'm dripping with need, desperate to impale myself on his length. I tease him by allowing just his tip to breach my entrance. He releases a strangled groan, his fingers digging bruisingly into my hips as he fights for control. The intricate black ink decorating his body ripples with tension—his neck arches as I drag my tongue up his corded throat.

He bucks upward, desperate for entry. I lift myself with a wicked smile, denying him what he craves.

I want him begging this time. His eyes burn into mine as a feral growl erupts from his chest, "Get that sweet pussy on my cock now." His voice is deadly. "Don't test me, Angel."

I remain motionless, savoring his restraint crumbling as I raise an eyebrow in defiance. I crash my mouth against his, biting his lip hard enough to taste blood. He groans deeply as he grinds against me with desperate intensity. Before either of us loses control, I pull away, torturing him further with my retreat.

"You think you can play with me? I promise you won't survive what comes next, sweetheart."

His voice drips with dark promise. I challenge him with a husky command—"Beg."

His response is immediate and brutal. Without warning, he grabs my hair, yanking my head back painfully as his massive cock slams into me. His punishing kiss smothers my scream of ecstasy as he pounds into me with savage intensity. His other hand grips my ass, forcing me deeper onto his length as I plead for more, moaning at his merciless invasion.

He tears his lips from mine, eyes blazing with possession. His rough voice cuts through my haze, "I don't beg, baby. I own every fucking inch of you." He emphasizes with a swipe of his tongue up my throat.

I wanted this domination. His commanding thrusts spear into me as I bounce on his hardness. He releases my hair, and I howl with pleasure as my head falls back in surrender. His guttural groans are devastatingly arousing, sending liquid heat coursing through me.

"You love being claimed by me, don't you? Let me hear those filthy screams as I fuck you senseless."

This is what I needed—to be completely owned, completely consumed.

His throbbing shaft stretches me to my limit, threatening to split me apart. I need him with desperate hunger. His merciless pounding drives me wild as my breasts bounce frantically between us.

"Rhy—" I gasp before his mouth crushes mine, swallowing my words.

He growls against my lips, "That's right, baby. Only one name leaves those lips—*mine*."

He feels incredible inside me that I'm losing my mind. The pleasure is too intense, too all-consuming. I match his savage rhythm, savoring every second of this delicious torture. His rough hands roam my body possessively, squeezing my breasts while his hot tongue teases my sensitive nipples. He's devouring me completely.

His cock swells impossibly larger with each brutal thrust. I feel my climax building to catastrophic levels. I grind against him frantically, craving more of his ruthless attention until I'm teetering on the edge of explosion.

He senses my approaching release as I tremble on the precipice, firmly grabs my hair at the nape and yanks me against him. His razor-sharp fangs pierce my throat, drawing a guttural moan from deep within me. I surrender to the forbidden blend of agony and ecstasy that electrifies every nerve ending. As the exquisite sensation of his teeth breaking my skin floods my veins like molten lava, I'm consumed by euphoria. My body goes slack as arousal rockets to heights I never knew existed. Everything becomes saturated with overwhelming pleasure, unlike anything I've ever known.

Rhyland's hands caress me tenderly as he drinks deeply.

Where Azrael's bite was caustic poison, Rhyland's is pure addiction—his bite sends waves of intoxicating pleasure coursing through me. I know I'll forever crave his savage intensity. The sensation is overwhelming as he deliberately slows, prolonging every second of this sweet torment.

He withdraws his mouth from my throat, keeping me impaled on his still-rigid length.

"Fuck, Angel. I need you. You're all I crave, and nothing else can satisfy this soul-deep hunger. I'm addicted to your body and every wicked pleasure it gives me."

I hover on the razor's edge of climax as he holds me motionless, denying my release.

I've never felt so consumed, so wholly possessed.

His voice turns primal and commanding, "Drink."

He produces a knife from nowhere—where the hell was he hiding that?—and draws it carefully across his throat. The intoxicating scent of citrus and musk fills my senses as crimson droplets escape the shallow wound.

I tremble as I realize this is the mating bond he's described. My body vibrates with need, my heart hammering against my ribs. As he holds me in place, I writhe desperately on his lap, craving friction. I'm quaking, breath coming in ragged gasps.

Thought becomes impossible—only sensation remains.

I press my lips to his throat, trailing my tongue along his skin. His blood pulses beneath my mouth, and he drops his head back with a groan as I taste him. A primal hunger awakens within me, and I latch onto his neck, drawing in my first taste of his essence. The flavor explodes across my tongue—rich and spicy like cinnamon—filling every cell with indescribable pleasure. I barely register his guttural moan as he continues to thrust deep inside me.

Pure ecstasy floods my system. His taste, his scent, his throbbing length—all overwhelm my senses simultaneously. My tongue eagerly laps at his crimson offering. His essence is addictive, and I crave more.

This is life-altering, but the pleasure is too intense to resist. He groans in ecstasy as I consume him. I know this will transform me forever, but nothing matters except this complete surrender. I drink his vitality as we both shudder with pleasure. He murmurs in some ancient tongue that sounds like pure carnal bliss.

A massive energy field envelops us, its power vibrating through our joined bodies. Initially, a gentle warmth spreads within me, like basking in sunlight. Then it erupts—raw power surges through every vein, illuminating each cell with blinding vitality. My entire being hums with newfound strength.

My awareness expands beyond physical limitations. I sense everything with supernatural clarity. Rhyland's breath scorches my skin, and each inhale I take feels impossibly pure, oxygen flooding my system with crystalline intensity. The world's hidden energies suddenly become visible.

This transcendent sensation...is this our bond completing? Or something more—some dormant power awakened by his ancient blood transforming me?

At first, I fear being consumed by it. Then Rhyland's powerful arms anchor me, his voice penetrating the roaring in my ears.

"That's enough, Angel," he commands, but I can't stop. It's too exquisite—too addictive.

His grip tightens painfully in my hair as he wrenches me away. "Enough, baby," he warns, our eyes locking in silent combat.

Whatever's happening to me, there's no going back now.

The atmosphere crackles with raw energy as he slams into me with increasing brutality. His ocean-blue eyes bore into mine as I struggle to match his savage pace. Our gazes remain locked even as our breathing turns ragged and desperate. I ride him frantically as he holds me close, our foreheads pressed together, his hand fisted in my hair, anchoring me to him, his other hand digging into my hip, controlling my movements as we share each desperate breath.

"*God*...Rhyland!" My inner muscles clamp down viciously, my senses impossibly heightened by our connection. The climax that rips through me is cataclysmic, shattering me from within. I scream his name as I convulse around his length.

"Christ, Dani—fuck!" His voice breaks, revealing the raw vulnerability beneath his dominant exterior. He erupts inside me with savage intensity, his primal roar of completion reverberating through my very soul and sending aftershocks of pleasure coursing through my trembling body as he floods me with his release.

In this moment, I am completely his—body, blood, and soul.

RHYLAND

47

We're tangled together, gasping for air after a mind-shattering climax. I hold Danica against me possessively, our sweat-slicked bodies fused as the aftershocks ripple through us.

She pulls back to search my face, those smoldering eyes full of questions. I brush her damp hair aside and claim that perfect mouth again, addicted to her taste. Our tongues battle desperately as we try to get even closer.

"Did you feel that?" she breathes against my lips between hungry kisses.

I nod, grinding my still-hard cock inside her. "Fuck yes, it was incredible."

I feel complete for the first time in my entire existence, bound to her in ways that silence my demons. I know she means the electric current that exploded between us when I spoke those ancient mating vows, and she drank greedily from my throat. Her mouth on my flesh sent heat through my veins, hurling me into an abyss of pleasure deeper than any I've known.

She gives me that innocent smile. "No, I meant the energy shift around us."

I draw a ragged breath, still coming down. A shockwave of raw energy burst from our joined bodies—her dormant power finally awakening in that moment of claiming. "I felt it, baby. You're mine now for eternity." I trace the curves of her face possessively.

She gazes up at me, eyes soft with wonder. "I know. It's like my heart is now an extension of yours."

I grin savagely, triumphant that she feels our profound connection. The instant our bond snapped into place, our souls fused into one unstoppable force. An unbreakable chain binding us forever.

"Was that the mating bond?" she asks, teeth grazing that swollen lip I just ravaged.

I drag my mouth down her neck, tasting her heated skin with my tongue, marking her with goosebumps. "Yes, and that was you tapping into your true power for the first time."

She stares up at me, confusion clouding those perfect eyes. "What do you mean?"

I take a deep breath, knowing we face a night of hard truths. But the time for secrets is over. My mate deserves to know everything.

I stroke her hair, my pulse quickening as I prepare to guide her into her destiny. "There are ancient secrets about who you really are, Angel. About what we've awakened together and the battle that's coming for us—"

Emily bursts from the bedroom and freezes dead in her tracks. We snap our heads toward her, catching that perfect deer-in-headlights expression—shock mixed with mortification.

Fucking perfect timing. She's walked in on her best friend riding my cock like a queen on her throne, both of us completely naked with me still buried deep inside my mate.

She slaps one hand over her eyes, spewing panicked excuses. "Holy shit—oh god! Sorry! Thought we were having an earthquake, but clearly you're the one making the earth move—FUCK!" she stammers. "I'm going back to bed before I'm scarred for life."

She flails blindly with her free arm, crashing into walls as she retreats down the hallway.

To my surprise, Dani erupts in wild laughter. She throws her head back, her whole body shaking with it, while I'm still inside her. The sight is fucking magnificent—her uninhibited joy has me grinning like a fool.

When she finally catches her breath, she fixes me with those golden eyes. "Agent Stalker," she says flatly, "you've got some serious explaining to do."

I cock an eyebrow, amused. "So I've earned a nickname already? Not sure how I feel about that one."

She gives me that smile that makes my cock twitch inside her. "Best I could come up with on short notice."

I lean in, breathing in her intoxicating scent. "You'll think of something better. We've got eternity for you to perfect it."

After cleaning up, we settle on the couch and I lay it all out—my desperate hunt for answers about her awakening power and the mind-blowing truth about her bloodline.

I break down the ancient prophecy, her crucial role in it, and the celestial/Fae legends Adrian uncovered. Danica's eyes go wide as her world tilts on its axis.

"There's something you need to see." She grabs a weathered note left with her as an infant. "Found this with me when I was adopted. The writing's like nothing I've ever seen."

She passes it to me, and I study the markings intently. The intricate sigils and flowing script hits me—unmistakable celestial language. "Holy shit. This is written in angelic script. Where did you get this?" I demand.

Danica looks shell-shocked. "It was with me when I was abandoned. My adoptive parents couldn't decipher it. You're saying these are actually celestial symbols?"

I trace the ancient letters with reverence, my pulse hammering. "This script predates human civilization."

She shakes her head, struggling with the weight of it all. "How could I possibly be connected to these celestial beings? Are you sure I'm...one of them?"

I grasp her hands firmly. "Nothing's certain yet. But this note, your awakening powers—something powerful lives inside you." I search those confused golden eyes. "I know it's a mindfuck. But we'll decode this mystery together. That's a promise."

Humans have dismissed these truths as myths for centuries. "My brother Adrian is the expert on this ancient shit."

"This is insane," she whispers.

"After decades of firsthand encounters and studying the prophecies, I've learned these beings are very fucking real. My library at home has extensive records," I tell her.

Fear and wonder battle across Danica's face as she processes my words. "I can't handle this, Rhyland. What if I can't control these powers? What if I fail?" Her voice trembles with raw vulnerability.

I pull her against my chest, running my fingers through her silken hair. "Look, it's normal to doubt yourself when faced with this crazy supernatural bullshit. I'll teach you to harness whatever power is awakening inside you." I lift her chin, locking onto those honey-gold eyes. "But get this straight—you're already stronger than you know, with a heart that outshines the darkness and enough stubborn fire to outlast any storm. This confusion doesn't stand a fucking chance against your light."

Danica clings to me like a lifeline, emotions crashing through her. "I'm trying to believe that. It's just—everything I thought I knew about myself is suddenly bullshit." She draws a shaky breath. "But with you, I can face whatever hellstorm is coming."

I kiss her hair, determination burning like wildfire in my veins. "Listen to me—it's you and me against this fucking mystery. I'll be right beside you, your goddamn warrior through every battle." My hand cups her face possessively."Centuries of existing meant nothing until you stormed into my world."

Danica presses those perfect lips to mine. "Just don't let go," she whispers.

"Never," I growl, pulling her hard against me. Our future's one massive question mark, but this unbreakable bond between us is solid steel. With trust as our weapon, we'll fight through the darkness together. Whatever cosmic shit storm is heading our way, we'll face it as one.

Danica

48

The ground beneath me might as well be vapor. My entire worldview is crumbling.

Thank God Rhyland's here—my one anchor in this hurricane of insanity. His presence alone fortifies me against the barrage of truth, demolishing everything I thought I knew. His revelations about my origins leave me grasping at fragments of an identity I never knew existed. This revelation would break someone weaker, but together, we can weather this storm.

I force a flippant tone to mask my terror. "So, any cheat codes or instruction manuals I should know about?"

"No," Rhyland's deep voice rumbles with authority. "Nothing. That's what makes this so dangerous. Adrian knows more than anyone. He'll uncover what we need—he's our only option now."

I climb eagerly onto Rhyland's lap, my body quivering with anticipation. His hands slide beneath my shorts to grip my ass possessively, sending electric currents through my core. I lose myself in those fathomless ocean-blue eyes. He's crashed into my life and transformed it irrevocably, marking my soul in ways no one else ever could.

"Where did you come from? What was your human life before all this?"

Rhyland's gaze turns distant as he recalls lifetimes of experience. "I lived during the Viking age," he says.

My eyes widen comically. "So you're basically a walking, talking fossil?" I tease.

His laugh reveals a dimple I hadn't noticed before—then his expression darkens.

"What?" I ask, wrinkling my nose in confusion. "What's wrong?"

"I was dying when my maker found me," he says flatly.

As he describes his mortal existence, awe washes over me. He paints vivid details—briny sea air, rough-spun clothing, raucous feasts by roaring fires, the weight of battleaxes, the thrill of conquest, the brotherhood of warriors.

But also gentler moments—carving toys for his children, verdant forests surrounding their settlement, his wife's quiet strength. These glimpses of his humanity move something profound within me.

"In my final years, darkness descended upon my people," Rhyland continues, his commanding voice edged with ancient pain. "Omens of destruction appeared—blood moons, shadows lengthening. Evil crept closer. Conflict with the English king grew volatile, violence inevitable."

How can someone carry so many years of memory and still function?

I squeeze his hand, sharing the weight of his dread. Rhyland's throat works visibly as he continues, "My youngest had just learned to say 'Papa.'"

My chest constricts painfully, imagining him leaving his family behind.

"That winter, I sailed reluctantly with my brothers-in-arms, our war cries echoing across the merciless sea toward our doom."

I brush away an unbidden tear, feeling the heaviness in his soul. As Rhyland describes what followed, I pale at the brutal violence. Yet I don't interrupt—he needs to purge these ancient memories.

"An enemy blade found its mark," he states with cold precision, "slicing through my gut—a mortal wound." He takes my hand, pressing it against the phantom wound. I shudder, imagining his agony. "As my blood soaked the earth, I collapsed in the chaos, my only thought of my wife and children." His voice fractures with centuries-old grief. I grip his hand fiercely.

Rhyland describes shadow-figures materializing, beckoning him toward death. Then a voice commanded: "It is not your time." Goosebumps erupt across my skin at those fateful words.

"I woke to find an ancient being standing over me. My fatal wound had vanished."

My eyes widen as he explains how this entity offered immortality and a greater purpose. I'm captivated by his description of that impossible choice after staring into death's face.

"Leaving my family tore at my soul. I returned to them only to find them slaughtered."

My heart shatters for him, feeling his agony at being torn between duty and destiny, only to discover his loved ones brutally murdered.

As Rhyland describes his rebirth under the dark skies, my pulse races. His account of acquiring supernatural powers and unquenchable hunger holds me spellbound.

"Through centuries with my maker, my mortal memories dimmed like distant stars." His beautiful eyes capture mine, blazing with intensity. "I never understood my true purpose... until I found you."

Tears stream down my face at his raw confession. I kiss him deeply, desperate to heal this old wound. If our meeting was prophesied, I silently vow to prove worthy of his eternal sacrifice.

Rhyland's lips curve slightly as we part, his thumb brushing away my tears. "Now I understand why I survived that battlefield. It was always for this—for you."

I cling to him, overwhelmed by emotion. Deep in my soul, I know it's true—our spirits are bound across time and realms. We were always destined to find each other. Fate has finally united us.

My eyes brim with tears as his words sink in. No one has ever shown such raw devotion. This man completely consumes me, our connection defying all rational explanation.

How can someone I've known so briefly feel like my entire world?

Desperately, I search his gaze, my hands framing his face as my fingertips brush against his rough stubble. "I know, I feel it too," I whisper, my voice barely audible.

My heart lies wholly exposed to him, vulnerable in ways I've never allowed before. Our connection transcends any physical reality.

Our lips move in perfect synchrony as his tongue claims mine. I dissolve into pure sensation as he devours me with increasing hunger. Each possessive touch ignites overwhelming pleasure, sending tremors of warmth radiating through every cell of my being.

"Do you see?" he softly queries, tenderly tracing his fingers over where Azrael left his mark. "It's all healed," he says with a smile.

There's that dimple again. I bring my fingers to my neck and feel smooth skin. The bite is no longer there, and the pain is gone. I had completely forgotten about it until now. "How did you...?" I start to ask.

"Our blood has healing properties in it," he answers.

Despite my extensive research on vampire blood, I need several moments to process this revelation. "Who else knows about this?" I ask as he adjusts my position on his lap.

"Few," he answers, his tone guarded yet authoritative. "We can't risk our abilities being exploited."

"Do you realize what this could do, Rhyland?"

"Angel, you need to understand why we can't share the secret of our blood's healing properties with the world."

I frown, my scientific mind racing. "But Rhyland, think of the potential good. It could transform medicine, save countless lives."

How many secrets does this man still hold? And how many more will I discover?

This explains why the institute restricts vampire blood testing. Do they already know these secrets? My mind races like a centrifuge, spinning with possibilities of how his blood could revolutionize medicine.

Rhyland acknowledges this with a measured nod. "Yes, it could," he concedes, "but it would unleash chaos and endanger both my kind and the balance of the supernatural world."

His expression hardens as he continues, "Imagine if humanity discovered a source of eternal life and healing. They would hunt us relentlessly. Governments would capture and experiment on us. We'd become nothing but resources to be harvested, stripped of all dignity."

How has this remained hidden? Or has it been known all along in certain circles? Is this the real reason for the black market trade?

My scientific mind spins frantically as I grasp the implications. "But we could use it selectively, help people without revealing the source."

Rhyland exhales heavily, ancient weariness momentarily breaking through his commanding presence. "Angel, history has proven that the pursuit of power and immortality corrupts even the purest intentions. Some would seek to control this gift for their own agenda. And if they couldn't control it, they'd destroy it, creating even greater devastation."

I release a heavy breath, recognizing the truth in his words. This is a battle for another day. "Thank you," I whisper. "Will you stay with me?"

His powerful hands move possessively across my body as he responds, "Baby, I'm *never* leaving your side." His tone shifts to practical concern, though his eyes remain protective. "But dawn approaches, and I need shelter from the sun."

He gestures toward my apartment's exposed windows, and I nod in understanding.

"Whaddya have in mind?"

RHYLAND

49

The suite door slams shut, severing the silence and dropping us into a pool of thick tension. My brothers' predatory gazes dissect the fragile human I've brought into our sacred circle. Heavy drapes shield us from the sun's deadly assault, bathing the room in shadow.

"Brothers, this is Danica," I announce, my voice steady as steel as I stand beside her, ready to tear apart anyone who challenges what's mine.

She's a vision of light amid our darkness, those golden eyes watchful but fearless. My chest swells with pride at her unwavering courage.

Erik steps forward first. "Danica, I am Erik. It is an honor to make your acquaintance." Respect glints in his silver eyes as she politely places her small hand in his formidable grip.

I nod shortly to my youngest kin. "Adrian." My eccentric brother materializes from the shadows, pale visage, dark brown eyes, and cryptic aura amplifying his ominous first impression. Danica shivers under that piercing stare but holds it unflinchingly.

"Interesting," Adrian muses, gaze clinical. "You are indeed the foretold one." His slight smile seems to unsettle Danica, but she stands resilient, spine straight.

Lucian circles her roguishly, lofty as a prince. "Well, well, miracles manifest—our lone wolf Rhyland snared by a mortal temptress. Nice to see you again, Kitten."

My warning growl only makes Lucian's grin widen. But Danica remains unshaken by my brothers' intense scrutiny. She stands tall, meeting Lucian's taunting gaze head-on.

"A temptress, am I?" She addresses Lucian wryly. "Funny, I don't recall using any mesmerizing art on you."

I nearly laugh when she lands that verbal jab, and Erik actually chuckles. Adrian looks like he's reassessing a worthy opponent, and I can't help but smugly smirk. But Dani just shrugs like she's at a coffee shop instead of surrounded by ancient killers.

"Anyway, pleased to meet you all, especially if you come bearing answers about glowy magical hijinks and destined soulmates or whatever." She gives me a pointed look. "Rhyland got a bit dramatic back there with talk of eternal bonds. But I'm reserving judgment until we figure this thing out."

I clear my throat, a little sheepish at how Dani's breezy demeanor lays bare the intensity of my feelings. Adrian and Erik seem to get a kick out of it, their expressions edging into smirks. Lucian, well, he just lets out a full-throated laugh, the sound ripping through the air, making it crystal clear he's damn impressed.

"Well, now, she's a lively one! Rare to meet a human so brazenly cheeky around us." He winks roguishly. "I like this girl, Rhyland. Well played!"

Danica smiles back. "I have my moments." She points at Lucian. "And your bullshit vague response regarding Rhyland's whereabouts could've been more forthcoming."

I watch my mate verbally bitchslap my brother with savage pride.

"How 'bout we wipe the slate clean, and you boys spell this freaky nonsense out for me? I'm trying to understand why my life suddenly resembles an acid trip through a National Enquirer."

She settles into an armchair, gazing at us expectantly.

Lucian stands there looking like his manhood just turned to stone. "Sorry, Kitten, I honestly didn't know jack shit until after I saw you."

My lips curl into a predatory smile. My mate's no simpering damsel—she's pure fire wrapped in silk and steel. What other surprises lie beneath that fierce exterior?

Adrian, the impatient bastard, cuts straight to business. "What do you know of your powers, Danica?"

I can practically see him cataloging every detail like the knowledge-hungry scholar he is.

"Um, well..." Danica hesitates, glancing at me as if seeking reassurance. I give her a subtle nod, hoping to instill confidence. After a bracing breath, she continues. "I can summon light and heat...small flames, illuminating darkness. I don't fully understand it all yet." Danica inhales unevenly before dropping the revelation casually. "Oh, and I may have turned Azrael into supernatural barbecue with some energy blast. Left him looking pretty crispy."

I nearly crush my crystal glass as horrified shock crashes through me. "You did? When the hell did this happen? Why didn't you tell me this earlier?"

"The night he ambushed me," Danica whispers, downcast eyes clouded with remembered pain. "And you sort of distracted me." After giving me a knowing look, she continues tonelessly. "Feeling his cruelty and your absence...something just erupted out of raw desperation."

Raw guilt rips through me like a blade. I pour whiskey with a shaking hand, fury and self-loathing warring in my gut. I should have been there protecting what's mine. We've got a fucking mountain of shit to deal with regarding Dani's awakening powers, but right now, I need to help her handle this chaos I've dragged her into.

"It wasn't your fault," Dani says softly, her voice gentle as summer rain.

"Like hell it wasn't," I snarl. "You faced that monster alone because I failed you."

Those honey-gold eyes find mine, filled with a warmth that drives back my demons. "You're here now," she whispers. "That's what counts."

Even in this storm of supernatural bullshit, her quiet faith in me sparks something fierce in my soul.

I feel her turmoil rippling through our new bond, and every instinct screams to shield her from it. But I force myself to stay silent, allowing her to breathe through this reality check.

"Well, this is all very touching," Lucian interjects, dramatically wiping an imaginary tear. "Should I start playing sad violin music, or are we done with the brooding power couple moment? Because I'm getting serious rom-com vibes here, and not the good kind—more like the 'everyone's about to die but first let's have feelings' kind!"

I shoot Lucian a withering glare, already calculating how many years it would take for him to regenerate if I ripped his tongue out through his ass.

"So what now?" Danica eventually demands, voice wavering slightly. "Does anyone actually know what I am or where I'm from?" She wraps her arms around herself. "What is my heritage?"

Before I can eviscerate my brother, Adrian steps forward. "Fortunately for all of us," he says with academic precision, "I've been conducting extensive research."

"Research into what exactly?" Dani asks, her brow furrowing with genuine curiosity.

"Ancient supernatural texts concerning the realms," Adrian explains, clearly pleased by her interest. He gestures toward the collection of weathered tomes and fragile scrolls piled nearby.

"Rhyland mentioned realms, but I'm still unclear what that means..." Dani admits, leaning forward intently. I feel something lighten in my chest as she engages despite everything she's been through.

Adrian's eyes light up with scholarly fervor. "There are seven principal realms, each containing unique dimensions inhabited by specific beings."

Dani tilts her head. "Seven realms? Can you tell me about them?"

"Luminara is the luminescent realm of the Fae," Adrian begins methodically. "Zephyria governs the skies, Aquaria the waters, Atheria houses the celestial races..."

He continues his list—"Pyrothos of fire, Unbra of shadows, and finally Mortalis, our realm of mortals and immortals." Dani listens with rapt attention, her expression a mixture of wonder and disbelief.

"According to ancient texts, these realms once existed in harmony until Moretemis shattered their connection," Adrian concludes gravely. "The prophecies speak of a savior who will reunite the realms and defeat Moretemis. We believe that savior is you, Danica."

I observe silently as she processes these revelations that will forever alter her existence.

"Let me get this straight—there's a bunch of magical worlds like Fairyland and Aquaman's Atlantis existing secretly out there? And I'm supposed to be an interdimensional warrior princess destined to defeat some big, bad, evil force?"

Sarcasm cracks her bewildered tone. Despite the gravity of it all, I suppress a smile—her fiery adaptability continues to impress me.

Danica exhales a sharp, borderline hysterical bark of laughter. "Wow, okay, no big deal or anything. Maybe let a girl ease into the whole 'congratulations, you're a foretold savior of the universe' thing, though?"

At least Adrian has the grace to appear somewhat abashed, blinking at her breakdown. But honestly, no one could fault Danica's strained reaction after having her entire understanding of reality shattered.

"Who's this ultimate evil Morty guy I'm expected to smack down if the multiverse depends on little ole' me?"

I speak up before Adrian can respond. "A being of a nightmare, from the prophecies of darkness. But nothing you need to worry over tonight." I give Adrian a quelling look so as not to overwhelm her further.

Lucian calls out, laughing from the bar. "Loving this firecracker! Think there's more where she came from, Rhy-Rhy?" He gives Danica an exaggerated wink.

Unfazed, she volleys back, “Sure, I think they’re on sale for 4.99 at the Hybrid Fae-Dragon Pet Emporium.” Lips quirking, she adds, “House training optional.”

Lucian nearly spills his whiskey while Adrian looks caught between scientific fascination and skepticism. I shake my head—my mate's razor-sharp tongue strikes again, even in the face of cosmic revelations. That mouth will be my fucking undoing.

Lucian roars with laughter. "Deadly AND delicious! All hail the queen!" He raises his glass in a mocking toast to Dani's defiant smirk.

Dani spins toward him, eyebrow arched dangerously. "Just your everyday apocalypse-stopping destiny, right? No pressure!" Even through her exasperation, I can't help the slight smile tugging at my lips. My mate is absolutely fucking fearless.

"If you're eager to battle ancient horrors immediately, I won't stop you," I reply, my eyes softening as I look at my fierce angel. "But perhaps starting with Lucian would be easier target practice."

My golden-haired brother flips me off while dramatically protesting about family betrayal. Still, I can see the wheels turning behind Dani's brave facade. Whatever cosmic bullshit awaits us, my faith in her remains unshakable...

Dani takes a shaky breath, the weight of revelation finally settling. "Do you really believe I'm from one of these realms?"

"Evidence strongly suggests it," Adrian confirms, his eyes gleaming with scholarly hunger. "The question is—which one?"

"Oh GREAT, a supernatural ancestry test! 'Congratulations, you're 50% badass with a dash of imminent doom!'" Lucian interjects, gesturing wildly with his glass. "Should we start taking bets? My money's on something flashy—no offense to the fish people, but our girl here definitely has more of a 'set things on fire' vibe than 'talks to seahorses'!"

I fix Lucian with a lethal glare. "If you don't shut your fucking mouth, I'll personally show you what 'set things on fire' looks like by shoving that glass so far down your throat you'll be pissing whiskey for the next week."

I turn back to Dani, my expression softening instantly. "Ignore him. He was dropped on his head repeatedly as a child. For centuries."

She takes a bracing breath before speaking hesitantly. "I may have a clue, actually..."

She mentions a cryptic phrase left with her adoption papers, hinting at celestial origins—my entire body tenses with certainty. Danica is undeniably the prophesied one we've been searching for. Adrian's intense focus tells me he's reached the same conclusion.

"I researched the term recently," Dani explains, her eyes finding mine. "It means 'ethereal being' in some ancient language."

Adrian leans forward, practically vibrating with academic hunger. "What was the exact word?"

"D'larayn," she answers without hesitation.

Adrian strokes his chin thoughtfully. "Unfamiliar dialect, but 'celestial' suggests specific dimensions. I'll need to research further." His eyes fucking sparkle at the intellectual challenge ahead.

She locks eyes with me then, unwavering and direct. I see pure courage and acceptance shining back at me in those golden depths. Once again, her strength leaves me humbled and hungry for our future together...

After this barrage of world-shattering revelations, plus the alcohol and our earlier physical activities, I can see she's reaching her breaking point.

"We should all get some rest," I announce, brooking no argument. Dani stands, giving me a grateful smile before bidding my brothers goodnight.

Safely alone, Dani exhales deeply as I draw her close. "My big, bad brothers didn't scare you off yet, I hope?" I smooth a hand over her hair, relieved to have her to myself.

Dani leans into me. "Oh, sure, it's a piece of cake being told I'm descended from aliens fated to battle ultimate evil." Her wry tone makes me chuckle.

I grin at her, acutely aware of each alluring curve pressed against me. "Mm-hmm, prophecy schmophecy. Clearly, you can handle anything, Supergirl."

Dani playfully smacks my chest, but can't hide her smile beneath the exhaustion. Fuck, she tempts me—those eyes gazing up through dark lashes. I brush my lips across her forehead, but the little minx tilts her face up demandingly, seeking more. Heat instantly surges through my veins.

"Careful asking," I warn, voice low. "Or I may get...ideas."

"Maybe I like your ideas," Dani retorts, hands framing my jaw daringly. The temptress knows precisely what she's doing, pressing her soft curves against my hardening body. Her tongue darts out to wet her lower lip—a deliberate invitation no man could resist...

With a muttered curse, my control shatters. I claim that smirking mouth with mine, swallowing Dani's sultry laugh—she thinks she can provoke the beast without consequences? My feisty angel is about to learn what happens when she plays with fire...

I devour her mouth hungrily, consumed by primal need. My hands pull her against me possessively as her fingers clutch my shirt. Our tongues battle for dominance, every nerve ending blazing to life.

I lift her effortlessly, her sexy legs wrapping around my waist as I lay her down on the bed, those expensive sheets framing her chestnut hair like a fucking halo.

Mine.

DANICA

50

I jolt awake to mysterious lights teasing my consciousness. Squinting through the darkness, I carefully extricate myself from Rhyland's possessive embrace. Can't disrupt Mr. Tall-Dark-and-Handsy's beauty rest after all.

Daylight blazes outside, but in here shadows reign. The heavy drapes block most of the afternoon sun, leaving the room in murky darkness. I'm not sure how long I was out, but something's illuminating the space—and it's definitely not coming from the windows.

I slip from between silk sheets, the strange glow intensifying as I approach. Curiosity mixed with trepidation quickens my pulse. Who's hosting an impromptu light show in our bathroom?

Stepping inside, I freeze mid-stride—an ethereal being bathes the space in radiance that ripples from within her flowing, gossamer gown. Translucent wings shimmer behind a face of impossible beauty, simultaneously alien yet naggingly familiar. My instincts battle between dropping to my knees in worship and calling a psychiatrist to report my apparent mental breakdown.

"Greetings, Danica." Her voice rings with harmonic perfection, instantly obliterating my doubts. "I am Seraphina, your guardian angel since birth. I've come to guide you."

I shake my head mutely, watching reality's fabric unravel before my eyes.

Guardian angel? Seriously?

Yet the inexplicable comfort washing over me at her presence confirms this impossible truth.

"Um, guide me where exactly?" I retort warily. "Cloud Nine day spa? Or straight to the psych ward since I'm clearly hallucinating?"

Her melodic laugh triggers strange déjà vu. "You are ready to learn about your true nature and destiny."

I blink in a slow, deliberate motion. "Yes?" The question hangs in the air, a question dressed up as an answer. Am I ready to go down this rabbit hole?

She smiles knowingly before continuing with urgency. "I've watched over you since you drew your first breath, dear one. But circumstances have changed, forcing us to accelerate your awakening. We have precious little time..."

Just when I thought dating a thousand-year-old vampire was the weirdest part of my week.

I blink repeatedly, questioning whether I'm dreaming or just completely losing my marbles while chatting with my glow-in-the-dark guardian angel. "Great. Rhyland is *so* not going to believe this when he wakes up..."

Seraphina glides closer, her radiance intensifying with each graceful step. "You are no ordinary mortal, Danica." Her voice carries gentle insistence. "I have waited for this awakening. You are destined for greatness as creation's own daughter."

My thoughts collide like atoms in a particle accelerator—wonder, doubt, and terrified awe. "What...what exactly does that mean?" I manage through suddenly desert-dry lips.

Compassion illuminates Seraphina's luminous gaze. "Your essence carries Elysium's divine gifts, though their meaning remains hidden from you."

I feel my grip on reality slipping as these revelations cascade over me. Elysium—the name resonates with mythic grandeur yet triggers inexplicable familiarity. "Who is Elysium?" I whisper.

"The radiant celestial ruler of Atheria—an embodiment of light and purity, beloved across all realms for his wisdom and benevolence." Reverent admiration permeates her musical voice. "His divine spirit infuses Atheria's very fabric, blessing his subjects with prosperity."

She continues relentlessly while I stand there like a cosmic deer in headlights. "Prophecies foretold that one blessed child of Elysium would arise to reshape destinies—a savior restoring balance and unity. Dear Danica, the god's own blood flows within you, awakening fated power."

Clearly, this celestial Tinkerbell has lost her marbles. Yet, some soul-deep recognition of this impossible truth demolishes my doubts—the mysterious note left in my crib with its angelic script.

Me—a daughter of a *god?*

Overwhelmed, I meet Seraphina's earnest, golden gaze. Reflected there, I see my unbelievable destiny staring back at me, waiting only for my acceptance.

My mind spins frantically, struggling to process it all—awe and uncertainty battle with this new awareness of fate's grand design. Being the daughter of an immortal celestial ruler is both an extraordinary blessing and a crushing responsibility.

One question burns through the chaos: "If this is true...why was I abandoned on Earth? Who's my mother?"

Pain flickers across Seraphina's timeless features. "Your father loved a mortal woman deeply. Their tragic tale must wait." Her voice softens with compassion. "Know that I've never stopped watching over you, dear one. An extraordinary destiny awaits, though it carries tremendous responsibility..."

Her words strike a chord of strange familiarity, igniting certainty and confusion. "Why show yourself now?" I demand.

Seraphina's expression clouds. "You have awakened, Danica. You've chosen one shrouded in darkness as your fated mate, a development I never anticipated." She hesitates, measuring her words carefully. "The prophecy speaks only of a destined union...but your father questions binding our realm's hope to a nightbound son fallen from grace."

I blink rapidly. "Wait—you're telling me my divine *Daddy* disapproves of Rhyland?" I let out a derisive snort. "Son fallen from—seriously? Is Rhyland secretly Satan or something? What does that even mean?"

Seeing my impending meltdown, Seraphina squeezes my hands reassuringly. "Be calm, dear one. True darkness doesn't dwell in Rhyland's spirit. But he remains vulnerable to the shadow's call and could easily stray."

I drag both hands through my tangled hair. "So what—vampires aren't good enough for the celestial country club? That's not prejudiced at all."

I wrap my arms around my middle as these revelations collide violently. Rhyland...unworthy? But our fierce connection feels cosmically ordained.

Adrian and Rhyland both swore up and down that a mate was supposed to trigger my powers. Well, they're definitely awake now, but something's not adding up. This makes zero fucking sense.

I fight against rising indignation and fear. "Rhyland? You question if he can stand with me against whatever's coming?"

Seraphina moves closer, her scent enveloping me—fresh rain mingled with jasmine. It somehow quiets my internal hurricane as she continues gently. "Not all light has abandoned Rhyland's spirit. But the darkness whispering in his blood presents eternal temptation few can permanently resist."

What the hell does that mean? This mystical fortune-cookie wisdom is seriously grating on my last nerve.

Great. Not only am I half-divine, but my boyfriend might have some cosmic darkness issues.

My eyes dart back toward the bedroom where Rhyland lies tangled in sheets, his powerful form barely visible in the darkness—the same sheets where passionate promises were exchanged mere hours ago. Or so I desperately want to believe. Could I have been that gullible? That wrong? Surely he remains the formidable protector sworn to stand beside me until death claims one or both of us. But doubt's familiar talons tear at my certainty...if Seraphina speaks truth, perhaps Rhyland's inner darkness might eventually consume us both in the trials ahead. Maybe I stand completely alone against destiny's approaching tempest.

Sensing my internal turmoil, Seraphina's expression softens. "There are things I must carefully reveal about your gifts...and troubling possibilities ahead."

I glance anxiously between her earnest golden eyes, similar to mine, and Rhyland's shadowed sleeping form.

Finally, Seraphina speaks with reluctant determination. "Your blood contains unique properties, Danica. When consumed by immortal nightwalkers, it grants them access to our celestial abilities, including walking in daylight."

My jaw drops in absolute shock, eyes widening to saucers as I stare at Seraphina in stunned silence. I can barely process this bombshell.

My blood lets vampires walk in sunlight? The concept seems utterly impossible.

"W-wait...you're saying my blood allows Rhyland to walk in the *sun*?" I finally stammer. I look at Rhyland, this beautiful, enigmatic vampire who has utterly captivated me, with new understanding and nervous energy crackling through my veins.

My mind floods with realizations that suddenly click into place—the overwhelming attraction between us and his intense craving for my blood. I shudder thinking how irresistible my blood must be, that other vampires and Azrael have tracked me like supernatural catnip.

Seraphina perceives my lingering doubt. "Rhyland possesses tremendous strength," she acknowledges. "He will challenge, protect, and fight for you relentlessly. But remain vigilant in determining whether he advances or impedes your destiny."

I shift uncomfortably, torn between my besotted heart and my cautious mind. No one can deny Rhyland's fierce devotion—the exhilarating clash when our equally stubborn wills collide, nor the possessive claim that has branded my soul irrevocably as his.

Yet...if my blood offers access to mythic privileges like daylight long denied his kind...has ambition rather than cosmic fate truly bound him to me?

Great. I'm not just dating a vampire—I'm his supernatural sunscreen. Talk about relationship complications.

"Rhyland isn't the only threat if this knowledge spreads unchecked." Sorrow clouds her luminous features. "If shadow legions discovered they could access our powers by harvesting your blood... apocalyptic war would inevitably follow."

Taking a steadying breath, I face Seraphina with newfound determination, burning away my doubts. "Alright. What's heroic task number one?"

Seraphina nods approvingly. "You must locate the Crown of Blessings—a powerful relic for uniting all realms against primordial darkness." She smiles confidently. "I know you're capable of this, daughter of Atheria."

Nervous excitement battles within me—apparently, my entire existence has been building to this cosmic wake-up call. "Great... Except, um, I don't suppose this crown comes with magical GPS coordinates or something?"

Serene confidence never wavers in Seraphina's ancient gaze. "You possess an inherent connection to the realms themselves. Focus your intention, and portals will manifest through concentration alone. Trust your intuition, dear one. Signs will illuminate your path."

My anxious exhale shifts to anticipatory intake. Uncharted magical territory stretching before me? "Wait—are you suggesting I can open a... *portal?*"

There's no way this is real. I pinch myself hard. Ouch! Definitely awake.

Seraphina squeezes my shoulder, her celestial touch somehow strengthening my resolve. "You were born for this, Danica. Never forget the power within you." Her voice resonates with absolute certainty. "Embrace this quest, and you'll be unstoppable."

As Seraphina's glowing form dissolves, her smile remains emblazoned in my mind—a beacon cutting through darkness. I'm still reeling from tonight's mind-blowing revelations. But destiny has called, and I'm determined to step up to this whole cosmic heroine gig.

Still, anxiety threatens to flatten me completely. I'm just one overwhelmed human woman with student loans. How am I supposed to achieve mythic greatness against ultimate evil?

Yet something deeper stirs within me—an unwavering inner fire whispering that I have the strength for whatever trials lie ahead. I was born to awaken this dormant potential and kick supernatural ass through dangers unimaginable.

Creeping back to bed, newfound purpose courses through me as I gaze at Rhyland's sleeping form, my thoughts racing. Seraphina implied his motives were suspect, but he's done nothing but protect me fiercely. Does selfish ambition explain such devotion? No, what exists between us feels too profound...or have I become too love-drunk to see the truth?

I slide cautiously beside this beautiful fallen warrior, studying his dark lashes, tousled hair, and relaxed stubbled jaw. Dangerous tempta tion...yet perhaps destiny bound our paths together, whatever celestial doubts my divine daddy might harbor. Intense darkness housed within a noble heart—the man, not the myth, has earned my trust.

Inhaling deeply, I try to calm my runaway thoughts. But stark reality can't be ignored—some prophesied holy crown now depends on my questionable mortal hands for retrieval, a task so absurd that it nearly tears me. How can I possibly locate this magical needle in a multiverse haystack before everything immortal comes crashing down?

I close my eyes, desperately blocking out frantic doubts and fears, trying to summon sleep's blissful temporary escape from crushing cosmic responsibility...

Typical. Discover you're half-angel, get tasked with saving multiple realms, and question if your vampire boyfriend loves you or your supernatural blood. No biggie.

Rhyland

51

I wake surrounded by darkness, the blackout curtains confirming it's still daylight—I'm immediately aware of Danica's heat pressed against me. Even in sleep, she's mine. Her delicate hands rest under her cheek—fucking beautiful even unconscious. There's something primal about watching her like this—all vulnerable softness, her chestnut hair spilling across my arm, her naked curves claimed by my hold. I can't resist; I pull back the sheets to reveal her perfection, my gaze devouring every inch.

My fingers trace the curve of her hip, watching goosebumps rise under my touch. Instantly, that familiar hunger roars to life—a savage need only this woman can satisfy.

My cock hardens instantly at the sight of her naked body, my muscles tensing with anticipation. While she sleeps, unaware, I claim her stomach with my mouth, exploring territory that belongs to me. She stirs slightly, and I reward her with a deliberate stroke of my tongue across her navel, consuming her intoxicating taste. A soft moan escapes her as I work my way to her neck, marking her with teeth and tongue, savoring the sun-warmed flavor of her skin.

This is the closest I'll ever come to feeling the sun again. This woman has given me something no creature of darkness should ever hope to possess.

My tongue claims a path back down her body, asserting ownership over every inch. Her full breasts demand my attention. I capture one perfect nipple, circling it with my tongue until it hardens against my hot mouth. I grip her curves roughly, possessively, as she begins to writhe beneath me. Her moans fuel my hunger as I bite her other nipple before soothing it with slow, deliberate licks.

"Rhyland..." She moans my name in her sleep, already wanting me.

"Angel," I growl against her skin before claiming those perfect lips with savage hunger that sets my blood on fire.

Her arms lock around me fiercely, staking her claim. I drink in every fucking second of this connection that's become as essential as breathing.

"Am I dreaming?" she whispers, her voice heavy with need. I smile against her mouth, pleased by her hunger.

"This is real," I whisper, restraint hanging by a thread. "And so is what I'm about to do to you."

Consumed with lust, I tear off my clothes with urgency. Without hesitation, I position myself between those perfect thighs, ready to claim what's mine. My mouth attacks her neck with hungry bites and sucking kisses that make her shiver beneath me. I capture her wrists in one hand, pinning them above her head in my iron grip. Her magnificent breasts rise and fall as she arches into me.

My fingers dig possessively into the soft curve of her hip as I devour her nipples with my mouth. When I finally slide my cock into her, she moans loud enough to wake the dead.

"Shhh, Angel," I command against her ear, feeling my control slipping with every second. "Don't want to wake everyone." But her cries only intensify as I drive into her relentlessly. Her tight cunt grips me like a vise, squeezing every inch of my cock.

With each powerful thrust, she cries out her pleasure while I try to muffle the sounds with my hand. Fuck, she's absolute heaven. I hammer into her with savage intensity, driving her toward explosive release.

Her muffled screams vibrate against my palm as I increase my pace. The sensation of her wet heat gripping my shaft is fucking addictive. Her tightness clenches around me with every thrust, leaving me desperate for more.

Her eyes roll back in ecstasy. I grab under both knees and spread her legs wider, fully exposing her to my hungry gaze. She gasps as my heavy cock drives deeper into her willing body, pushing until I'm completely buried inside her.

With a possessive growl, I position myself above her and thrust deep with brutal intensity.

My lips crash down on hers as I rumble against her mouth, "You like it rough, baby? You just love," I thrust harder, "getting fucked," another powerful thrust, "by my hard cock."

Her lips part, eyes glazed with pure desire.

I lock my gaze with hers, demanding, "Tell me now, Angel." I drive into her deeper, pushing her closer to the edge.

She cries out in overwhelming pleasure, "Yes...yes...oh god."

Mine to take. Mine to claim. Mine forever.

Pride surges through me as my angel surrenders completely. She craves the carnal sensations I can give her, which only urges me further. My filthy girl loves it when I fuck her with such passion.

My hand grips her plump ass, squeezing as I mercilessly drive into her. Her cries echo against my lips. I own her now, staking my claim with each savage thrust.

I tangle my fingers in her hair, taking what I crave, tugging tightly as I take control of her body and own it like an animal. I'll brand her body with mine until she can't walk or think straight. Her surrender is my drug, and I'm addicted to her sweet cries.

“Bite me,” she whispers, "Please..." begging to experience the same pleasure I’ve given her.

I trace my lips along the delicate curve of her neck, feeling her pulse quicken beneath my touch. "Craving my dark kisses, Angel?" I ask against her throat, my voice rough with the need to taste her.

With a growl, I claim her offering. My teeth pierce her delicate skin, unleashing a flood of pure ecstasy as her essence fills me. Her blood—sweet sunshine and raw power courses through me like liquid fire. She trembles beneath my fangs before surrendering completely, her body yielding to the ancient pleasure of my bite.

The dual sensation of drinking her life force while claiming her body drives me to the edge of sanity. Each drop pushes me further into feral possession, my control shattered by her breathless moans.

With a burning desire, I flip her onto her stomach in one fluid motion, positioning her exactly how I want her. My hands grip her hips with bruising intensity, preparing to stake my claim in the most primal way possible.

"Lift that sexy ass of yours," I order. She complies without a word; her perfect round ass is now spread before me, glistening with arousal, and my mouth waters in anticipation. I pry apart those succulent cheeks, exposing her tight little hole to my gaze.

My tongue darts out, licking at her from behind as she squirms beneath me.

"Rhyland!" she gasps in embarrassment, not expecting such an intimate gesture from me.

But I'm in control here, and I remind her of that with a loud slap on her ass, accompanied by a deep warning growl, "Don't. Move."

She cries out in pleasure as I hungrily devour her most sensitive area. I massage her clit, wild with desire.

She moans into the bed. "You like it when I'm being a filthy bastard, don't you, Angel?" I purr.

"Y-yes!" she pants, almost breathless.

"Beg me to eat this ass," I demand.

She hesitates. So I smack her ass again.

"P-please," she stutters nervously.

I can tell she isn't used to men dominating or asking what she wants, but I want to ensure she feels comfortable enough to do anything with me and tell me exactly what she desires.

"Please, what?" I gently ask, still teasing her sensitive hole with the tip of my tongue.

"P-please eat my… ass," she says in a throaty whisper.

"Mmm, my sinful girl," I purr and increase the speed of my finger circling her clit.

I devour her delicate spot with my mouth as if it were a priceless delicacy. My moans and gasps of pleasure amplify my desperate craving for more.

I need to claim every part of her—my mate, my territory to explore and conquer.

Her passionate cries fuel my dominance as I slide my fingers into her dripping pussy, feeling her body respond instantly to my touch. Her whimpers grow desperate as I work her inner walls, drawing out her pleasure with expert precision. I withdraw my fingers, slick with her arousal, and trace them over her back entrance.

"You better open for me, baby."

I'm not going to fuck her ass yet, but I am going to tease her.

I smirk. Playtime has just begun.

Danica

52

Holy *shit*, this man is pure sin incarnate, and I'm addicted. He's exploring territories I never knew existed, making me flush crimson as his wicked tongue trails where no one's dared before. Each skillful swipe ignites molten heat, pulling uncontrolled moans from my throat.

All that exists is Rhyland and his deliciously dark desires consuming me completely.

Cosmic destiny can fucking wait. Right now, I'm being devoured by a thousand-year-old Viking vampire, and it's goddamn glorious.

He slips his thick thumb inside, and I curse into the pillow, "Fuck!"

"Relax, baby. Focus on your clit."

He continues rubbing the throbbing nub, sending pleasure through my body until I'm ready to come undone."That's it. There you go," he encourages.

His dick slides deep inside my waiting pussy, and I purr at his invasion. "*Fuuuck*, baby. You're so tight. You're doing so good."

He picks up his pace and pounds against me. His thumb pushes deeper into my sacred hole as I roar into the bed. “That’s right, baby,” he grunts. “Let me fill up all your holes and take you straight to heaven.”

He grabs my hair, wrenching my head back. I'm entirely at his mercy as he pounds against me. His thrusts are relentless and intense as his thumb jams past its limit.

His masterful dominance awakens every sense, his control giving me an intense thrill while filling my heart with security and love.

How can I ever question that Rhyland isn't my soulmate?

I'm speechless, overwhelmed by the sheer pleasure he delivers. His beastly grunts only amplify the arousal coursing through every inch of my body.

"Goddamn, baby...you're so fucking beautiful taking all of me," he grunts. "Christ. I can't hold out much longer."

The heat starts low in my back as I prepare for orgasmic bliss.

"Come for me, Angel. While I fuck both your holes.” His perversion is almost too much to bear!

My body melts under his words. His filthy instructions drive me wild, and I'm powerless against his command.

I scream, my body contracting before exploding into waves of pleasure radiating from every nerve ending.

He thrusts harder and faster, his seed spilling inside me until I overflow. My screams echo through the room while intense spasms wrack my body.

We lay sprawled on the bed, panting. He pulls me back against his chest. Neither of us speaks; we hold each other in the afterglow of what we just experienced.

I finally break the silence.“That was...oh my god...”

A playful smile tugs at the corner of Rhyland’s lips.“Incredible?” He completes for me, and I nod in agreement, still trembling from pleasure.

“Will it always be like this?” I ask.

Rhyland passionately kisses my neck before whispering against my ear, “It’ll only get better.” He chuckles.

Rhyland claims my mouth, his powerful body holding mine. His calloused fingers grip my face with possessive gentleness while his tongue invades with commanding precision. His kiss devastates me—equal parts tender worship and primal claiming that sends molten heat cascading through my trembling body.

This isn't just a kiss—it's a goddamn declaration of ownership.

“Holy shit! Someone shut these assholes up before I take matters into my own hands. I'm sure the whole damn city can hear you all!” Lucian shouts from the other room.

I'm so embarrassed that I can't help but laugh and cover my mouth with my hand. I shake my head. “Oh my god.”

Rhyland retorts, “Ain't nobody stoppin' you, Lucian. You can dip out anytime you want.”

Rhyland's thumb traces my cheek, joy wrinkling his eyes. Clearly, it's been a while since he felt such delight. A whisper floats in my mind—"*I love you.*"

I jolt in surprise. "What was that?"

Rhyland looks equally startled, asking if I heard his voice internally. He explains that some vampires communicate telepathically once they are bonded. Now that our connection has formed, I can access this intimate exchange.

"Try projecting back to me," he encourages.

Unsure how to focus my thoughts intentionally, I questioned him further. "Relax your mind and feel our bond thrumming between us. Then voicelessly share whatever words you wish me to hear."

I close my eyes, my senses attuning to the vibrant connection between us. Feeling bold, I form the words silently, projecting them toward Rhyland's waiting consciousness— *"I love your massive cock."*

Rhyland erupts with thunderous laughter.

I can't help but giggle. "Did it work? Did you hear me?" I ask eagerly.

"Hell yes," he says with satisfaction. "That's exactly the kind of thing you should be sending me."

He captures me in his powerful arms, his nose dragging possessively along my neck. "You're a quick study," he declares, his deep voice vibrating against my skin with unmistakable pride.

At least my first telepathic message was memorable.

Rhyland

53

As we dress, Danica halts me with a startling revelation. "Remember how you thoroughly distracted me this afternoon? I actually had a pretty wild convo with an angel named Seraphina while you slept early this morning."

I blink hard. "You...spoke with an *angel*—are you certain?"

Dani explains Seraphina's counsel about portals, celestial lineages ...and disturbing doubts about whether my darkness can truly assist Danica's fated quest.

"Wait—you can travel between realms?" That's all I can manage.

According to legend, it has been lost to memory for many years as the realms have been shut off.

"I guess." She says softly.

"Did Seraphina explain anything about the reasoning for your abandonment?"

Dani shakes her head. "Only that I need to speak to my father about it when the time is right."

I embrace her with understanding before saying, "We will, Angel, and we will get the answers you deserve."

She mentions finding a relic linked to her heritage. I frown in puzzlement. "A relic?"

She nods. "Yeah, but I have no clue how to even start."

My fingers rake through my hair in frustration. How can I help her if I'm bound by darkness? I take a deep breath, "Okay...we will figure this out, but I don't think I can be of much assistance if—"

Dani interrupts me with palpable excitement, clapping. "Oh, oh! This is the best part! My blood's properties will allow you to be in daylight."

My fucking brain misfires as if I just heard her say her blood can allow me to walk in the sunlight. "What?" I ask, stunned.

She continues explaining that her blood is a source of light itself and will allow me to walk in the sun—something no vampire has ever been granted before.

I shake my head in disbelief. "No fucking way," I utter.

It has been centuries since I have roamed the land during the day. If I were to step foot in the sun, I would immediately turn into a pile of ashes. I've got no choice but to rely on her words, to trust in her. But damn, is she right? Can I take this leap of faith on her say-so alone? The truth feels like a gamble with stakes higher than I've ever known.

"Rhyland, I swear it's the truth. Why would Seraphina lie about something like that if it wasn't true?"

She's dead serious as she lays down the law—this stays between us. Spilling these beans could paint a target on her back the size of the realm. It clicks now why Azrael and the other nightwalkers can sniff her like bloodhounds. There's this fire in her eyes as she spells it out for me, and the gravity of it all presses down like a goddamn anvil. If the vampiric world gets wind that her blood is the holy grail, the cure for our cursed existence, they'd swarm her from every shadowy corner of the globe. We've got to keep this under wraps, or she's as good as a lamb in a den of lions.

I nod, grab her hand, and open the door.

We walk into the main living area to find all of my brothers already there, seemingly in a trance-like state. Adrian is engulfed in a book while Lucian and Erik nurse their drinks at the bar.

Before I can utter a word, Lucian breaks the silence with his loud voice. "We heard every moan, whisper, and squeak of that damn orgy you two had." He snickers.

Dani's eyes shoot at me with panic.

"Don't worry, your pretty little head about us telling anyone, girl. Man, *alive*, that was some major intel you just dropped on us!" Lucian says with excitement.

I walk to the bar and pour myself a scotch. Dani takes a seat on the pristine white couch.

Lucian smirks. "So when are you gonna get the balls to give her 'Sunny D juice a go?"

I gulp down my scotch. "First thing in the morning," I comment with a smirk.

Adrian whistles, impressed. "Damn. You lucky son of a bitch." He coughs and continues. "I started researching Atheria—since now we know where Dani is from."

Damn, Adrian sure is efficient. He's a scholar and research extraordinaire! I peer at him. "And?"

He shifts awkwardly in his seat. "There is an ancient relic that her guardian has talked about, a crown or tiara, depending on how you look at it. It was lost to this realm many moons ago, so much so that some thought it was just a fairy tale. However, the item symbolizes unity."

"Any idea where it could be?" I ask.

Adrian gets up to wander around the space. He informs us that the document mentions its last known location was in the Valley of Ancients, concealed deep within the thick Amazon jungle. It is said to be under the watchful eye of ancient guardians and surrounded by powerful magic, making it almost impossible for adventurers to explore.

"Alright, let's begin there." Dani quips.

"Do you all have those nifty magic rings that teleport, or are you all taking the slow route by air?" Lucian chuckles.

Dani gives a bewildered shake of her head. "I don't understand how to teleport. It's crazy to think about it."

Adrian sits beside her and asks, "Did Seraphina tell you what you must do? How to make it happen?"

Dani shrugs, "She just said that I needed to concentrate on my destination, and that would be enough."

Erik ends his contemplative silence with a confident statement, "Dani, you are capable of great things if you just trust in yourself and have faith. There is much more to this universe than meets the eye."

She snorts, rolling her eyes. "Thanks, Erik. I've gathered enough insanity these past few days to last me an eternity." She smirks. "But you already knew that, didn't you?"

Erik laughs. "Indeed. We all have."

I push into her mind with encouragement and support. "*We can make it through this, Angel. I'm here for you every step of the way.*"

A hopeful smile appears as she answers me. "*I know.*"

DANICA

54

We stayed up for hours, devouring the ancient tome of Atheria until dawn's light crept through the window. My eyelids finally surrendered to exhaustion, and I passed out in bed with Rhyland well into the afternoon. When consciousness finally returns, my stomach growls ferociously, demanding immediate attention.

I descend the marble spiral staircase and navigate through the hotel lobby, weaving between pretentious potted palms. The intoxicating scent of bacon wafts from the Grab-n-Go Deli, and I settle on a turkey sandwich. I hand over cash to the bored-looking employee and trudge back up to Rhyland's ridiculously luxurious suite.

Rhyland looms at the bar, brooding over a glass of scotch. When I push through the door, his head snaps up, and his eyes instantly darken as he abandons his drink and stalks toward me. His powerful frame radiates tension, and his jaw is clenched tight as he demands to know why I left without my phone.

Daylight still cracks through the curtains, and guilt pinches at me for causing him stress. "I didn't want to wake you," I offer lamely. "Just needed some food."

He captures me against him, strong arms locking possessively around my waist. "Next time, you come to me and tell me what you need," he commands, his voice brooking no argument.

I snort derisively, "Seriously, Rhyland? I'm a grown-ass woman. I don't need a knight in shining armor for a sandwich run. I've been feeding myself quite successfully for years, thanks." I punctuate this with a sarcastic wink.

"Oh, baby, we both know you can handle yourself." His lips curl into a predatory smirk. "But that's not what I meant. I need you safe, especially with our current situation." The authority in his tone makes it clear this isn't a request.

I relent with a sigh, "Fine. I get it."

He claims my forehead with a possessive kiss, his stubble scraping deliciously against my skin. His smile reveals that devastating dimple, sending my pulse into overdrive. I saunter to the dining table, practically salivating over my pathetic sandwich. Perched on the table's edge, I tear into the paper wrapping and devour the layers of meat, vegetables, and cheese.

The sharp bite of pickle and the comfort of melted cheese assault my taste buds. I take another massive bite, my neglected stomach practically singing with relief. My eyes roll back in embarrassing ecstasy, barely containing the moan threatening to escape.

Christ, when did I last eat actual food? Between vampire drama, celestial revelations, and mind-blowing sex, basic survival needs have taken a backseat.

Being half-divine doesn't eliminate the need for processed deli meat. Good to know.

I demolish my meal like a starving animal, barely pausing to breathe. Glancing up, I catch Rhyland's intense stare fixed on me. Heat floods my cheeks as I hastily wipe crumbs from my mouth. "Sorry, I must look like a feral beast," I laugh awkwardly under his predatory gaze.

Rhyland stalks over with lethal purpose. My pulse skyrockets as he claims the space between my thighs. "Never apologize for your hunger, Angel," He snatches my sandwich and launches it across the room in one fluid motion.

"What the hell! You can't be serious!" I protest around my mouthful. "I wasn't finished!"

His eyes devour me. "Hungry, baby?" he purrs with wicked intent. "Watching you ravage that sandwich is making me jealous."

I force down my bite. "Seriously? You're envious of processed meat and limp lettuce?" I challenge, arching an eyebrow.

He chuckles darkly. "No. If you want something to savor, I've got something much better for those pretty lips."

I smirk back. "Oh really now?"

He claims my neck in searing kisses. His touch ignites a different kind of hunger, and thoughts of food evaporate instantly. I eagerly reach for his belt, desperate to feast on the pleasure he's offering.

He tears my shirt open with savage intent, exposing my bare chest to his burning gaze. His scorching mouth claims my neck while his hands possess my breasts. His tongue blazes a trail down, expertly tormenting my nipples until I'm begging shamelessly for more, arching into his hungry assault.

My heart stutters as I suddenly remember his brothers sleeping just one room away.

Rhyland senses my tension, biting my nipple with delicious warning before growling against my flesh. "Don't worry... they're dead to the world."

Fuck the sandwich. This is a much better meal.

I surrender with a shaky breath as his powerful hands lock me against him. My legs wrap around his waist, feeling his hardness straining through denim. Every piece of clothing between us feels like torture—I need skin on skin *now*.

We tear at each other's clothes frantically, his shirt shredding under desperate hands. The electric tension crackles as we struggle with remaining barriers.

Finally naked, he claims his place between my thighs. His thick, veiny cock slides against my aching clit, as I claw at his back. He fists my hair, drawing a wanton moan as I submit. His blazing eyes capture mine as he yanks my head back—our ritual of dominance and surrender. His tongue teases my lips while I pant shamelessly.

"Say it, baby." His voice drips sin against my lips.

But what if I resist? What delicious punishment awaits my defiance?

I taste him hungrily, melting as I arch against his hard body. My whimpers betray my desperate need.

"Beg." His command vibrates through me.

Make me.

I meet his gaze with defiant heat, daring him to punish my disobedience. His eyes flash dark promises as I drag my tongue up his neck, hands exploring every muscled plane. His chest heaves against mine, restraint wearing thin.

"Oh, you want to play dirty, baby?" he growls, voice pure predator.

Fuck yes I do. Show me what happens to defiant little humans who don't beg properly.

"What will you do to me if I don't beg?" I purr wickedly, eyes challenging.

His gaze ignites as he drags me to the edge of the table. "You asked for it, baby."

His hot breath teases my thigh before his mouth claims my clit. That wicked tongue torments with devastating skill, electricity shooting through me. His hands grip under my knees, spreading me wider as his groans vibrate against my pussy.

Oh god, his mouth is sin incarnate.

Heat blazes through my body, my nipples aching. His merciless assault has me moaning shamelessly as he devours me like a starving man.

"So fucking delicious," he growls against my flesh.

I grip his hair, grinding desperately against his mouth. "Oh fuck! I'm gonna—"

Rhyland freezes suddenly, and I stare down in disbelief. His hands cage me, crackling with strange electricity unlike anything I've felt before. "What... what the hell are you doing?"

The heat at my clit turns icy, my orgasm hovering just out of reach. My core pulses desperately for release as I whimper for him to finish what he started.

"Beg," he commands with dark satisfaction.

Oh, this magnificent bastard. He's playing dirty now, edging me into submission.

Fine. Two can play at this game, big boy. Let's see who breaks first.

His merciless tongue drives me higher and higher, only to deny release at the last moment. Again and again, this beautiful bastard pushes me to the brink before pulling away.

"Goddammit... Rhylaaaand!" I snarl, desperate and aching.

His dark laugh vibrates through me before he slaps my throbbing clit. I yelp at the exquisite shock. "Beg me to fuck you. I'll give you pleasure you'll never forget."

Another slap lands. "Such a dirty little angel. You love this. Submit."

His fingers plunge deep, curling wickedly as his tongue torments my clit. My whimpers turn to screams, body coiling tighter—until he stops again.

I can't take it anymore.

I lunge up, yanking him against me as my legs lock around his hips.

Fine. He wins this round.

I grind against him frantically. "Please... make me scream," I beg shamelessly, desperate for relief from this sweet torture—my body can't take anymore. I'm dripping and aching to have him buried inside me.

He moves with inhuman speed—but instead of giving me what I need, his rough hands tear me from the surface, spins me around, and slams me onto the unforgiving table. My sensitive nipples press against cold wood as Rhyland grinds his thick cock against my ass.

"Rhyland... please..." I whimper pathetically.

His breath scalds my neck. "Want to play games, sweetheart? I can play." His dark promise makes me shiver. "Game on, Angel. And I never lose."

The crack of his palm against my ass draws a cry of pure ecstasy.

Oh fuck. What have I started?

I revel in the delicious sting. "Spread those legs," he commands. "Wider," he barks with absolute authority. I comply instantly.

He grips my ass possessively, his wicked tongue exploring my dripping core. I shudder helplessly in his grasp.

"This ass," he purrs. Another sharp smack makes me yelp. "Mine."

Yes, yours. All yours.

I'm trembling as his tongue eats me out from behind, drawing desperate moans. Bent over the table, I'm completely at his mercy—devouring me, pinning my hips against the wood.

The forbidden position sends electricity through me. Each flick against my clit brings me closer to the edge.

He spreads me wider, burying his face deeper as animalistic groans vibrate through my core.

"I've got centuries of patience, Angel," he taunts between licks.

"Please, Rhyland... I can't... please..." I beg.

Tension coils tighter with each stroke of his masterful tongue. I grind shamelessly against his mouth, desperate moans filling the room as I writhe on the table.

So close... please...

Just as my climax builds, the beautiful bastard stops again.

"Fuck!" I snarl in frustration.

Centuries of patience? Fuck you and your immortal stamina, Viking.

He rises, pressing his powerful body against mine. "Want to come, baby?" he rumbles darkly.

I barely hesitate before answering, "Yes, goddammit!" Frustration edging my voice.

"Ready to stop playing games?"

With reckless defiance, I whisper, "Never."

My challenge hangs in the air.

He fists my hair brutally, yanking me back against him. "Is that so?"

His scorching breath fans my skin as his thick length presses against me. I grind back teasingly, drawing feral groans.

"We'll see about that," he growls.

His fangs pierce my neck as he slams inside me. My screams of pleasure echo off the walls.

"This what you need, Angel?" He pounds into me savagely, his balls slapping against my skin. The obscene sounds of our coupling fill the air.

Yes, destroy me.

He grips and pulls my hair harder, making me gasp. His burning palm finds my breast, kneading with delicious cruelty.

"Answer me, Dani," he demands against my ear.

"Y-Yes!" I stammer desperately.

Who needs food when you can feast on Viking cock?

"That's my good girl. You love this thick cock stretching your needy pussy," he pants, yanking my head back to expose my throat.

His thrusts turn savage as I writhe and moan, begging shamelessly for more. He seizes my throat in an iron grip, forcing my head back while his other hand remains tangled in my hair. His sinful breath intoxicates me as he locks me in his dominant embrace.

He drives relentlessly deeper, leaving me utterly helpless to his assault. His raw power consumes me until I can only surrender to his will.

His burning gaze captures mine. "Are you gonna be my filthy angel?" His lips claim me brutally as he holds me immobile. His breathing turns ragged as he breaks away to growl, "Answer me."

His grip tightens on my throat as pleasure blazes through me. I teeter on the edge of a devastating orgasm as I gasp, "Yes! Fuck...*yes!*"

Rhyland growls against my neck, stoking my desperate need as he pins me down against the unforgiving table. "Good. Now be a good girl and come all over my cock," he commands.

His thrusts turn punishing as I submit to his primal claiming. Our bodies collide with brutal force as he dominates me completely, and I revel in every exquisite second.

"You'll remember this lesson," Rhyland grunts as his fingers dig into my hips and he slams home. I cry out as incredible pleasure detonates through me, erupting into an earth-shattering orgasm.

Rhyland follows with a feral roar, his release triggering another wave of ecstasy.

I bite my lip, breathless. "Good. I'm loving your *lessons.*"

Danica

55

After our steamy dominance play, Rhyland and I shower together. My phone buzzes—John's name flashes urgently. I freeze, gripping the device as conflict churns inside me. Rhyland's piercing eyes lock onto mine, his powerful frame radiating protective tension.

"It's John..." I murmur.

The Playful Pint needs me, but guilt wars with fear. John's been family to me, yet Azrael's sinister presence still lurks in the shadows.

I scan the text, anxiety gnawing at my gut. "The bar's slammed. He needs help..." The words tumble out defensively.

Rhyland's jaw tightens. "It's not safe, Dani. Azrael's still out there."

Guilt twists deeper. Abandoning John feels wrong after everything he's done for me. Despite having loving adoptive parents, John became another pillar in my life—the one who listened to my excited rambles about DNA sequencing breakthroughs at closing time, who remembered every publication date, who celebrated each small victory in my research. The Playful Pint became my sanctuary when lab pressures mounted, a place where John's steady presence and dad jokes could always lift my spirits.

I still remember how he'd stepped in when my ex wouldn't take no for an answer, his normally jovial face turning stone-cold as he escorted the persistent jerk out with a firm hand and a whispered threat that ended the harassment for good. John protects his own.

But Rhyland's warning sends dread through my veins. I bite my lip, torn between loyalty and survival.

"I have to go," I say, meeting his gaze. "John's been covering for me while his mom was in the hospital. He canceled his fishing trip to help me out. I can't bail now when he finally asks for something in return." My voice comes out stronger than intended, fueled by years of John's unwavering support.

Rhyland crowds closer, his scent overwhelming me. "Promise you'll stay alert. No risks," he demands, his intense gaze searching mine. "Text me when you arrive and when you leave."

"I promise," I whisper, the words feeling pathetically inadequate against the danger we both know lurks out there.

I squeeze his hand, pleading for understanding. "John's family—not by blood, but by choice. He's been there for every crisis and triumph. I can't abandon him now." The memory of John sitting with me through my meltdown after a critical experiment failed flashes through my mind. "Trust me."

Rhyland finally nods, though worry still darkens his eyes. He crushes me against his chest in a fierce embrace. I melt into him, grateful he's letting me make this choice despite his fears.

"I'll sense any danger," he whispers against my hair. "Call me and I'll come—no matter what."

"Thank you," I murmur. With a final look at his stormy expression, I grab my coat and step into the afternoon sun.

The streets are eerily quiet this late in the day. Each step toward my car makes my pulse race faster as Azrael's threat looms in my mind. John's been my rock for years, but is my loyalty worth risking everything?

Please let this not be a horrible mistake.

The wall of sound hits me as I push through the heavy door—laughing drunks, clinking glasses, thumping music. John's exhausted face lights up when he spots me.

"Thank fuck you're here, Dani! We're getting killed," he calls over the chaos of bodies packed shoulder-to-shoulder.

I tie my apron and dive into the familiar dance of slinging drinks. But gnawing dread sits heavy in my gut, impossible to ignore. My eyes snap to the door every time it opens, half-expecting Azrael's menacing bulk to materialize.

Azrael's a vampire—he can't exactly stroll in here while the sun's up.

Still, dark whispers of doubt refuse to leave me alone. The rational part of my brain knows I'm safe in daylight, but fear isn't always logical.

During a brief slowdown, John catches my jumpiness. "You good?"

"Yeah... just paranoid," I mutter, Azrael's face flashing unwanted through my mind.

"We've got you covered," John says, squeezing my shoulder before plunging back into the madness. His words do nothing to ease the doom crawling up my spine.

I throw myself into the work, drowning in the packed bar's deafening noise and suffocating heat. Stale beer and sweat hang thick in the air, coating my skin. I focus on drink after drink, desperately trying to ignore the darkness growing inside me.

Please let me get through this shift without everything going to hell.

After hours in the chaos, John finally orders me to take a break. I practically throw my apron at him, desperate to escape the overwhelming crush of bodies and noise.

After the bar's din, the back hallway's silence hits like a physical wall. But even here, dread coils tighter in my gut. A leaky faucet's steady drip echoes ominously through the empty space, setting my teeth on edge.

"Get your shit together," I mutter, heading for the bathroom. The air shifts the moment my fingers touch cold metal. Pressure builds around me, making each breath a struggle through the suddenly thick atmosphere.

"Don't. Move." The menacing growl freezes my blood.

Brutal hands seize me, slamming me against unforgiving tile with crushing force. A massive palm silences my startled cry. Feral yellow eyes bore into mine with predatory hunger—Marcus Welch. My stomach lurches in recognition.

"Scream and you die," he snarls, putrid breath hot on my face. His imposing frame towers over me, scarred muscle rippling with barely contained violence.

I'm trapped. Alone. When he slowly removes his hand, survival instinct takes over—my palm cracks across his stubbled jaw in desperate defiance.

Marcus's answering roar is pure animal rage. His retaliation is devastating—a savage backhand that explodes stars behind my eyes. Before I can recover, iron fingers crush my jaw as he slams me back into cold tile.

"Stupid fucking bitch!" he seethes, eyes promising brutal retribution.

I thrash uselessly against his overwhelming strength, but I'm helpless against his raw power. His hand clamps down again, muffling my terrified screams.

Through the blur of tears, I see the syringe in his hand before he brutally jabs the needle into the side of my neck. Liquid fire erupts under my skin, radiating agony through my veins as the sedative rapidly takes hold. The edges of my vision dim as Marcus's snarling face swims above me.

Just then, the bathroom door bursts open with a crash. John appears, gripping an aluminum baseball bat. False hope leaps in my chest. But Marcus moves with preternatural speed, whirling and lunging for John's exposed throat before he can react.

"No! Leave him alone!" I shriek, but it's useless.

With chilling efficiency, his hands close around John's neck, thick fingers digging ruthlessly into flesh. A wet crack echoes off tile walls. The bat clatters uselessly as John's body crumples, eyes already empty and staring.

"JOHN!" My scream tears raw from my throat. Marcus whirls back, face twisted in demonic fury. Tile bites into my spine as he slams me against the wall.

I claw desperately at our bond, but darkness creeps in at the edges. Marcus's voice filters through cotton wool, stuffing my head. "You're coming with me."

Blackness crashes over me like a wave. His final whisper follows me down: "Sweet dreams."

My head lolls to the side as he hoists my limp body over his shoulder. The floor seems to tilt and spin as he carries me from the bathroom, my unfocused eyes landing on John's broken form sprawled on the grimy tiles. The aluminum bat is lying useless next to his outstretched hand.

Bile rises in my throat as the hallway stretches out endlessly before me. I try to scream, to struggle, but my limbs refuse to obey, weighed down as if my veins are filled with lead.

Faces flash through my fading consciousness—Mom, Dad, Rhyland, Emily... John. Everyone I've failed. Marcus's warning echoes as darkness claims me—

"Scream, and you die."

I'm so sorry...

Cold metal presses against my cheek. Everything spins as drug-induced fog clogs my thoughts. Rough rope bites into my wrists and ankles, drawing blood with each desperate twist. The trunk's cramped darkness crushes in, reeking of motor oil and fear.

Rhyland... please hear me...

I scream into the void between us, but only silence answers. My clumsy attempts at telepathy scatter like smoke in the wind.

How the fuck does this bond even work?

Duct tape muffles my raw screams until they're nothing but animal sounds. My body thrashes against unyielding bonds, skin splitting and weeping—exhaustion wars with terror as the car lurches and sways.

When my throat finally gives out, darkness creeps back with velvet fingers. I gulp stale air through my nose, fighting to stay alert. But sedatives drag me down like iron chains, my consciousness fracturing at the edges.

No... have to stay awake... have to...

The trunk becomes my metal coffin as blackness claims me once more.

I jerk awake again as I'm hauled crudely onto a massive shoulder. Disoriented, I glimpse a dense forest flashing past through the gloom. We must be close to wherever these psychos are taking me. In the distance, I hear loud, angry voices.

A harsh woman demands, "About damn time. Toss her ass in the cellar."

I'm carelessly dropped to the freezing dirt floor of a cramped hole in the ground. The impact sends shock waves of pain through my battered body. Heavy footsteps approach, and I see Marcus leering down at me, eyes glowing with sick malevolence in the dark.

He crouches next to me, lips twisted into a feral mockery of a smile. "Shame about your boss," he taunts. "Died trying to play hero to a useless cunt."

Rage and anguish surge within me at the memory of John's gruesome fate. If not for me, he would still be alive. I'll never fucking forgive myself for the tragedy my presence caused him. For now, consumed by fear and adrenaline, I can only clench my jaw in defiant silence.

Sneering, Marcus continues, "You won't be leaving this shithole anytime soon. Get comfy, bitch." He gestures mockingly around the cramped, windowless cellar before turning on his heel and departing, the door slamming with an echoing finality behind him.

Alone again, I take stock of my limited options. With my limbs bound and no clear avenue of escape, panic creeps in. What exactly do my captors have planned for me? Rhyland's absence leaves me untethered, set adrift in a violent sea with no anchor. He's my only hope, yet impossible to reach. I wrestle against the ropes anew until exhaustion takes over.

Curled on the freezing dirt, I slip into fitful unconsciousness, John's lifeless body haunting me even in my fucked-up dreams.

RHYLAND

56

"I FELT her fucking terror!" I roar, whirling on Adrian and Erik, my control hanging by a thread.

I stalk the hotel suite like a caged predator, rage building with every passing second. The moment darkness fell, I tore through the city to that worthless bar, but Danica was already gone. The stench of werewolf hung in the air like a threat. My blood turned to ice when I discovered her boss John's lifeless body sprawled across the filthy bathroom floor. I tore that place apart searching for any trace of her, my mind conjuring increasingly violent scenarios.

Marcus. That cold-blooded enforcer from Leavenworth. His loyalty to Azrael is absolute, unbreakable. The way that animal looked at her with those dead eyes... calculating how to claim what's MINE. The thought of his hands on her makes my fangs descend with murderous intent.

We all agreed Azrael's underground human trafficking operation was our first target. When we arrived, Lucian and Adrian threw everything they had at those warded entrances, but even their combined power couldn't break through. Erik and I stormed the perimeter, hunting for any weakness.

I'm desperately reaching through our bond, straining to catch even the faintest whisper of her presence, but there's nothing but deafening silence. She's not here—no scent, no trace, nothing. The rage building inside me is primal, volcanic, demanding blood and vengeance.

A roar of pure anguish tears from my throat, echoing into the darkness.

Every attempt to touch her mind slams into an impenetrable wall. Our connection—severed or blocked—leaves me clawing at emptiness where she should be. Her phone is equally useless, ringing endlessly with no answer. Each unanswered call drives my fury higher, the repeated tones mocking my failure to protect her.

As night bled into dawn, we tore through every shadow and crevice of the surrounding area, finding nothing but emptiness where her scent should be.

Now, with the first light breaking over the horizon, the brutal truth hits me like a stake through the heart. I'm forced to wait out the entire fucking day, trapped and useless while my mate is in the hands of that animal. The knowledge that I can do nothing—absolutely nothing—to reach Danica burns like acid in my veins.

My fist obliterates the wall, plaster exploding into dust. The destruction does nothing to ease the savage beast clawing inside me.

"Control yourself, Rhyland," Adrian cautions, fear edging his voice as he surveys the destruction. "This rage won't help us find Danica."

His words slice through me, momentarily stunning me before feeding the inferno of my fury. My brother stands there, still not comprehending the hell unfolding around us.

"Was it Azrael?" Adrian asks tentatively.

At that bastard's name, my last thread of control snaps. "It was Marcus, you ignorant fuck!" I snarl, my voice barely human. "He took her for himself!"

The room practically vibrates with my violence. I'm ready to tear apart anything–or anyone—standing between me and my mate.

Erik steps forward, trying to be the voice of reason. "Rhyland, listen. We will find her, no matter what it takes."

As if he could possibly understand the black void consuming me. The knowledge that Marcus and his pack could be hurting my Danica while I'm trapped by the fucking sun makes me want to tear my own skin off.

"Don't you think I know that?" I growl, beyond reason. "I'll burn the entire world to ash if that's what it takes to get her back!"

Erik takes a measured breath, his voice deliberately calm. "I understand you're in hell right now, but we need clear heads to get Danica back. Why would Marcus specifically target her?"

I collapse into the nearest chair, raking my hands through my hair, desperation clawing at my insides. My mind tortures me with images of Marcus at Dani's parents' house—the raw hunger in his eyes when he looked at her, like a predator sizing up prey. The memory makes my stomach twist with violent rage.

Was it power he wanted? Some sick, twisted satisfaction? Or both, festering in his depraved mind?

Through clenched teeth, I detail every interaction with Marcus, my voice barely controlled as I describe his unwavering loyalty to that snake Azrael. My hands shake with suppressed fury, knuckles white as I grip the armrests.

Erik nods grimly. "You're right. Given their connection, Marcus must be holding Danica as leverage for something bigger. We need to uncover his endgame."

"I don't give a fuck about his endgame," I growl, a deadly promise in my voice. "I'm getting her back, and then I'm tearing his fucking throat out with my bare hands."

Lucian chooses that moment to saunter in, reeking of cheap perfume, with the audacity to wink at me.. "So sorry I'm late to the party, gentlemen. I'm afraid I got rather delightfully distracted by a particularly lovely barmaid downstairs."

Pure hatred flashes through me. I fix him with a look that would make most men crumble. "Now is not the fucking time for your bullshit theatrics, Lucian," I snarl. "Danica is with a bunch of murderous psychopathic mutts. So, please enlighten me. Why in the hell do you seem to think a jocular tone is appropriate right now?"

Lucian's teasing expression instantly morphs into one of sincere remorse. He quickly holds up both palms in a gesture of peace and apology. "Those reprehensible heathens are holed up somewhere remote in the Cascades, correct?" he asks, all joking aside.

At my short nod of confirmation, his jaw locks tightly, a storm brewing in his eyes."Well, tickle my taint. We have a wolf hunt in our future, boys."

Erik stands swiftly, posture radiating authority and command. "It's decided then. We mobilize and depart the moment dusk falls. No excuses."

The hours until nightfall stretch like an eternity of torture. My mind conjures increasingly violent images of what Danica might be enduring—each one driving me closer to madness. The bond between us remains terrifyingly silent, a void where her presence should be.

Is Azrael pulling the strings? Is Marcus acting on orders or for himself? And the question that sends ice through my veins—what do they want with her?

Sunset can't come soon enough. When it does, I'll hunt like I never have before.

And God help anyone who stands between me and my angel.

DANICA

57

The dank, musty air of the cellar feels oppressive as weak daylight filters through cracks in the wooden boards, casting feeble strips of illumination on the cold, damp ground. I blink slowly, my vision swimming as I struggle against the restraints binding me to the rusty chair. My head throbs relentlessly, and my mind is still fogged from whatever shit they injected into me.

I groan, my voice barely a rasped whisper as I strain futilely against the ropes digging cruelly into my wrists and ankles. Sick panic rises within me, my heart racing uncontrolled, as the terrifying gravity of my situation sets in. I have got to get the fuck out of here. No telling what these sadistic werewolf bastards have planned for me.

The loud creak of a heavy door echoes through the cellar, and my eyes widen in renewed fear as Marcus, the ruthless alpha leader of the pack, strides into view. His cold gaze meets mine, a twisted grin spreading on his lips.

"Well, well…look who's finally awake," he sneers, voice dripping maliciously.

My throat constricts, and each swallow feels like I'm forcing down razor blades. My muffled cries of desperation are met only with his mocking smile.

"What's that, girlie?" he taunts, exaggeratedly cupping his hand to his ear. "I can't quite hear your pathetic whimpering down there."

I writhe and twist uselessly against the ropes, every muscle burning in protest. Suddenly, he lunges down, viciously ripping the tape from my mouth in one savage motion. White-hot pain explodes, but I summon every ounce of defiance left inside me.

"What the hell do you want from me, you sick bastard?" I scream, my voice wavering uncontrollably.

Marcus slowly circles the chair like a predator toying with cornered prey, his heavy footsteps echoing through the confined space."You're a rare prize, my dear. One Azrael is most eager to acquire. Which makes you very useful leverage for me," he spits, eyes glinting with cruel excitement.

"Leverage for what?" I demand, my anger and frustration fueling my courage. "What could that snake possibly offer you?"

A sinister chuckle escapes Marcus's lips at my questions. "Let's just say he has something of great value that belongs to me. Something I aim to take back."

I grit my teeth as understanding dawns, the pieces of his vile game falling into place. "You're a goddamn fool if you think that bastard will just hand anything over to you."

Marcus throws his head back, laughing coldly at my response, the sound reverberating through the cellar and sending dread slithering down my spine."No, you naive little bitch," he says, amusement lacing his words. "Azrael's hunger for power is unmatched. And you..." He inhales deeply as if trying to catch some scent in the air. "You possess a kind of power he craves desperately."

My body tenses involuntarily at his words, a looming unease twisting in my gut. I force my voice to remain steady, determined to gain any information. "What could he possibly have that's so valuable you'd exchange my life for it?"

Marcus resumes his slow, deliberate pacing, considering my question. After a few endless minutes, he drags a creaky wooden chair from the corner into the center of the room and sinks into it. Even seated, his imposing, muscular frame dominates the small space. He leans forward, regarding me intently.

"Many years ago, Azrael and I made a solemn pact. A blood oath," he begins. "In exchange for granting me the dark power and strength to protect my pack, I promised to deliver a certain precious artifact to him. One of great worth."

I stare at Marcus, listening intently despite the distraction of my raging thirst and pounding headache. "What kind of artifact?"

"It's known as the Soul Stone," he explains. "An object tied to primal dark energy and shadow itself. Incredibly potent." His tone radiates reverence and greed. "I aim to take back what's mine. And you are the leverage I will use to get it."

I squirm helplessly against the ropes, biting into my skin, desperate to escape this nightmare. "Please, you don't have to do this," I plead. "You can't possibly think he'll uphold any deal with you."

Marcus rises slowly to his imposing full height, his expression unreadable. Suddenly, he kicks the chair violently across the room, the wood clattering loudly against the far wall. He's inches from my face in two swift strides, and his expression twisted into a menacing sneer.

"Oh, he'll make the trade alright. I can smell it on you, whatever power you hold," he growls through gritted teeth. "He won't be able to resist possessing you. And then I'll finally have back what's rightfully mine."

Rage boils up inside me. "You're a delusional fucking moron if you think that snake will uphold any deal," I spit defiantly.

Marcus's massive hand shoots out, clamping around my throat and cutting off my air. "You dare insult me, you worthless bitch?" he roars, tightening his grip.

I gasp uselessly for breath, vision darkening at the edges. After an endless, terrifying moment, he releases me.

"He will make the exchange," Marcus declares coldly. "Or I will end your pathetic life without hesitation."

The true direness of my situation crashes down on me. I have to find some way to warn Rhyland. Mustering every ounce of focus, I strain desperately against the ropes, trying to summon my powers, but they remain maddeningly out of reach.

Marcus looms over me, satisfaction twisting his features. "You won't be escaping, girl. Your fate will soon be decided."

I glare up at him defiantly. "You can't hurt me unless Azrael agrees to your pathetic deal. I'm untouchable by the likes of you."

My taunt hits its mark. Marcus's eyes blaze with unrestrained rage. Before I can react, his massive fist slams into my face, the force of the blow sending me and the chair crashing sideways to the ground.

Pain explodes through my skull and shoulder from the impact. I cry out, the taste of blood filling my mouth. Above me, Marcus towers like a vengeful demon.

"You think being Azrael's bargaining chip makes you safe?" He punctuates this with a vicious kick to my unprotected ribs. I hear a sickening crack, blinding agony lancing through my side."I'll teach you some respect!" Marcus roars.

Through the pain and blood, I cling desperately to one thought—I have to survive this. Rhyland is coming.

Marcus unties me from the chair and grabs a fistful of my hair, wrenching me up. "Let's see you spew more of that defiant trash now," he snarls before slamming my face into the unforgiving ground.

As darkness creeps into my vision, I retreat deep within my mind. *Just hold on,* I tell myself. Rhyland will find me. He has to...

He tears my underwear from my body with brutal force. I scream in terror as he rips my shirt off, exposing my breasts to his malicious gaze. His meaty hand clamps around one of them, squeezing forcefully until I can't help but cry out for mercy. My tears mingle with the dirt on my cheeks as I struggle hopelessly against his crushing grip, my feeble attempts to fight back powerless against his strength. His fingers trail down to my core, where he pushes them into me rough and rugged, making me writhe in pain and anguish.

"You like that, slut?" he sneers in my face between gritted teeth. "How about a real dick instead of a dead one inside you?"

A cry of agony rips through my throat, "STOP!"

This can't be happening again, and I'm powerless to stop it. Though I fight, my abilities have been silenced as if a switch had been flipped—rendering Rhyland inaccessible. Even if I can reach him, what could he possibly do?

I clench my eyes shut, gritting my teeth as Marcus's weight bears down on me. I dig deep within myself, searching for the source of my power. It simmers beneath the surface, and I focus. The rage that sweeps through me is a turbulent storm fueled by fear and desperation.

As I struggle violently against Marcus's iron grasp, my magic suddenly burns within me like wildfire, lashing out at him with force beyond my control. Before I can even process what's happening, Marcus rockets clear across the cellar with the power of a freight train, crashing thunderously through the far wall in an explosive shower of splintered wood.

His body lies crumpled against shattered debris, eyes wide with disbelief. My hands tremble violently as residual energy crackles across my skin. This wasn't my usual steady flow of warm, familiar magic.

This was pure devastation—a tsunami of raw power that erupted without warning or control. My chest heaves as drug-addled thoughts try to process what just happened. I took down an alpha werewolf by accident. And I have no fucking clue how to handle this new, volatile force surging through my veins.

THUD. THUD. THUD.

Heavy boots thunder down wooden stairs. My head snaps up as a massive wolf charges into the destruction. His eyes dart from his fallen alpha to me, and his face twists with dawning rage.

Oh shit.

The air grows thick with accusation as understanding hits him. I stand frozen in the wreckage, waiting for the other shoe to drop.

He whirls to face Marcus, who is slowly dragging himself up from the rubble, murder blazing in his enraged eyes."What the hell happened here, Marcus?" the wolf bellows, voice booming through the confined space. "We had strict orders not to lay a single hand on the girl!"

Marcus pulls himself to his full imposing height, muscles coiled and jaw clenched. "Watch your tone with me, boy!" he roars. "I'm still the leader around here. I'll do as I damn well please, and no one will question me!"

Heavy footsteps at the top of the stairs signal another arrival. A fierce-looking woman with eyes of pure flaming rage appears in the doorway, fixing first me, then Marcus, with a scorching glare. "Marcus! Get your pathetic worthless ass up here right now!" she screeches with venom.

Marcus holds my frightened gaze for a long, endless moment, his cold eyes piercing my soul. "Drug her again. Immediately," he orders the other wolf. "I don't care what the hell she is; we cannot allow another magical...outburst."

The apparent threat behind his words sends real fear through me. As the reluctant pack member approaches me, I cringe back instinctively, pleading uselessly for mercy or restraint. But his large hands roughly grab and lift me to my feet as if I weigh nothing.

"I'm sorry, but I have my orders," he mutters before draping a scratchy blanket around my trembling shoulders and forcing me back into another chair.

His ominous words echo through my panicking mind, each syllable ringing with terrifying finality. I'm almost out of time and options now.

As darkness begins creeping into the edges of my vision, I cling desperately to one single thought—Rhyland is coming for me.

He has to be...

RHYLAND

58

The engine howls as I slam the accelerator to the floor, the speedometer needle climbing past 120. Outside, darkness swallows the last traces of daylight—a perfect mirror to the black rage consuming me. Lucian's matte-black SUV devours the asphalt, suspension groaning in protest as I take each curve with reckless precision.

Knuckles white against the steering wheel, jaw clenched until teeth threaten to crack. In the rearview mirror, Lucian's mouth moves, something about strategy and caution, but all I hear is the thundering of my own pulse and the phantom echoes of Dani's terror cutting through our bond.

Rain begins to lash against the windshield, fat droplets racing across the glass like tears. Fitting. Nature itself weeps for what I'm about to unleash.

The SUV fishtails as I wrench it off the main road, tires spraying gravel like shrapnel. We skid to a halt beneath towering pines, their shadows offering cover as the engine falls silent.

We emerge like wraiths into the forest. No words needed—just the synchronous movement of predators on the hunt. The earthy scent of rain-soaked soil mingles with pine, but beneath it all, something foul. Wolf. My nostrils flare, tracking the stench.

I reach through our bond again, fingers of my consciousness grasping at empty space where Dani's light should be. Nothing. The void where she should exist stabs deeper than any blade.

Something electric pulses beneath my skin—not her thoughts, but her essence. It pulls me forward like a compass needle finding true north. My pace quickens, and my boots barely touch the forest floor as I surge ahead, my brothers' footfalls whispering behind me.

My fist shoots up, freezing us in place as the encampment materializes through the trees. Firelight flickers against canvas tents and crude wooden structures nestled in a natural depression. Hulking shadows move between fires—more wolves than before, at least twenty new bodies among their ranks.

The air reeks of unwashed fur and blood. Fresh blood.

Adrian's hand grips my shoulder, his eyes asking the question his lips don't form. I nod once, and he dissolves into shadow, slipping between trees toward the camp.

Minutes stretch like hours. Rain patters against leaves overhead. A wolf laughs somewhere in the camp, the sound like broken glass in my ears. My fangs descend involuntarily, tongue tasting copper as I bite the inside of my cheek.

Adrian's voice slides into my mind, grim and urgent. *"There are too many. More underground. We should retreat..."*

"No!" The word tears from my throat, primal and raw. "We act now!"

We descend on the camp like angels of death. No battle cry, no warning—just the whisper of displaced air as I materialize behind the first guard. My fingers lock around his throat, crushing his windpipe before he can draw breath to scream. Fangs plunge into his neck, tearing through muscle and artery with savage precision. His body convulses as I nearly separate head from shoulders, hot blood cascading over my chin and chest. I discard the twitching corpse like garbage.

I pivot toward the next target, gore dripping from my chin, fangs bared in a feral snarl. The remaining guards scramble to shift, panic in their eyes as they realize death has come for them.

Erik moves like liquid silver, his ancient blade whistling through the night. A wolf's desperate howl cuts short as steel cleaves flesh from collarbone to hip. The beast's insides spill steaming onto the forest floor, the copper stench of death thickening the air.

My hands find another wolf's skull, vise-like, as my teeth tear through his throat. Arteries rupture between my jaws, the hot rush of lifeblood flooding my mouth. I spit chunks of gristle to the ground, scanning for my next kill.

A massive gray wolf launches at me, fully shifted, claws extended for my gut. I move fast. I snatch the beast mid-leap, twisting its spine with a sound like wet branches breaking. When I slam it to the ground, the impact sends tremors through the ground, bone fragments puncturing fur as the creature's body caves inward.

Nearby, Lucian delivers a kick that sends a wolf crashing into a pine trunk with bone-liquifying force. "Down, Fido! Bad dog!" he cackles, providing a flurry of blows that reduce the creature to a fur-covered meat puzzle.

Blood-soaked and relentless, we carve through their ranks, yet their numbers barely thin. Through the haze of violence, a towering figure catches my eye—Marcus, his cold gaze meeting mine across the battlefield.

My world narrows to a single point. Him.

Marcus bolts, a shadow slipping between moonlit trees. My muscles coil and release as I surge after him, each footfall like thunder against the earth. The forest blurs around us—branches whipping past, undergrowth crushed beneath our supernatural chase.

He skids to a halt in a small clearing bathed in silver moonlight. Surrounded by sentinel pines, he turns to face me, yellow eyes gleaming with feral malice in the darkness.

"Here for your precious little human pet, Rhyland?" His lips curl back, revealing teeth too sharp for a human mouth.

I stalk toward him, every muscle vibrating with violence. Blood from earlier kills, still warm on my skin. "Where the fuck is she, you worthless piece of shit?!"

Marcus's face twists into a taunting smirk. "Wouldn't you just love to know?"

Something snaps inside me—the last thread of control severed. "What could you possibly want with her, you psychotic bastard?" Blood flies from my mouth, fangs fully extended.

He throws his head back in laughter—the sound like broken glass scraping across my nerves. "She's insurance, Rhyland." His eyes glitter with cruel knowledge. "You've somehow got yourself a truly rare and valuable prize in that girl, though I doubt you fully comprehend the true nature of the power she harbors."

My jaw clenches until my teeth threaten to crack. "Enough bullshit, Marcus." My voice drops as talons extend from my fingertips. "Tell me where she is, or I fucking end your worthless life right here in this goddamn clearing."

He steps closer, sizing me up with cold calculation. Behind his bravado, fear flickers in his eyes—the instinctual recognition of a superior predator.

"Well now, guess you'll never find out what I have planned then," he taunts, false confidence wavering.

Something primordial breaks loose inside me. A roar tears from my chest—not human, not vampire, but something ancient and terrible. I launch at him, a blur of rage and vengeance. My body slams into his with bone-shattering force, driving us both to the ground with impact enough to crack the earth beneath us.

The hunt ends now.

My fingers find his throat, digging deep into flesh until I feel the pulse beneath my grip. Blood wells around my fingertips as I bear down with my full weight, pinning him beneath me. His eyes bulge, veins standing out against reddening skin as his oxygen depletes.

Marcus's fist connects with my jaw—a desperate, glancing blow. The momentary distraction loosens my death grip. He twists free, gulping air into his starved lungs, crimson rivulets streaming from the puncture wounds in his neck. He staggers backward, that infuriating smirk still twisting his bloodied mouth despite the fear in his eyes.

"You're too late!" Blood sprays from his lips as he speaks. "You can't possibly stop what's already been set in motion. Azrael will have your precious Danica soon, no matter what futile machinations you attempt here."

"That will NEVER happen while I still draw breath." Each word drips with lethal promise.

Marcus's body contorts unnaturally before me. Bones crack and reshape with wet, sickening pops. Skin splits as coarse black fur erupts across his frame. His face elongates into a muzzle, human teeth falling to the forest floor as dagger-like fangs take their place. Where a man stood seconds before, a massive black wolf now crouches, yellow eyes burning with hatred. Saliva drips in viscous ropes from jaws that could crush bone.

I stand immobile, my fangs bared in challenge. The beast stalks toward me, each step cracking the earth beneath massive paws. The stench of wet fur and blood fills the clearing. Marcus throws back his lupine head, unleashing a howl that vibrates through the night before lunging at my throat.

I sidestep with preternatural speed, seizing him mid-leap by the scruff of his neck. With a roar that tears from my very core, I pivot and hurl his massive form throat-first into a towering pine. The impact splinters wood and bone alike—a sickening symphony of destruction. His yelp of pain pierces the night, high-pitched and pathetic.

Blood matting his fur, Marcus peels himself from the shattered remains of the tree. One leg hangs at an unnatural angle, bone jutting through skin. Still, he launches himself at me again, jaws snapping for my jugular. I raise one palm, unleashing a wall of telekinetic force that blasts him backward through underbrush and saplings, leaving a path of destruction.

Impossibly, he rises again, yellow eyes burning with such pure hatred that I know this ends only with death.

As he charges once more, I unleash my full power. My hand extends, fingers splayed. Marcus's massive body lifts from the ground, suspended in my invisible grip. His legs thrash uselessly as I slowly close my fist, crushing his windpipe. His whimpers turn to gurgles as I savor his suffering before slamming him down with enough force to shatter his bones.

Without pause, I follow with a telekinetic-enhanced punch that sends him rocketing backward through the forest, trees splintering in his wake like matchsticks.

I stalk toward Marcus's broken form, now reverted to human shape—too shattered to maintain his wolf. Blood bubbles from his lips with each labored breath, ribs jutting through torn flesh like broken cage bars. His eyes widen as I loom over him, terror replacing defiance.

Without hesitation, I plunge my arm into his chest—flesh parts. Ribs crack. Hot blood cascades over my forearm as I thrust deeper, fingers closing around his frantically beating heart. The organ pulses against my palm, desperate and alive.

Marcus's mouth opens in a silent scream, eyes bulging as he feels my grip tighten around his very core.

"Go fuck yourself," I growl, voice barely human.

One savage twist and pull—his heart tears free from its moorings with a wet, sucking sound. Arterial spray coats my face and chest as the organ continues to pulse in my hand, muscle memory refusing to acknowledge its separation.

Marcus's body convulses once, a final spasm before stillness claims him. Blood pools beneath his corpse, soaking into the forest floor. I examine the heart, still quivering in my grip, veins and arteries dangling like obscene ribbons. With contempt, I let it fall—a wet, meaty thud as it lands beside its former owner.

"Rot forever in hell, you worthless bastard." My spit lands on his vacant, staring eyes.

Erik's voice slices through my bloodlust. *"Rhyland. We need you here now!"*

I materialize at his side instantly, finding us surrounded by a fresh wave of wolves—hackles raised, teeth bared. My hands drip crimson, Marcus's blood still warm on my skin. I unleash a roar that shakes leaves from branches, primal and terrifying.

"Get the fuck out of here if you want to live." Each word cuts through the night air like a blade.

Uncertainty ripples through the pack. Ears twitch. A muscular gray wolf shifts, bones cracking as he takes human form, naked and vulnerable.

"Marcus is dead? Truly?" Fear threads through his voice.

"Yes." My voice drops to a lethal whisper. "And you'll share his fate unless you flee. Now."

Erik, Adrian, and Lucian form a deadly perimeter around me, power radiating from them in palpable waves. Blood from earlier kills still drips from Erik's silver blade. Adrian's hands glow with arcane energy. Lucian's eyes gleam with gleeful anticipation.

The pack tightens their circle, jaws snapping with foam-flecked rage. We're outnumbered twenty to one, but I welcome their attack. Death hangs in the air, waiting to claim more souls tonight.

A single nod passes between my brothers. We brace as the wolves surge forward—a tide of fur, fang, and fury.

Danica

59

Agonized screams pierce the night silence—human cries dissolving into wet, gurgling howls. My eyes snap open, drug-fog scattering like roaches in sunlight. The sounds above can only mean one thing: Azrael has come to collect.

Ice floods my veins as rough wool scratches against bare skin. The filthy army blanket reeks of mildew and old blood, its coarse fibers catching on every raw patch of flesh. Fluorescent zip ties bite deeper into my wrists, cheap plastic cutting through layers of dried blood and inflamed skin. Each desperate twist sends fresh blood down my fingers. My throat feels like I've swallowed broken glass—Marcus's idea of "breaking" his prey.

Move. NOW. While there's still time.

My legs tremble like a newborn colt's as I force them to bear weight. The cellar's single bare bulb swings wildly overhead, casting manic shadows that dance across mold-slicked walls. The world tilts violently sideways as darkness creeps in from the edges. Packed earth rushes up to meet my face as my knees give out.

Heavy boots thunder across wooden floorboards above. Seconds left before—

CRACK!

The door explodes inward in a shower of splintered oak. Jagged shards pierce my exposed flesh like wooden needles, drawing tiny beads of blood. A sound between a sob and scream tears from my ravaged throat as I scramble backward on bleeding knees. The rough earth wall presses against my spine—nowhere left to run.

Boot heels strike each rotting stair with deliberate force. My heart slams a desperate rhythm against my ribs, blood roaring like storm-tossed waves. Stale air burns in my lungs, thick with the stench of earth and fear. Every nerve ending screams to flee, but I'm trapped in this underground tomb with only darkness and those approaching footsteps.

Please, god, don't let it be Azrael. Don't let me die in this hole like a trapped animal.

The footsteps stop. A shadow falls across the dirt floor.

"Dani—Angel, where are you?"

That voice cuts through the darkness like lightning. My heart stops.

Rhyland?

Reality blurs at the edges—is this another drug-induced dream? I inch forward from the shadows, throat raw and bleeding. "Rhy...?"

"Stay there, baby. I'm coming." Desperate urgency colors each word.

My legs give out as hope crashes through me. Tears carve tracks through dirt and blood on my cheeks. In two strides, he's there, crushing me against sandalwood, leather, and *home.* I cling to solid muscle, terrified he'll dissolve like morning mist if I dare loosen my grip.

"Shh, you're safe now, sweetheart. I've got you." His voice wraps around me like a shield.

A sob rips through my shredded throat. Strong fingers cradle my face as ocean-blue eyes anchor me to reality. My body convulses with silent screams, vocal cords too destroyed to make sound.

Powerful arms lift me from hell's pit. Pain lances through cracked ribs—Marcus's parting gift. Sweet night air floods my lungs as Rhyland lays me in cool grass. Every breath becomes more manageable, but terror still whispers this is another beautiful lie.

"Get these fucking ties off her." Rhyland rumbles.

Metal flashes as Lucian's blade sets me free. I throw leaden arms around Rhyland's neck, ignoring screaming ribs to press closer. Raw desperation drives me to cling tighter—if he vanishes, I'll wake back in that cellar's darkness, this rescue nothing but another cruel dream.

"You're safe, baby. I've got you." His whisper wraps around my fractured soul.

A broken sound claws past ravaged vocal cords.

Rhyland's jaw hardens like granite. "I need to heal you, Angel."

Please let this be real. Please don't let me wake up.

But Lucian urges sharply, "We've got to bolt before Lord Fuckwad shows up to claim his unwilling bride!"

At his words, memories of Marcus's vile plan come crashing back. Frantic, I push the horrific tale directly into Rhyland's mind, unable to speak it aloud.

Rhyland's ephemeral touch surrounds me as he takes in my panicked warning. "I hear you, baby. We'll get you out of here," he vows.

Relief courses through me that our mental bond remains true.

"We need to move. NOW." Adrian's voice cracks with urgency.

Rhyland hesitates, loathing to see me suffering yet unwilling to risk Azrael's wrath. His protective instincts war with logic, two dire threats poised on either side. Before we can flee, Azrael slides from the shadows, leering like a viper poised to strike.

"Leaving with my prize so soon?" Azrael's serpentine voice drips poison. Bile rises as his obsidian eyes devour me. "The girl stays. She's mine now."

He lazily mentions Marcus's grisly end: "Should've known better than to trust that mongrel." The casual cruelty freezes my marrow.

Rhyland's arms become steel bands around me. "Back the fuck off! She's not yours to take."

Lucian and Erik flank us, predators ready to pounce. Thunder rumbles in Rhyland's chest as they face down evil incarnate. Even wounded, he refuses to yield.

Rhyland tries a telekinetic blast, but Azrael deflects it easily, sending a writhing spear of shadow to knock Rhyland off his feet like a shotgun blast, wrenching me from his arms. I hit the cold earth hard, barely stifling a scream.

Before I can move, inky tendrils bind Rhyland in midair. He howls in fury as more shadows slither over me, slowly dragging me towards Azrael's clutches.

Lucian and Erik launch themselves at Azrael, but he swats them aside like insects. They crash limply to the ground, groaning.

"Now, my pet," Azrael croons, caressing my face as I cringe away. "Time to take your rightful place at my side..."

Though every fiber of my being recoils, some last reserve of defiance rises within me. I will not surrender silently—better to fight with my final breath.

As Azrael's shadows drag me toward his clutches, hate and rage ignite within. I will not surrender quietly to this fiend. "I will...never...be yours," I rasp, my damaged voice ringing with conviction. Mustering every ounce of strength, I channel all my fury into pure white heat.

Azrael's gloating eyes widen in alarm as I unleash a blazing orb of energy at his chest. He dissipates into smoke and shadow, narrowly avoiding obliteration. The blast leaves me spent, but triumph flares for this small victory.

Before I can collapse, familiar arms catch me. Rhyland cradles me close, tenderness and pride mingling in his gaze. I cling weakly to him, drawing comfort from his solid strength.

Around us, Lucian, Adrian, and Erik groan, struggling to rise after Azrael's onslaught. Though battered, determination still burns in their eyes. My brave defenders gather around us once more.

"Remind me not to piss you off, Firecracker," Lucian mutters with a pained chuckle. Erik squeezes my shoulder in silent solidarity.

Rhyland sweeps me up and blurs into motion, his speed leaving us a vanished ghost in the darkness. I cling to him as we race to safety, my head swimming and stomach roiling with every jostling step.

We reach the car, and Rhyland gently climbs in with me. Lucian pushes the SUV recklessly as Rhyland cradles me in his lap. Shivering uncontrollably, I'm pathetically grateful when he removes his shirt to cover my nakedness. Still, I tremble, wracked by bone-deep shock and the lingering drugs in my system. Lucian continues hurtling down the highway while I battle the twin demons of fear and nausea.

"Drink, Angel," Rhyland urges, pressing his bleeding wrist to my lips.

I eagerly swallow the thick, coppery blood, citrus, and cinnamon, feeling its restorative effects spread through me. Under its influence, my wounds begin knitting together, and bones snap back into place. I drink desperately until the raging fire in my throat finally ebbs.

"Thank you," I rasp, voice still a ruined echo of itself.

Rhyland smiles tenderly, leaning in to kiss me softly. "There she is," he whispers.

His evident relief at hearing my voice almost undoes me, but I blink back grateful tears. Pulling him close, I breathe him in, savoring this quiet stolen moment together.

As the aches slowly recede from my muscles, I notice Rhyland's untreated injuries, guilt flooding me. "You're hurt; let me help you," I plead urgently.

But Rhyland gazes at me with bottomless love and protection. "I'm alright, Angel," he assures me, kissing my lips gently. "Just rest now. You're safe."

Too drained to argue, I relax into him. His arms around me are a balm, allowing me to finally block out the memories of fear and pain, if only for now.

"About an hour out," Lucian informs us briefly from the front. I let my eyes fall shut, focusing only on the reassurance of Rhyland's presence.

Soon, I'll have to reckon with all that was done to me, all I now know. But, cradled against the only soul who makes me feel whole, I can pretend the world has disappeared. If only for this one perfect, stolen hour.

Rhyland

60

I cradle Danica against my chest, her fragile form weightless in my arms. Even unconscious, tremors ripple through her body—echoes of terror that refuse to release their grip. Her chestnut hair spills across my bloodstained shirt, her breath warm against my skin.

The hotel lobby parts before us like water around stone. Humans glance up, curious eyes quickly averted when they sense the lethal energy radiating from me. Smart. Tonight is not the night to test my restraint.

Inside our suite, I lay her on the king bed gently, as if she might shatter under rougher handling. The white sheets frame her vulnerable form—a stark canvas highlighting every mark those animals left on her. My blood has healed the visible wounds, but some scars run deeper than flesh.

She sighs in her sleep, turning instinctively toward my lingering warmth. The primal rage that's been consuming me since her abduction banks slightly at the sight. She's here. She's alive. She's mine again.

My fingers brush a stray lock from her face, committing every detail to memory—the curve of her lips, the flutter of eyelashes against her cheeks, the steady pulse at her throat. Mine to protect. Mine to avenge.

I force myself away, closing the door with barely a whisper of sound. The suite's opulent living area feels like a battlefield compared to the sanctuary of her presence.

My brothers look up as I enter, their hushed conversation dying instantly. Erik's silver eyes lock onto mine, his stoic mask slipping just enough to reveal genuine concern.

"How is she?" The question hangs in the air between us.

Words stick in my throat like broken glass. I turn away, pouring three fingers of whiskey with a hand that betrays the slightest tremor. The liquor burns a path down my throat, doing nothing to wash away the taste of rage.

"She's asleep." My voice emerges as a raw, dangerous thing. "She needs time."

What I don't say hangs heavier in the air: that some wounds never fully heal, that the girl sleeping in that bed may never be the same carefree soul she was before Marcus took her.

And for that, more blood will flow.

Lucian runs his blood-stained hand through his hair, genuine shock cracking through his usual flippant facade. "Jesus Christ, what in the actual fuck is Azrael playing at here, Rhyland?" His voice drops an octave, all traces of humor evaporated. "I knew that sadistic creep had underworld connections, but werewolves? That's a special kind of stupid even for him."

The disgust in his eyes mirrors the acid churning in my gut. This nightmare has spiraled beyond anything I anticipated. Azrael's obsession with Danica runs deeper than simple possession—it's a sick hunger that would drive him to break her entirely to rebuild her in his twisted image.

The thought of what Azrael planned for her sends rage coursing through me like liquid fire. Marcus must have had something truly damning over Azrael's head to make him risk such an alliance. What unholy bargain exists between them? What shared darkness connects werewolf enforcer and vampire criminal?

More importantly, how do I shield my angel from a predator willing to burn the world to claim her?

"We guard her with our lives," I growl, voice dropping to a dangerous rumble. "No mistakes. No weaknesses. If Azrael gets his hands on her again..." I don't finish the thought. I don't need to.

Adrian and Erik nod, the gravity of the situation etched into their faces. For once, even Lucian doesn't have a smart remark.

After a weighted silence, Adrian speaks carefully, "A powerful cloaking spell could hide Danica from magical tracking. I could weave protections around her that would mask her presence from divination."

"It's a start," I concede, mentally cataloging every resource, every ally, every weapon at our disposal. The storm brewing on our horizon will require everything we have and more.

Erik has remained uncharacteristically silent up until this point, his piercing, almost colorless gaze boring into me relentlessly from across the room. Even without utilizing words, my oldest friend and ally has a singular gift for forcing ugly, brutal truths to be confronted head-on rather than avoided. And I can tell by the weight of his stare that he's silently imploring me to voice the dark question haunting our thoughts, though no one has yet found the courage to speak it.

"Rhyland, based on your gifts and your bond with Danica..." Erik begins gravely, never one to shy away from ripping off the bandage, no matter how much it may sting. "What do you believe they truly did to her when she was held captive? How badly do you think she's suffered?"

I instantly close my eyes against the vivid horrors that have been cycling through my imagination since I first felt Danica frantically reaching out to me in stark terror through our mental bond. During my darkest moments of doubt and helplessness, gruesome images of the violation and pain she endured play out like an endless nightmare behind my tightly shuttered lids.

It was a devastating slideshow of all that may have been inflicted upon her delicate flesh and fragile psyche while I was trapped, utterly useless, unable to prevent her anguish or even bear faithful witness. I want nothing more in this world than to bury my head in the sand and forget this evil was ever allowed to befall someone so wondrous and precious.

But I know with sinking dread that sooner or later, I will need to find the strength to face even the most devastating possibilities head-on if I ever hope to truly aid Danica in healing her deepest wounds. The task threatens to overwhelm me.

Lucian silently takes my empty glass, refilling it without spilling a drop. His eyes speak volumes as he slides it back.

I nod grimly, downing the liquor. Anything to blur the horror show behind my eyes.

"Rhyland, look at me, brother." His usual snark gives way to rare sincerity.

I meet his gaze, finding unexpected compassion there.

"Dani has a will of iron and the spirit of a warrior goddess," he says quietly. "She'll find her way back. Have faith in her strength, as you always have."

His words ignite something in my chest. He's right—Dani's strength has never failed. I need to trust in that now more than ever.

My glass slams against the marble countertop with decisive force. "Adrian." My voice cuts through the tension like a blade. "I want every entrance warded. Every threshold sealed. The strongest protection runes you can conjure."

Adrian's eyes meet mine, no questions, just understanding. A single nod conveys his commitment.

When they finally leave me to my thoughts, my feet carry me instinctively back toward her—my mate, my purpose. The scent reaches me before I cross the threshold—lavender and steam curling from the partially open bathroom door, beckoning me like a siren's call.

Through the veil of mist, I find her—a silhouette behind frosted glass, motionless beneath cascading water. Her forehead presses against cool tile, shoulders slightly hunched, letting the scalding spray pound against her skin as if trying to wash away memories that water alone can't touch.

I slip inside like a shadow, discarding blood-stained clothes that reek of death and vengeance. The steam envelops me, hot and thick with lavender and her unique scent—honey and sunshine, now tinged with lingering fear.

My arms encircle her waist, skin against slick skin. She turns instantly, pressing her face to my chest where water and tears mingle indistinguishably. Her body trembles against mine, small hands clutching at my shoulders as if I might disappear.

I smooth back her saturated hair, tilting her chin upward gently. "Talk to me, Angel." My voice barely carries over the pounding water. "Let me help carry this burden with you."

She shakes her head, droplets flying from her lashes. "Not yet. I can't." Her voice breaks, raw and fragile. "Please, Rhyland, for now...I just...need you."

Her plea slices through me like silver. No pretty words can erase what she's endured. No empty promises can bypass the healing ahead. But I can give her this—a temporary escape, a sanctuary in my arms.

I brush wet strands from her cheek, feeling her pulse flutter beneath my fingertips. Her eyes—those honey-gold eyes that captivated me from the first time—look up with naked vulnerability, silently begging me to understand.

"Then let me take you far from this place tonight. At least in spirit," I murmur against her temple, inhaling the clean scent of her hair as I capture her mouth in a kiss that promises both tenderness and oblivion.

My hands work meticulously, lathering scented soap across every inch of her skin. I'm determined to erase every trace of those animals—every scent, every touch, every memory that clings to her perfect form. They had no right to lay their filthy hands on something so precious, so wholly mine.

She belongs only to herself and me tonight, as it should be. I'll scour away the darkness that dared to claim her, restore the brilliance those bastards tried to dim. Her light will blaze again, fierce and untamed, and I'll tear apart anything threatening to extinguish it.

This I swear on my immortal soul.

DANICA

61

The days after John's death stretch endlessly, each hour filled with unbearable grief and soul-deep guilt. I've tortured myself with how things might have ended differently if I'd stayed home that night. Without my friend and mentor, loss sits like a suffocating blanket, pressing down until I can barely breathe.

Rhyland stays constantly at my side, his touch anchoring me each night as he whispers protection, apologies for not arriving sooner, and promises of unending love. I wake frequently before dawn, sleep shattered by nightmares of Marcus, Azrael, and John's violent end.

Rhyland quickly envelopes me, reassuring me I'm beyond their reach. During my darkest moments, speaking about the Soul Stone and Marcus's revelations proves cathartic. Sharing these burdens lightens their crushing weight.

In the aftermath, Rhyland and I have reached a profound intimacy. We know with certainty how essential the other has become, our souls so entwined that separation would devastate us both.

I wish I could forget the horrors of my captivity. But deep down,

I know healing will require time. Some scars run too deep to fade completely.

When Emily visited, horror and empathy shone in her eyes as she listened to my abduction story and John's fate. Without words, she guided me to sit beside her.

We stayed in companionable silence; the only sound was my occasional ragged breaths. Eventually, the burden became too much to contain.

When I found my voice, it emerged hoarse as I recounted everything—what happened and what I'm becoming. Emily listened with infinite patience as I released the anguish suffocating my spirit.

No platitudes were offered, only a sympathetic ear when I needed it most. When my tears slowed, Emily wordlessly embraced me, gently brushing away the dampness from my cheeks.

"He wouldn't have wanted you to blame yourself for this tragedy, girl," she whispers into my hair. "No one could have foreseen or prevented what happened that night."

Though part of me resists accepting her absolution, Emily's voice feels like a healing balm on my emotional wounds.

Sensing my doubt, Emily squeezes my shoulder. "Whatever this is that you have to do to save us all from darkness...I truly believe only your badass can accomplish it."

Despite her kind words, tears continue slipping down my face as I silently disagree. My thoughts spiral darker, imagining how events might have unfolded without my alien gifts drawing powerful monsters to my once-insignificant life. The guilt threatens to swallow me whole.

I take a deep, bracing breath before solemnly going across the verdant, rolling hills of the cemetery where John is to be laid to rest. The pervasive aura of grief here is nearly palpable as I join the gathering of friends, family, and loyal patrons who have come together to mourn our beloved friend and mentor. The ordinarily vibrant Seattle sky seems to mirror our collective sorrow today, heavy, leaden clouds overhead, unleashing a dreary downpour of rain. The cold raindrops mingle with hot tears on my cheeks, rolling down my face in steady rivulets as we say goodbye.

John's son Mark stands solemn and straight-backed beside me, clearly trying to remain strong, though anguish shines bright in his kind eyes.

After the funeral, those gathered return to the Playful Pint for an informal wake celebrating John's life. Usually bustling with laughter and lively chatter, the bar resonates with a subdued melancholy hush tonight. Dimmed lighting casts a warm amber glow over the familiar worn oak counters and polished taps that John so lovingly maintained. Framed photos of him in happier times now adorn the walls, capturing memories of his easy laughter and talent for fostering community and camaraderie. Though his physical absence is still keenly felt, the images bring bittersweet comfort.

As friends and loved ones raise glasses and share stories, the pub becomes a place of solace and reflection for all who knew John. The nostalgic air is thick with memories, while the muted clinking of glasses and murmur of voices fill the void left in his wake.

I stay until the last guest finally wanders out. Mark pauses to take in the room, expression wistful. "I promise to keep my father's legacy alive, Dani. To maintain this place just as he would have wanted," he vows.

I nod, genuinely touched by the resolve shining in Mark's eyes despite his palpable grief. It's the legacy John deserves, carried on through those who loved him most.

DANICA

62

Dawn paints Rhyland's penthouse in watercolor pastels. The air crackles with anticipation—my blood might be his salvation from eternal darkness. His massive frame radiates tension as he watches pink light creep across marble floors.

"Either this works," he growls, midnight-blue eyes gleaming, "or you'll be scraping vampire barbecue off Fifth Avenue. Better have the meat wagon on speed dial for my crispy ass."

I roll my eyes, sweeping chestnut waves aside to bare my throat. "Such an optimist. It'll work—Seraphina wouldn't steer us wrong."

His powerful arms cage me against solid muscle. "How much do I need, baby?" Warm lips brush my pulse point.

"No idea." My breath hitches. "Guess we're winging it."

A rumble vibrates through his chest. Calloused fingers trail fire up my spine as he nuzzles my neck. His tongue traces delicate patterns that sends heat straight to my core. My head falls back, a throaty moan escaping as his thick length presses against me.

"Keep making those pretty sounds," he purrs, "and we'll miss our daylight debut."

I arch closer, shameless. "Maybe stop wielding your massive sword like a weapon, then." Heat floods my cheeks. "Can't help it if you're walking sex on legs."

Since my rescue, he's been uncharacteristically gentle, letting me heal at my own pace. The restraint must be killing him.

His dark chuckle raises goosebumps. "Never apologize for wanting me, Angel. Your body knows exactly who it belongs to."

God help me, he's right.

His fangs pierce my throat with exquisite care. My back arches violently, a desperate cry tearing from my lips as liquid fire races through my veins. Each pull of his mouth ignites a primitive need deep within my core—a hunger that could never be sated, no matter how often he drinks. I clutch his broad shoulders as he groans against my skin, the vibration sending shivers cascading down my spine.

"Rhyland," I gasp, fingers threading through his raven hair. The dual sensations of pleasure and surrender overwhelm me, leaving me dizzy and clinging to his solid frame.

His large hand cradles the back of my head as he takes what he needs, what I freely give. The connection between us pulses with each draw of blood, our bond strengthening into something tangible that shimmers in the air around us. When he finally withdraws, his tongue sweeps across the puncture wounds, sealing them with tender care.

"You taste like fucking sunlight," he murmurs against my skin, voice rough with need and something deeper—hope.

We rush toward the balcony doors, anticipation and terror crackling between us. Morning light spills across Italian marble like molten gold. Rhyland hesitates at the threshold, jaw clenched tight. No matter how strong the will, a thousand years of instinctive fear doesn't vanish in a moment.

"Ready to see if I become barbecue?" His attempt at humor doesn't mask the vulnerability in those ocean-blue eyes.

I squeeze his hand. "If Seraphina's right, you're about to get reacquainted with an old friend."

He extends one muscled arm cautiously into the brightness, centuries of ingrained fear evident in the tension of his powerful frame. The sleeve of his black Henley rides up, revealing the intricate tattoos that map his forearm. We both watch, barely breathing, as sunlight caresses skin that hasn't felt its touch in a millennium.

Silence stretches between heartbeats. Nothing happens.

His savage grin breaks like dawn itself.

"Holy fuck," he whispers, flexing his fingers in the golden light.

I hold my breath as he steps fully into sunlight that hasn't touched his skin since the Viking age. Radiance bathes his chiseled features, illuminating him from within. Each deliberate step makes the luminescence around him pulse brighter—not the deadly inferno we feared, but a gentle aura that dances across olive skin.

The morning light reveals new dimensions to him—subtle variations in his hair color I'd never noticed, the exact shade of stubble along his jaw, tiny scars from a human life long forgotten. Sunlight transforms him from beautiful to breathtaking.

"Holy shit, it's working!" His voice cracks with raw emotion. "I can feel the heat—it doesn't burn!" He turns his face upward, eyes closed in reverence as sunshine bathes his features. "It's warm, Angel. I'd forgotten how fucking warm it is."

Tears stream unchecked down my cheeks as I launch myself into his waiting arms. "Well, looks like you can finally work on that pasty-ass complexion!"

His laughter—full and unreserved—rumbles through his chest as he lifts me effortlessly, spinning us both in the golden morning light. The warmth kisses our skin as we twirl across the balcony, drunk on possibility.

"Do you know how long it's been?" he asks, setting me down but keeping me locked in his embrace. "It has been over a thousand years since I've felt the sun without pain. A thousand years of darkness and shadows." His calloused thumb wipes away my tears. "And you gave it back to me."

The enormity of this moment settles around us. No vampire in recorded history has ever conquered their fatal weakness to sunlight. What this means for Rhyland, for vampires everywhere, is nothing short of revolutionary.

"Thank you, Angel." Bright, beautiful blue eyes glisten with unshed tears, vulnerability raw on his face. "You've given me the fucking sun."

He claims my mouth with devastating tenderness, pouring a millennium of darkness and longing into the kiss. I melt against him, giggling against his lips when we finally break apart.

"Just think of all the beach sex we can have now."

He throws his head back and laughs, the sound unfettered and joyous. "Is that all you think about? Getting me naked?"

"Can you blame me?" I gesture to his ridiculous perfection. "Besides, I'm a scientist. I need to run extensive tests on your newfound sun tolerance. Preferably with you wearing as little as possible."

His eyes darken with hunger. "I like your scientific method, Dr. Pierce."

We stand together in the warm embrace of morning light, possibilities stretching before us like the endless horizon. Rhyland's face is transformed by wonder as he watches dust motes dance in the sunbeams. For the first time since I've known him, the ancient weight of his curse seems lifted from his shoulders.

"What do you want to do first?" I ask, tracing the contours of his face with my fingertips, memorizing this moment.

His smile is breathtaking—boyish and mischievous in the golden light. "Everything, Angel. Absolutely fucking everything."

Let the daylight adventures begin.

RHYLAND

63

Standing in raw sunlight feels like claiming territory I never thought I'd conquer. My angel—my Dani—has given me back the sun, a gift no vampire in history has ever possessed. After weeks of methodical testing and her unwavering determination, we've established my limits—two days of sunlight guaranteed on a single feeding, three days pushing my luck. By hour forty-eight, the sun starts biting back; hit seventy-two and the burn becomes a warning I can't ignore. We've settled on feeding every other day—a precaution I won't compromise on.

We've been mapping the parameters of this miracle with scientific precision. Her blood in my veins creates something unprecedented—a vampire who walks in daylight. We've calibrated the perfect amount I can take without weakening her, a delicate balance that keeps us both strong.

With our system locked down, we've shifted focus to the Valley of the Ancients. Dani's fixated on creating a portal directly there, armed with rainforest photographs and coordinates that might lead us to answers.

I watch her brow furrow in concentration, hands extended as she tries to manipulate energy she's only beginning to understand.

"This is hopeless," she finally snaps, frustration radiating from her like heat. "No matter how hard I concentrate, nothing happens. What am I doing wrong?" Her hands land on her hips, defiance masking disappointment.

I cross to her in three strides, pulling her against my chest where she fits perfectly. "Try to relax, baby," I murmur into her hair, breathing in her scent—sunshine and honey. "You're just beginning. None of us expects perfection immediately."

She exhales against me, tension slowly unwinding from her shoulders. "I should take a break and grab some food," she concedes.

"Allow me." I move to the phone, ordering enough to sustain her energy for another attempt later. Behind me, her phone rings—Emily checking in—and she steps away to take the call.

Adrian approaches while I finish the order, suggesting he and Erik accompany us on the hunt for the relic. I clap his shoulder, appreciating his loyalty. We've fought side by side for centuries, but his dedication to Dani—to her safety and her mission—means more than he knows.

"That would be great," I acknowledge, gratitude evident in my tone.

Dani emerges from the bedroom looking defeated, shoulders slumped, hair escaping her usually neat braid. She collapses beside me on the couch with a sigh that carries the weight of expectations she's placed on herself.

"Food will be here soon," I offer, watching a faint smile cross her lips.

Thirty minutes later, a knock comes, and I open the door to find a deliveryman balancing a tray of steaming dishes. Dani practically levitates from the couch, her earlier frustration momentarily forgotten as she digs into her meal with appreciative moans that stirs something hot in me.

Our peace shatters when the evening news cuts to an urgent bulletin that freezes the blood in my veins.

"A savage double homicide has rocked the nearby small town of Leav-

enworth. The victims, Tom and Louise Pierce, were brutally mauled in their homes. Authorities suspect a vicious animal attack by a creature never before encountered. Shock and fear ripple through the community."

The words slam into me and I can't breathe. My throat closes, lungs refusing to work as the implications crash through my mind with devastating clarity. I turn to Dani, watching her face transform as understanding dawn's—first confusion, then disbelief, finally horror so raw it's like watching her soul fracture before my eyes.

She's frozen, eyes wide and glassy, lips parted in a silent scream that can't find its way out. Every step I take toward her feels like wading through concrete, the distance between us impossibly vast. When I finally reach her, the ocean of grief in her eyes threatens to drown us both.

I pull her against me with desperate force, as if I could somehow absorb her pain through skin and bone. My rage builds like a gathering storm—black, violent, and all-consuming. I should have hunted down every last one of those mangy fuckers. Should have torn out their throats when I had the chance. Instead, I'd shown mercy, and now Dani pays the price for my weakness.

Her lips part, trembling violently as she struggles to form words. "No." Just that single syllable—broken and raw—before tears spill down her cheeks in hot, silent rivers.

My arms tighten around her instinctively, knowing no words can touch this kind of devastation.

Guilt hammers through me as her body shakes against mine. Those wolf bastards we let live have exacted their revenge in the most brutal way possible—not against me, but against the innocent people who raised the woman in my arms. The woman whose world I swore to protect.

Each of her sobs is a blade between my ribs. Her grief soaks through my shirt, branding my skin with the consequences of my failure. She'd barely begun processing John's senseless murder, and now this—her parents slaughtered like animals, their blood on my hands as surely as if I'd wielded the claws myself.

I will hunt down every last wolf responsible. I will make them suffer deaths so horrific that stories of their ends will echo through generations of their kind.

But first, I have to hold the shattered pieces of my mate together as her world collapses around her. I press my lips to her hair, breathing in her scent now tinged with the sharp tang of grief.

"I've got you," I whisper against her temple, knowing it's not enough—nothing could be enough in this moment. "I've got you, Angel."

And silently, I make a vow that will stain my soul darker than any act in my centuries of existence—every wolf connected to this slaughter will die screaming my name.

DANICA

64

The news of my parents' murder crashes over me like Arctic waves, stealing breath and reason. My hands shake violently as I fumble through my bag, numb fingers finding a ridiculous white tennis skirt and neon pink tank top—summer clothes for a winter nightmare. I pull them on mechanically, the bright fabric jarring from the darkness consuming me.

They're gone. They're really gone.

The highway unspools beneath Rhyland's Audi, each mile marker ticking down to ground zero of my grief. Pine trees and mountain vistas blur through tears I refuse to shed. The leather seat creaks beneath me as I shift restlessly, unable to find comfort in a world suddenly tilted on its axis. Rhyland's hand finds mine across the console, his thumb tracing gentle circles on my palm. His touch anchors me, but even his supernatural strength can't hold back the tsunami of loss threatening to drown me.

The future stretches before me—a vast, terrifying wilderness without their guiding stars. No more Sunday phone calls with Mom. No more awkward dad jokes or fishing trips with my father. No one to call when I achieve something great or need comfort when I fail. The finality of it hits me in waves, each realization a fresh wound.

My parents' home appears around the bend, its cheerful blue shutters now obscene against my shattered world. Mom's hanging basket of fuchsias, planted last spring, still sways in the gentle breeze—impossibly alive while she isn't. My legs turn to concrete as I exit the car, each step toward that familiar red door requiring monumental effort. The weight in my chest threatens to crush my ribcage.

Inside, the air hangs wrong, stagnant and empty. No cinnamon and coffee scents from Mom's Sunday baking. No classic rock filtering from Dad's ancient stereo. Just hollow silence where life used to overflow. The grandfather clock in the hallway continues its steady tick-tock, obscenely normal in a world that will never be normal again.

My fingers trail compulsively over family photos and knick-knacks—the porcelain lighthouse Dad brought from Maine, Mom's collection of vintage spoons, the silly ceramic frog I made in third grade that they insisted on displaying despite its lopsided eyes. Each object is a knife twisting deeper. These treasures, once alive with stories, are now just... things.

The living room carpet still bears the indentation of Dad's favorite recliner, moved by investigators during their search. A half-finished crossword puzzle sits on the side table, his reading glasses folded neatly beside it. He'll never complete 23-across now. Mom's knitting basket rests by her chair, a partially finished blue sweater spilling from its depths. Was it meant for me? I'll never know.

Detective Alvarez approaches from the dining room, compassion etched into his weathered face. Coffee stains dot his rumpled shirt, evidence of the sleepless hours he's poured into this investigation. "Ms. Pierce, my deepest condolences. We're pursuing every lead to find who did this."

I nod mechanically, his words washing over me like distant waves. Justice feels like a cruel joke—what punishment could possibly balance this loss? What prison sentence could fill the void where my parents should be?

Rhyland and I both know exactly who's behind this sick, twisted mess. But what the hell would telling Detective Alvarez accomplish? Nothing but blank stares and a fast track to the psych ward.

"Can you tell me if anything seems out of place or missing?" he asks gently. "Sometimes family members notice details others might overlook."

I scan the room through tear-blurred vision. Everything is simultaneously precisely as it should be and horribly wrong. "I don't—I can't—" My voice cracks and falters.

Rhyland's steady presence at my back gives me strength. "We'll take our time, Detective. This is a lot to process."

The kitchen destroys me. Sunlight streams through gingham curtains, casting cheerful patterns across the worn linoleum floor where my mother's blood has been meticulously cleaned away. Mom's favorite teacup sits in its usual spot in the open cabinet, delicate blue flowers faded from decades of morning rituals. My fingertips trace the rim as memories ambush me—thunderstorm afternoons with cookies and gossip, late-night confidences over steaming Earl Grey, her gentle laugh when I'd mimic her proper pinky extension.

The refrigerator door is plastered with photographs and magnets from their travels—the Grand Canyon trip three summers ago, their anniversary cruise to Alaska, and the tacky flamingo magnet I sent from Florida. A grocery list in Mom's flowing handwriting is stuck to the freezer door: "Eggs, milk, pot roast for Sunday dinner, " a dinner she'll never cook.

Rhyland's warm hand envelops mine, anchoring me as grief threatens to sweep me away. His ocean eyes reflect my pain, absorbing some of its crushing weight.

"They were here," I whisper, voice breaking on each syllable. "Just days ago, they were right here, making plans, living their lives. How can they just be... gone?"

A golden sunset floods the violated rooms as the coroner's team arrives. They move with clinical efficiency, their black body bags stark against the floral sofa where I once opened Christmas presents and celebrated birthdays. Mom's hand slips from beneath the zipper—pale fingers that braided my hair and wiped my tears are now limp and waxy. The diamond anniversary ring Dad gave her last year catches the fading light, one final spark of brilliance before they zip her away

I collapse against Rhyland's chest as they carry my parents out, his arms the only thing keeping me upright as my world crumbles to dust.

Rhyland pulls me into his strong embrace as dusk deepens around us. "We will make them pay for this atrocity," he vows, steely resolve etched in the tension of his jaw.

I steel myself with the promise of justice, turning to meet his fiery gaze with my own. If this evil comes for me again, it will not find me such easy prey. “Justice is not enough, Rhyland. I will ensure that no one else has to endure this pain. No more shattered lives due to this evil.”

Silence hangs thick between us, punctuated only by the rhythmic thrum of tires against asphalt as we drive back to the hotel. My fingernails dig into my palms until tiny crescents of blood form—physical pain to distract from the emotional avalanche threatening to bury me.

John's body sprawled on cold bathroom tiles. My parents' blood-soaked living room. So much death. So many lives extinguished because they had the misfortune of loving me.

How many more will die before this is over?

"Their deaths are all my fault," I whisper, the words falling like stones into the suffocating quiet.

Rhyland's knuckles turn bone-white against the steering wheel before his warm palm finds my thigh, anchoring me to reality.

"No, Angel. None of this is on you," he says, voice low and steady as ancient bedrock. "Don't shoulder the burden of others' evil. The fault lies with those who chose violence, not with you for existing."

Something snaps inside me—a dam breaking against tsunami force. White-hot fury floods every cell, drowning grief in its molten current. My hands shake violently as I rake them through tangled hair.

"Whose fault is it then?" The words explode from me, sharp-edged and dangerous. "If I weren't some cosmic fucking science experiment with freak blood, everyone I love would still be breathing! Tell me how that's not on me!"

Tires screech as Rhyland swerves onto the shoulder, gravel spraying beneath us. The engine dies with a turn of his wrist. In one fluid motion, he's facing me, massive hands engulfing mine, ocean eyes capturing my wild gaze.

"Danica." My full name—rare from his lips. "I would tear out my own heart if it would ease your pain." His voice cracks, centuries of carefully maintained control fracturing. "What I feel through our bond right now... It's gutting me. But listen to me—this evil existed long before you. It will exist long after. You didn't create it and are not responsible for its actions."

His forehead touches mine, his breath warm against my tear-stained cheeks.

"I understand this is overwhelming," Rhyland murmurs, his voice a velvet rumble against my skin. "But you're not alone, Angel. Every ounce of strength I've gathered over a thousand years is yours. Every breath I take is to keep you safe. Whatever you need to survive this, I'll provide."

His passionate vow vibrates through the confined space of the car, lifting the crushing weight from my chest like Atlas taking the world from my shoulders. Shame washes over me for lashing out at him—this ancient warrior who offers his immortal heart so freely.

His calloused fingers thread through my tangled hair, each gentle stroke soothing the storm raging inside me. Those ocean-blue eyes hold mine with an intensity that feels like physical contact—sheltering, protective, consuming.

Words fail me. I lean forward instead, tilting my face to his. Our lips meet in silent communion, and my eyes flutter closed as he groans deep in his chest. His tongue slides against mine, tasting of ancient power and desperate need. He carefully explores my mouth, as though mapping territory he intends to claim for eternity.

His massive hand wraps around the nape of my neck, controlling the angle with possessive pressure. I gasp against his mouth as he deepens the kiss, tilting my head to grant him better access. Heat radiates from his body, thawing the ice that grief had crystallized in my veins. Every touch melts another layer of pain, replacing anguish with primal hunger.

Make me forget. Just for a moment, make me forget everything but this.

With supernatural speed, he releases my seatbelt and hauls me across the console onto his lap. The leather seat groans as he slides it backward, reclining nearly horizontally with one fluid motion. My body responds instantly, core clenching with desperate need as his hardness presses against me through layers of fabric.

He makes quick work of his zipper, shoving his jeans down just enough to free his impressive length. My breath catches at the sight—thick and straining, a drop of moisture already gathering at the tip. His powerful hands slide up my thighs with determined purpose, fingers digging into the soft flesh of my hips before cupping my ass with possessive force.

With one savage motion, he tears my delicate underwear aside. I arch against him, surrendering to the primal comfort only he can provide.

Yes. This. Make everything else disappear.

I yank my tank top down in one desperate motion, freeing my heavy breasts to the cool air. His eyes darken to midnight as they lock onto my exposed flesh—hungry, predatory, worshipful.

"Take me," I command, voice raw with need. "Make everything else disappear."

He surges forward like a starving man offered salvation, capturing one sensitive peak between his lips. His tongue circles the hardened bud with exquisite precision while his hand claims its twin, fingers expertly rolling and teasing. Electric currents race from these points of contact straight to my core. I arch against him, offering more, demanding everything.

Now. Need him now.

Desperation claws through me as I position myself over his colossal cock. I plant one knee on either side of his powerful thighs, the leather seat creaking beneath our weight. Without preamble or gentleness, I impale myself on him in one brutal stroke. The delicious stretch borders on pain—exactly what I need. My body convulses around his invasion as a primal cry tears from my throat.

"Fuck," he growls, the sound vibrating through his chest and into mine.

I roll my hips in savage circles, grinding myself against him with punishing force. His fingers tangle in my hair, gripping the strands at the base of my skull. The slight sting only heightens my arousal as he uses this leverage to slam upward, meeting my downward thrusts with bruising intensity. Each collision sends shockwaves of pleasure radiating outward, my cries bouncing off the fogged windows.

"Shit, baby," he rasps, voice strained as his hips piston relentlessly upward. "You feel so fucking good wrapped around me."

Something awakens within me—a need to dominate, to control something when everything else has spiraled beyond my grasp. I wrap my fingers around his throat, feeling his pulse hammer against my palm. His breath catches, pupils dilating further as I force myself harder onto him, setting a punishing pace.

A dangerous rumble builds in his chest, his massive body tensing beneath me. "Fuck, baby. That's it," he commands, voice dropping to that deep register that makes my inner walls clench around him. "Take what you want from me."

My nails dig crescents into his flesh as I ride him with savage abandon, chasing oblivion in the slick friction between our bodies. The obscene symphony of skin against skin and breathless moans fills the small space. Power surges through me with each roll of my hips—I may have lost control of my life, but in this moment, I own his pleasure completely.

"Goddamn, Angel," he grunts. "Ride this fat cock." His words vibrate against my constraining fingers, filthy praise sending fresh heat pooling between my thighs.

In this moment, there is no grief. No destiny. No death. Just his body beneath mine, and the mounting pressure coiling tight at my center.

Headlights slice through darkness, casting fleeting illumination across our tangled forms. Cars rush past on the nearby highway, but we exist in our own universe—a bubble of sensation where nothing matters but this primal connection. My hips rise and fall in relentless rhythm, driving my slick heat onto his thickness with reckless abandon. Let them look. Let the whole world see.

Let me feel something other than pain.

His magnificent body remains relatively still beneath me, understanding without words that I need this control—need to reclaim some small territory when my entire world has been conquered by chaos. Only his hands move, guiding my pace with bruising pressure on my hips. Each downward stroke drives him impossibly deeper, his impressive girth stretching me to the edge of pleasure-pain.

The car windows fog completely as our bodies generate scorching heat. Sweat beads between my breasts, rolling down to where our bodies join in this violent dance. The obscene soundtrack of flesh meeting flesh fills the confined space—wet, urgent, desperate.

Pressure builds at my core, a gathering storm of sensation. "Oh god... Rhyland," I gasp, voice barely recognizable.

His breathing turns ragged, jaw clenched as he fights his own release. Veins stand out on his neck with the effort of restraint. "That's it, baby," he pants, fingers digging deeper into my flesh. "Come for me. Let me feel you fall apart."

The command shatters my last threads of control. My inner walls clamp down on his length as liquid heat gushes between us. A primal scream tears from my throat as white-hot pleasure obliterates thought, grief, time—everything but the exquisite sensation pulsing through every nerve ending.

His cock swells impossibly larger inside me. With a guttural roar, he erupts, hot pulses filling me as his powerful body bucks beneath mine. His climax triggers aftershocks through my oversensitized flesh, drawing out my pleasure until I collapse against his heaving chest.

Strong arms encircle me immediately, creating a fortress of muscle and warmth. His heartbeat thunders against my ear—steady, reliable, eternal. For the first time since hearing the news, the jagged edges of my grief soften slightly. Not gone, never gone, but momentarily bearable within the sanctuary of his embrace.

We remain locked together as minutes stretch to hours, neither willing to break this fragile peace. His fingers trace gentle patterns along my spine while his lips press reverent kisses to my temple, my cheek, the corner of my mouth. Each touch is a silent promise: *I am here. You are not alone.*

In this moment, suspended between day and night on an anonymous stretch of highway, I find a temporary shelter from the storm.

Danica

65

The past week dissolves into a haze of half-remembered moments. Time loses meaning as I burrow deeper into my nest of tangled sheets and grief, emerging only when absolutely necessary. The call to my lab supervisor passes in a fog—clinical words explaining unimaginable loss, her sympathetic murmurs promising my position will remain secure—small mercies in an unmerciful world.

Rhyland moves through our shared space like a silent guardian, anticipating needs I can't articulate. He brings food I barely taste, draws baths I soak in until the water turns cold, and holds me through nightmares that leave me screaming for parents who will never answer again. His strength becomes my anchor when darkness threatens to swallow me whole.

Emily arrives daily with coffee and fierce determination, forcing windows open to let stale air escape. She doesn't flinch from my tear-streaked face or hollow eyes. "You don't have to be okay," she whispers, brushing tangled hair from my face. "Just be here."

The funeral materializes like a surreal painting—black clothes, somber faces, meaningless platitudes. I stand beside twin caskets, numb and disconnected, until a familiar figure cuts through the crowd.

"Dani."

My brother Damon's voice shatters my fragile composure. Joy and devastation collide as he enfolds me in arms that smell of motor oil and the same aftershave Dad used. His shoulders shake with silent grief as we cling to each other—the last remaining branches of our family tree. His presence soothes and intensifies the ache, making our parents' absence more starkly real.

By the seventh day, something shifts within me. The luxury of uninterrupted mourning is one I cannot afford. With trembling hands, I force my grief into a locked compartment—not gone, but contained. The Crown of Blessings won't wait for my heart to heal.

"The secondary ward should overlap here," Adrian demonstrates, elegant fingers tracing invisible patterns in the air. His dark eyes reflect concentration as he and Rhyland debate arcane technicalities. "When properly aligned, the runic sequence creates a metaphysical barrier no malevolent entity can penetrate."

I watch from the bed as Adrian inscribes ancient symbols around our hotel room with practiced precision. The runes seem to shimmer momentarily before fading into the wallpaper—invisible to ordinary eyes but humming with power I can somehow sense.

"We procured these from the Arcane Emporium," he explains, noticing my interest. "A hidden establishment that caters exclusively to practitioners of the esoteric arts. The proprietor owed Lucian a favor after an incident in Prague last century."

I tug my cardigan tighter around my shoulders. "Couldn't we just go to my apartment? It has actual security, and no one can enter without an invitation."

Rhyland's jaw tightens almost imperceptibly. "This is safer, Angel. Trust me."

I don't press the issue, suspecting his reluctance stems from pride rather than practicality. The thought of immortal vampires crowded into my modest suburban apartment probably offends his ancient sensibilities. Some battles aren't worth the energy I don't have.

Hours blur together as Adrian and I pour over yellowed texts, searching for the key to opening a portal to the Valley of the Ancients through sheer will. Despite combining his centuries of arcane knowledge with my intuitive connection to the crown, success remains frustratingly elusive.

"The text mentions 'desire aligned with destiny,'" I mutter, rubbing tired eyes. "What does that even mean?"

Adrian frowns at the ancient parchment. "Perhaps it's less about technique and more about intention. The crown chose you—there must be resonance between your essence and its purpose."

I slump back in my chair, defeat etched in every muscle. My fingertips press against throbbing temples as the beginnings of a migraine pulse behind my eyes. Across the table, Adrian's jaw tightens with impatience as he flips through a crumbling leather tome, his movements growing increasingly agitated.

"Perhaps the crown requires a specific emotional state," he mutters, not quite meeting my eyes. Something about his twitchy demeanor raises red flags in my mind.

Why is he so invested in this? So pushy?

When Rhyland ducks his massive frame through the doorway to check our progress, I remain silent, letting Adrian summarize our spectacular lack of success. The three of us bounce theories off each other for nearly an hour, each suggestion more far-fetched than the last. The conversation circles endlessly like water down a drain, leading nowhere.

"I need a break," I announce, pushing away from the table. My back pops in three places as I stand—how long have we been at this?

After choking down a sandwich I barely taste, I return to find Adrian hovering, his dark eyes unnervingly intense.

"Your emotional turmoil is blocking progress," he declares with clinical detachment. "Portal creation demands absolute concentration and serenity. You must purge disruptive thoughts and recenter yourself."

No shit, Sherlock. Sorry, my parents' brutal murder is inconveniencing your schedule.

"Easy, Adrian." Rhyland's voice drops to that dangerous register that makes the air vibrate. "That's my mate you're speaking to."

Adrian raises his hands in surrender, but the flash of something—annoyance? Frustration?—crosses his features before he can mask it.

Adrian's advice isn't entirely wrong despite my irritation at his bedside manner. I close my eyes and consciously unclench my jaw, releasing tension from my shoulders to my fingertips. Each deliberate breath carries away fragments of grief and fear, creating space for something else to emerge.

Inhale clarity. Exhale chaos.

Gradually, warmth blooms in my core—a gentle vibration that feels foreign and intimately familiar. It pulses in time with my heartbeat, growing stronger with each cycle of breath.

"Now visualize your destination," Adrian instructs, his voice softer but still carrying that edge of urgency. "See the rainforest canopy, the emerald leaves, and vibrant flowers. Hear exotic birds calling. Feel humid air against your skin."

I follow his guidance despite my lingering wariness. Something about his intensity doesn't sit right—like he's pushing toward an agenda beyond helping me. When this is over, we'll need to establish some boundaries about his approach to my "training."

But for now, I focus on the image forming behind my closed eyelids: a lush, primeval landscape pulsing with ancient power. The vision grows sharper with each breath, until I can almost smell the rich earth and feel misty air against my face.

Show me the way forward.

The rainforest materializes in my mind with startling clarity—not just an image but a sensation that floods every sense. Something stirs within me, responding to the deliberate summoning. My blood hums with dormant power awakening, like electricity finding a forgotten circuit.

I grasp this ethereal thread, directing the energy outward through my fingertips. My palms begin to glow with soft luminescence, casting pearl-white shadows across my skin. The hotel room dissolves around me as the rainforest vision consumes my awareness. Each heartbeat sends pulses of energy radiating through my body.

"You have the power within, Danica." Adrian's voice reaches me as if from underwater. "Let the portal form naturally. Trust your instincts."

I inhale deeply, steadying the tremor in my hands. The air before me ripples like heat waves above summer asphalt, distorting reality itself. Tendrils of light weave together, forming intricate patterns that defy comprehension. Gradually, these nebulous ribbons coalesce into something recognizable—a shimmering doorway suspended in midair, revealing glimpses of emerald canopy beyond.

Magic dances at my fingertips, responsive and alive. The realization hits me with dizzying force: *I'm creating a doorway between worlds.*

My concentration fractures with excitement, and the portal dissolves like morning mist under hot sun. But the momentary success leaves me breathless with possibility.

"Holy shit, it worked!" I bounce on my toes, laughing with childlike wonder. "Did you see that? I actually made a freaking portal!"

Adrian's serious demeanor cracks into genuine pleasure. "Beautifully done. I knew you had it in you."

Riding the high of success, I throw my arms around him in an impulsive hug. "Thanks for pushing me, Adrian. But seriously, maybe dial back the drill sergeant routine? Portal creation wasn't exactly covered in my genetics PhD program."

He chuckles, eyes crinkling at the corners. "My apologies. It's not every day I encounter someone with your potential."

"So why the intense interest?" I raise an eyebrow. "What's your stake in all this?"

A cryptic smile plays across his features. "Let's just say my scholarly pursuits have allowed me to read about the universe's secrets—not experience them firsthand."

Before I can press further, Rhyland's powerful arms encircle my waist from behind. He spins me around, capturing my lips in a kiss that curls my toes. When he pulls back, his ocean eyes shine with unmistakable pride.

"I knew you could do it," he murmurs against my mouth.

Erik emerges from the adjoining room, silver eyes widening slightly—the equivalent of shocked amazement in his stoic expression. "You succeeded?"

I nod, still floating on adrenaline and accomplishment.

"Impressive," he says, the single word carrying genuine respect.

Rhyland's hand settles at the small of my back. "We should prepare to leave at first light."

I glance toward the window where night has fallen over Seattle's skyline. Tomorrow we venture into the unknown—a reality that should terrify me. Instead, I feel a strange calm. After everything that's happened, moving forward is the only option that makes sense.

Danica

66

We spend the rest of the evening methodically preparing for our expedition. Rhyland's massive hands move with surprising precision as he packs two weathered rucksacks, his focus absolute as he arranges survival gear with military efficiency. Erik and Adrian departed hours ago to gather their own supplies, promising to return by dawn for our departure.

Tension crackles in the air like the moment before lightning strikes. My mind races with everything that's happened—and everything still to come. Something feels wrong. The temporary sanctuary we've created feels suddenly fragile, like thin ice creaking underfoot. Rhyland's jaw tightens as he glances toward the door, confirming my suspicion that he senses it too.

The explosion of splintering wood shatters the silence.

Our hotel door blasts inward, ripped from its hinges. Dark figures pour through like liquid shadow, flowing into our sanctuary with predatory grace.

I freeze as primal fear floods my system. In the dim light, I make out pale skin stretched over inhuman features. Blood-red eyes survey us with cold calculation—hunters assessing prey.

The leader prowls closer, twisting thin lips into a sadistic sneer, baring jagged fangs. "You managed to slither away..." he hisses, eyes focused on Rhyland. "But you won't escape us again."

Rhyland places himself between me and danger. His lip curls back as a vicious snarl rips from his throat. "You'd better back the fuck off right now, Cade, before I rip your goddamn head off."

Cade laughs—a sound like breaking glass. He shifts to peer around Rhyland, dragging his gaze down my body with naked hunger.

"Ah, Danica," he purrs. "I've looked forward to meeting you." His unnaturally long tongue slides across cracked lips. "Once I dispose of this worthless meat shield, you and I will take a long...journey together."

"You won't lay a fucking finger on her," Rhyland vows, icy calm lacing each syllable.

I reach through our mental connection, desperate for answers.

"Who the hell is this?"

"The Shadow Brotherhood. The same twisted bastards who confined me, and the reason I was kept from you."

My stomach drops, my heart in my throat as the other five figures spread out, slowly encircling us with a clear, hostile intent. Their faces remain obscured by hooded cowls, but I can feel the violent anticipation coming off them in waves, like ravenous wolves closing in for the kill.

“Cut the bullshit, Rhyland. You don't stand a chance against us here," Cade states.

Dread coils tighter within me. Whoever these monsters are must wield significant influence and dark power to have captured someone as formidable as Rhyland before. We're outmatched.

"When I give the signal, run like hell, and don't look back!"

I tighten my grip on his hand in acknowledgment, though I know deep down that I won't abandon him willingly to this fate. Before I can brace for the clash, Cade launches himself at Rhyland with blinding speed.

"Go, now!" Rhyland bellows, grappling with his attacker.

Chaos erupts. Rhyland and Cade collide with bone-crushing force. They move with lethal precision—a macabre ballet too fast for human eyes.

A scream tears from my throat as iron bands constrict around my chest from behind. I kick wildly as my captor wrenches my arms higher.

Rhyland's head snaps toward the sound, ocean eyes blazing with fury. Something ancient and terrible awakens in his face—the predator beneath the man. With a roar that shakes the walls, he seizes the nearest attacker's head between his massive hands and *twists.* The sickening crack of vertebrae separating echoes through the room as the body crumples, head lolling at an impossible angle.

Without pausing, Rhyland extends one hand toward another advancing figure. The air ripples between them, and suddenly, the attacker is airborne, hurled across the room by an invisible force. He slams into the far wall with enough impact to crack the plaster before sliding to the floor in a broken heap.

Holy shit. He has telekinesis?

The revelation hits me with stunning force. In all our time together, I've never seen him use this power. The raw energy radiating from him now is terrifying and magnificent—primal forces barely contained.

Three more attackers rush him simultaneously. Rhyland pivots and delivers a roundhouse kick with such devastating force that the first attacker's ribcage visibly caves inward. The second receives a palm strike that literally lifts him off his feet, sending him crashing through the coffee table in an explosion of splintered wood. The third hesitates just long enough for Rhyland to seize his throat, crushing his windpipe with a single savage squeeze.

Cade uses this momentary distraction to strike, leaping onto Rhyland's back and locking powerful arms around his neck in a chokehold. Rhyland rears backward violently, slamming the crown of his skull into Cade's face. The wet crunch of cartilage giving way is followed by a spray of crimson as Cade's nose shatters.

I watch in awe as Rhyland moves with agility and ferocity I have never seen before. He attacks with a wild abandon that seems fueled by an inner fire. This is genuinely the fighting style of the Vikings—savage, relentless, and unyielding.

Cade lunges forward, pale fingers locking around Rhyland's throat in a death grip. Without hesitation, Rhyland slams his forearms downward, breaking the hold brutally. He drives his forehead into Cade's already-shattered nose in the same fluid motion. Fresh blood erupts in a crimson spray as Cade staggers backward, momentarily stunned.

Rhyland presses his advantage with merciless precision. His fist punches straight through Cade's chest cavity with a wet, tearing sound. Cade's eyes bulge with shock and agony as Rhyland's fingers close around his still-beating heart. Their gazes lock in silent combat—predator and prey frozen in the moment before death.

"What's it gonna be, Cade?" Rhyland's voice is ice over steel. "I can end this quickly or slowly. Your choice."

The cold kiss of metal against my throat halts everything.

"I'd reconsider that move if I were you," purrs the creature holding me, pressing the blade deeper against my skin, drawing blood.

Rhyland freezes, his entire body rigid. His eyes flood with something I've never seen before—naked fear.

Long seconds stretch into eternity as we remain suspended in this deadly tableau. Finally, with glacial slowness, Rhyland withdraws his bloodied hand from Cade's chest. The injured vampire collapses to his knees, clutching the gaping wound as he gasps and sputters.

My captor increases pressure on the blade, forcing me to arch my neck awkwardly to avoid deeper cuts. I can feel his satisfaction radiating like heat.

"Don't, Rhyland. Kill him," I plead, willing him to understand through our bond. *"Don't give up your advantage. Not for me."*

But the savage predator who moments ago ripped through enemies with terrifying ease has vanished, replaced by a man paralyzed by the sight of his mate in danger. For all his power and supernatural abilities,

Rhyland has one devastating weakness.

Me.

Sneering at Rhyland's momentary compliance, the cocky brother restraining me loosens his grip fractionally. It's just enough.

In one smooth motion, I rear my head with as much force as I can muster, feeling the crunch of cartilage and bone against my skull. The brother howls, his grip instinctively flying to his gushing nose. I use the distraction to stomp down hard on his instep and lurch free of his faltering hold.

Rewarded by my defiance, Rhyland shoots his hand back out to crush Cade's windpipe in a viselike grip. Face mottled, Cade claws frantically at the unyielding fingers, cutting off his air supply.

But in the chaos of the brawl, neither of us notices one of the remaining brothers circling behind Rhyland, murder etched on his inhuman face. My warning comes too late—before Rhyland can react, the hulking figure violently twists his head, and a sickening crunch fills the air and sends him toppling lifelessly to the floor.

"NO!" I scream.

My brain short-circuits, unable to process what I just witnessed. Rhyland—my immortal warrior, protector, and *everything*—crumpled like a broken doll on the hotel room floor. Still. Silent. *Gone.*

This isn't possible. He can't just... die.

Nobody told me vampires could die like this. In all our time together, through every conversation about his immortal nature, this vulnerability never came up.

Cade straightens, grinning maliciously at Rhyland's lifeless body, then turns his gaze toward me, a sinister grin twisting his lips. "Your precious Rhyland can't save you now," he sneers with an evil hiss.

His cold fingers seize my jaw, wrenching my face toward his with bruising force. "Such spirit," he rasps, his fetid breath washing over me. "I look forward to taming that fire, girl."

Revulsion churns in my stomach as his gaze rakes over me like a physical touch. I want to unleash a torrent of defiance, but fear constricts my throat. All I manage is a trembling whisper: "I won't let you do this."

Finding one last spark of courage, I gather saliva in my mouth and spit directly into his face. "Screw you," I growl.

Cade's expression darkens dangerously as he wipes the spittle from his cheek. The remaining vampires circle closer, their hungry gazes fixed on me with predatory intent. I close my eyes, desperately trying to summon the power I know. It's like a damn floodlight on a dimmer switch, and I still haven't figured out how to make it stay bright. Panic rises, and I squeeze my eyes shut.

One of the brothers seizes my arms from behind, his grip crushing enough to leave instant bruises. Cade leans in, his face hovering just inches from mine. He inhales deeply at my neck, like a connoisseur sampling fine wine.

"So this is what all the talk's about?" he murmurs, pulling back to study me with newfound appreciation. "The human who will supposedly bring our destruction."

Something shifts inside me—grief, rage, and terror crystallizing into a single molten core. My parents' murder. John's sacrifice. Rhyland's now dead on the floor. Each loss feeds the growing inferno within.

I meet Cade's gaze directly, arching one eyebrow in defiance. "Care to fuck around and find out firsthand what all that talk is about?"

Electricity crackles through the air, raising the fine hairs on my arms. Cade's lips pull back in a feral snarl, exposing elongated fangs dripping with anticipation. He lunges forward, murder written in every line of his face.

As his hands reach for my throat, something inside me *shatters*.

The scream that erupts from my lips carries all my suppressed rage, grief, and power—a sound no human should produce. Light explodes outward from my body in blinding waves, filling the room with impossible brilliance. The stench of charred flesh invades my nostrils.

Let them burn.

The world explodes in blinding white light.

A miniature sun ignites within me, radiating outward with catastrophic force. The shockwave pulses through the room, shattering windows and splintering furniture. The very air combusts as debris whirls in chaotic patterns. My ears fill with the deafening roar of unleashed power.

The intensity threatens to tear me apart. Liquid fire courses through my veins, burning and cleansing simultaneously, consuming everything in its path—including my attackers.

Then the light recedes, leaving eerie silence broken only by smoldering embers. Moonlight streams through shattered windows as dust motes dance in the destruction.

The room lies in ruins—furniture reduced to kindling, walls scorched black, ceiling partially collapsed. Nothing remains of Cade and his brothers but fine ash drifting like macabre snow. The destructive power I've unleashed staggers me.

My legs buckle. I crawl through wreckage toward Rhyland's motionless form. He lies sprawled amid devastation, neck bent unnaturally, eyes closed. Somehow the blast obliterated our attackers but left him physically intact.

Exhaustion crashes over me as I reach him, hands trembling uncontrollably. I brush debris from his face, his skin cold beneath my fingertips. The magnitude of potential loss constricts my chest until breathing becomes nearly impossible.

Please be alive. Please.

I've seen him heal from injuries before, but a broken neck? My limited knowledge of vampire physiology offers little comfort as I stroke his icy cheek.

"Rhyland, please..." My voice breaks. "Don't leave me, goddammit!"

I shake him gently, then more forcefully. Desperation builds inside me like a pressure cooker, hot tears splashing onto his face. What good is this power if I can't save the one person who matters most?

Rage and grief collide as I pound my fists against his broad chest. "Rhyland!" I scream, the sound tearing from my raw throat. "Come back to me!"

A faint cracking sound stops my fists mid-descent. Beneath my palms, something shifts—subtle movement followed by bones realigning. A groan rumbles through his chest as his head slowly rights itself, vertebrae audibly snapping back into place.

Ocean-blue eyes flutter open, clouded with pain. His hand rises shakily to touch his neck.

Relief crashes through me with such force that I collapse against his chest, arms wrapping around him with desperate strength. "Oh, thank God you're alright," I whisper, breathing in his familiar scent.

"I'm sorry, Angel," he murmurs weakly, his arms encircling me despite his weakened state.

I pull back to see his face, drinking in his eyes—alive, aware, mine. "For what?"

"For failing to protect you." Self-recrimination darkens his features. "I should have—"

I silence him with a fierce kiss, pouring all my relief and love into the contact. When I break away, I rest my forehead against his. "I think I just proved I can protect myself," I whisper, a fragile smile forming.

The ruins smolder quietly around us—a stark reminder of the destructive force awakening within me and the enemies still hunting us. But for this moment, in his arms, I allow myself to feel nothing but gratitude for his survival.

We're still here. We're still fighting.

RHYLAND

67

I drink from Danica, her blood flooding my veins with renewed strength, healing wounds that run deeper than flesh. Pride surges through me at her raw courage, but it's tainted by crushing shame. Some fucking protector I turned out to be—brought to my knees while trying to shield my mate. Her reassurances that I did everything possible against impossible odds ring hollow against the thundering chorus of self-loathing in my head.

Yet here she is, trying to shoulder the blame herself, claiming she should have unleashed her power sooner to help me. Even after the horror she's endured, she puts my pain before her own. The selfless strength of this woman splits me open—she's trying to be my shield when I should be her fucking fortress.

As I recount how Danica explained she turned our enemies to ash with celestial fire, Adrian and Erik listen with stunned faces. The raw power she commands is beyond anything we've witnessed in centuries of existence. It's like watching an avenging angel channel heaven's wrath through mortal flesh.

Adrian's face mirrors my bewilderment when I press him about the failed wards. His expression darkens as he theorizes that only ancient, primordial evil could have breached such powerful protection—magic older than time itself.

The implications hit like a sledgehammer. Moretemis isn't just lurking in the shadows anymore—he's actively manipulating Azrael and his entire operation, using them as conduits to gain power in our realm. Those human prisoners aren't just Azrael's twisted experiments; they're unwitting sacrifices to a demon god.

When Danica mentions the Soul Stone again, my blood runs cold. If this relic is real, and Azrael has it in his possession, we're facing a threat beyond anything we've prepared for. I order Adrian to dig up everything he can about its origins, powers, and weaknesses. Anything that might give us an edge.

"This goes beyond Azrael's usual depravity," Erik observes, silver eyes hard as steel. "He's either knowingly serving Moretemis, or being played like a puppet, thinking he's the master when he's just another pawn."

Both scenarios are fucked. A willing servant of Moretemis is bad enough. But Azrael—thinking he's in control while being played? That's a time bomb waiting to detonate.

"We move tomorrow," I command. "Find the relic. Unlock Dani's power."

One thing's crystal clear—we're out of time for playing it safe. Every moment Dani spends untrained is a risk we can't take. Too many lives at stake, and hers is one I won't gamble with. The shadows are coming, blind to what they're hunting. We may not know her full potential yet, but it's time to unleash my angel's true power.

This ends now. Heaven help anyone who tries to stop us.

Steam rises around us in the massive clawfoot tub, candlelight dancing across the water's surface. Dani's body fits perfectly between my thighs, her curves pressing against me as water laps at the swell of her breasts. Vanilla scent mingles with her natural sweetness—honey and sunshine—as I trace lazy patterns across her skin, memorizing every inch of her.

I bury my face in her neck, inhaling deeply. Even after the battle, after the blood and shadows, she smells like home.

"I'm just glad you're alive, Rhyland. Please don't beat yourself up over this." Her voice vibrates through me, straight to my core.

I let my head fall back against the tub's edge with a dull thud, exhaling slowly. "I know, Angel. It's easier said than done, though." The weight of failure still sits heavy in my chest, but her presence soothes the jagged edges.

My hands wander across her water-slicked skin, claiming rightfully mine territory. "You did good, baby," I murmur against her ear, voice dropping to a primal register that makes her shiver against me.

She melts further into my embrace as my fingers find her breasts, teasing the hardened peaks until she arches with a throaty moan that sends blood rushing to my cock. It throbs against the small of her back, hard as steel and aching for her.

"You can fight with poise, heal with grace, and be the most beautiful woman alive," I rumble against the heated flesh of her neck, grazing it with my teeth. "My angel is truly a badass."

Her giggle vibrates through her body and into mine. I tighten my grip possessively, need building with every breath.

"I was so scared," she confesses, vulnerability raw in her voice. "I thought I lost you."

My arms lock around her like living armor, a silent vow to protect her from ever feeling that fear again. "I know, Angel. I'm sorry for causing you to worry like that." I quickly explain the limited ways vampires can truly die, wanting to ease the terror I'd seen in her eyes.

"By the way," she says, turning in my arms that makes water cascade from her curves. Her fingertips trace the old scars and tattoos on my chest, eyes locked on mine—those golden depths that see straight through my centuries of carefully constructed walls. "Aren't you a sly fox! You've been hiding your special talents from me. Care to explain how you pulled off that telekinesis trick? Are you a wizard, Rhyland?" Her lips quirk mischievously. "Can I call you Merlin?"

A genuine laugh rumbles from my chest. "Yeah, lots of vampires have unique gifts. Mine is telekinesis, and it's been a part of me for ages." Pride edges my voice—not for the power itself, but for the wonder it brings to her eyes.

"You just get even more incredible each day." Her smile hits me like a physical force, bright enough to chase away the lingering shadows.

"You're my world, Rhyland. I can't imagine life without you." Her raw honesty strips me bare, leaving me more vulnerable than any physical wound could.

Before I can respond, she claims my mouth with fierce hunger. I groan against her lips, fingers tangling in her wet hair as my tongue explores the sweet heat of her mouth. When we break apart, the look in her eyes—desire mixed with something deeper, something that terrifies and exhilarates me—steals my breath.

I lift her from the water in one fluid motion, rivulets streaming down her perfect form as I carry her to our bed. Her skin feels like living silk beneath my palms as I lay her across the sheets, her eyes never leaving mine.

That look—trust and desire and something I'm not ready to name—is all the invitation I need. I cover her body with mine, determined to show her with actions what I can't yet say with words: that she's become essential to my existence in ways I never thought possible.

With every kiss, every touch, every shared breath, I pour out lifetimes of longing I never knew I carried until she awakened it.

DANICA

68

After my little supernova obliterated our suite, Rhyland asked to switch rooms, and the hotel kindly accepted, no questions asked. I mean, an atomic blast goes off in this place, and all you get is a nonchalant "Sure thing, sir, right this way to your new room."

Gotta appreciate the discretion—though I can't imagine the bill that's going to cost Rhyland. Hope his black Amex has an unlimited super-natural credit line for "Act of Goddess" damages.

As we gather in the new suite at sunrise, I pass vials of my precious blood to Erik and Adrian. Nothing like a bit of Vitamin D from Dani to grant these nightwalkers the gift of strolling in the sun's radiance. Because nothing says "thoughtful travel companion" like being a walking SPF 10,000.

"One serving of liquid sunshine, gentlemen. Don't say I never gave you anything," I quip, watching them drink my blood with reverent care.

We've got a long, dangerous trek ahead into the uncharted rainforest of the Amazon to reach the mythic Valley of the Ancients. No biggie. Just your average Amazonian vacay—jungle trekking, ancient secrets, potential death at every turn.

I take a few deep, centering breaths and consciously tune out all external distractions. My heartbeat aligns with something ancient and powerful—the cosmic rhythm section keeping beat for the universe's most complicated dance number.

As I focus on manifesting our doorway to elsewhere, a brilliant spark ignites between my palms, expanding into a swirling vortex of light. It's like having a tiny supernova growing between your hands—which, after yesterday's explosion, is apparently my new party trick.

Rhyland's solid presence beside me acts like an anchor, his quiet strength making me feel like maybe, just maybe, I won't accidentally open a portal to the dinosaur era or something equally catastrophic.

I glimpse Erik and Adrian from the corner of my eye as the portal stabilizes into a shimmering oval of otherworldly iridescence. It pulses and ripples like the universe's most spectacular mood light, practically screaming, *"Step into the unknown. What could possibly go wrong?"*

"Well, this is it, gentlemen. Grab your machetes and bug spray," I announce with a quirked eyebrow. "Ready to take the plunge into the great unknown?"

Erik and Adrian exchange one of those meaningful, immortal looks that somehow pack decades of conversation into two seconds. Must be nice to have that kind of communication efficiency—meanwhile, humans need emojis just to clarify when we're being sarcastic.

Rhyland's warm hand engulfs mine, his thumb brushing reassuringly across my knuckles. "Together, Angel," he murmurs, voice rumbling through me like distant thunder.

The four of us step into the shimmering vortex in unison. Reality folds around us like cosmic origami before snapping back into place with a disorienting lurch.

Suddenly, we're standing in the heart of the Amazon rainforest. The air hits like a wet blanket—hot, heavy, and scented with a thousand exotic plants. Towering trees stretch impossibly high overhead, their canopies creating a living cathedral. Filtered sunlight dapples the forest floor in shifting patterns while unseen creatures provide the jungle's greatest hits soundtrack.

"By the gods above and below..." Erik murmurs, his eyes wide with genuine wonder.

Meanwhile, Adrian completes a slow 360-degree turn, his head tilted back in undisguised wonder as he absorbs every detail of our surroundings. "This place is... utterly beyond anything I could have envisioned," he breathes, sounding more like an excited grad student than a centuries-old sorcerer. "The sheer biodiversity teeming around us is astonishing!"

I catch Rhyland's eye, sharing a moment of quiet satisfaction. There's something profoundly moving about watching these guys experience sunlight in a rainforest for the first time—like watching someone taste chocolate or hear music after a lifetime of deprivation. My blood has given them this simple joy, and despite all the chaos, that feels like a win.

"Alright, gentlemen." I continue with a clap of my hands. "This is only the antechamber of wonders. Shall we see what other secrets this valley is hiding? Maybe we can find a mystical crown before lunchtime?"

Adrian tears his attention away from a particularly fascinating orchid. "Well then, which direction first?" he asks, suddenly all business again. "Any sign of where we might pick up the relic's psychic trail?"

I close my eyes, letting my awareness expand beyond normal senses. It's like tuning a radio to pick up a distant station—static and interference gradually giving way to a clear signal. After a moment, I feel it—a subtle but unmistakable pull, like a cosmic fishing line hooked somewhere behind my navel.

"This way," I announce, pivoting on my heel and striding confidently into the undergrowth. "Try to keep up, vampire squad. Mystic treasure hunting waits for no one!"

We push deeper into the valley's steamy embrace, moving as quickly as the dense vegetation allows. Every step is a battle against nature itself—vines grab at ankles, massive ferns block our path, and hidden roots seem determined to send us face-first into the loamy soil. My hair plasters to my neck with sweat, and my clothes cling uncomfortably to every curve.

"You know," I pant, hacking at a particularly stubborn liana with my machete, "in the movies, they just cut to the heroes arriving at the temple. Nobody shows the part where you get eaten alive by mosquitoes and have sweat in places you didn't know could sweat."

The jungle provides its own soundtrack—a constant symphony of shrill insect calls, exotic bird cries, and distant monkey howls echoing through the green cathedral around us. No sign of human presence appears anywhere—this might as well have been Earth a million years ago or an alien planet entirely.

Just as my legs begin to seriously protest the endless trek, the cramped sea of green abruptly gives way. We emerge into a sun-dappled clearing that stops us all in our tracks.

Before us lies a scene straight from a fantasy novel—a pristine jungle oasis centered around a crystal-clear pool. A waterfall cascades from a rocky precipice, sending up a fine mist that catches the late afternoon sunlight and scatters ephemeral rainbows across the lagoon's cerulean surface. Thick, verdant grasses carpet the shoreline, while massive umbrella-shaped trees provide dappled shade where small, curious mammals have gathered to drink.

The air itself feels different here—charged with an ancient serenity that soothes away the tension of our arduous hike. It's as if we've stumbled upon Eden itself, a pocket of paradise untouched by time.

"Well," I breathe, unable to maintain my sarcastic facade in the face of such beauty, "I guess the travel brochure wasn't exaggerating after all."

Before I can fully appreciate the view, Erik and Adrian have already stripped off their shirts and are racing toward the water like teenagers at spring break. Their exuberant whoops shatter the tranquil silence, sending birds and small mammals scattering in momentary alarm. The dignified immortals I've come to know are suddenly transformed into jubilant boys, splashing and diving with unrestrained joy.

A pair of scarlet macaws observes the spectacle from a high branch, their expressions somehow conveying avian judgment at these noisy intruders.

I burst out laughing at the absurd sight of centuries-old vampires cannonballing into a jungle pool. "And here I thought Erik didn't know how to have fun," I gasp between giggles. "Someone should be recording this for blackmail purposes."

Rhyland chuckles beside me, shaking his head at his brothers' antics. The rare sound of his laughter rumbles through his chest. His blue eyes gleam with mischief as he turns to me.

"Wanna get wet, baby?" he asks with a suggestive quirk of one eyebrow.

"Was that an innuendo, Mr. Eriksson?" I tease, already pulling my sweat-soaked tank top over my head. "Because I'm choosing to take it as one."

Unable to resist the call of cool water after miles of humid trekking, I strip down to my bra and panties and wade in to meet him. The moment the water touches my overheated skin, I sigh with pure bliss. We float and splash, momentarily unburdened by prophecies, ancient relics, and enemies hunting us.

For one perfect hour, we're just four people enjoying a secret paradise, as carefree as children at play.

Eventually, the slanting afternoon light reminds us of our purpose. We reluctantly emerge from the tranquil oasis, duty calling us back to reality. As the others dress and gather their gear, I linger at the water's edge for one final moment, committing every detail to memory—the rainbow mist, the crystal waters, the perfect peace.

Back in cargo pants, hiking boots and a fresh tank top, I hoist my rucksack onto my shoulders and step back onto the trail. The swim has rejuvenated us all, washing away the morning's fatigue. As afternoon light filters through the canopy in golden shafts, we continue our trek, casting long shadows across our path.

The terrain gradually changes, leading us down into a rocky gorge where the first evidence of past human presence finally appears. At first, it's subtle—a too-straight line here, a weathered step there. Then suddenly, the jungle parts to reveal its secret heart.

"Holy Indiana Jones," I breathe.

Magnificent ruins rise from the emerald undergrowth like the bones of sleeping giants. Crumbling pyramids of pale stone reach skyward, partially reclaimed by vines and roots that snake across their once-perfect geometry. Fallen columns line what must have been grand processional ways, now carpeted with moss and ferns.

Most striking are the intricate carvings that still adorn many surfaces—mysterious glyphs and stylized figures locked in eternal ritual. As I trail my fingers over the eroded patterns, an uncanny sense of recognition washes over me. These symbols feel familiar, as though they were etched directly onto my soul long before they were carved in stone.

"Incredible," Erik murmurs, examining a weathered astronomical chart that spans an entire wall. The stoic vampire's silver eyes are wide with scholarly reverence. "This civilization had an advanced understanding of celestial mechanics. Look here—they tracked not just solar and lunar cycles but planetary conjunctions across multiple systems."

"This place was a center of learning," Adrian adds, brushing away vines to reveal more symbols. "A repository of sacred knowledge."

I move deeper into the ruins, drawn by an invisible thread. These weren't just buildings—they were temples to cosmic understanding, observatories of the heavens, schools where ancient wisdom was preserved and passed down.

And somewhere among them lies the relic we seek.

Adrian traces concentric circles carved into a fallen monolith. "These depict ancient celestials and elemental forces," he explains. "They held beings like yourself in great reverence, Danica."

I approach a wall where a radiant winged figure dominates the scene. Something about it resonates within me. "This place calls to me," I whisper, placing my palm against the stone. "Like I'm following footsteps laid down before I was born."

Rhyland covers my hand with his. "The past is written, but you write what comes next. Trust your instincts."

As my fingers trail over weathered hieroglyphs, energy surges through the stone. The faded carvings illuminate as if lit from within, transforming into three-dimensional scenes of astonishing detail.

"Holy shit," I breathe, transfixed by the spectacle.

The static carvings become living history, projecting holographic visions of a civilization in its prime. Phantom figures move through phantom streets, conducting commerce and performing rituals.

"It's as if we're witnessing their actual society," Adrian says, eyes gleaming. "Their customs, philosophies, cosmology..."

The images reveal a world where winged celestial beings walked freely among humans—not distant gods but partners in a cosmic dance. Knowledge and blessings flowed between realms in mutual respect.

I reach out instinctively, and figures spring to brighter life at my proximity, responding to something in my essence—their energy calls across centuries to something deep within me.

Suddenly, the joyful images twist into nightmares as writhing shadows consume the light. Celestial warriors battle valiantly against encroaching darkness, but cannot stem the tide. Civilizations collapse as balance shatters.

"This corrupting darkness tore the realms apart," I whisper. "It drove the celestials into exile and destroyed unity."

Silence falls as the visions fade, leaving only weathered stone. Rhyland's expression hardens.

"Moretemis," he states grimly. "His poison turned fellowship into chaos."

Adrian nods. "This was no mere physical battle. It was a war of ideals that consumed everything."

We survey these ruins with new understanding—monuments to a cosmic tragedy still echoing through time. The same darkness that destroyed this civilization now threatens all realms again.

I place my hand on the wall one final time, a silent promise to those long gone. Their suffering will not be in vain.

"Let's find that crown," I say with quiet determination. "We've got work to do."

Danica

69

As we venture deeper down, an unnatural darkness creeps in, thickening the air and settling heavy in my lungs. Cold sweat prickles my skin while that familiar sixth sense of danger raises the hairs on my neck. Without hesitation, I summon a radiant orb of pure light into my upturned palms and launch it toward the shadowed ceiling. It hovers like a miniature sun, scattering beams into every crevice and banishing the oppressive gloom.

I catch Rhyland's eye with a playful grin. "Not too bad, eh? And to think I used to need a flashlight app."

He shakes his head, one corner of his mouth quirking upward—his version of a beaming smile. "You're becoming quite adept with your abilities, Angel," he says with a wink that makes my stomach flutter after everything we've been through.

The relic's call grows stronger with each step—an insistent tug beneath my breastbone, pulling me forward like an invisible thread. My inner compass points unerringly toward some hidden inner sanctum.

"This way," I murmur, following mystical currents invisible to the others. We proceed in a single file, guided by my floating light that casts wavering shadows over cracked walls covered in more symbols and scenes.

The passage narrows and descends, leading us down precarious stairs cut directly into bedrock—the ceiling bristles with stone icicles and mineral formations that resemble grasping fingers. Despite the unnatural silence surrounding us, tension draws tighter with each downward step.

The ground beneath us grows increasingly uneven as we enter what feels like the heart of this ancient complex. I pause to catch my breath, suddenly sure what we seek lies ahead.

"Welcome to the Valley of Ancients," I whisper, barely disturbing the weighted silence. "I have a feeling this is just the beginning."

Erik and Adrian follow closely behind us, their forms casting elongated shadows that dance like specters across ancient walls. The weight of centuries presses down as we venture deeper into the temple's heart, my conjured light barely holding back the primordial darkness.

Without warning, the stone floor convulses beneath our feet. A deep rumble builds from within the earth itself—not like an earthquake, but something deliberate, awakened. Jagged fissures race across the rock like lightning, splitting the ground into unstable islands.

"Move back!" Rhyland shouts, but it's already too late.

The rain-slicked surface offers no traction as the floor tilts sharply downward. My feet scramble uselessly against crumbling stone. I hang between stability and chaos for one suspended moment—then gravity claims me.

I plunge into darkness, the world dissolving into a blur of motion and terror. My companions' faces flash beside me, frozen in identical expressions of horror as we hurtle downward. My fingers claw desperately at passing rock, nails tearing and leaving bloody streaks as I grasp for any handhold.

The void below yawns wider, a hungry mouth waiting to swallow us whole. Wind rushes past my ears, drowning out even my screams as I accelerate toward certain death.

Then—impact. My body slams against an outcropping with bone-jarring force. Pain explodes through my shoulders and spine as momentum carries my lower half over the edge. By some miracle, my fingers find purchase on a narrow ledge, leaving me dangling over the abyss.

My makeshift light, still hovering above, reveals the true scale of our predicament. The chamber has opened into a colossal cavern stretching impossibly far below. Distant crystal formations catch and reflect the light in eerie patterns, like stars in an underground sky. One slip means plummeting hundreds of feet into that waiting darkness.

"Dani!" Rhyland's voice cuts through my panic. I look up to see him sliding down the tilted floor toward me, every movement calculated despite the urgency in his eyes. He anchors himself against a jutting stone, stretching his arm toward me.

"Give me your hand!" he commands, his voice steady despite the fear I can see behind his eyes.

I reach up with trembling fingers, my shoulder screaming in protest. Our hands strain toward each other, inches apart but might as well be miles. My grip on the ledge weakens with each passing second.

"I can't—" I gasp, feeling my fingers slipping.

"Yes, you can," Rhyland growls. "Look at me, Angel. Only at me."

With one final desperate lunge, our fingers connect. His hand closes around mine like an iron manacle, refusing to let go. Every muscle in his massive frame strains as he gradually pulls me upward, fighting gravity to save me.

With a final heave, he drags me back onto relatively solid ground. I collapse against him, gulping air into starved lungs, my entire body trembling with adrenaline and relief.

"I've got you," he murmurs against my hair. "I've always got you."

As my racing heart gradually slows, I take in our new surroundings. My floating light reveals a vast underground chamber that must have remained untouched for millennia. The walls glitter with embedded crystals and more elaborate carvings than those above. This is no ordinary cave—it's the true heart of the temple complex, hidden from casual explorers by its deadly entrance.

"Well," I manage shakily, attempting to reclaim my usual bravado, "I guess they really didn't want visitors."

My heart thunders against my ribcage like a trapped animal, each frantic beat a celebration of survival. I struggle to draw proper breath into lungs that seem to have forgotten their purpose, the world still spinning in dizzying arcs around me.

Rhyland crushes me against his chest with almost desperate strength, his face buried in my hair as if to reassure himself I'm truly still here. One hand cradles the back of my head protectively while the other moves across my body in a frantic inventory, checking for injuries his enhanced senses might detect.

Though he remains silent, the storm raging behind his eyes speaks volumes—bone-deep terror at nearly losing me again, battling with raw fury at the universe that seems determined to tear us apart. I've come to recognize that look—it's the face of an immortal confronting his greatest vulnerability.

I cling to him weakly, his solid presence the only anchor in a world that just tried to swallow me whole. With effort, I manage a faint nod to signal I'm unharmed, though my trembling body betrays the lingering shock. The image of that endless void yawning beneath me has burned itself into my memory—another nightmare to add to my growing collection.

"Dani! Rhyland!" Adrian's voice echoes through the darkness above, tight with barely controlled panic.

"We're here!" I call back, my voice surprisingly steady despite everything. Relief washes through me at the confirmation that the others survived as well.

Rhyland and I exchange a brief look before beginning our cautious ascent up the treacherous slope. Each handhold feels like a small victory as we navigate back toward solid ground.

When we finally reach them, Erik's normally impassive face shows uncharacteristic concern. " Are you okay?" he asks gruffly, his silver eyes scanning us for injuries.

"We're fine," Rhyland answers, his grip on my hand betraying the casual tone he attempts. "Just another day of near-death experiences."

Adrian surveys the massive cavern stretching around us, scholar's curiosity temporarily overriding fear. "This place is remarkable," he murmurs. "A hidden sanctuary beneath the temple complex."

"We can't stay here," Erik interjects pragmatically. "That collapse was no accident. This place has defenses—who knows what might trigger next."

I direct my floating orb of light higher, illuminating the full scope of our surroundings. The cavern extends in all directions like an underground cathedral, its walls embedded with crystal formations that catch and refract my light into countless prismatic patterns. The ground beneath us slopes downward into deeper shadows, while stalactites hang from the distant ceiling like stone daggers.

"Look there," Rhyland points toward the lower reaches of the cavern where a faint but distinct glow emanates from what appears to be a passageway. "That light isn't natural."

"No," I agree, feeling the familiar tug beneath my breastbone growing stronger. "And that's exactly where we need to go."

I take a steadying breath, shaking off the last of my vertigo. "The relic is down there. I can feel it calling."

We pick our way cautiously down the slippery decline, every step heavy with purpose. The slick ground is treacherous, making our slow and laborious progress all the more excruciating. But we press on, lured onward by the promise of another opening, a hidden cavern to explore that lay just beyond our reach.

As we descend lower into the cave, the air changes from warm to cool. My light grows dimmer, casting soft shadows on the walls of a forgotten sanctuary.

We navigate cautiously across the slick stone floor, our footsteps splashing through shallow rivulets that wind between our feet. The air hangs heavy with moisture, each breath tasting of mineral-rich earth and ancient secrets.

Fallen pillars line our path like the skeletal remains of giants, their ornate carvings still visible despite centuries of erosion. Broad ceremonial staircases, now choked with rubble and draped with persistent vines, lead to various chambers and alcoves around the perimeter. This wasn't merely a temple—an entire subterranean complex designed for gatherings of significant spiritual importance.

Every available surface bears testament to the artistic devotion of its creators. Elaborate bas-reliefs depict mystical ceremonies, fantastical creatures, and celestial beings in scenes of worship and communion. Some show winged figures bestowing gifts upon kneeling humans; others portray cosmic battles between light and shadow that mirror the visions we witnessed above.

"It's like a hidden city," I whisper.

Erik nods, silver eyes wide as he takes in the architectural achievement surrounding us. "Indeed. An entire civilization flourished here, hidden from the world above."

Adrian points toward a set of narrow stairs carved directly into the bedrock, descending deeper into shadow. "Should we continue?"

Rhyland turns to me, seeking my guidance. In matters of mystical navigation, I've become our reluctant compass.

I close my eyes and draw a deep breath of the mineral-rich air, consciously extending my awareness beyond physical limitations. My mind reaches out like invisible tendrils, probing the ancient darkness that shrouds this hallowed place.

For what feels like endless moments, only silence answers my wordless call. Then—just at the threshold of perception—a faint harmonic hum vibrates against my consciousness. It's distant but unmistakable, a subtle resonance that calls to something primal within my blood.

My eyes snap open, newfound certainty coursing through me. "It's down there," I say, nodding toward the descending stairway. "I can feel it singing."

Danica

70

Step by step, we descend deeper into the earth. The air grows cooler and heavier with each level, carrying the weight of millennia. This hidden place feels alive with secrets waiting to be uncovered.

Massive stone statues line our path, towering sentinels standing at attention every few feet. Their faces are stern, carved with intricate symbols that spiral down their torsos.

"What do you think these are?" I ask, my voice barely above a whisper.

Adrian examines one statue, fingers tracing the mysterious glyphs. "Guardians," he finally says. "I've read about them. Ancient protectors imbued with magic to defend sacred treasures. If activated, they unleash devastating power against intruders."

"Activated?" I ask, dread knotting my stomach.

"They're dormant now, but if they sense a threat..." He leaves the implication hanging.

Rhyland tightens his grip on my hand as we proceed with exaggerated caution, each footstep placed deliberately. The weight of unseen eyes follows our progress. The slightest misstep could awaken whatever ancient power is hidden within this place.

A bone-chilling growl echoes through the tunnel, followed by the scrape of claws against stone. From the darkness ahead emerges a pack of skeletal wolves—emaciated creatures with exposed bone visible through patchy fur. Their eyes glow with unholy light as they circle us, jaws dripping with putrid saliva.

"Bone-howlers," Adrian hisses. "Created by ancient sorcery—souls ripped from the afterlife and bound to physical form. Neither dead nor truly alive."

Rhyland shifts into a protective stance, positioning himself between me and the unnatural predators.

"What can we do?" I whisper, feeling the light in my palm flicker against the encroaching darkness.

Adrian's face is grim. "Their vile power roots them here, an insurmountable barrier keeping out all who seek the relic. I fear we cannot pass."

The howlers continue prowling, their guttural utterances setting my teeth on edge. Those gnarled yellow fangs look capable of quickly rending flesh from bone. Rancid drool spills freely down their jaws, anticipation coming off them in waves. They mean to feast on us.

Rhyland shoves me securely behind him, muscles coiled with tension as he braces for their attack. "Stay close to me, Danica. Do not leave my sight." I nod mutely, throat tight with dread.

Then Rhyland addresses the nightmarish pack, fury blazing in his eyes. "I'll be damned if a bunch of mangy fucking walking carcasses stop me."

Adrian and I trade uneasy looks, knowing the situation is dire. The beasts continue circling with chilling coordination as we debate our next move.

Cold, fetid breath hits the back of my neck. I spin to face glowing eyes mere inches from mine—an alpha howler, massive and terrible, its gaze fixed on me with predatory intent.

It launches forward in a blur of bone and matted fur. My scream echoes as its claws tear through my clothes into flesh beneath. I hit the ground hard, pinned under its weight, putrid breath washing over me as fangs lunge for my throat.

"DANI!" Rhyland's roar cuts through the chaos.

The crushing weight vanishes as the beast slams into the far wall, shattering on impact. Horror freezes my blood as bone fragments skitter across stone, reassembling before my eyes.

"They won't stay down!" I gasp, scrambling upright.

Another howler lunges at Rhyland, who barely twists away. He retaliates with a telekinetic blast that sends it flying, but it rises unfazed, bones snapping back into place.

Adrian chants in an ancient tongue, hands extended. The air vibrates with building energy until a shockwave explodes outward, scattering the pack like leaves. Seconds later, they reform, advancing with unnatural persistence.

"Normal attacks are useless!" Erik shouts, his silver blade cleaving through a howler that immediately begins reconstructing itself.

A massive howler leaps for Rhyland's throat, jaws unhinging impossibly wide. Blood sprays as fangs sink into his shoulder. His agonized roar echoes through the chamber as he tears the beast away, ripping its head from its body.

"Rhyland!" I scream, sending a bolt of celestial light streaking across the chamber, disintegrating another attacker.

Adrian's eyes widen with sudden realization. "We must return them to the earth!" he roars over the chaos. "It's their only weakness!"

Erik's blade becomes a silver blur as he hacks through the oncoming pack. Bone splinters and rotten flesh parts beneath his sword, the severed limbs twitching with unnatural life where they fall. "They keep coming!" he shouts, kicking a still-snapping skull into a nearby crevice.

A massive howler launches itself at his exposed back. I send a bolt of celestial energy that catches it mid-leap, its skeletal form disintegrating in a flash of holy light. Another immediately takes its place, jaws unhinging to impossible width as it lunges for my throat.

Rhyland intercepts it with brutal efficiency, his fist connecting with such force that the creature's skull explodes into fragments. But even as it falls, the pieces begin skittering back together like a macabre puzzle.

"Their numbers are endless!" Adrian shouts, blood streaming from a gash across his forehead. Three howlers circle him, their movements coordinated with terrible intelligence.

The largest beast darts forward, teeth slashing toward Adrian's exposed throat. He drops to one knee, hands weaving complex patterns as ancient words tumble from his lips. A shimmering barrier materializes just as jaws snap closed—teeth scraping against magic instead of flesh.

"Get back!" Adrian commands, his voice resonating with power. His eyes blaze with arcane energy as he slams both palms against the stone floor. "Aperio terra consumere!"

The ground beneath us trembles violently. Hairline fractures race across the ancient stone, spreading outward in complex geometric patterns. With a deafening crack, the floor between us and the howlers splits open—a yawning chasm revealing bottomless darkness below.

Howlers tumble into the void, their unearthly shrieks echoing as they fall. Those at the edge scrabble desperately for purchase, claws leaving deep gouges in the stone. One by one, they lose their grip and plummet into the abyss.

Adrian's face contorts with effort, veins standing out on his temples as he channels more power. "Claudo terra sigillum!" The edges of the chasm begin to close, earth and stone flowing like liquid to seal the breach.

A final howler lunges in desperate fury, clearing the narrowing gap. Its jaws clamp around Adrian's forearm, tearing through fabric and flesh. He cries out but maintains his spell, even as blood streams down his arm.

Rhyland tears the creature away, crushing its skull between his hands. The remaining fragments of bone and sinew are sucked into the closing earth as Adrian completes his spell with a final word of power.

The ground solidifies once more, though faint scratching sounds still emanate from below—the entombed howlers already seeking escape.

"That won't hold them long," Adrian pants, clutching his mangled arm. Sweat pours down his ashen face. "We need to move. Now!"

We sprint down the only path available, the muffled howls of our pursuers driving us forward. Each step sends waves of agony through my shredded flesh.

"Here," Rhyland pulls us into a narrow alcove, his face etched with concern. "I need to heal Dani."

"I'm fine," I protest weakly, though blood soaks my torn clothing. "We don't have time."

"Don't argue, Angel." His voice brooks no opposition. "I can feel your pain. Let me help you."

The battle may be temporarily won, but the war for survival in these ancient depths has only just begun.

I collapse against the wall, finally acknowledging the devastating damage. My arm hangs uselessly, skin in ribbons where claws tore through. Every breath ignites fresh torment.

Rhyland kneels before me, bringing his wrist to his mouth. His fangs pierce his own flesh, releasing a crimson stream. "Drink," he commands softly.

I press my lips to the wound, drawing in his ancient blood. Power surges through me immediately—a lightning storm in my veins that rushes to my injuries, knitting flesh and mending bone.

"Your turn," I insist, noting his pallor and the deep gashes across his chest and shoulder.

"I'm fine," he dismisses, though blood saturates what remains of his shirt.

"Rhyland—"

"We move," he cuts me off, eyes scanning the darkness behind us where distant growls still echo.

With renewed strength flowing through my healed body, I push off the wall. "Then let's finish this before our furry friends return for round two."

The tunnel narrows ahead, leading us deeper into the mountain's heart—and closer to what we came for.

RHYLAND

71

My mind snaps back to those ancient chamber walls—stone tablets telling of darkness devouring everything in its path. I know that darkness intimately. It's the same shadow that ripped my mortal family from me over a millenia ago, the same evil I fought as a warrior before watching it consume everything I loved.

When death came for me that day, something intervened. As my blood soaked the battlefield and shadows closed in, some unknown force pushed back the darkness. What power sealed away that encroaching void? What entity decided I deserved to survive while others perished? The question has haunted me my entire immortal life.

Dani's voice cuts through my brooding. "I feel it! It's pulling me in here." Her eyes gleam with certainty as we round the bend.

The stone sentinel looms before us—massive, imposing, a warning carved in granite. My muscles tense instinctively at the sight. Ancient power radiates from every inch of this chamber, from the obsidian floor beneath our boots to the black and red symbols etching history into walls that seem to breathe with forgotten magic.

We move silently, respecting the crackling energy that surrounds us. This place demands reverence. The guardian's eyes burn like coals in its stone face, radiating heat that hits us in waves even from a distance. Its gaze is calculating, measuring our worth against some ancient standard we can't begin to comprehend.

"You dare approach the sacred relic?" Its voice rumbles through the chamber, vibrating in my chest like an earthquake. "Only those deemed worthy may lay eyes upon it. The relic is meant for a special individual."

The guardian's words hang in the air between us—a challenge, a warning, and perhaps a promise.

We face the towering sentinel, its form wreathed in ethereal light. I step forward, voice steady and commanding. "We understand the relic's power and will wield it only to restore balance and defend the realms."

The guardian remains motionless, its stony gaze boring into us with ancient judgment. Adrian moves beside me, his tone respectful yet firm. "We stand before you as the ones destined to fulfill the prophecy. We've found the one who will restore balance—the Light-Born."

The chamber trembles as the guardian responds, its voice like boulders grinding together. "The ancient prophecies are shrouded in metaphor. Many have claimed to be Light-Born. All have failed to prove their worth."

I motion Dani forward with a confident nod. "Tell him who you are."

She straightens beside me, her small frame suddenly radiating power. The flickering light catches the gold in her eyes as she steadies herself, squaring her shoulders.

"My name is Danica, daughter of Elysium. And I'm here to save your ass."

A smirk tugs at my lips. Even facing an ancient guardian, my mate doesn't lose her fire.

The sentinel leans down with a sound like mountains shifting, heat blasting from its molten eyes. "Daughter of Elysium... and under which sign were you born, child?"

Dani's pulse quickens—I can hear it from where I stand. Adrian and

I exchange glances. This is it—the prophecy's test.

"Well," Dani says, cocking her hip, "if I were to believe in horoscopes, which I don't, then being born in August would make me a Leo." Her lips curve into that defiant smile I've come to crave. "You know, the lion's sign... in case you didn't catch that."

The stone bastard just stands there, still as death.

She throws me a look before turning back to our rocky roadblock. "Hey, Mount Rushmore! You deaf under all that granite?"

"The prophecy speaks of the Lightborn of two celestial houses, not one."

The words hit like a sledgehammer. What the fuck?

"How the fuck does one person share two celestial houses?" I growl, patience wearing thin with these cryptic stone riddles.

I lock eyes with Adrian, silently demanding answers.

"Dani," my brother asks, his voice tight with sudden understanding, "exact birthday?"

"August 22nd," she snaps, clearly done with this shit.

The Golem shudders, stone grinding against stone. "The cusp of Leo and Virgo..." Its voice rumbles like an avalanche. "The lion and the maiden...born when day and night stand in perfect balance. The child of two realms. Now, prove yourself."

My mind races. The balance point between two signs—just like the balance between light and shadow. Fuck me, this prophecy runs deeper than I thought.

Confusion flashes across Dani's face as she looks to me for guidance. I mentally urge her to summon her light, giving her an encouraging nod. Her eyes close in concentration, and the air around her hands begins to shimmer.

Energy gathers between her palms, first a soft glow that rapidly intensifies into a brilliant sphere of pure light. She cradles this miniature sun, her face serene as she meets the guardian's gaze.

"My services aren't free," she declares boldly. "I'll take that trinket you're hiding as payment."

Pride surges through me as I watch her—this fierce, impossible woman facing down an ancient being with nothing but nerve and raw power. The guardian's silence stretches, and tension builds with each passing second.

When it finally speaks, there's something new in its rumbling voice—respect, perhaps even awe. It fixes Dani with its burning gaze. "You carry a great burden. Much needs to be done, and it may cost you your life. Are you aware of this? Are you ready—"

"Listen up, pebble nuts," Dani snaps, her patience visibly shattered. "I'm exhausted and monumentally pissed off. I've nearly died a dozen fucking times on this bullshit quest. Nearly falling to my death upon arrival in this shithole cave, which was a cosmic mindfuck. Savage-ass dogs tried to rip my damn face off. Oh, and my parents and very good friend were freaking brutally murdered! All for the sake of some ancient prophecy that says I must save all your asses."

My jaw slackens as she unleashes hell on this ancient being. Beside me, Adrian's face contorts with pure horror, his eyes darting between Dani and the guardian like he's watching a train wreck in slow motion. The silence that follows her outburst is deafening—clearly no mortal has ever dared speak to a guardian with such blistering disrespect.

"So how about you stop with the vague mystical horseshit and move your stony ass out of my way," she continues, chest heaving. "I'm the Light-Born, fucking Chosen One, Princess of goddamn Destiny. Just let me get this relic to finish what I'm destined to do. Then, we can all get the hell on with our lives. Comprende?"

Blood rushes south instantly. My cock hardens painfully against my jeans as primal possession surges through me. This fierce, foul-mouthed creature is *mine*. I want to grab her by that smart mouth, pin her against the nearest wall, and fuck that defiance right out of her. I'd tangle my fingers in her hair, growl commands in her ear while she takes every inch of me as punishment for that filthy tongue.

Erik and Adrian exchange glances, surprise morphing into barely suppressed smirks. But my focus remains locked on Dani, mesmerized by the fire burning in her.

She stares down the guardian, cocking her head with a smirk that promises trouble. "Do I pass your inspection, oh wise one?" Sarcasm drips from every syllable as she waits, unflinching.

For one breathless moment, I prepare to defend her from whatever wrath she's unleashed. Then, impossibly, the guardian begins to move. Stone grinds against stone as it steps aside, clearing our path forward. Dust settles around us as Dani stands victorious, her chin lifted in defiance.

"Shall we?" she suggests, as casual as if she's just asked us to dinner.

I can't help the predatory smirk that curves my lips. My feisty little angel has no idea what she's awakened. The moment we're alone, I'll remind her exactly who she belongs to—pinning her beneath me, claiming that smart mouth, and fucking her until she's begging, submissive and spent.

But for now, I follow my mate forward, pride and desire warring within me as she leads us toward our destiny.

DANICA

72

Maybe I didn't need to sass-talk a ten-ton rock monster, but after everything I've been through, I wasn't about to take attitude from an overgrown paperweight. I just want to grab this stupid relic, check "save the world" off my to-do list, and maybe—just maybe—get a full night's sleep without something trying to kill me. If that makes me bratty, well, add it to my growing list of character flaws.

A chill crawls up my spine as we step through the arched doorway. The hulking stone guardian's empty eyes seem to track our movement even as it remains motionless. My heartbeat thunders in my ears, echoing off ancient walls as we enter the inner sanctum.

"By the gods," Adrian whispers.

In the chamber's center lies an expansive mosaic of intricate symbols etched into the floor, each line glowing with faint blue luminescence. The tapestry of interconnected shapes and swirling patterns is breathtaking in its complexity—clearly not decorative, but functional.

I approach cautiously, drawn by an instinct I can't explain. My boot brushes against a slight depression in the floor—an indentation that seems deliberate rather than worn by time.

A low hum instantly fills the chamber, vibrating through stone and bone. The floor splits open with a grinding rumble, ancient slabs parting to reveal hidden mechanisms below. A marble pillar rises slowly from the opening, ascending until it stands waist-high before me.

Carved into its surface, glowing with ethereal blue light, symbolizes three interlocked wavy lines.

"Wow," I breathe, unable to formulate anything more eloquent.

Adrian steps closer, hand tracing over the carving. "Water," he murmurs.

Rhyland and his brothers spread out instinctively, each finding similar depressions across the mosaic floor. As they press down, more marble pillars rise in response, each bearing a different glowing emblem.

"This one is fire," Rhyland announces, indicating a stylized flame dancing with orange-gold light.

"Air," Erik calls from across the chamber, standing before a pillar marked with swirling currents.

"I believe this represents light," Adrian says as I join him beside a carving of a radiant circle.

I examine two more pillars in turn. "Earth," I identify easily, recognizing the mountain symbol. But the last carving—a complex circular pattern with intricate internal geometry—remains unfamiliar.

"What do you think this is?" I ask, gathering the others around.

"Magic," Adrian declares with dawning realization. "Of course—magic has to represent the Fae realm."

I look around at the six pillars, each marked with symbols of the different realms. "So what now? Where's the crown?"

Adrian attempts to rotate a pillar while I push against another. Neither budges despite our efforts. After several frustrating minutes, I step back, wiping sweat from my brow.

I circle the pillars, studying each one carefully. Above them, elaborate carvings emerge from shadow—mythical guardians watching over each element. A vivid green dragon with flaming breath looms over the fire pillar. The water column has a bubble-blowing blue mermaid. A being with black wings spread flies above the air—a woman wearing a cloak hovers over the Earth pillar. An angelic figure with wings stands above the light pillar, while a unicorn sits over magic.

"Look!" I point upward. The others follow my gaze, expressions shifting to wonder at the celestial menagerie.

Inspiration strikes like lightning. "Let me try something," I announce, dashing to retrieve my pack.

Returning with my water bottle, I approach the water pillar. Heart racing, I pour liquid over the carved symbol. Immediately, the pillar illuminates with ethereal blue light as water cascades down its sides. With a deep rumble, it rotates clockwise.

"Their elements activate them!" Adrian exclaims, eyes wide with revelation.

We scatter to different pillars. Rhyland strikes a match and sets it atop the fire column. Flames dance across the stone, igniting a golden glow as they turn smoothly. Erik creates a small whirlwind for the air pillar while Adrian crumbles soil onto earth.

Rhyland gestures toward the light pillar with a playful smirk. "This one's yours, Angel."

I focus inward, summoning a sphere of pure light that hovers above my palm. Gently, I place it atop the pillar. Radiance erupts instantly, the column rotating with a satisfying click.

"And magic is yours, Adrian," I say, nodding toward the final pillar.

He conjures a shimmering emerald orb of arcane energy and presses it against the symbol. Green light pulses through ancient stone as the pillar completes its turn.

The chamber trembles as hidden mechanisms awaken after centuries of slumber. Gears grind somewhere deep within the walls. With a scraping of stone against stone, a previously invisible doorway materializes in the far wall.

Cold air rushes from the opening, carrying scents of mineral and mystery. The crown's energy surges around me, its pull undeniable—a magnetic tug toward whatever waits beyond.

The passage stretches before us, ancient torches igniting at our approach. Vivid murals line the walls—scenes of mythical realms and forgotten legends, their colors impossibly preserved. With each step, the relic's presence grows stronger, its energy resonating through my very bones.

We emerge into a vast circular chamber that steals my breath away. Constellations of luminous crystals stud the domed ceiling and walls, casting prismatic light across the space. At the center rises a stone dais with four carved sections representing the primal elements. Atop a central pedestal hovers a perfect crystalline orb, pulsing with inner light.

Erik examines the platform's intricate symbols. "It appears we need to align the elements somehow."

Adrian gestures toward metal levers protruding from the walls. "Perhaps these control the mechanism?"

"Let's find out," Rhyland says, moving toward one lever.

We each take a position at a different control, the cold metal biting into my palm. On Rhyland's count, we pull simultaneously. The chamber rumbles to life—flames ignite along circular channels, water flows through transparent conduits, wind whistles through hidden vents, and sections of the floor shift like tectonic plates.

The orb responds immediately, swirling with chaotic colors that clash discordantly. The harsh vibration sets my teeth on edge.

"Wrong combination," I mutter, releasing my lever. The chamber returns to stillness.

Erik studies the wall carvings with renewed intensity. "These aren't just decorative—they're instructions."

"Look here," Adrian points to interconnected symbols. "The elements must flow in harmony, not opposition."

Rhyland and I exchange understanding glances. "Balance," I say simply.

We try different configurations, adjusting the levers with increasing precision. With each attempt, the orb's colors shift, sometimes violently clashing, sometimes almost harmonizing. Finally, as we settle on a specific arrangement, a perfect resonance fills the chamber—a melodic hum that vibrates through stone and body alike.

The orb transforms, radiating concentric shells of color—emerald, sapphire, ruby, amber, and pure white light at its core—the perfect harmony of all elements. As it reaches peak brilliance, a section of the wall dissolves to reveal a hidden doorway framed in glowing runes.

"I feel like Lara Croft!" I laugh, the sound echoing joyfully as we approach the threshold.

Beyond lies our prize—and perhaps, if we're lucky, another piece of the puzzle that might just save everything.

Danica

73

We cross the threshold into absolute darkness. For a moment, we're blind, but then our eyes adjust to reveal an immense circular chamber unlike any before. The walls appear to absorb light rather than reflect it, yet they shimmer with faint constellations and arcane symbols—cosmic cartography etched in luminescent ink across obsidian stone.

At the chamber's center stands a raised dais, and upon it—the crown.

Even from here, I can see the intricate metalwork catching little light, the single brownstone embedded in its circlet glowing with inner fire. My scalp tingles, then burns with recognition as we approach. The crown's energy resonates within me like a tuning fork struck against my soul.

"My god," Erik whispers, his voice unnaturally loud in the perfect stillness.

Rhyland reaches toward the artifact—only to jerk back as crackling electricity erupts around the crown, forming a dome of dancing blue-white energy. The barrier hums with warning, sparks illuminating our shocked faces.

"What the hell?" Rhyland breathes, taking an involuntary step back.

Adrian extends his hand cautiously toward the shimmering wall. The energy intensifies, pushing against his approach. "Some kind of enchantment," he concludes. "Ancient protection magic."

"Allow Dani to try?" Erik suggests, his silver eyes calculating.

Rhyland's gaze meets mine, concern battling understanding. "Are you certain?"

I nod. "Yes. I think I'm the only one who can."

"Be careful," he urges, reluctantly stepping aside.

I approach the dais alone, the crackling barrier intensifying with each step. The energy field presses against me like a physical wall, raising the hair on my arms—testing, evaluating. I close my eyes and reach out with more than just my hand, extending my awareness toward the crown.

I am here. I have come for you.

The electricity parts like a curtain before me, recognizing what flows in my veins. The path is clear.

My skin prickles as if recognizing something ancient and familiar—a connection beyond understanding.

With trembling fingers, I reach toward the shimmering dome. The moment my palm touches the energy field, everything changes. Warm light radiates outward from the point of contact, illuminating dormant runes carved into the stone floor. The symbols awaken, twisting with serpentine grace across the chamber.

The barrier doesn't repel me—it recognizes me. Like water parting, the energy field dissolves beneath my touch, leaving the crown exposed and vulnerable.

My hand hovers above the artifact for one breathless moment before making contact. The metal feels impossibly smooth, warm as living flesh despite centuries of entombment. The solitary brownstone pulses with inner light, sending electric currents through my fingertips and up my arm, resonating with my racing heartbeat.

I lift the crown from its ancient resting place. Its weight feels substantial yet perfectly balanced—two pieces of a cosmic puzzle finally reunited.

Turning to face the others, I see awe reflected in their expressions. This journey has forged something unbreakable between us—strangers weeks ago, now bound by forces beyond comprehension.

Tears stream unbidden down my cheeks as the enormity crashes over me. My old life—deadlines, coffee dates, scientific papers, and mundane worries—feels like a distant dream. The world is vaster and more perilous than I ever imagined. Anxiety and wonder war within me.

Rhyland's eyes shine with fierce pride. "You found it," he says softly, his fingers intertwining with mine.

Adrian and Erik exchange resolute nods. "We must plan our next steps carefully," Adrian states.

Before anyone can respond, a deep rumble shudders through the floor. The temperature plummets as an ominous groan reverberates through ancient stone. The constellation patterns tremble, then fracture as chunks of ceiling crash around us.

"The whole complex is collapsing!" Erik shouts.

"We need to go now!" Rhyland pulls me toward the exit as larger stones begin to fall.

I clutch the crown against my chest, its energy pulsing in time with my racing heart as we sprint for survival. Our journey has only begun if we live long enough to continue it.

Rhyland sweeps me into his arms without hesitation. "Hold on!" he commands, already moving with inhuman speed.

I clutch the crown against my chest with one hand, the other gripping Rhyland's shoulder as he sprints through the disintegrating chamber. The ground bucks beneath us like a living thing, ancient stone giving way after millennia of silence.

Massive chunks of ceiling crash down mere inches behind us, pulverizing ornate statues that have existed since immemorial. The air thickens with choking dust and powdered stone, visibility shrinking to mere feet.

"There!" I gasp, spotting a narrow fissure in the far wall—a service passage perhaps, or a structural weakness.

Rhyland pivots instantly, powerful legs propelling us forward as the floor begins to sink beneath our weight. We hurtle through the opening seconds before the chamber's ceiling collapses with a deafening roar, sealing the crown's resting place forever.

The impact sends us sprawling. I land hard, crown still clutched to my chest, lungs fighting for clean air in the dust-filled passage. Every breath burns as I force myself upright, body protesting each movement.

The respite is momentary—the collapse spreads through the complex like an infection. The tunnel groans ominously as fractures race across its ceiling.

"Move!" Rhyland pulls me to my feet as a massive stone crashes where I'd been lying. He lifts me again, navigating the treacherous passage with preternatural agility.

I glimpse Adrian and Erik behind us, their faces pale smudges in the darkness as they leap between falling debris. The entire underground city is dying around us, burying its secrets for eternity.

Rhyland skids to a sudden halt, nearly sending us both crashing into a wall of collapsed stone blocking our path. My heart plummets.

"What's wrong?" I gasp, though the answer is brutally obvious.

"The way's blocked," he confirms, voice tight with controlled panic. "We're trapped."

I look down at the crown glowing softly in my hands, its single stone pulsing like a heartbeat. We've come too far to die here, entombed with the prize we sought.

"There has to be another way," I whisper, refusing to accept defeat as the mountain collapses around us.

Danica

74

A shower of boulders crashes from the ceiling. Instinctively, I throw my hands up. White-gold light erupts from my palms, creating a shimmering barrier. The rocks hover momentarily before Rhyland yanks me aside as they shatter against the ground.

His eyes lock with mine. "How did you—"

"I don't know," I gasp.

He wastes no time, launching down the newly revealed passage with inhuman speed. The slap of his boots against ancient stone echoes through the collapsing tunnel. Behind us, Adrian's hands glow electric blue as he deflects falling debris with precise magical bursts, his face contorted with concentration. Erik weaves through the chaos like liquid silver, his movements a blur as he navigates the destruction.

A violent tremor rocks the cavern, deep and primal. The ground splits beneath Rhyland's feet with a sickening crack, throwing me from his protective arms. I slam against jagged stone, the impact forcing air from my lungs in a painful rush. My body tumbles across razor-sharp rubble, each point of contact sending fresh waves of pain through my battered form. My fingers find the crown, clutching it desperately as the floor gives way completely beneath me with a sound like thunder.

Then I'm falling.

My scream tears through the abyss as darkness rushes up to claim me. The wind whips my hair violently as gravity pulls me toward certain death. In that suspended moment, my life flashes before me like opening credits to a movie I'll never finish—

Impact. Not with unforgiving stone, but with Rhyland's iron embrace. He caught me mid-fall, his body a living shield against the collapsing world. His ocean eyes burn with desperate determination, dust and sweat streaking his face.

"I got you, baby. Hang on!" he commands, voice raw with urgency.

We hurtle through collapsing tunnels, each leap more desperate than the last. Rhyland lands on crumbling ledges that disintegrate seconds after we launch forward, the sound of stone giving way pursuing us like a ravenous beast. The crown pulses against my chest, its energy thrumming with ancient power, somehow guiding us toward daylight like a supernatural compass.

Ahead, a sliver of blinding light cuts through the darkness—the exit. With one final, superhuman effort, Rhyland launches me through the opening. I hit the ground outside as sunlight sears my dust-filled eyes, momentarily blinding me as fresh air fills my burning lungs.

Turning back, my heart stops. Rhyland clings to the crumbling edge of the opening, muscles straining as the cavern collapses beneath him. Rocks cascade into the void, the mountain itself seeming to devour him inch by inch. Without thinking, I dive forward, landing hard on my stomach. My fingers lock around his wrist, his skin slick with sweat and grime.

"Rhyland!"

I pull with everything I have, muscles screaming in protest, tendons threatening to snap under the strain. He surges upward with a primal roar, crashing onto solid ground beside me as the entire mountainside rumbles like a dying beast. We scramble backward on hands and knees, watching in awe as the ancient city vanishes forever, swallowed by the earth with a thunderous finality.

Rhyland scoops me up again, putting distance between us and the collapsing terrain until we reach stable ground. He sets me down gently before collapsing to his knees, chest heaving, his powerful frame covered in dust and blood.

I clutch Rhyland fiercely, heart hammering against his. "Erik, Adri an... are they okay?" My voice cracks with barely contained panic.

He shakes his head, dust cascading from his sweat-soaked hair. "I... I don't know." The words fall between us like stones, heavy with unspoken fear.

I can see the worry etched in the hard lines of his face, the tightness around his eyes. My heart grows leaden as a lump forms in my throat, threatening to choke me. I had lost track of them after my tumble down that treacherous slope—what if they're trapped in that stone tomb forever?

A wave of nausea surges through me as bleak thoughts crowd my mind. Tears blur my vision, hot and stinging against dust-caked skin. The crown in my hands suddenly feels like a curse, its weight the price of lives I wasn't willing to pay.

Footsteps crunch on gravel behind us. I spin around so quickly my vision swims, steadying myself against Rhyland's solid frame.

Erik and Adrian emerge from a different opening in the mountainside, their faces lined with exhaustion, clothes torn and bloodied. Erik's silver hair is matted with dirt and something darker, while Adrian's hands still pulse with fading magical energy.

"Glad to see you two made it out," Erik manages between labored breaths, his usually immaculate appearance now ruined by their desperate escape.

Relief crashes through me like a tidal wave, washing away the dread. I launch myself at them, wrapping both men in a desperate embrace, feeling their solid warmth—alive, here, safe. "I was so worried," I choke out, tears finally breaking free to carve clean tracks down my filthy cheeks.

Rhyland bows his head, his broad shoulders sagging with visible relief. The tension that had been coiled in his massive frame slowly unwinds as he watches us.

Adrian returns my embrace briefly before gently disentangling himself. His dark eyes scan the horizon, ever vigilant. "I think it's time we get going," he says, voice rough from the dust and exertion.

I feel Rhyland's presence before his touch, that distinctive energy that seems to charge the air around him. His arm wraps around my waist, pulling me against him with almost desperate strength. His entire body trembles slightly, the aftermath of adrenaline and fear making itself known in the mighty Viking's frame.

He pulls back just enough to look into my eyes, his ocean-blue gaze boring into mine with such raw intensity that I'm momentarily stunned. He searches my face as though memorizing every detail, like a man who has glimpsed death and found new appreciation for what remains.

His gaze softens, the fierce warrior giving way to raw vulnerability. His lips tremble with emotion barely contained. "I thought I lost you," he whispers, voice breaking on the last word, the admission torn from somewhere deep and primal.

I kiss him fiercely, tasting dust and blood and life. "Remember—nothing in this world or any other can keep us apart." The promise hangs between us, both comfort and challenge to whatever forces might try.

Amid the death throes of the ancient city, I grasp the crown tightly in my dirt-encrusted hands. It responds immediately, a soft golden light illuminating the surrounding jungle in ethereal radiance. A gentle breeze caresses our faces as we step away from the ruins, carrying away the scent of ancient dust and destruction.

I focus my mind on opening a portal to Rhyland's hotel room, drawing on the newfound power that hums beneath my skin like electricity. "Hang on," I say. He gives me a puzzled look, ocean eyes widening as the air before us begins to shimmer and distort.

A sudden realization hits me—returning to the hotel feels dangerously unwise after the Shadow Brotherhood's attack and the failed rune security. "Maybe we should go to my place instead, just for now until we figure out our next move?" I suggest, my voice rough from screaming and dust.

Adrian and Erik nod immediately, their exhaustion evident in every line of their bodies. Rhyland hesitates, his protective instincts warring with practicality, before finally agreeing, "For now." The reluctance in his voice speaks volumes about his desire to keep me somewhere he controls.

I focus harder, visualizing my living room with perfect clarity—the worn leather couch, the mismatched throw pillows, the stack of scientific journals on the coffee table. The air shimmers and parts like a curtain, revealing my familiar space through a doorway of pulsing light.

"Gentlemen," I manage a tired smile, the effort almost more than I can bear, "please come in."

We step through together, Rhyland's arm still protectively around my waist. The portal seals behind us with a sound like a sigh, my ordinary apartment materializing around us like a protective embrace after the chaos we've survived.

Adrian and Erik collapse onto the couch without ceremony, daylight's toll finally claiming them as their eyes drift closed. In my bedroom, I place the crown reverently on my dresser, its central stone catching lamplight and scattering tiny rainbows across my walls like fragments of another world.

Steam fills the bathroom as I let scalding water pound my battered body, washing away blood and grime in rivulets down the drain. This mundane ritual somehow grounds me after a day spent defying reality itself.

For tonight, at least, we're safe. Tomorrow brings new challenges—the next step in a destiny I never chose but can no longer avoid.

RHYLAND

75

I stalk after Dani into her room, primal hunger coursing through my veins. Steam billows from the shower, and I strip quickly to join her, my body already responding to her proximity.

After we clean up, she stands before the mirror, water droplets trailing down her curves like a map I want to explore with my tongue. I cage her with my arms, pressing against her back, our naked bodies reflected in perfect clarity. *Mine.* The thought burns through me like lava.

Pride and possession surge through my chest as I study her reflection. This fierce creature who faced down death multiple times today, who stands unflinching before ancient guardians and supernatural horrors—all mine—each time she nearly slipped through my fingers, only stoked the inferno of need burning in my core.

"I'm so proud of you," I whisper against her ear, watching her honey-gold eyes darken with desire in the mirror.

She flashes that defiant smile. "None of it would have been possible without you and your brothers," she challenges, that familiar fire dancing in her words.

My cock hardens against her lower back as I recall her fearless command of the situation, how she faced every obstacle with a blend of courage and sass that drives me wild. Our eyes lock in the mirror, and the heat between builds like an inferno. Her desire hits me like a physical force—sweet, intoxicating, demanding.

"I haven't forgotten how naughty your mouth can be, Angel." My voice drops to a dangerous register. "In fact, I've been craving the taste of it and thinking about giving you a good spanking."

Her lips curve into a wicked smile. "Is that a promise?" she purrs, arching against me.

"Oh, it's definitely a promise," I growl, gripping her hips possessively.

She spins in my arms and attacks my mouth with savage need, her skin burning against mine. I lift her onto the cool marble counter, swallowing her gasp as the cold surface meets her heated flesh. My hands claim every inch of her body as I devour her mouth.

I break the kiss to look down at her, spread before me like a feast. "You'd like that, wouldn't you—getting spanked?" I murmur against her throat.

My tongue traces a path down to her breasts, teasing each nipple until they peak in my mouth, drawing desperate moans from her lips. She arches against the mirror as I drag her to the counter's edge, positioning her exactly where I want her.

"I'm famished for some angel food," I growl against her breast, ready to feast on every inch of my defiant mate.

I've restrained myself with Dani while she adjusts to her new reality—the losses, the trauma, everything she's endured. Only let her feel real power when she climbed on my cock in the car and fucked me like the wild little thing she is.

Tonight, I'm done holding back. Time to remind this little firecracker exactly who owns this sweet pussy and who's really in charge—one brutal, punishing inch at a time.

I hoist her legs onto the counter, exposing her glistening pussy like an offering. She gasps, thighs falling open in wanton invitation. The sight of her wet and ready nearly undoes me. "Don't move," I command, voice rough with need.

Dropping to my knees, I worship at the altar of her body. She's a feast laid out before me, and I'm a starving man. My hands map her curves, reveling in the searing heat of her skin. Her pretty pink slit beckons, and I can't resist its call.

"Fucking scream for me," I demand before diving in.

My tongue traces her soaked petals, savoring her nectar like a man lost in the desert. I lick, swirl, tease—drawing desperate whimpers from her throat as I focus on her swollen clit. She squirms under my assault, hips bucking for more.

I grip her thighs, pinning her in place. "Keep yourself open for me. Don't make me tie you up, Angel." The warning is a dark promise.

Her taste is my addiction, her pleasure my drug. I feast on her like a man possessed, drunk on the power I hold over her body.

She fists her hands in my hair, head thrown back as she rides the edge of ecstasy. Her moans shoot straight to my cock, making it throb with savage need. Reaching down, I fist my length, stroking in time with the thrusts of my tongue. I'm so fucking hard it hurts, desperate to bury myself in her tight heat.

"Rhyland," she keens, "I need you now."

Ignoring her plea, I take my time trailing back up her body, worshipping sun-kissed skin with lips and teeth. I linger at her throat, sucking a bruise into delicate flesh. "You're going to beg," I rasp against her ear.

My hands map her curves with fevered intensity, claiming every inch as mine. I capture a dusky nipple, sucking hard before giving the other the same attention. Fingers find her clit, circling, teasing, keeping her suspended on the knife's edge of release.

"Rhyland..." This time, it's a broken plea. Her body trembles, wound tight and desperate for completion.

But I'm not done with her yet. Not even close.

I claim her mouth in a brutal kiss, tongue delving deep to taste her sweetness. She moans into me, the sound vibrating through my chest as I plunder every corner of her. Her pleasure fuels my own, making my cock throb with savage need.

I've given her control lately, letting her set the pace as she heals. But my restraint has reached its limit. Tonight, I'll remind her who she belongs to—dominating her until she screams my name, until she's ruined for anyone else.

Her eyes meet mine, pleading and desperate. Her body trembles, strung tight with anticipation.

"Yes, Angel?" I purr, waiting for the words that will unleash the beast inside me.

"Rhyland..." she whimpers, squirming against my fingers. "Don't be an asshole."

I tsks, eyes narrowing. "Asshole? Oh, your filthy mouth will get you in trouble, Angel." I rub her clit roughly, making her cry out. "Fucking tell me you want me."

Her moans echo off the walls, her body shaking with need. I revel in the power I hold over her, the way she comes undone at my touch.

"Rhyland, I want you... I always fucking want you. I need you." It's almost a demand, laced with breathless arrogance.

"Well, since you asked so sweetly..." I slam into her, burying myself to the hilt. Her scream is music to my ears, primal and raw.

"You... complete... bastard," she gasps as I set a punishing pace, nails scoring my back. But the fire in her eyes tells me she craves this just as much as I do.

I devour her mouth, kissing her with bruising force as I pound into her tight heat. This isn't about romance or making love—it's about possession, about claiming what's mine.

And fuck, does she love it. Every desperate buck of her hips, every ragged moan torn from her throat, every clench of her walls around my cock—it all screams her need for me.

I grip her hips, slamming her back against the mirror as I drive deeper, harder. She tenses, hovering on the edge of oblivion. Her eyes blaze with insatiable hunger, begging me to give her what only I can.

"More," she pleads, nails digging into my shoulders. And I'm happy to oblige.

I fuck her with relentless force, chasing our mutual destruction. The bathroom fills with the slap of skin on skin, the wet sounds of our joining, the symphony of her cries mingling with my grunts. It's raw, animalistic—a primal claiming that leaves no doubt who she belongs to.

I lift her effortlessly, hooking my arms under her knees and spreading her wide. She clings to me, nails digging into my shoulders as I grip her ass and slam into her with punishing force—her heart races against my chest, skin electric where it meets mine.

Her desperate need fuels my own, driving me to take her harder, faster. I pull her ass cheeks apart, giving the mirror a perfect view as I pound into her—soaked and wanting more. Each thrust is relentless, designed to shatter her completely.

I catch her gaze in the reflection, eyes dark with promise. "Watch me rip you apart, Angel."

Shifting my stance, I make sure she has a front-row seat to her own destruction. She stares back, pupils blown with lust as I drive into her again and again. Her moans bounce off the walls, her body writhing in ecstasy.

"See how goddamn gorgeous you look when you take every inch of me," I growl, punctuating each word with a savage thrust.

"Rhyland..." she whimpers, "it's too much."

I crack my palm across her ass, making her yelp. "That's one—you will take every inch of this cock like the filthy angel you are."

I pound into her relentlessly, the obscene sounds of our coupling filling the room. She writhes against me, desperate to escape the overwhelming pleasure. I hold her captive, my grip unyielding.

The raw need in her eyes drives me wild. Her walls pulse around my cock, signaling her approaching release. Each moan begs me to take her harder.

She arches, exposing her throat in surrender. Her eyes burn with invitation. "Do it," she commands, offering her essence.

Primal hunger surges through me. With a savage grin, I sink my fangs into her flesh, claiming her completely. Her moan vibrates against my lips, my balls tightening with the need to fill her.

She shatters around me, walls clamping down as she comes with a scream. Her release floods over my cock as I continue my assault, drawing out her pleasure while holding back my own.

I'm nowhere near finished. Mad with need, I crave more of her sweet destruction. She'll be ruined for days after this—sore and satisfied, branded inside and out as mine.

And we've only just begun.

RHYLAND

76

I withdraw abruptly, leaving her aching and empty. Stalking to the bed, I toss her onto the mattress and cover her body with mine. She melts into me as I claim her mouth in a searing kiss, tongues tangling in a battle for dominance.

Her moans fill the room as I ravage her with lips and teeth. "Up on your knees and turn around," I command, voice rough with need. She trembles beneath me, obeying without hesitation.

She crawls slowly, hips swaying in a tantalizing display. Her cheeks are flushed, eyes heavy-lidded with desire as I move behind her. My cock nestles against her slick pussy, throbbing with the need to bury myself deep. Fisting a hand in her hair, I tug sharply, forcing her back into an arch. She gasps at the delicious sting, body taut with anticipation.

I nip at her earlobe, growling low. "Beg me to fuck your ass."

Her breath catches, tension thrumming through her. But I'm determined to push her boundaries, to show her pleasure she's never dreamed of. The thought of finally claiming her tightest hole, making it mine, has me harder than steel.

"Rhyland... I..." she protests weakly.

A sharp smack to her ass echoes through the room. She yelps, the sound morphing into a moan as I soothe the sting with a gentle caress.

"That's two—you'll love what I do to you, baby. Now beg for it." My fingers find her clit, circling the swollen nub. She writhes against me, caught between apprehension and need.

I tighten my grip on her hair, tilting her head back. "Beg me, Dani."

Defiance flashes in her eyes. "Fuck you."

A groan rumbles in my chest at her bratty response. "Oh, that is *exactly* what I'm gonna do to you." Another slap to her ass, more brutal this time. She cries out, the scent of her arousal thickening the air. "That's three. Want more?"

Gripping her ass, I spread her wide. The sight of her glistening pussy and tight rosebud has my mouth watering. I gather saliva, letting it drip onto her forbidden entrance. Slowly, I slide two fingers into her soaked channel, coating them liberally before tracing them around her back door.

Lowering my head, I lick her with my tongue, teasing the tight ring of muscle. She bucks against me, whimpering as I work her open with lips and teeth. Pressing the tip of my tongue inside, I groan at the exquisite heat. "Ready for this cock, baby?"

Her answering moan is all the encouragement I need.

She rocks back against me, whimpering as I land another sharp smack to her ass. Slowly, I feed just the tip inside her tight opening, savoring the exquisite pressure.

I keep my movements gentle but insistent, easing her open with patience and skill. Inch by inch, I'll show her the heights of ecstasy this forbidden act can bring. By the time I'm fully sheathed, she'll be begging for more.

A gasp tears from my throat as her tight ass chokes me. Pushing deeper, her body tenses, and a shattering scream echoes off the walls.

"Relax," I murmur, circling her clit with feather-light touches. Her breathing shifts, pleasured moans replacing pained whimpers. With careful persistence, I slide forward as she squirms beneath me.

"Is it... in?" she asks breathlessly, a hint of innocence in her voice.

I chuckle, nipping at her shoulder. "Just an inch, sweetheart. About seven more to go."

A violent shudder wracks her body as I sink deeper, a guttural moan falling from her lips. "Fuck."

Pausing, I struggle to control my ragged breathing. "That's it, Angel," I rasp, hands roaming her trembling form. "You're doing amazing."

She whimpers, teeth sinking into her lower lip as sensation overwhelms her.

Savoring the intimate connection, I whisper against her skin, "Ready for me to move, baby?"

At her shaky nod, I begin with slow, shallow thrusts. Her tightness is almost unbearable, wringing every ounce of pleasure from my aching cock. It takes every shred of control not to pound into her mercilessly.

Gradually, I increase my pace as she quivers uncontrollably. "It's too intense!" she cries out, hands fisting in the sheets.

I stroke her soothingly, murmuring words of encouragement. "Just relax and let go, sweetheart. I'll take you somewhere new, somewhere amazing."

My movements gain depth and rhythm, angling to hit that sweet spot deep inside her. Under my patient guidance, she'll experience bliss she's never known.

I bring her to the edge slowly, treasuring every gasp and moan, every flutter of her tight walls around my shaft. By the time she's taken my full length, she'll be addicted to this pleasure only I can give her.

Gripping her hair, I yank her head back and drive forward, burying myself to the hilt in her perfect ass. She cries out as I fill her completely, the sound echoed by my own guttural moan.

"Fuck, you feel incredible," I groan, savoring the exquisite vice of her body. "So tight, so perfect."

With that, I begin to move earnestly, claiming her as mine—body, heart, and soul.

"Look at you, fucking desperate for it," I snarl, voice thick with dominance. "Say it, Angel. Beg me to destroy this perfect ass like the filthy girl you are."

I dominate her ruthlessly, one hand fisted in her hair while the other pinches and rolls her sensitive nipples. She writhes beneath me, a symphony of pleasured cries spilling from her lips with each punishing thrust.

"Yes!" she sobs, the word torn from her throat. "God, yes! Use me, fill me, ruin me..."

"Fuck yes, take it all, baby," I growl, slamming forward with punishing force, watching my thick cock disappear into her perfect ass. "Made for this—made for me to ruin."

Her answering moan is pure sin, a sound that shoots straight to my aching balls. I pound into her mercilessly, the wet slap of skin on skin obscenely loud in the otherwise quiet room. Danica meets every thrust eagerly, grinding back against me like a bitch in heat.

"Fuck... harder... please!" she keens, desperation coloring her voice.

Using my grip on her hair for leverage, I comply with savage intensity. Each stroke seems to split her open, my thick length stretching her impossibly full. Danica's screams of ecstasy fill the air, spurring me on as I chase our mutual ruin.

I feel her start to tighten, her body tensing as pleasure builds to a crescendo. "That's it, baby," I urge, angling my hips to hit that spot deep inside her. "Come from my cock in your ass, like a good girl."

My filthy words push her over the edge. With a shattering cry, she comes undone, her release gushing hot and slick down her thighs. I fuck her through it ruthlessly, prolonging her climax until she's a babbling, incoherent mess.

"Fuck!" Dani screams, her orgasm making her shake.

"Look at my angel, so fucking greedy for this cock." My voice drops a dangerous octave, thick with need. "Is this what you crave, to be filled and wrecked and left bruised? To be completely and utterly mine?"

She can only whimper in response, too far gone to form words. I continue my relentless pace, each stroke dragging her sensitive walls. Before long, she's cresting again, a second orgasm ripping through her spent body.

"Rhy... I can't..." she gasps, even as she grinds back against me wantonly.

"You can and you will," I command, my release building at the base of my spine. "One more, baby. Give me one more, and I'll fill this greedy ass with my cum."

Reaching around, I circle her swollen clit with clever fingers. She bucks wildly, overstimulated nerves sparking with pleasure-pain. I rub the sensitive bundle harder, my thrusts becoming erratic as I near the edge.

"Now, Dani," I demand, sinking my teeth into the curve of her shoulder. "Come. Now."

Her body obeys, a final climax crashing through her as she clenches like a vice around my cock. With a roar, I follow her over, painting her insides with jet after jet of my release.

I collapse against her back, both of us gasping for air as aftershocks roll through us. Slowly, reluctantly, I pull out, admiring the sight of my seed leaking from her abused hole.

Flipping her over, I gather her boneless form into my arms. Her eyes are glazed, face slack with sated bliss as I carry her to the bathroom.

Setting her on the cool marble, I drink in the sight of her—flushed and panting, thoroughly ravished. "Jesus Christ, Rhyland!" she manages breathlessly. "You have to be the dirtiest man alive."

"Yeah?" I shoot back with a wicked grin. "But you love it."

After another shower to wash away the evidence of our passion, Danica and I rejoin the others in the living room. We gather around the crown, admiration warring with confusion as we take in the six empty settings and lone amber stone at its center.

What is the meaning of these missing pieces?

Adrian examines the crown with intense focus, his dark eyes narrowed in concentration. The empty settings taunt us with their hollowness—where have the other gems vanished to? Why did this solitary amber stone remain when others were taken? The questions multiply, breeding like shadows in the corners of my mind.

Dani collapses onto the couch beside me, her face a portrait of confusion. The scent of our recent passion still clings to her skin, mixing with the subtle fragrance of her soap. "Seraphina said she'd contact me once I retrieved this," she says, frustration edging her voice. "Maybe she can explain?"

"Is there any way for you to contact her first?" I ask, my fingers itching to touch her again, to ground myself in her warmth while my thoughts race toward dangerous possibilities.

Dani shakes her head, uncertainty twisting those full lips I'd ravaged just an hour ago. The memory of her taste lingers on my tongue, distracting me momentarily from the mystery at hand.

"Why not call out for her?" Adrian suggests, breaking my reverie. "It's worth a try."

Dani's hands twist in her lap, nerves getting the better of her. She takes a deep breath, then calls into the room's stillness. "Seraphina? Are you there?"

The silence that follows is deafening. We all hold our breath, straining for any hint of a response. But there's nothing—just the heavy weight of unanswered questions hanging in the air.

She tries again, her voice tinged with desperation. Still, only emptiness echoes back. With a huff of defeat, she throws up her hands. "Guess not," she sighs, slumping back against the cushions.

As night falls, Adrian and Erik slip out to feed, leaving Danica to seek solace in sleep. But rest eludes me. My mind races, turning over the puzzle of the crown as I study its gleaming surface.

Adrian's words keep circling back—he'd mentioned the seven realms—seven settings, seven stones... Could it be that each realm holds one of the missing gems? The thought sends a thrill of anticipation through me, and my heartbeat quickens.

Does the amber stone symbolize Danica's light realm? What other treasures might we find scattered across the other domains? The possibilities are dizzying, each one leading down a different path of speculation.

We've cracked the first code, but it's clear now that this is just the beginning. A labyrinth of riddles and challenges stretches before us, waiting to be unraveled.

I set the crown aside and slide into bed beside Danica. Her body instinctively seeks mine, molding against me with perfect familiarity. Tomorrow, we'll begin unraveling this enigma. But tonight, I focus solely on her soft breaths against my chest and the silken heat of her skin against mine. The future, with all its dangers, can wait—this moment, with her safe in my arms, is all that matters.

Danica

77

A soft glow seeps under my eyelids, dragging me from exhausted slumber. I blink awake to find my bedroom bathed in ethereal light, shimmering particles dancing through the air like cosmic dust. Seraphina materializes before me, her form translucent yet radiating power. Her golden hair floats as if underwater, wings folded neatly against her back.

"You've recovered the ancient crown," Seraphina says warmly. "A crucial step towards reuniting the fractured realms."

Burning with questions, I blurt out, "Thank you. I've been desperately awaiting your return."

She acknowledges my attempts to summon her. "I heard your call, but couldn't respond immediately. You have many questions." Her soothing voice calms my nerves. "Ask, and I will illuminate what I can."

Meeting her wise, ancient gaze, I ask, "What happened in the Valley of Ancients? Why did such an advanced civilization collapse?"

Sorrow clouds Seraphina's luminous face. "Long ago, before darkness tainted existence, the realms coexisted harmoniously. Mortals and celestial beings collaborated through open portals, creating a peaceful universe." Her expression darkens. "Then evil emerged from the void."

"Moretemis," I whisper, a chill running through me.

Seraphina nods gravely. "Moretemis brought chaos and ruin. He sought to consume light and hope. Elysium had no choice but to exile him to the Shadow Realm and seal the portals, separating the realms for their protection."

"But why couldn't my father destroy Moretemis completely? Why only banish him?"

Seraphina's eyes hold deep sorrow and grim resolve. "Moretemis's sinister power had grown too immense. Elysium couldn't defeat him. Sealing Moretemis away was the only way to safeguard the realms from his evil."

I absorb her tale of shattered unity and lost hope. "So isolating the realms destroyed their harmony," I say heavily.

Seraphina nods. "Yes. Moretemis still infiltrates the realms from the shadows, using agents to spread chaos. His dark power has only grown in the void. Now he craves to fully return, extinguish all light, and engulf everything in eternal darkness."

Azrael springs to mind. A cold dread grips me. "And that's where I come in, right?"

"Yes, Dani. Only you can bridge the sundered realms, weave them back together. The crown is a guiding light on your destined path."

Profound purpose shines in Seraphina's timeless gaze. "It will take a tremendous collective force from all realms to defeat Moretemis and his fathomless dark power. Elysium couldn't do it alone. But now it falls to you, Dani, to unite the worlds, proving yourself as the prophesied savior to lead them against the ultimate evil."

My mind spins like a centrifuge, struggling to process the cosmic responsibility being placed on my shoulders. I'm just one woman—a scientist who, until recently, thought vampires were strictly fictional.

"This is insane," I whisper, sinking onto my bed. "How am I supposed to accomplish what a literal god couldn't?"

"It will not be easy," Seraphina acknowledges.

"Understatement of the millennium," I mutter.

"But you possess what Elysium himself did not—the ability to unite rather than divide. To build bridges where others erect walls." Seraphina's light pulses gently. "The power to stand as a beacon against darkness lives within you, Danica."

Contradictory emotions war inside me—exhilaration clashing with terror, determination wrestling with doubt. Yet beneath this emotional tempest, I recognize an uncomfortable truth: I can't walk away from this—not now, not knowing what's at stake.

"Thank you for coming," I say, voice unsteady. "For helping me understand."

Seraphina's radiance intensifies, bathing my bedroom in golden warmth. "You do not walk this path alone. You have guidance from above, allies at your side, and strength within that you've barely begun to tap." Her voice resonates through me. "The journey ahead is perilous, but remember—you carry the hopes of every realm upon your shoulders."

Her form begins to fade, light diminishing like a sunset.

"Wait!" I lunge forward desperately. "I still have questions!"

Seraphina's dissolution pauses, her presence lingering though her form grows transparent.

"Why me?" The question bursts from me, raw and honest. "Out of everyone in existence, why would Elysium create me specifically for this cosmic shit-show? Couldn't he have picked someone with, I don't know, actual qualifications? Or at least someone who knew what they were signing up for?"

A ripple of something like amusement passes through Seraphina's fading light. "It is precisely because of who you are, Danica. Your father needed someone capable of true compassion, of seeing beyond differences to find common ground—qualities abundant in mortal souls but often lacking in eternal beings."

I shake my head incredulously. "So out of billions of humans, I'm somehow special enough for this?"

"You are his daughter," Seraphina says simply. "Light of his light. But also uniquely human—capable of growth, adaptation, and understanding in ways immortals cannot comprehend. Your very nature bridges divides."

The crown pulses on my dresser, as if responding to her words.

Seraphina's light ripples across my bedroom walls as she continues. "You are uniquely positioned at the crossroads of two worlds—mortal compassion and celestial power in perfect balance."

I lean against my headboard, trying to absorb the cosmic bombshell she's dropping. "So it's not about raw power? It's about... connection?"

"Precisely." Her voice softens with approval. "Mortals possess an innate empathy celestial beings struggle to comprehend—an intuitive understanding of the bonds between all living souls. Your divine heritage amplifies this gift exponentially."

"Great," I mutter, rolling my eyes. "So I'm basically a cosmic social worker with superpowers."

Though her form has nearly faded, I feel Seraphina's amusement. "To reunite the fractured realms requires more than strength or magic. It demands someone who can relate to every realm's struggles and forge genuine understanding between disparate peoples. Someone mortal, yet touched by divinity. This is why Elysium created you."

The crown rises from my dresser, hovering between us. Its single stone gleams, surrounded by six empty settings.

"Each empty socket awaits its stone," Seraphina explains, gesturing to the first vacant setting. "The Shadowstone of Unbra grants mastery over darkness itself—controlling shadows, creating invisibility."

Her finger traces to the next socket. "Pyronyx from Pyrothos, the Realm of Flame. Its bearer commands fire, remains unburned by infernos, and shapes wildfire at will."

She indicates the third setting. "Aquanite from Aquaria's depths. Connected to water's adaptable nature, it allows control over all liquid forms—from gentle streams to raging tsunamis."

Two more settings gleam empty in the crown's circlet. "Faerite from Luminara enables communion with all magical creatures. Zephyrite from Zephyria grants dominion over wind and the power of storms."

I count the settings. "That's five. What's the sixth?"

"Atherite," she says softly, "embodies your father's blessed Light Realm. It's pure energy shall empower you to pierce any shadow, heal any wound, and strike down wickedness with hallowed light."

The enormity of my task settles over me—intimidating yet strangely exhilarating. I'm terrified, but something deeper stirs within me—a purpose I never knew I was created for.

"Fine," I say, straightening my shoulders. "I'll be your realm-uniting, shadow-fighting chosen one. But I'm doing it my way—with science, sass, and style."

I hear Seraphina laugh for the first time—a sound like silver bells. "We would expect nothing less, Danica."

The crown hovers between us, its single brownstone catching the moonlight. I stare at the gleaming gem.

"What about this one?" I ask, pointing to the stone already set in the crown. "What realm does it represent?"

"That, Danica, is the Terraglide stone—the embodiment of Mortalis, your Earth.

"Mortalis is far more significant than many realize," Seraphina explains. "The Terraglide stone connects its bearer to the very essence of your world—granting extraordinary physical abilities, combat prowess that rivals immortal warriors, and wisdom drawn from humanity's collective journey."

I study the crown's empty sockets, my mind racing to process everything. "To defeat Moretemis, I have to become some kind of interdimensional jewelry thief collecting magical gems for my cosmic tiara?"

Seraphina's laughter fills the room like wind chimes. "You have a unique way with words, Danica. But essentially, yes. Each stone represents a realm's essence. United in the crown, they will grant you the power needed to rally all worlds against the darkness."

I exhale slowly, feeling the weight of impossibility. "Where the hell do I even start?"

"Your first destination is crucial. It will set the course for all that follows."

I wait, heart hammering against my ribs.

"Begin in Luminara, the Fae Realm," she finally says. "The Faerite stone grants communion with all magical creatures—allies you'll desperately need. Many beings there possess knowledge lost to other realms."

"What kind of creatures?" I ask, curiosity overriding my anxiety.

"In Luminara, you'll speak with the fae. They know pathways between worlds that even I cannot perceive. Should you earn their trust, their wisdom will illuminate your journey forward."

Her light brushes against my cheek, warm as sunshine. "Trust your instincts, Danica. The crown will guide you to each stone in turn. Each acquisition will reveal the path to the next."

I nod slowly, trying to absorb the enormity of what lies ahead.

Seraphina's light wraps around me like a warm embrace. "You do not walk this path alone, dear one. Your allies stand ready to aid you. And Rhyland—" her voice softens "—your mate will be your anchor through the storms to come."

As Seraphina's radiance begins to fade, the weight of what she's asking settles over me. Collect magical stones, unite fractured realms, and defeat an ancient evil? Part of me wants to dive under my covers and pretend this is all a weird dream.

But that's not an option anymore. Dear old Dad didn't make me his chosen one, so I could chicken out when things got tough.

I straighten my shoulders, chin lifting with determination. "Alright, Morty," I whisper to the darkness. "Get ready to have your shadowy ass kicked by a scientist with style."

RHYLAND

78

I cut through Karma's writhing masses, the club's chaos fading behind me. No sign of Lucian among the strobe lights and bass-heavy beats. He's likely in his office—the only sanctuary from this sensory overload.

I burst through the door unannounced, catching Lucian balls-deep in some nameless woman bent over his desk, tits bouncing with each thrust. The girl spots me and freezes in horror, begging him to stop. Lucian responds with a harsh slap to her ass, ordering her to stay put.

Without missing a stroke, he tosses me a casual "Be done in a sec, brother," like I've just interrupted a business call rather than a fuck session.

I stride to his bar, pouring myself a generous whiskey while he finishes pounding the mortified girl. After a final grunt, he zips up and drops into his chair with a self-satisfied smirk. The woman scrambles out, face burning with humiliation. Lucian's unfazed—the perverted bastard probably gets off on the audience.

"Glad you're back in one piece," he drawls. "That oozing ass-pimple

Azrael was sniffing around for intel on you and your firecracker."

My fists clench reflexively. "What did that shit-gargling fuck want?"

"Oh, harmless stuff—your whereabouts, info about Dani. A friendly chat over tea and biscuits."

That bloodsucking parasite is already tracking us after the ambush. "So what did you tell him?" I demand through gritted teeth.

"I informed Mr. High-and-Mighty that ignorance is bliss. And that my club isn't the ideal spot for a game of twenty questions." His grin turns predatory. "Far more impactful than simply saying 'fuck off.'"

Lucian studies me with sudden interest. "Which reminds me—you've been gone for over a week. Did something happen on your nature hike, or did you just decide to get lost for shits and giggles?"

"That's impossible. We were only gone a day, tops."

At his confused frown, I explain our discovery of the Valley's civilization and Dani's immediate consultation with Seraphina about the crown.

"Well, bend me over and fuck me sideways—looks like you crazy kids did some bonafide time travel!" His eyes gleam mischievously. "Maybe you can grab some winning lotto numbers from the past, Marty McFly."

Ignoring his childish jokes, I cut to the chase. "What intel did you gather on Azrael's blood trade?"

Lucian's smirk vanishes instantly. He slams a thick dossier onto the desk. "Feast your eyes on this steaming pile of dirty secrets."

I rip through the pages, each revelation stoking my fury like gasoline on fire.

"Senators, CEOs, philanthropists—all tied to this sick operation?" I growl.

Lucian's fingers drum against his jaw. "Either that lumpy jizz-stain is harvesting souls with a crazy straw for Moldy-wart, or he's stockpiling blood and bodies to build a goddamn undead army."

His eyes burn with intensity. "Let's ram this evidence down the council's fossilized throats! No more slipping through the cracks. Time to end this deviant creep!"

The vampire council enforces our laws with iron fists. With this proof, they can't ignore Azrael's escalating atrocities.

"Get it done. Now," I command.

He sighs dramatically. "Dealing with those crusty vampire farts just sucks balls. But for you, brother, I'll make them squirm." His grin turns predatory.

Leaning forward, Lucian prods, "So, spill it. What happened during your little adventure?"

I detail everything Dani learned from Seraphina—her destiny to find the missing stones and harness each realm's unique energy.

"Holy shit." Lucian's face darkens. "Those realms won't just hand over their magical rocks." His laugh is sharp and humorless. "This ain't gonna be no pleasure cruise. Every world's gonna have its share of challenges and villainous ass-clowns."

I clench my jaw, resolve hardening. "I fucking know. It'll be brutal. But we'll do whatever it takes to stop that evil bastard from spreading more chaos and destruction."

The weight of our mission settles on my shoulders—heavy, but one I'm born to carry. For Dani. For all the realms.

Lucian meets my gaze with an exaggerated wink. "You know I'm ride-or-die for Team Save-All-The-Realms! I'll round up whatever motley crew of misfits we need for this suicide mission."

Despite his maddening personality, I grip his shoulder firmly, genuinely grateful for his loyalty through the centuries. Having Lucian's considerable power and inability to shut the hell up on our side will prove... something.

Cracking his knuckles with theatrical flair, he bounces on his heels. "So what's our play, Captain Broody-Pants? Step one in Operation Don't-Let-The-Universe-Get-Royally-Fucked?"

I outline Danica's directive to start with the Fae Realm—bonding with its inhabitants to secure their stone.

"Ooooh, fairy land!" Lucian claps his hands like an excited child. "Tiny wings, sparkly dust, and beings who'll probably turn our intestines into party streamers if we look at them wrong! Sign me up for THAT death trap! Think they have chimichangas there?"

I scowl at his inability to take anything seriously. Then I remember another critical matter. "We also need to train Dani to master her emerging powers. She must access their full potential."

Lucian's face lights up like he just won a murder lottery. "Hold the phone! Little Miss Sunshine needs power training?" He fans himself dramatically. "I volunteer as tribute! I've got centuries of experience helping women discover their... hidden talents." He waggles his eyebrows so aggressively they might fly off his face.

My vision goes red. I barely resist slamming him against the wall as I snarl, "You so much as look at her wrong, and I'll rip off your balls and shove them down your fucking throat."

"Whoa there, Testosterone Tornado!" Lucian throws his hands up, mock terror on his face. "Your precious angel's virtue is safe from my devilishly handsome clutches. Besides, I'm pretty sure she'd turn me into a crispy critter if I tried anything." He mimes an explosion with his hands. "POOF! Lucian flambé!"

His expression shifts to something almost serious—as serious as Lucian ever gets. "But for realsies, once Dani goes full Super Saiyan with her celestial mojo, she'll need a Yoda to her Luke. Untamed magic is like me at an open bar—chaotic, destructive, and likely to end with something important on fire."

I nod grimly, envisioning the potential chaos. "You're right. Know any trustworthy magic practitioners?"

"Funny you should ask!" Lucian spins in his chair like a demented child. "There's this ancient wizard dude named Tenzin who's owed me since dinosaurs roamed the earth. Total hermit now—lives in the mountains, probably talks to rocks and has meaningful relationships with squirrels." He shrugs dramatically. "But when it comes to magic, he's basically Dumbledore, Gandalf, and Doctor Strange having a three-way mind-meld. Perfect for our little light-bringer!"

Relief washes through me. Finally, a solid lead—if I can trust anything coming from Lucian's mouth.

Danica

79

Rhyland returns from his meeting with Lucian, tension evident in his stance.

"Will the Vampire Authorities really contain Azrael?" I ask, doubt coloring my voice.

"The Authorities have methods for those who break their laws," Rhyland assures me.

We settle onto the plush sofa, fingers intertwined, stealing a fragile moment of peace. The warmth of Rhyland's body against mine and the gentle tick of the mantel clock create an illusion of normalcy—a delicate bubble of safety about to shatter.

The door explodes inward with a thunderous crack that reverberates through my bones. Splinters of mahogany spray across the room like deadly confetti. In the ruined threshold stands Azrael, but not as I remember him. Darkness writhes around his form like living smoke, coiling and slithering with sentient hunger. His coal-black eyes gleam with malice, reflecting no light—bottomless pits into some primordial abyss. The air temperature plummets, my breath crystallizing before my face as his presence fills the room—heavier, more malevolent than before—as if something ancient and terrible now wears Azrael's skin like an ill-fitting suit.

"Perfect," he snarls, his voice a layered abomination of sounds—Azrael's tenor overlaid with something deeper, older, scraping against my eardrums like rusty nails. "Two souls to harvest in one strike." His gaze locks onto mine, the weight of his attention crawling across my skin like insects. "I'll enjoy breaking you piece by piece, my dear."

My heart hammers against my ribs. *"How the hell can he enter?"* I project desperately to Rhyland.

"It's not just Azrael anymore," Rhyland's voice cuts through my terror. *"Moretemis works through him now."*

The name sends ice through my veins—the shadow lord himself has found us.

Rhyland launches himself at Azrael—a savage blur cutting through space. Their collision rocks the foundation, the impact reverberating through the floorboards like an earthquake. The chandelier sways violently overhead, crystal tinkling an ominous melody. Paintings crash to the floor, frames splintering. Each exchanged blow thunders like cannon fire in the confined space.

Despite Rhyland's ancient strength, Azrael matches his fury. Darkness coils around Azrael's fists like living smoke, extending his reach with every strike.

I claw desperately at my power, finding only paralyzing terror. My heart hammers against my ribs while my limbs turn to stone. Useless. I'm utterly useless as Rhyland battles for our survival.

Azrael's fingers slice through air—a midnight tendril lashes out, striking with cobra-like precision. It wraps around my torso, colder than Arctic waters, constricting with impossible strength. My lungs burn for oxygen that won't come. I can't scream, can't move—can only watch in silent horror as darkness seeps through my skin like black ink bleeding through paper.

The shadow violates my mind. Memories flood in—my parents' betrayal projected in high definition, their abandonment dissected frame by agonizing frame. Rhyland's devotion warps into calculated deception before my eyes. Every insecurity I've buried erupts to the surface like magma breaking through earth.

Through vision blurred by tears and shadow, I see Rhyland's fist connect with Azrael's jaw. The sickening crunch precedes Azrael's body hurtling through my coffee table. Wood explodes into deadly projectiles. But the darkness binding me only tightens, crushing until my vision tunnels to pinpricks of fading light.

Seraphina's voice pierces the void like a silver arrow. *"Use your light, Dani!"*

Before I can respond, Azrael recovers impossibly fast. He tackles Rhyland with inhuman speed. They crash to the floor with a bone-jarring impact that rattles my teeth. Azrael straddles Rhyland's chest, unleashing a barrage of blows. Each sickening impact sprays crimson across white walls. Blood patters against my cheek—hot, metallic, terrifying.

One desperate glance my way—Rhyland's eyes lock with mine across the battlefield of my living room. In that fractured moment, something primal passes between us. With a roar that seems torn from the depths of centuries, he heaves upward. The movement catapults Azrael into the wall. Plaster fractures like spider webs, white dust billowing around his crumpled form.

Rhyland staggers upright, face a mask of crimson. He lurches toward me, my name breaking on his bloodied lips—"Dan-i"—each syllable a desperate prayer.

"You're pathetic..." the shadows hiss directly into my consciousness, their voice like steel scraping bone. *"Your parents wanted to die rather than be with you..."*

Something snaps inside me. With a cry that tears from my soul, I reject their poison. Light erupts from my core, searing through darkness like a supernova. Shadow tendrils recoil, writhing like wounded snakes.

Azrael rises from destruction with a roar that vibrates my skull. He charges Rhyland again, their bodies colliding in a symphony of violence. Each blow cracks the air like lightning strikes, impact waves rippling through my flesh.

I reach desperately for that wellspring of light, fingers grasping at power that slips through them like water, leaving me hollow and gasping in its wake.

Fucking fantastic. My cosmic mood ring abilities choose now for a coffee break? What's the point of having powers if they don't show up when needed?

Time fractures as Azrael drives a jagged wooden shard—a splintered table leg—into Rhyland's chest with savage precision. The wet *thunk* of penetration echoes in my ears like a death knell. Rhyland's ocean-blue eyes flood with shock—massive hands clutching the protruding stake, fingers already crimson-slick as blood blooms across his shirt like a grotesque flower.

Rhyland's eyes lock with mine in shocked disbelief. His massive hands rise slowly, trembling as they clutch the protruding shard. Blood seeps between his fingers, dripping with sickening rhythm onto the pristine floor.

"NO!" The scream tears from my throat, painful and raw.

Cruel laughter echoes as his knees buckle. His towering frame crumples, first to his knees, then sideways with terrible finality. The impact of his body against marble sounds like the end of my world.

Terror floods my veins with ice. My lungs forget how to function. My heart forgets how to beat. One suspended moment of pure, crystalline horror before I'm lunging forward, scrambling across blood-slick marble.

I crash to my knees beside him, the impact jarring my bones. "No, no, no, God, please no!" Desperate prayers spill from my lips as my hands hover uselessly over the gushing wound. His lifeblood spreads beneath him, a growing scarlet pool reflecting my shattered expression.

Rhyland convulses, a violent cough spraying blood across my face, warm and metallic. His beautiful features twist in agony as deathly pallor creeps across his skin like winter frost.

"Stay with me! Please, *please*, stay with me!" Tears blind me, hot and relentless. I clutch his massive hand between mine, feeling his immortal strength ebbing away with each labored heartbeat. The enormity of what's happening crashes over me in suffocating waves.

"You'll be okay—just hold on," I plead desperately, the lie burning my throat. My entire body shakes with terror as I watch his life drain away.

This can't be happening. Not him. Please not him.

His chest heaves with rattling breaths. Each one shallower than the last. His eyelids flutter, ocean-blue disappearing behind heavy lids.

The silence that follows is deafening.

"Rhyland, hang on!" My scream. But he lies motionless beneath my bloodstained hands, his powerful chest still as stone.

Blind panic claws through me. I grasp the stake with shaking hands, fingers slipping in blood. Bile rises in my throat as I wrench it free with one desperate pull. The obscene sucking sound as it exits his flesh will haunt me forever.

I fling the bloody shard away and gather his massive frame against me, cradling him like something precious and broken. Violent sobs tear through my body as I rock him, my tears falling onto his ashen face.

A stake through the heart.

The discussion we had flashes through my chaotic mind. Wasn't that what Rhyland explained just days ago? The details blur as panic floods my system, my thoughts scattered like broken glass.

Does it kill them instantly? Or just immobilize them?

I strain to remember his exact words, but terror clouds everything, leaving only fragments of knowledge when I need certainty most.

Did the stake pierce his heart or miss by inches?

The question hammers in my skull, relentless and terrifying.

Maybe not direct? Please, not direct.

Azrael turns predatory eyes toward me, pupils blown so wide they devour the iris. His lips curl back in a twisted smile that reveals too many teeth. "Ah, the lovely little sorceress," he purrs, voice dripping venom. "You've caused quite a stir. How did you escape my shadows?"

I tremble violently, rage and terror fusing into something primal in my chest. "Fuck you," I spit, voice raw. "We want nothing to do with you."

His chuckle echoes through the room, cold and hollow as he circles me with predatory slowness. "You may not want anything to do with me, but I want everything to do with you."

A sudden, desperate gasp breaks the tension—Rhyland's eyelids flutter, chest heaving as he draws in a ragged breath. Relief floods through me, washing away despair as his formidable healing abilities begin knitting flesh and repairing the damage. The color gradually returns to his face as his body fights back from the brink.

With inhuman speed that blurs my vision, Rhyland launches himself at Azrael. They collide with a thunderous crash that shakes the walls. Blood slicks the marble floor beneath my feet, making it treacherous as I struggle to stand. Azrael raises both hands with a guttural incantation, unleashing an ebony wraith that envelops Rhyland in suffocating darkness.

Rage overtakes fear as I watch the man I love being consumed. "Aren't you just a pathetic shitstain sucking off the dark lord for scraps of power?"

Azrael's eyes blaze with hatred as he abandons Rhyland, moving toward me with terrifying speed. Before I can react, he backs me against the wall, viciously fisting my hair and yanking my head back. "I'll rip that filthy tongue from your mouth."

His icy presence presses against me, the cold emanating from him unnatural and bone-deep. Defiance wells up despite the terror clawing at my throat. I refuse to break under his gaze, even as pain shoots through my scalp from his cruel grip.

He slams me against the wall with brutal force, driving the breath from my lungs in a painful rush. Through swimming vision, I see Rhyland across the room, ensnared in slithering shadows that tighten around his massive frame. Raw fear twists his features as he struggles against the darkness invading his mind.

Tears stream down my face, hot trails cutting through dust and blood as I scream uselessly, watching darkness slowly devour Rhyland's essence.

Azrael clamps my chin between his fingers, nails digging into my skin hard enough to draw blood. "You'll be mine, whore." His rancid breath blasts my face as he leans closer, his features distorted with malice.

I shut out his presence, focusing all my attention on Rhyland across the room. "Fight it!" I call out desperately. "Don't listen to its lies!"

Red rage overrides fear. I gather crackling energy until electricity swirls around me. With a guttural roar, I drive a blazing orb directly into Azrael's face. The impact hurls him against the far wall.

"Listen here, asshole. I'm already taken, and you don't stand a chance. I'm your worst nightmare. So, back the fuck off!"

I suppose my abilities don't always manifest when I want them to, but better late than never. I've got my glow back and ready to kick some serious ass.

Adrenaline surges through my body as my brain switches into fight mode.

Azrael rises slowly, shadows deflecting most of my blast. Blood trickles from his mouth as he cackles wetly. "Claimed you, has he? Mated to you?" His glance toward Rhyland ignites fury in my core.

I hurl bolts of light toward Rhyland's prison, but Azrael intercepts each one with shadow barriers. My light consumes darkness before dissipating.

"You smell like the goddamn sun," he snarls, features contorting with disgust. "Your presence pollutes the air with that revolting hum."

He looks absolutely unhinged—a total lunatic. His eyes are murky voids, humanity long vanished. The dark tendrils continue dragging Rhyland deeper into despair while my frantic mind scrambles for solutions.

Suddenly, Azrael's body unravels—skin morphing into roiling smoke and shadows. His transformation is horrifyingly complete, an unstoppable embodiment of primordial darkness. With an inhuman bellow, he launches a tidal wave of churning shadow toward me.

The sight triggers flashes of the Valley of Ancients, obliterated by this same malevolent force.

Instinctively, I throw up my hands and squeeze my eyes shut. When I dare to look, a shimmering barrier of blazing white light surrounds me, thrumming with power that vibrates through my bones.

Azrael batters the shield with relentless force. I grit my teeth, limbs shaking with effort. Sweat drips down my face as I channel every ounce of energy into maintaining the protective dome. It could shatter at any second.

"No. It can't be true!" he roars over the whine of warring energies. "You shouldn't be alive!"

His words bounce off my steel focus. Nothing matters now except holding this line—between light and shadow, between life and death.

Before Azrael can strike again, the door bursts open. Adrian and Erik explode into the room like avenging furies. Erik slams Azrael to the floor with bone-crushing force while Adrian locks his arms around the shadow-man's neck in a blur of motion, attempting to decapitate him.

With an unearthly howl that shakes the walls, Azrael releases a tsunami of darkness from his amorphous form. It crashes over Adrian and Erik, who convulse in agony as the shadows leech the life out of them. Across the room, Rhyland chokes and gasps within his own suffocating prison.

My shield wavers as I watch three vampires—ancient, powerful beings—brought to their knees by this darkness. My heart hammers against my ribs while I desperately channel what little energy remains into maintaining my protection.

Azrael's monstrous roar reverberates as he shifts into a towering column of smoke and shadow, his human form completely abandoned.

Something breaks inside me. Tears spill down my cheeks as emotions surge like a tidal wave—fear, rage, desperation, love. I unleash a primal scream that tears from the depths of my soul.

Blinding light erupts from my core, flooding the room in a supernova of pure radiance. Windows shatter outward in a crystalline explosion. Azrael's shadowy form dissipates like mist before a hurricane, his scream fading into nothingness.

The others collapse as their torment ends. I fall to my knees, sobs wracking my exhausted body. This power exacts a terrible toll, but I'd pay any price to protect those I love.

Rhyland stirs with a pained moan, struggling to rise. I sprint to him as he sits up, pulling me into a fierce embrace. His relieved sigh tickles my ear as he strokes my cheek, eyes scanning my face with naked concern.

"Thank you," he whispers hoarsely before releasing me. "I heard you, Angel. I fought it as hard as I could."

Adrian and Erik rise unsteadily, faces shocked at what they've witnessed.

I cling to Rhyland, adrenaline fading into bone-deep fatigue. Questions can wait. Explanations can wait. For now, we're alive, and Azrael has retreated once more.

But one truth burns bright in my mind—this is only the beginning.

Rhyland

80

I rise in one fluid motion, arm locking possessively around Dani's waist as I process what we just witnessed. "It wasn't Azrael pulling the strings—it was Mortemis using him like a fucking puppet," I growl.

Erik staggers into the living room, collapsing onto the couch. His eyes fix on Dani with wary respect. "What the hell did you just do?"

Dani shrinks under our scrutiny, shaking her head. "I–I don't understand it myself. I just… channeled everything I had at him."

Adrian's voice trembles with awe. "It's her light—powerful enough to force that shadow-dwelling bastard out."

My mind races through our options. We're exposed here—vulnerable. We need a fortress. "The citadel," I decide, brooking no argument. "Its ancient wards will shield us from his reach."

A knowing smirk crosses Adrian's face. "Perfect. The Library of Secrets houses extensive Fae lore. Finding what we need won't be a problem."

Erik strides toward the door with purpose. "I'll alert Lucian. You two move now—we'll follow."

Dani's golden eyes widen. "The citadel? Where is that?"

I step closer, dominating her space. "Oregon. Grab your things. We leave immediately."

She hesitates, uncertainty clouding her face. I grasp her shoulders firmly, my voice dropping to a commanding rumble. "I know you have questions. Everything's happening fast. But trust me—we'll be safe at the citadel. I'll explain on the way."

After a tense moment, she nods, determination hardening her delicate features. Watching her, pride swells in my chest. Thrust into this dangerous world against her will, yet she faces each challenge with unwavering courage. Her inner strength only makes me more resolute in my mission to protect what's mine.

No matter what darkness comes for her, it will have to go through me first.

I push my Audi to its limits, weaving through Seattle's late-night traffic like it's standing still. The engine roars as I slice between lanes, claiming the road as mine. Beside me, Dani clutches the door handle, her knuckles white.

My phone lights up—Lucian calling. I answer through the dash, keeping my eyes locked on the road.

"Helloooo, Team Apocalypse Aversion!" Lucian's voice chirps through the speakers. "Your friendly neighborhood backup squad is hot on your tail! Got the super-secret, ultra-damning paperwork of doom right here! Should I have laminated it? I feel like evidence against world-ending shadow demons should be laminated."

I clench my jaw, already regretting answering. "Just bring the documents and try not to narrate the entire drive."

"Roger that, Captain No-Fun! Sucking all joy from life in three, two—"

I hang up before he can finish.

I glance at Dani, her exposed legs and generous cleavage drawing my eye like a magnet. Unable to resist, I grip her thigh possessively, my fingers inching higher with clear intent. She stares out the window, worrying her lip between her teeth.

I squeeze her leg, marking my territory. "It'll be okay, Angel. Nothing will touch you."

She turns, brow furrowed. "What about what Azrael said—that I shouldn't be alive? He looked like he'd seen a ghost."

The comment stirs my suspicions about Dani's origins and her mother's secrets. "They know something about you. We'll find the truth."

Her golden eyes meet mine, warm but determined. "Tell me about this vampire council. Who are they?"

"The Council governs all vampires globally," I explain, my tone authoritative. "They enforce our laws, punish transgressions."

She arches a brow. "So, dictators of the undead?"

I chuckle darkly. "Essentially. They ensure we maintain order now that we exist alongside humans." I continue, "Seven members represent regions worldwide—Viktor, Randal, Killian, Cole, Garrett, Eva."

"And your role?" she probes.

I meet her gaze, power radiating from me. "I'm the Leader. Have been for decades. I make the final decisions that affect our kind."

Her lips curl into a teasing smile. "The Leader, huh? By merit or might?"

I flash her a predatory grin. "It suits my nature perfectly, wouldn't you agree?"

The charged air between us ignites something primal. Her barely-there smirk makes my cock stir. I slide my hand higher up her warm thigh. "I was made to dominate, baby. In every aspect of life." My voice drops to a seductive rumble.

We drive in loaded silence until we reach our destination deep in Oregon's forest. The citadel rises before us, weathered stone silhouetted against the night sky—centuries of history and magic hum in the air.

Gravel crunches as another car pulls up. Erik, Adrian, and Lucian approach, their expressions grave—except Lucian, who practically bounces with manic energy.

"Welcome to Castle Grayskull!" Lucian announces, arms spread wide. "Time to show those crusty vampires our presentation—"'Azrael's all-you-can-eat blood buffet and freaky soul smoothies—it should be a real shit show. Maybe we can even get front-row seats to watch those ancient dickbags piss themselves in fear when they see what that black hole-looking motherfucker's been up to with Moldy Voldy."

I pinch the bridge of my nose, barely containing my rage. "For fuck's sake, Lucian, can you be serious for five goddamn minutes?"

"Serious?" He gasps, clutching his chest. "In this economy? Sorry brother, but gallows humor is all I've got left besides my devilishly good looks and—"

"Shut. Up." I growl.

Lucian turns to Dani, waggling his eyebrows. "Speaking of devilishly good looks, how about you ditch Mr. Grumpy-Fangs and run away with me, sunshine? I'll show you a much better time..."

Dani crosses her arms, matching his theatrical tone. "Sorry, but I prefer my men broody and built, not chatty and desperate. Maybe try Tinder?"

"Ouch!" Lucian staggers back like he's been shot. "Your words wound me deeply! But I do love a woman who can match my wit. Are you sure I can't tempt you with my—"

"Finish that sentence," I snarl, stepping forward, "and I'll rip out your tongue."

"Kinky!" Lucian winks. "But save that energy for your firecracker here. Speaking of which, these walls are pretty thick, so feel free to get loud—"

I move to throttle him, but he dances away, cackling like a madman.

As Adrian rushes off to research, we face the imposing citadel. Its towering spires disappear into darkness, stone gargoyles perched along the edges like sentinels frozen in time.

I watch Dani take in the intimidating structure, her eyes wide but determined. I squeeze her hand possessively, a silent promise of protection.

Our footsteps echo through the cavernous entrance hall, ancient banners bearing the council's crest hanging from vaulted ceilings. Dani's fingers tremble in mine as we pass artifacts of vampire history, the weight of centuries pressing down on us.

The path ahead remains shrouded in uncertainty, but one thing is clear—Mortemis must be stopped. And I'll destroy anything that threatens my girl.

Danica

81

Holy shit, this place is intense-like medieval-castle-meets-supernatural-courtroom intense. The council chambers are straight out of a Gothic horror movie—all dark wood, dancing shadows, and enough gravitas to sink a battleship.

The elders glide in like a parade of highly judgmental ghosts, their robes whispering across stone. They take their seats at a table that probably cost more than my student loans, staring at us like specimens under a microscope.

Don't fidget, don't fidget, don't—damn it. I shift under their ancient gazes. These are the beings who decide immortal fates, and I'm the human crash-testing their worldview.

Their eyes drill into me like they're trying to extract a confession through sheer force of staring. Great. Just what I needed today—soul-searching from creatures who've probably seen the fall of Rome firsthand.

We gather under chandeliers that definitely weren't bought at Home Depot. The flickering candles cast everyone in that perfect "I might eat you later" glow.

Lucian clears his throat, slipping into his best impression of courtroom drama. "My liege council," he announces with enough sarcasm to fill a swimming pool. "I've gathered you fine, wrinkly specimens here today because—surprise!—Azrael's being a complete dickwad again. Exhibit A: his super illegal blood-trafficking operation that makes the cartels look like amateurs."

He slaps down documents with the dramatic flair of a game show host revealing the grand prize. The council members rustle and murmur like gossipy hens at a church social.

Rhyland steps forward, all brooding intensity and power. "Azrael is working with Moretemis," he states, his deep voice rumbling through the chamber like distant thunder. "He seeks not just profit, but to create a foothold for darkness in our realm."

The council members do the immortal equivalent of clutching their pearls, exchanging looks that scream *"oh shit"* in twelve different languages.

"What evidence links Azrael to Moretemis?" asks a stern-faced woman.

Rhyland's jaw tightens, a muscle ticking in his cheek. "Eva, the truth cannot be denied. Azrael attacked us with shadow magic that goes beyond vampire abilities. He invaded our minds with darkness that could only come from one source. His underground network isn't just trafficking blood—it's trafficking humans to Moretemis himself."

Eva narrows her eyes. "You've witnessed these captives?"

"In living, breathing, terrified-out-of-their-minds color," Lucian quips, examining his nails like we're discussing the weather instead of supernatural human trafficking.

The room falls silent as every ancient vampire eyeball swivels toward little old me. Great.

The eldest councilor, who looks like he personally witnessed the Big Bang, fixes me with a stare that could freeze lava. "Explain yourself, girl. Why have you come before this assembly?"

Oh, good. My favorite part is explaining to ancient vampires why they should listen to the human lab rat.

I straighten my spine under the weight of approximately ten million years of judgmental vampire stares. "I am Danica, the one foretold—" *Shit.* "—sir."

The elder's lip curls like he just smelled week-old blood. "I am Viktor. Do not address me so."

"Viktor—sir!" *Jesus Christ, mouth, pick a lane.* Rhyland squeezes my hand as I mentally facepalm.

The council sits statue-still, only my nervous breathing breaking the silence. Then, like someone hit play on the world's most intimidating focus group, they unleash a barrage of questions.

Rhyland raises his hands, his alpha-male voice cutting through the chaos. "Silence! One at a time." *Damn, that commanding tone does things to me.*

The youngest council member—who still probably remembers the Bronze Age—leans forward. "What proof have you that you are the prophesied one?"

I lay out my case: the powers, the crown, the whole chosen-one package deal. Some council members look like they're sucking lemons, others like they're watching a fascinating science experiment.

Eva's gaze could cut diamonds. "Before we entertain this farce, tell us your plan to save the realms. Time grows short."

No pressure or anything.

I explain how the crown can unite different worlds against evil.

"Time to bag Az and kick his ass out of Dani's orbit," Lucian drawls, gesturing to his evidence like a demonic game show host. "I'll be here with popcorn and pom-poms."

The council exchanges looks that practically scream *"what the actual fuck?"* before the dark-haired one speaks. "Very well. We'll handle Azrael while you focus on...the realms."

Rhyland stands, radiating authority like a sexy nuclear reactor. "It's good to know we are all on the same page. Let's get ready for our grand exit, shall we?"

The Library of Secrets lives up to its dramatic name—endless shelves stretching toward a ceiling lost in shadow, ancient tomes bound in materials I probably don't want to identify, and enough knowledge to make Google weep with inadequacy. The air tastes old, like breathing in centuries.

Adrian hunches over a book thick enough to stop bullets, his dark hair falling across his forehead as he mutters to himself. When he spots me, his face lights up like I've just offered him unlimited research funding.

"Dani! Perfect timing!" He practically bounces from his creaky chair. "I've found something—a spell to permanently bind the crown to you."

I fish the crown from my bag, it's metal cool against my fingers. "You mean so no one can steal it?"

"Exactly." He points to a standing mirror that looks older than America. "Put it on."

What could possibly go wrong?

I approach the ornate mirror, its tarnished surface reflecting distorted images of the endless bookshelves behind me. With a deep breath—*here goes nothing*—I place the crown on my head.

It's surprisingly light, like it's made of air rather than metal. The engraved gold catches the light, making my chestnut hair look almost red beneath it.

Then—*holy shit*—the crown erupts with light, its swirling patterns beaming like miniature suns. Energy pulses through me from scalp to toes, like I've just grabbed a live wire. I gasp, spinning to find three vampires staring at me with identical expressions of shock.

"Did you see that?" I whisper, though I already know the answer.

Rhyland's hands settle on my shoulders, warm and grounding. "I think it has bound itself to you," he says, voice low with wonder. "The crown has chosen."

Adrian blinks rapidly. "Well, that was unexpected. Guess my spell won't be necessary after all."

I turn back to my reflection, barely recognizing the woman wearing a glowing crown. She looks powerful. Regal. Terrifying.

Rhyland wraps his arms around me from behind, his breath tickling my ear. "You look like a queen," he murmurs.

Experimentally, I reach up to remove the crown—and it's like trying to move a mountain. My fingers strain against something immovable, muscles screaming in protest.

"So it's stuck?" I ask, already knowing the answer.

Adrian's smile is both triumphant and sympathetic. "That's the idea. So no one can steal it."

Great. Permanent magical headwear. Just what every girl dreams of.

I sigh, still adjusting to my new permanent accessory. *At least it matches everything.*

Rhyland's grin is infuriatingly sexy. "Get used to it, Angel."

Easy for you to say, Mr. I-Don't-Need-Magical-Headwear.

Adrian's gasp cuts through my crown-related sulking. His fingers hover reverently over an illustrated page. "I've found it—the Book of the Fae." His voice practically vibrates with academic excitement.

My heart does a little jump as I approach. The book looks ancient enough to have witnessed the birth of literacy, its binding held together by what I suspect is pure stubbornness and maybe a little magic.

Adrian reads aloud, his voice painting pictures of a world that makes Disney look amateur. I lean in, completely hooked as he describes Fae that would make supermodels jealous—human-sized beings in colors that probably don't exist on the mortal spectrum, wielding enough elemental power to make the Avatar feel inadequate.

His enthusiasm is contagious as he explains their society. "Lords and ladies rule them," he says, eyes shining like a kid explaining their favorite video game, "but the queen is supreme. She embodies the realm's essence, maintaining harmony between her people and nature itself."

I absorb this fairy-tale political lesson before asking the million-dollar question: "Is there any mention of where they're keeping our stone?"

Adrian shakes his head. "Not yet. But listen to this—"

He launches into a description of the Five Courts that sounds like the most epic fantasy RPG ever. There's Floriana's Court of Blossoms (flower power central), Lord Oberon's Court of Elemental Magic (where physics goes to cry), and Lady Nadia's Court of Hidden Springs (underwater real estate goals). Lady Mirella runs the Court of Sylvan Creatures (Doctor Dolittle's dream job), while Lord Corallus handles the Court of Mystical Beasts (basically a supernatural zoo on steroids).

Great. Five different courts to potentially piss off. This stone-hunting business just keeps getting better.

My eyes bug out at mentions of unicorns and ogres. Rhyland chuckles at my fish-out-of-water reaction, which earns him my best scientist glare. "Excuse me for being excited that fairy tales are apparently National Geographic specials!"

Adrian geeks out over illustrations of the faerie queen, suggesting she must have our stone. Because, of course, the most powerful being in the realm has what we need.

Lucian saunters in with his signature dramatic timing, nursing what I'm betting isn't apple juice. He collapses into a leather chair like it's a therapy couch. Meanwhile, Adrian scurries off to text someone, grinning like he's got a secret. *Suspicious much?*

"Don't get too starry-eyed, firecracker," Lucian drawls. "That realm's got more teeth than Disney lets on."

Rhyland kicks him. "Can you try not being a dick for five minutes?"

"Fine." Lucian's grin turns wicked. "Life is like a box of chocolates—full of crap and surprise shits."

I snort-laugh before I can stop myself. Rhyland looks ready to commit fratricide until he sees my amusement. *Crisis averted.*

"See?" Lucian preens. "She appreciates my poetic soul."

Rhyland changes subjects before he gives in to brotherly murder. "What's the council's plan for Azrael?"

"Off to Seattle for some political ass-kissing and prison prep." Lucian waves his glass. "No rest for the wicked!"

I exhale, relieved that at least one psychopath will be dealt with. *Now we just have to worry about everything else trying to kill us.*

Adrian returns, his professor-mode activated. "We should start planning our Luminara expedition. Details matter."

"Agreed." Rhyland's voice turns commander-mode. "And Danica needs combat training. Immediately."

My stomach does an anxious flip. The whole chosen-one thing gets realer by the minute.

Lucian smirks. "I know some excellent motivation techniques." His eyebrows do a suggestive dance.

Rhyland's glare could freeze hell. "Touch her and I'll make you permanently dead."

Lucian laughs off the death threat. They fight like cats and dogs, but I've seen how far they'll go to protect each other.

Danica

82

Rhyland's brow furrows into that sexy concentration face I'm starting to catalog. "Adrian, any news on the Soul Stone?"

Adrian shakes his head, fingers nervously combing through his dark hair. "Still digging..."

A light bulb clicks on in my brain. "Wait—Seraphina said the Shadow Stone controls darkness itself, right? And Marcus mentioned the Soul Stone having similar powers." I look between them, connecting dots. "What if they're the same thing?"

Rhyland's eyes widen. "That would explain Azrael's alliance with Moretemis. He's using the stone to access the shadow realm."

My stomach does a backflip with extra anxiety. "So I just need to take an all-powerful shadow artifact from a homicidal vampire who's BFFs with the lord of darkness?"

"Well, this is a clusterfuck supreme," Lucian announces helpfully from his chair.

I shoot him a glare. "Your contribution is noted, Lucy."

He winks. "Just keeping it real, sweet cheeks."

Rhyland paces like a caged tiger, his boots probably wearing grooves in the floor. He rakes his hands through his hair—*hello, sexy stress response.* "We stick to the plan. Fae Realm first, Azrael's stone later."

I nod, relieved to postpone the "steal from psycho vampire" portion of our quest. Still, the question hangs in the air—when exactly is the right time to confront someone who can manipulate shadows and has already tried to kill us twice?

Adrian buries himself deeper in his books while Rhyland wears a path in the floor. Lucian watches us all like we're his personal reality show, occasionally sipping his drink with dramatic flair.

"Well, this is productive," he finally drawls, standing with theatrical slowness. "While you kiddos figure out your little scavenger hunt, I'll be draining every pretty neck I can find. Play safe!" He saunters out, leaving exasperated silence in his wake.

And the award for Most Helpful Vampire goes to... literally anyone else.

After a night of cramming Fae etiquette like it's finals week, today's finally the day we jump between worlds. My stomach does nervous backflips while my heart races with equal parts excitement and terror. But with three impossibly hot vampires backing me up, I'm feeling weirdly confident. This definitely beats my usual Saturday routine of Netflix and lab reports.

Adrian has drilled me on every nuance of the Court of Blossoms until I could recite their customs in my sleep—if I'd actually gotten any. I'm as ready as I'll ever be to open a freaking interdimensional portal.

Surprisingly, Lucian's insisting on joining our magical field trip. Make that *four* impossibly hot vampires.

"Are you sure you want to come?" I ask, eyebrow raised. "Won't your club fall apart without your micromanaging?"

Lucian waves dismissively. "And miss the chance to get down and dirty with some fairies? Not a chance, sweet cheeks." His leer could power a small city.

I shake my head, fighting a smile. He's obnoxious and crude, but somehow I've developed a soft spot for Lucian's particular brand of chaos.

Rhyland sits nearby, lost in thought. I saunter over and plop myself in his lap. His ocean-blue eyes focus on me, and that slow smile spreads across his face. Our kiss ignites like a match to gasoline.

"Ready for this?" I whisper against his lips.

He pulls me closer with a growl that vibrates through my entire body. "Yes. I'm ready to have you right now until you scream." *Holy hell.*

Rhyland nips at my neck, and I arch against him embarrassingly fast. "Not what I meant, you insatiable man," I manage, though my body's voting a hard *yes.*

"I know, Angel," he chuckles, and I'm caught between disappointment and anticipation.

I tilt my head, offering my throat. His fangs pierce my skin with that exquisite sting that sends heat flooding through me. My nipples tighten and my core aches as he drinks slowly.

Focus, Dani. There are people watching.

Lucian's gravelly chuckle confirms we have an audience. "Don't mind me. Consider this educational viewing..."

"Lucian, shut your damn trap," Erik snaps from across the room.

I ignore them both, shamelessly grinding against Rhyland's very obvious arousal. His bite always short-circuits my brain. Before I can completely embarrass myself, Rhyland's iron grip on my hips stops my movements.

Rhyland pulls back, his face a masterclass in restrained hunger. His kiss is urgent, demanding—and I'm instantly ready to forget about quests, crowns, and saving the world.

"Keep that up," he growls against my lips, "and everyone's getting a show." The heat in his eyes suggests he's not entirely opposed to the idea.

I reluctantly extract myself from his lap and catch Lucian's hooded gaze.

"My turn?" he rasps with a smirk.

Rhyland's growl could register on the Richter scale. "Touch her and die. Again."

"What?" Lucian shrugs innocently. "I just want a sip from the juice box."

I roll my eyes and retrieve the blood vials I'd prepared. "This should last you two days—three max," I say, handing them out like party favors.

Being den mother to vampires wasn't on my career vision board.

They drink deeply, and suddenly it's showtime. The room crackles with anticipation as everyone looks to me.

I close my eyes, reaching for that strange power that hums beneath my skin. With a deep breath, I focus on the Fae Realm, picturing it as Adrian described. Magic responds, dancing around me like static electricity. My fingers tingle as I reach out to part the veil between worlds.

The air shimmers, then splits open into a kaleidoscope portal fragrant with exotic blooms.

"You're almost there!" Adrian urges.

With one final push, the passage stabilizes. I'm staring through a window into another reality—a place where physics took hallucinogens and decided to get creative.

Lush meadows stretch toward a horizon painted in colors that shouldn't exist. Atop a distant hill stands a palace that seems grown rather than built, its marble walls draped in cascading flowers.

Rhyland's hand finds mine as we step through together. Wonder washes over me like a wave. Trees tower overhead, their branches heavy with blossoms that glow from within. The grass beneath our feet is thick and springy, emitting a soft luminescence with each step. Butterflies the size of dinner plates drift by on wings that shimmer like stained glass.

Jewel-toned birds swoop overhead, calling to each other in musical trills as they investigate the strange newcomers. Their songs blend with bubbling springs and rustling leaves into a symphony that feels alive.

"What in the actual fuck..." Lucian breathes, for once at a loss for words as he takes in the technicolor wonderland around us.

Dorothy, we're definitely not in Kansas anymore.

Adrian kneels reverently, letting the luminous grass sift through his fingers. "The true Faerie Realm," he whispers, academic detachment crumbling. "No text could capture this magnificence."

I drift forward in a trance. Flowers burst with colors that shouldn't exist, perfuming the air with intoxicating sweetness. My skin tingles when I touch a petal that seems to pulse with its own heartbeat. This entire world breathes magic.

Rhyland squeezes my hand, grounding me. "Nothing could have prepared me for this," he murmurs. I cling to him, overwhelmed by beauty that borders on sensory overload.

"Which way now?" Lucian asks, staring up at the distant palace. "Tinkerbell sure has upgraded her real estate. Let's go crash the party."

I close my eyes, trying to sense the Faerite stone's pull. There's something—a muted tug in my chest like a distant magnet—but I can't pinpoint a direction.

Rhyland reads my frustration instantly. "We'll find it," he promises, his certainty a balm.

The stillness hits like a thunderclap. Birdsong cuts off mid-note. The air thickens with malevolence, raising goosebumps across my skin. I motion for silence, every instinct screaming *danger*.

We spin toward an unnatural ripple behind us—a viscous portal black as spilled oil. Foul tendrils unfurl from its surface, blindly grasping at nothing.

My lungs freeze as Azrael materializes, his fathomless eyes bleeding darkness. I'm rooted in place, fight-or-flight response short-circuiting at his vile presence.

"Dani," he purrs, savoring my name like a delicacy. "Thank you for sharing your remarkable gift."

His meaning hits like a wrecking ball. Rhyland exhales sharply beside me, vibrating with fury and dread. Azrael's gaze slides to him with sadistic anticipation.

"How?" I demand, fear eclipsed by desperate need to understand.

Azrael's mouth twists cruelly. "Isn't it obvious? Your power creates a path I can follow. I simply piggyback on your gift, accessing realms in your wake."

His words turn my blood to ice. He sneers with twisted pleasure, turning to Rhyland. "Your toothless council can't save you now. But my thanks for the warning, *Adrian.*"

The name drops like a bomb between us.

Horror creeps up my spine like a venomous spider. Adrian steps forward, refusing to meet our stunned gazes.

Rhyland explodes. "You motherfucker. I'll rip your goddamn heart out!" His hands flex like he's already imagining Adrian's blood on them.

"Ah yes, Adrian." Azrael's casual tone makes this nightmare even worse. "You thought he was helping you?" He tsks mockingly. "No, my dear. Adrian is merely my personal lapdog."

The realization hits me like a physical blow. Adrian was never on our side.

Rhyland turns on his brother, fury radiating from him in waves. "You backstabbing bastard," he snarls, coiled tight like a predator. "You called the Brotherhood, didn't you? That was you and had us chained like animals?"

Adrian shifts nervously under our collective glare. "I've been searching for the prophesied one for eons," he murmurs. "Then you deliver her to my doorstep. I had no choice but to inform Azrael."

No choice? White-hot rage burns through me. This pathetic excuse for betraying us all, for betraying his own brothers.

Shame flickers briefly across Adrian's face. "Azrael hired me long ago to find the one prophesied—"

"The one who will die by *my* hand," Azrael interrupts, satisfaction oozing from every pore. His eyes gleam with malice. "You shouldn't have been born, little prophet. Your existence is a mistake I plan to rectify. One I thought I'd already handled with your *mommy.*"

Ice floods my veins. He moves toward me like a shark scenting blood, each word a knife twist.

"You were foretold to stop Moretemis's destiny. To prevent the dark future we've worked toward." His lip curls. "But I will end you before you fulfill that tiresome prophecy."

My chest constricts painfully. *My mother?* Horrible scenarios spiral through my mind as tears threaten. Nausea twists my gut like barbed wire. I want to scream, to punch something, but despair weighs me down like lead.

I shove my grief deep down where it can't touch me. *Not now.* Fear gets shelved next to it. My mind flips a switch—survival mode activated.

Truth first. Breakdown later. If we survive this.

"Anakin fucking Skywalker reborn," Lucian spits at Adrian. "Figures your dark magic obsession would lead to this."

Erik edges closer to me, coiled to strike. Azrael extends his hand, eyes cold as space. "The crown. Now." His voice allows no defiance.

"Yeah, sorry, not on the menu today," I snap, surprising myself with the steel in my voice.

Something ignites inside me—rage burning away fear like paper in a furnace. Magic detonates through my veins, howling for release. It's stronger now, more accessible. With a primal scream, I hurl a nuclear fireball that blasts both Azrael and Adrian back through the oozing portal. The doorway seals shut with a sickening slurp.

"Dani, run!" Erik shouts.

Rhyland seizes my arm with bruising force as we bolt into the woods. We race wildly, breaths sawing, feet barely touching the spongy earth. Glancing back, I see Erik and Lucian sprinting behind us, no sign of pursuit yet.

But they'll return—that's the one certainty in this nightmare. Azrael can piggyback on my ability to cross realms. *Talk about a monkey wrench in the operation.*

As we tear through the forest, my lungs burn for air just like Adrian's betrayal burns in my gut. *How could he do this to me? His own broth ers...*

Ahead, a frothing river slashes through the forest like a liquid blade. "Jump!" Rhyland bellows.

We leap as one into the mountain runoff's lethal embrace. Glacial chill shreds through me, stealing my breath. Vicious currents instantly pull me under into a blurry aquatic hellscape. My lungs spasm as I battle toward the distant, wavering sunlight. I break the surface with a ragged gasp, clinging weakly to Rhyland.

Then disaster strikes. The ruthless river tears our hands apart, indifferent to our panicked cries. Rhyland is ripped away into the rapids—my anguished scream lost in the roaring waters.

"Rhyland!" I scream hoarsely, but the churning current swallows him whole.

The river carries me onward, alone and terrified, my mate torn from my grasp by nature's casual cruelty.

Lucian and Erik vanish downstream as I'm tossed like driftwood through the rapids. I grab at passing branches only to be wrenched free repeatedly. The freezing water steals my strength with each passing second.

I claw toward the shore, fingernails scraping against rocks and roots, but the current keeps dragging me back. My vision blurs with exhaustion. Ahead, the river narrows and drops away—a waterfall.

Oh god, no.

I'm sucked under again, hands grasping futilely at nothing but liquid darkness. Terror claws up my throat as I sink deeper, lungs screaming for air they can't have.

My foot scrapes the rocky bottom. With one desperate push—my last reserves of strength—I propel myself upward. I break the surface with a ragged gasp, swallowing precious air before the current sweeps me over the edge.

The world tilts sickeningly as I free-fall through misty spray. My stomach lurches into my throat, nerves jangling with primal terror. A scream tears from my lungs as I plummet toward the churning pool below.

Everything goes black as the freezing cascade envelops me. Impact knocks the remaining breath from my body. Paralyzing cold penetrates to my bones as merciless currents toss me like a forgotten toy.

Which way is up? I can't tell—my vision useless in the murky depths, my chest spasming with the need for air. I have seconds of consciousness left.

Is this my fate?

Alone and afraid in an alien realm, without even saying goodbye to Rhyland? Without fulfilling my destiny? Despair pulls me down as surely as the dark water.

The cold numbs everything, offering a strange comfort as I sink deeper. My thoughts grow sluggish, disconnected fragments floating away like debris.

So this is how my light goes out...

THE SEVEN REALMS

1. Atheria. The Realm of Light and Creation. It is a realm of divine beauty and purity where celestial beings and creatures of light reside. It is a place of harmony and enlightenment, where the power of creation flows freely, shaping the fabric of existence.

2. Aquaria. The Realm of Water. Aquaria is a vast world with vibrant marine life and mystical creatures, such as Merfolk, Skelkies, and Pirates. It is a realm of serenity and fluidity where the ebb and flow of tides hold great power.

3. Luminara—The fae reigns supreme in the realm of Luminara, a world filled with enchanting beauty and mystical wonders. Luminara is a realm of ethereal forests, shimmering lakes, and glowing meadows, where the natural world is interwoven with magic and wonder.

4. Mortalis—The Mortal Realm, where humanity resides with immortals and explores the boundaries of their existence. It has diverse landscapes, bustling cities, and uncharted territories. Humans navigate their everyday lives in Mortalis, unaware of the existence of other realms.

5. Pyrothos—The Realm of Fire. Pyrothos is a land of perpetual flames and scorching heat, where volcanic landscapes and fiery mountains dominate. It is a realm of passion and intensity, where the essence of fire fuels the powers of its inhabitants. Pyrothos is home to powerful fire elementals, fire-breathing creatures, and ancient fire temples.

6. Unbra—The Realm of Shadows. A world consumed by eternal darkness, where pure evil lurks, and creatures of nightmarish origins dwell. It is a realm shrouded in mystery and treachery, harboring ancient secrets and maleficent forces.

7. Zephyria—Realm of Sky and Air— Zephyria is breathtaking, with endless skies and gentle breezes. No one knows what this realm is besides vast expanses of open air, where the wind guides the movement of everything.

Acknowledgements

This book simply would not exist without the support of some very special people.

To my incredible beta readers—Kerry Taylor, Ellie Hohestein, Stephanie Young, and Samantha Parisi. My amazing Critique Partner, Ayn Kennon. Thank you for taking the time to read early drafts of this book and providing such thoughtful feedback. Your enthusiasm kept me going through the challenging parts of the writing process.

Also, to a very great supporter, Talia Harris, for believing in me and helping me through the entire book writing process. Thanks to your keen insights and suggestions, this book is vastly improved. I'm so grateful for your friendship and belief in my writing.

I could not have produced this book without the help of my village. Your faith in my ability to bring this story to life means more than you know. My deepest thanks for making this dream a reality.

Join Dani and Rhyland in Book Two
As they find themselves in the wondrous realm of Luminara, where the lines between dazzling dreams and reality blur into an adventure like no other. Watch as they navigate this enchanting world where the fae holds sway, and every glittering glen hides mysteries untold. Will the light of Luminara reveal the depths of their destiny?

FOLLOW ME HERE TO STAY UP TO DATE—

A.L. Hampton

www.ingramcontent.com/pod-product-compliance
Lightning Source LLC
Chambersburg PA
CBHW070551310726
48982CB00011B/1545/J

* 9 7 9 8 9 9 9 1 5 4 1 0 1 *